DRUMBLAIR

Dear Bill,

In appreciation of the opportunity you gave to this Jamaican to become your School Librarian and Housemistress in Alex House at Brentwood; for your abiding support and confidence in me, I thank you sincerely.

With warm affection,
Eileen Mais

June 2000.

DRUMBLAIR

*Memories of
a Jamaican Childhood*

Rachel Manley

VINTAGE CANADA
A Division of Random House of Canada

VINTAGE CANADA EDITION, 1997

Copyright © 1996 by Rachel Manley

All rights reserved under International and Pan American
Copyright Conventions. Published in Canada by Vintage Canada,
a division of Random House of Canada Limited, Toronto. Originally
published in hardcover in Canada by Alfred A. Knopf Canada, Toronto,
and simultaneously in Jamaica by Ian Randle Publishers Limited, in
1996. Distributed by Random House of Canada Limited, Toronto.

Canadian Cataloguing in Publication Data

Manley, Rachel

ISBN 0-676-97083-4
I. Manley, Rachel.   2. Manley family.
3. Jamaica - History.   4. Jamaica - Biography
I. Title

FI887.M35 1997   972.92'05'0922   C96-930997-X

Text design: Sharon Foster Design
Cover design: Concrete Design Communications Inc.

Inner photographs courtesy of The Norman Manley Foundation,
The National Archives of Jamaica, and the author.

Printed and bound in the United States of America

10 9 8 7 6 5 4 3 2 I

To Pardi & Mardi
Love,
Pie

Many people helped,
but very specially:

Michael and Glynne Manley
Douglas Manley
Louise Dennys, Susan Burns, Gena Gorrell
Ian Randle
Melanie Martinez
Joan Beckford
Tony Bursey and Cookie Kinkead
Rex Nettleford and Tony Bogues

and Israel, without whom...

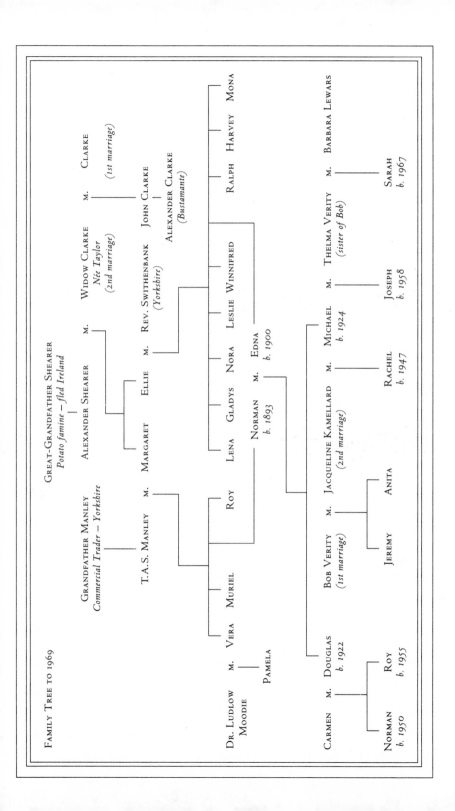

FAMILY TREE TO 1969

GREAT-GRANDFATHER SHEARER
Potato famine – fled Ireland

GRANDFATHER MANLEY
Commercial Trader – Yorkshire

ALEXANDER SHEARER

WIDOW CLARKE
Née Taylor
(2nd marriage)

CLARKE
(1st marriage)

M.

REV. SWITHENBANK
(Yorkshire)

M.

JOHN CLARKE

ALEXANDER CLARKE
(Bustamante)

T.A.S. MANLEY   M.   MARGARET   ELLIE

LENA   GLADYS   NORA   LESLIE WINNIFRED

RALPH   HARVEY   MONA

ROY

NORMAN
b. 1893

M.

EDNA
b. 1900

MICHAEL
b. 1924

M.

THELMA VERITY
(sister of Bob)

M.

BARBARA LEWARS

VERA   MURIEL

BOB VERITY
(1st marriage)

M.

JACQUELINE KAMELLARD
(2nd marriage)

M.

RACHEL
b. 1947

JOSEPH
b. 1958

SARAH
b. 1967

DR. LUDLOW
MOODIE

M.

PAMELA

DOUGLAS
b. 1922

JEREMY   ANITA

CARMEN   M.

NORMAN
b. 1950

ROY
b. 1955

PROLOGUE

I am three or four years old, and I have a bear on my bed with whom I share a till-death-do-us-part love. There is a tall, white-haired woman who wants to be my grandmother. I like her, but I remember that I have one already back home who is not restless or wild, and who likes to be called Granny. This new one tells me to give her a name that will make her ancient and timeless. I name her Mardi.

People looking for names. Names looking for people. . . . Daddy and Mummy are names looking for people. Daddy will soon have a person, I'm told, for he is coming to join me, but Mummy is a word without a person. I try not to say that word, and sometimes, when I do, it lands numbly, like the moo of the mute in Harbour Street with a little flourish at the end.

And there's a brown man here who I know is my grandfather. I always see his clean, cracked black leather shoes first; then, farther up, his waistcoat with a shining little chain. He is always dressed the same, and when I look at his face he is smiling at me under his nose, but I know he looks serious as soon as he turns away, or he removes the two small dimples of mischief out of his smile. I love his nose, it is smooth and strolls down his face on a comfortable walk, and I know I can depend on him with that nose. Each morning I pick a red rose-bud for his nose. He sniffs it like a Vicks inhaler, then puts it in a buttonhole on the front of his jacket, for it hasn't got a button.

I know he loves me, and I call him Pardi.

There's a white dog called Wog who always wants to be with me, and a yellow-eyed cat called Percy whom I sometimes stroke, till I get the feeling he believes me; then, if I can, I grab him by his tail and spin him. He is always so surprised and betrayed, and fights against the torrent of passing air and seems to yowl through his tail till I lose my grip and he runs away for days. I mean it; it's not a game. I hear and see his pain; I cause it. I am glad it's not happening to me.

At night my grandparents are mostly out, and I discover I own the top floor of this big house. The doors are large and heavy, and they obey me, their stiff handles plunging their tongues in and out, opened and closed. This amazes me. But the glass windows on their rough, dry sashes are too stiff for me. When Mardi and Pardi are out, there is a large, singing woman called Edith in a lot of bright cloth who comes through the door sucking peppermints. I think she belongs to me.

Things are brighter here. I have never seen such colours before. There's a much younger sun who visits us every day, bringing this nice old lady, Miss Boyd, with her hair in a bun and a broken-down voice, and she sometimes brings a sewing machine, which makes all the wooden things in my room purr.

But my very best friend in the world is this big, wooden house. Soon I know all its secrets, its cottony-dusty areas along the spaces left by cupboards not flush with the walls, which hide pencils and stamps and a green swirly marble; I know the way the boards join each other like skin to fingernails; I know there's a bird's nest under the roof just left of my window, and one for ants under my grandfather's window-sill. I know it's a grumpy house sometimes, but I can get it to smile. It is called Drumblair.

✳

In late 1949, at two and a half years old, I arrived in Jamaica for the first time. I had crossed the Atlantic by air from England. My Jamaican father was studying in London, my European mother was sick, so in true Jamaican style I was sent home to my grandparents. Norman and Edna Manley lived in the suburbs surrounding the capital, Kingston, in a house called Drumblair. I knew nothing about them—they were strangers to me—but they were household names in Jamaica.

It would be years before I understood the significance of the home in which I found myself, and of the two extraordinary human beings who were suddenly part of my life. This serious man who saved his dimples for me would one day be Jamaica's premier, "Father of the Nation" to many people, and my own father would be prime minister of Jamaica for three terms. It would take me half a lifetime to understand our history and my family's contribution to it, and to see, past the thicket of my own feelings and ties, how they were pivotal to so much more.

Our history is only five hundred years old. The story of British colonialism's triangular trade to help finance the industrial revolution is well known. The first passage of the journey began in England with ships loaded with goods destined for Africa, where they were exchanged for slaves. This new cargo of souls was in turn transported to the Caribbean and sold for use as labour. The ships were then reloaded with sugar for a final passage home to England. When I was a child I learned these facts briefly and harmlessly in a gentle, competent school where many of my teachers were in fact British. In my home I learned a different version of history:

of the betrayal of one tribe by another, and the human horror of the Middle Passage.

"History has left us with deep insecurities," my grandmother would sigh. It seemed to explain many things to her. "We lack that hammock of national belonging which cradles a people against historic falls," I heard someone else say, maybe my grandfather. I guess some nations feel they've been there since the world began. We cannot think that. Our migrations, some forced, some voluntary, are too recent. All of us are new arrivals—the Spanish, English, French, African, Indian and Chinese. Those early inhabitants who could have sensed an original belonging were destroyed by the arrival of Columbus. With this brief and humiliating past, and a divisive geography of islands, we have had to invent ourselves.

Modern Jamaica grew out of no single act of collective violence. The Caribbean islands were too small to fight their own wars and define themselves by some glorious moment. We did not win our emancipation; it was an expedient concession made to us by the British Emancipation Act of 1833, arguably motivated as much by economics as by morality. Labour, now having to feed itself, actually became cheaper. The slaves who flew from bondage soon had to return to the plantations at starvation wages, with no political rights to do anything about it. Their freedom proved to be as much myth as reality. The British West Indian islands had a seemingly permanent underclass which lived in poverty and had no voice. A tiny middle class began to emerge in the nineteenth century. It was made up of mulattos, the offspring of plantation owners and female slaves. Plantation society could not function without supervisors and bookkeepers, lawyers and doctors; this class began to provide some of the skills, and helped keep Caribbean society functioning. Its members were always grateful not to have to earn a living in the cane fields.

My grandfather was a product of this middle class. In this vivacious, macho, often vulgar region, Norman Manley was an unlikely hero. He was shy, sensitive and reclusive. He loved the arts and music, both of which he wrote about. His life was an extraordinary series of achievements. He was the greatest schoolboy athlete of his period; a Rhodes Scholar and a decorated First World War hero who returned to Jamaica and went on to become the greatest lawyer and courtroom advocate in Caribbean history. He never lost a murder case, and was the first Caribbean advocate to appear before the judicial committee of the Privy Council, the Commonwealth equivalent of the U.S. Supreme Court. The woman he married became a legend in her own right. Edna was his cousin, whom he met in England. She had grown up in Cornwall with a Jamaican mother and an English father. She studied art and became a sculptor. Her vital spirit had always been at odds with the grey landscape of her Edwardian youth. In Jamaica that spirit rejoiced in the other side of her heritage. She quickly became bored with the verandas of middle-class Jamaica, and impatient of the timid, imitative culture she found there. Instead she buried herself in the landscape and colours and forms of her new country. She opened new doors for herself and for other artists in discovering our island soul. In their marriage each life complemented and ignited the other; they were like two beacons searching out the limits of a common coast.

He was a moral man, concerned for those less fortunate than himself, and he was a proud nationalist who wanted more for his country. Yet nothing he achieved as a Jamaican meant anything to him unless he was his own man.

No epic moment validates my grandfather's role in our history. There was no Battle of Hastings from which he could emerge as conqueror. Though most major epochs of the world are identified with a beginning, a place or a moment, in Jamaica there was only a landmark where no battles were fought, no soldiers buried, no monuments built. It was the house they called Drumblair.

I grew up in that house with my grandparents. This is my story of them. It is not history. It is memory.

Part One

EDITH

As ONE WOULD say the name of a planet or a continent, Venus, Earth, Africa, so on the island one spoke the name "Drumblair". Even now, many decades later, it evokes the sense of an age ... the Stone Age, the Iron Age, the Drumblair Age.

As a child I thought it belonged with its rhymes; with here, there, somewhere, nowhere, everywhere and Drumblair. It was its own category, one of the big, intrinsic alternatives of language and life.

There was nothing spectacular about the old wooden two-storey house set far back from the road. It was not even in a fashionable area, but rather poised precariously on the journey between the city and its ghettos, and the lofty slopes of the suburbs. It has often been described as elegant, but it was too visceral and self-willed a place to be so, for elegance is a product of control. The gate, a plain iron grille hinged to a cracking square cement post, always hung open lazily, despite the thick "Chinese hat" hedge on either side guarding the house from view. The companion post carried the inscription of the name in frank block capitals on a marble inset. The initial slope of the circular driveway was steep enough that even a car needed a burst of new energy to make its way up. And there, at the top of the encircled front lawn, stood the house. It appeared not to take itself very seriously. It was large, but not in the sense of having many rooms—more in the way that you look at a puppy's paws and say, "These are large paws; this will be a big dog." It was just meant to be a large house. It looked out at the world from under a shady sombrero of shingles. At its waist, a similar frill of roofing adorned it like a fat ballerina's tutu. A veranda enclosed by a criss-cross wooden railing circled the ground floor like the dash of a hasty signature.... Drumblair.

All of my earliest memories lie within that house.

❋

Miss Boyd was the housekeeper at Drumblair. I remember her sitting with me, as she often did, in my room upstairs. Her sewing-basket lay on my low white table with childhood's graffiti of Plasticine bits, spills and pencil scrawls. It was purple and yellow, made of woven Guatemalan straw, fat as a pumpkin, with a lid attached by a thread of straw.

Miss Boyd was engulfed in the large white wooden chair, and her tiny feet dangled way above the floor, adorned by pretty socks and severe black laced shoes with thick heels. She was only four feet ten inches tall.

She was darning a sock on a stone, her thimble clicking rhythmically against the needle.

"Brumus needs an eye, Aunta," I announced, holding my mangy polar bear under her nose. People called her Miss B. But I called her Aunta.

"Not now, Ray dear. I'd have to go right through the basket and see if I can find two buttons that match."

Everyone except my grandfather called me Ray unless they were cross with me, in which case I reverted to being Rachel.

"But he only needs one eye. He has the other," I explained irritably.

"Yes I know that. But I don't have another button like that glassy one, so I will have to find two matching ones and throw that one away. You don't want the poor bear to have two different eyes. People will think he's crazy!"

I threw Brumus back on the bed. He'd been there from my very beginning, I was told. He'd been with me before Mardi and Pardi, before Aunta. But maybe not before Daddy, I thought, for Daddy was there at my very, *very* beginning.

I called my grandfather Pardi because it was the grandfatherly version of Mardi. And I called my grandmother Mardi because she didn't like to be called Grandma...so I turned it around to be Margrand...somehow I must have heard of Mardi Gras and made a leap of association.

"Can I go downstairs, Aunta?"

"Lord, child, you know you're only going to disturb your Mardi. She's terrible busy this morning."

"Terrible busy." She said it with a protracted whir of R's for emphasis, but this incorrect adjective was the single lapse in her observance of perfect standard English. She was quick to correct each successive generation of children who deliberately or inadvertently strayed into the music of local dialect.

"Busy doing what?"

"Oh, Ray, you know what it's like when she has to be on the back veranda, serving the country for your grandfather."

It seemed to me that "serving the country" provided thousands of reasons why I couldn't be with my grandparents.

"But what is she dooooing?"

"Child, you just don't know.... Your Mardi has a heart of gold."

Miss Boyd knew about duty and sacrifice and hearts of gold. When she spoke of these things, one sensed that she recognized them within her own being. I remember an edge of resentment creeping into her voice as she shook her head knowingly on "you just don't know." There was some moral high ground from which she frowned, ever so gently, upon the world. As a child I sensed but could not identify the implicit rebuke.

She was the youngest child from a large family of Boyds. She had lost her mother at an early age, and accepted the responsibility of looking after her ageing father when the need arose. This she did with care and gentleness, never questioning her duty or regarding it as a burden. Her sisters had lived their own lives, made their own families. After her father's death Miss Boyd was left with the modest family home on Hope Road and her irreversible spinsterhood.

As time passed and problems arose, each one was placed in Miss Boyd's capable hands. Not only did she foster her sisters' children and their children after that, but like homing pigeons the elder sisters would come back with their broken lives, and finally their old age and senility, and she would continue to nurse and care for them all, counting them like rosary beads through her fingers as they returned. Her home became filled with the pets they left behind, the last of which was a parrot called, predictably, Polly, who was said to be ninety when sister Blanche died.

She brought the same martyrdom of service with her to Drumblair. And like another bead in her rosary I became one more small burden she had to bear.

I don't remember my arrival, but I have often heard Mardi tell the tale. I had disembarked from the plane tired and petulant, clinging grudgefully to an indifferent polar bear.

"I am your grandmother," a strange lady attempted to explain as she scooped me up into her arms at the side of the plane.

"You are not my gwanmuffer, you are NOT my gwan-muffer!" I raged, as I battered her grey head with the bear. The only grandmother I knew was my mother's mother, a petite Frenchwoman with piercing dark eyes who in no way resembled this woman.

A look of bewilderment passed between the couple. They hadn't expected me to have an English accent.

Edna Manley had embraced the idea of my arrival with impetuous zeal, seeing it as a chance to fulfil her role as a true Jamaican grandmother; now she seemed tentative. Both their sons were grown, educated, married men. She was not particularly proud of her record as a mother, but they had somehow survived, with a lot of muddling along and help from the staff in the house.

Norman Manley was not only overworked as a barrister, but deeply involved in the island's political process as the founder of its first national party. His wife was finally able to disappear into her sculpture studio and create the beings she felt she was really competent to produce. Her days were filled with her husband's fledgling political life and the island's nascent art movement. Until this afternoon I had been no more than a namesake of Rachel, one of her carvings—

born the day before her husband's birthday on July fourth, and therefore a Cancerian; the subject of small photographs mailed by her younger son, Michael, from England. Now I had arrived. How were they to cope?

They set off for home, trying in vain to subdue my screams of fury. Along the way, Norman parked the car on the gravel at the side of the road, looking for a diversion. We faced the listless harbour, where we could see the predatory dives of pelicans and the faraway ships. But the sound of my paroxysms still filled the car, and I fought for my next breath from a desperate, ruddy face.

On a narrow bank on the driver's side of the car, a couple of goats chomped on some salt-faded bushes, balancing nimbly on the verge of shifting beach stones.

"Look at the goats!" Edna commanded, as though the most commonplace thing in this world might somehow distract me from a grief that I felt was inescapable.

And it did.

I had never seen a goat. I lunged from Edna's grip into the small space on my grandfather's lap in front of the steering wheel, and he diligently explained the sure-footedness of goats.

A bond had been established.

The lap I saw the goats from became my vantage point, one that I always took for granted. My grandfather was the object of my needs and my energy, and I was quite unconcerned with the pressure of his work, the sanctity of his thoughtful silence and the brooding reticence and even shyness of his disposition. By now, over a year later, I had not a single memory of any life before Jamaica.

"But Aunta, you never listen. What is she doooing?"

"All those poor people you see waiting on the veranda"
—she tugged the needle despairingly, pulling the line of
stitches into place and surveying the grey area of sock with
gravity—"she has to help them in hard times. You don't
know what the good Lord in his wisdom makes some people suffer in this country."

"Yes, Aunta, but what is Mardi *doing?*" I enunciated each
word with careful deliberation, still hoping for a more specific answer.

"She has to help all those people find clothes and houses,
recommend them for jobs, even get medicine for their sick
children!"

"Why?"

"Lord, child, you ask a lotta questions. You better give me
a break so I can get my darning done."

"Well, can I go and help her?"

"The best way to help her is to stay here with me and
keep the house quiet for her," she said with satisfaction, as
though the conversation had led inevitably to a conclusion
she had withheld until this perfect moment.

"Then can I go down and see Edith?"

At the back of the house, below the kitchen, was a small
basement. Tucked into the damp earth, it was cool and
secret. The concrete of walls and floor was uneven, and the
structure slumped into a comfortable shrug under the weight
of Drumblair. On a hot day it was a relief to push open the
scraping wooden door and enter the subterranean shadows
there. This was the province of Edith—Edith was a province of Drumblair.

She had arrived as a laundress, and retired slowly over
the years into the landscape. The basement, with its great

concrete sinks where she squashed and squeaked clothes to utter softness before starching them, had become her domain.

Edith also made guava jelly; she was known in the parish of St. Andrew as the guava-jelly woman. The basement had a Dover stove at the back, big and black. Here she made her preserves in huge pots, feeding the oven with wood from time to time, heaving the latest batch of her vintage across the stove-top and out of the way. As the wood cracked in the ravenous fire she would observe, "Yes Lawd, as de sparks fly h'upward...." On replacing the pot, she would lift the lid to give the lethargic mixture an encouraging prod with a wooden spoon.

The smell of clean clothes and hot damp guava.

Edith was a huge woman, tall by comparison to my child-hood smallness. Over the years, her fat had settled stealthily around her, giving her the appearance of a complete island setting sail whenever she embarked on a movement. Her skin was soft and creamy, a gentle brown. It bore no wrinkled tributaries, but stretched thick and firm across her surface, occasionally falling into a definite fold. Her face carried no rumour of age, only occasional bunches of moles like grapes which I enjoyed pointing out to her. She would smile. Edith always smiled. It seemed that her time on earth was a state of limbo in which she existed, and which she greatly enjoyed, without deep commitment. Her life and inner light had a separate schedule later and beyond.

"When dat great bugle blow, me will be ready!" she'd say.

In the meantime she remained patient in her hibernation, simmering on a low flame, her bubble of life escaping as slowly as that of the guava jelly.

When she was not drifting sleepily through her jelly making, or pounding the laundry, she would be in her end room at the back of the house, singing hymns knowingly to herself.

"No, dear, you can't. Edith's not here today. She's gone to town to see the doctor."

"Is she sick, Aunta?"

"Pressure. Terrible pressure," she said, as she lifted her forehead into lines of acknowledgement that caused her tight bun to bob at the back of her head.

Aunta's grey hair looked almost straight when it was scraped back. Straight hair meant good hair on the island. And straight hair, thin lips and a small nose were coveted features of beauty according to the national psyche. There were of course gradations, particularly when it came to the question of colour. The whiter the better. Light was good; dark wasn't. That was how our people saw themselves, through the prism imposed on them by their colonizers.

Since I had heard these notions, and was myself a creamy mulatto colour and had waves in my hair, I asked Pardi if this was good or bad.

"It is a matter of total indifference," he told me. "Your muscles tell you if you're strong or weak, your mind tells you if you're smart, but your colour tells you nothing. Colour is incidental. How you look is incidental. What counts is your mind, my dear, and your heart. Pray those are strong and interesting."

And that was how he lived, and how he saw himself and others. Curiously, that noble concept failed him in his attitude to bald heads. They seemed to amuse him. When we went to the pantomime at the big Ward Theatre in Kingston, he joined me in the little alcove beside the special box where he usually sat, and we aimed peanuts at the shining bald pates underneath, ducking back into our seats if we scored a hit. More than once, we missed and our missiles lodged in a lady's hairdo.

Miss Boyd was definitely of mixed blood, and the proportions came out in her favour. Her skin was a light beige with the aura of grey that seems to cling to fair skin after fifty. Her tiny limbs, where they were uncovered, revealed freckles, goading reminders of the "lick of the tar-brush." Her oval face under its prim spectacles had a girlish quality, for her cheeks were puffy and mischievous. Her nose was unsophisticated, a little button like her thimble; it even had pin-sized indentations.

"Your nose is like a strawberry with holes," I would tell her, and she would chuckle. She was quite without vanity, having surrendered whatever seed of her feminine being might have complicated the straightforward issues of her life. And yet, old as she seemed, she was pretty. Or maybe her kindness seemed pretty.

"What's pressure?" I asked, for I was continuously hearing that grown-ups had pressure.

"Well," she said, as she frowned at the sock and then shifted her studious gaze to rest on the basket, "it's a thing with the blood. Like it's pushing too hard."

"Could it make you burst, Aunta? Will Edith burst?"

"No," she laughed, resting the ensocked stone on her lap, "I don't think it's that bad."

"Well she mustn't burst before tomorrow. 'Cause what's tomorrow?" I asked.

"It's April Fool's Day. And I hope you're not coming with one of your tricks!"

"But what else is tomorrow, Aunta?" I repeated, flopping my elbows onto her pint-sized lap with the ailing sock.

Struggling to regain the thread now pulled out of the needle, she answered absently, "What else... you tell me, child."

"It's Edith's birthday!"

"Good Lord.... You're right, you know.... I must see to that at once.... You know what you can do for me? Run down to the garden and see if you find Batiste. Ask him to cut a good pineapple for Edith. Tell him to make sure it's sweet. Have you got her a present?"

"Mardi took me to Kong's. I got April Violets."

"What's that?"

"Powder. Edith likes powder, Aunta." I was becoming exasperated.

"Oh, powder! It's *called* April Violets! See what a nice girl you can be. Now go and tell Batiste, and when you come back we'll have a good look and see if we can find a pair of eyes for old Brumus."

Batiste was the gardener at Drumblair. He was a tall, lean man, but with a fat man's apathetic disposition, a lethargy of the soul. And yet he was not the least bit lazy; he just did things slowly, like a tree growing in a garden. Although he lumbered, he moved easily, at one with his shadow passing, and when he stopped one hip would sling to the side, as though he were a sack half-filled and his contents shifted when let go. His face was smooth and gentle with little expression, just an agreeable dreaminess. He spoke seldom, except to the plants; he would praise or admonish them for their accomplishments, or lack of them.

By his nature he became a mediator, a slow-roving diplomat between the plants and the people of Drumblair. With careful digging and planting, and long hours of watering, he was able to coax some order out of the land's natural defiance. He sensed the wayward spirit of both the land and Mardi, the woman who wanted a garden here. The land, he knew, would rather be a jungle.

He moved deftly between these two forces, pruning a shrub here and an expectation there. The result was contradictory. The alamandas, though planted in a row, failed to form a hedge. Their blooms tore up into the sky on long, wilful stalks that refused to link arms in any form of co-operative camaraderie. The bougainvillaea grew heavily and without symmetry towards their favoured side, but their blooms were intense and joyful as they choired across the landscape.

Some afternoons I would sneak to the fridge and get a Red Stripe beer for Batiste, or a few cigarettes from the box on one of the little living-room tables. Thus armed with safe passport into his private world, I would stand beside him as he watered, nudging the hose up and down as though to encourage the plants. He would drink his beer out of the bottle as I prattled on about school or told him stories from inside the house. He would grunt or smile and continue to stand still in the cool late afternoon with the spray of water tickling the light, himself like a plant.

I had found out his secret from the whisperings in the kitchen, but I never let him know I knew. People would say, "Batiste cyan 'ave no pickney."

Not to be able to have children was obviously proof of some terrible failure in a man, but Batiste seemed peaceful and serene despite this cruel fate.

I found him clipping an oblong bed of plumbagos at the bottom of the garden. "Of all the flowers they are the most true," Mardi would say, "for they bloom even in the drought." Batiste was bent over, his body like a stem broken in a strong wind. And he clipped and pulled. Beside him a freshly bathed Wog lay drying in the sun, chained to a distant tree.

Wog was a valiant white mongrel with unlikely mastiff claims. His name—an acronym, really—called for endless explanations, as it was a term used by racist Englishmen to describe people of colour. Neither Mardi nor Pardi had known this when they christened the animal "Wrath of God".

Wog was not a handsome dog, but he was loved for his sense of adventure and his kind heart. Though his legs were short, he was strong and would pull us, holding onto his tail, up and down hills and across the pasture.

Although there were always cats at Drumblair, like Sun Yat and Tang Hai and Percy, it was by its dog that each era was recalled. Pardi said that Mardi loved horses but was faithful to dogs.

To the right of Batiste, the weary constituents of the island's poverty pulled their way up the drive towards the side of the house. They had come because they needed jobs or housing or school fees for their children, or medical attention or help to get a visa for a farm worker's job in America. They would always leave with something, a letter or money or a telephone call made on their behalf. Batiste continued without the least curiosity, their presence no more than a familiar reflection of a common state.

I waited beside him until he straightened as though coming up for breath. I handed him my offering of a couple of Albany cigarettes grabbed on the way out.

"T'anks, chile," he said, nodding more in approval of my gesture than at me. "See I wash your friend Mister Wog!"

"Batiste, you know tomorrow is Edith's birthday? Aunta says please to cut a pineapple for Edith."

Holding his side with his hand, he looked in the direction of the pineapple patch at the back of the house, though the house itself stood in the way. He frowned thoughtfully, seeming to study the implications of what I had said, and then resumed his pruning.

"She says to make sure it's sweet," I added.

Batiste laughed sardonically, shaking his head. "Look like Barrista cyan grow nuttin' sweet!" A lot of people called Pardi "Barrister" because his feats as a trial lawyer had become legendary on the island. When his murder cases were reported in the daily newspaper, many people who could not read would get a literate person to read the court report aloud in a local rum shop as entertainment.

Batiste was once again lost in the monotony of his own movements as he hovered over the bed. I checked the ground for ants before I sat on the soft grass beside him.

"What 'appen? You miss you Mardi?"

Indeed I did miss Mardi. But she wouldn't be through for a long time yet. Along the side of the lawn people were waiting, some sitting on the tiny retainer wall that edged the pathway, others resting under one of the big oak trees at the top of the lawn. The haphazard queue tailed off silently, like patients in a doctor's office, preoccupied with their fate. I watched with angry resentment. Each one was an intrusion into my home and my life. Each person would take a portion of Mardi's day away from her and from me.

Batiste for the first time looked towards the source of my anger.

"What a whole 'eap o' people! You Mardi cyan go to de studio again today."

He turned sadly towards the grass-piece at the far side of the house. It seemed to lurk with wayward abandon as an alternative to the responsibilities on the other side of the house. As a child I thought it was the "grass-peace". It was the place from which Mardi always emerged peaceful. She would take her huge horse, Gay Lady, for rides through the long grass, pounding up the hill at the far side. It was also where she had built her sculpture studio. There were other things in life she did, but in that little wooden room she *was*. She became whatever the essential being of her restless spirit was.

"Me will 'ave to wet de clay firs'," he explained, and after a moment I realized he was weighing his priorities, the embryonic mound of clay on the stand, which would become the working maquette for a new carving, taking precedence over Edith's pineapple.

Pardi and I had to be invited or granted permission to enter Mardi's studio. We would be there for the patting of the wood for good luck before the work began. We would be there for the "laying on of hands". From time to time we were asked for an opinion. But only Batiste had free access.

He would lift up or take down the huge forms, rub the wood with delicious linseed oil or wet the clay daily, gently wrapping it in its myriad damp towels, layer by layer. He nursed her fledgling creations continually, bringing comfort to each on the many days when Mardi's duties kept her away.

I loved the smell of the studio with its sweet wood chips and rummy turpentine. Sometimes Mardi would let me watch her work as the wood chips were flying, or as she gouged out form from the clay, her teeth biting the side of her tongue as though to set an example for her hands. She was tall and very fair, with an excitable head of white-grey wavy hair that parted itself in the middle and always looked much the same way. A first impression of Mardi was always dominated by her sharp nose, like the asparagus tips we got out of tins but without the notches. It was a curious nose, but not a nosy nose. Somehow its curiosity appeared to be sensitive. When she spoke or laughed, a pair of substantial yet attractive front teeth would take over. But her face was a narrow lantern that shielded the flickering curiosity of the light blue-grey eyes she had inherited from her Yorkshire father.

She would set me to work on a bar of soap with fine wire tools, or on sheets of paper to fill, so large I had to crawl over them to work with a paintbrush or charcoal. I had to be quiet. When I had run out of interest I would watch from outside a world which had shrunk to a log of wood, and a restless, angular woman with strong hands and a mallet and chisel, as she entered that person she really was, finding her way by imagination.

Having finished the bed, Batiste set off as his twofold mission required, with me trailing behind uninvited, and Wog at a gallop sniffing adventure until he abruptly stopped, having used up the length of his chain.

At a distance the high grass looked like the well-groomed mane of a palomino, sandy-coloured and ready for silage. The grass-piece seemed to brood, waiting for the thump and throb of a thousand horse hoofs and the tat, tat, tat of the wooden mallet, listening for the next beat of its own heart.

In the evenings, if I was lonely, I would ask Edith to come and stay with me and sing her hymns while I went to sleep. She would promise to try to come, but always later; never then, with me. Sometimes Mardi would ask her to stay with me if she and Pardi were both going out.

It was a rare treat when she came.

I would hear her lumbering up the stairs, resting after every three or four steps and whispering to the Lord.

I can still hear her: "Lawd, me Jesus, ah comin', ah comin'."

Her dresses were often faded from laundering, and so thickly starched that they arrived around the door before she did, like an annunciating flag. Beneath, her stockings had settled around her ankles in bunched folds, despairing of travelling farther up those insurmountable legs.

She would stand at the door for a while, holding her hips and blowing. That is how she arrived that night. She had come to baby-sit.

"Wha' 'appen to Miss Badness dis time?"

"Come here, Edith," I shrieked with delight as I bounded out of the small single bed to drag her the last few feet of the way.

"Wait nuh, chile... you wan' fe kill me! You doan see dat me can 'ardly ketch me bret...me soon a go 'ome to me Lawd, chile."

She slumped heavily into the white chair next to my bed, produced her large plastic fan with a Chinese motif and proceeded to fan herself in time to the rhythm of her breathing. I jumped back into bed beside her.

"You jus' wan' company 'cause you Mardi gone an' lef' you again. Weh she gone, chile, she gone a meetin'?"

"I don't know," I singsonged, holding onto the crisp corner of her skirt, feeling the comfort of her presence in the large old house. Its emptiness at night without Mardi and Pardi seemed to knot its diffuse shadows into a silent black fist.

"Are you better, Edith?"

"Me nat better! Me did go an' see de Injan doctor today."

"Have you got pressure?"

"What you know 'bout pressure?" She was laughing. "Yes, 'im say I 'ave pressure. 'Im gimme more pill weh cos' summuch money an' nu do nuttin'. So coolie man stay!" She sucked her teeth in resignation.

"How old will you be tomorrow?" I asked her.

" 'Ow ol'? Me na know... plenty ol', plenty ol'...."

I felt the heaviness of her warm hand on my back as she started to stroke me to sleep. From the very centre of her massive chest her voice rose sadly, like an old crying practised night after night. Some bloom of melody succoured the tune within the hoarse cobwebs of her throat.

"Swing low, sweet chariot..."

She had once heard Paul Robeson sing this at Drumblair, "all we ancestor dem weep when it roll out from inside of 'im." It seemed she was still remembering that evening as she carefully retrieved each word from its place of memory.

The chariot was coming forth to carry her home, and it was coming forth to carry me to sleep. I did not even feel the corner of her skirt escape my grasp when she left me.

Soon after I opened my eyes the next morning, I remembered Edith's birthday and set off to deliver her present. Before I could cross the hall to start down the stairs, Mardi appeared in the opposite doorway. It seemed such a long time since I'd seen her, though it was really only a day. I ran to her, throwing my arms around the top of her legs. I hugged her and hugged her. But I knew by her gentleness and impotence that something was wrong.

"It's Edith's birthday," I said tentatively. I looked up at her face for an answer.

But she told me Edith was gone. She had gone last night. They had taken her away.

"But she hasn't got the April Violets!"

This seemed to sum up my predicament. I had never encountered death and had no idea of its implications. But over the following days I began to realize that there would be no more singing at bedtime, no more guava breezes wafting from the basement. Dearest Edith had gone—propelled up into heaven, I presumed, by the pressure of her blood. Or had that chariot come to collect her? Or had whoever ordains these things simply played a cruel trick on me and on Drumblair on April Fool's Day?

Late that evening, with Maria Callas straining at the bridling walls, I climbed into Pardi's lap. "Hi Pie . . . listen to Callas . . . she may have the finest voice in the world today!" He always called me Pie, though I didn't know why at that time, for I was not particularly sweet, or unusually gluttonous.

"When I am quite big I won't eat any more. I'll stop eating," I told him.

"Oh," he said as he settled me, "you will come to an end and everything will be finished for you."

Perhaps he felt my bony limbs go suddenly still, as still as the first time I sat in his lap.

"Do you mean you won't live any more?"

"Yes," he said softly under the glorious, commanding soprano.

"Why?"

"Because you can't live without eating." He took a deep breath. "Everything eats. The dogs, the cats, the cows."

There was a prolonged silence between us, and Callas seemed to relax without the distraction.

"Even the lovely Maria Callas must eat," he added. He had recently heard that the soprano was in danger of losing her voice through dieting.

"Pardi, when you're not alive, is it dark?"

"Yes, I suspect so," he answered.

"Why?"

"It's like that," he said sadly.

"Do you have to sleep?"

"Yes."

I was quiet for a long time, though my body squirmed and settled, finding some place to curl its spirit. I had already decided that it was shadows and not light that defined my life.

As the music ended, I said from a temporary stillness, "I suppose you must sleep, or you could not find the way out..."

When I went to bed that night, it was Mardi who sang to me, in her high, uncertain voice. It was a haunting lullaby that felt smaller and yet safer than Edith's; a reassuring one with fairies coming down the shut-eye road, and brownies coming with them too, to watch over me, and she put in my name, and I heard when she changed the eyes from blue to brown like mine.

But I was thinking of Edith. Her songs had belonged to some great river of human suffering whose comfort lay beyond this world.

Wherever Edith was now, I felt sure she was singing to the notes of that bugle she had listened out for in her dream on earth. She was gone to the heavenly hosts of angels and her beloved Lord with whom she shared all her secrets. Most of all, I began to realize, she was gone from me.

All that remained of her in my life was her arduous effort to join up the letters of her name on a page in my autograph book: "Edith".

Nomdmi

LET ME TELL you about my grandfather.

Pardi was a handsome man. As far as I was concerned he was the most handsome man in all the world. His father, Thomas Albert Manley, was the son of a travelling English tradesman and a black Jamaican woman. Looking at the only picture that exists of him, I believe he must have had some East Indian blood. His mother, Margaret, was a mulatto who appeared more white than black. The mixtures produced an uncommon harmony in Pardi. He had comparatively aquiline features, with deep-set communicative eyes, a "noble Roman nose" that made his face strong and distinguished, and a slight mouth which actually seemed unintrusive rather than mean. His face expressed all of the good qualities in life: intelligence, kindness, generosity, strength and courage, humour, gentleness, compassion and love. He was five feet ten inches tall, with long, slim limbs and slender feet which Mardi claimed were aristocratic. His being was one of quiet thoughtfulness. He was the colour of mahogany, warm and glowing.

Pardi was, as I have said, a Rhodes Scholar. Pardi was a war hero with a medal in a box in his top drawer which he didn't like to wear, and two letters M at the end of his name which he didn't like to use either. Pardi once held the world school-boy record of ten seconds flat for the hundred-yard dash, and there is no point arguing that it was only the island school-boy record, for that's not how I got the story in my head.

He was the brightest and best barrister in all the world. He was the only person I knew who played a mouth organ, and by the time I came on the scene he had become what Miss Boyd called a "nation-builder". This last pursuit had apparently begun in 1938 with what was generally described as "national unrest", which always made me think that every-one on the island of Jamaica had been unable to sleep one night.

In 1938 there had been an important strike in Jamaica. The strike had started with sugar workers on plantations and had spread to the dock workers in the capital city, Kingston. The strike had been called by Pardi's famous elder cousin, Alexander Bustamante, fondly called Busta by most people. My family said this was his last attempt at being radical in his life. His fervour for the working class cause got him thrown into jail. Pardi negotiated with the British gov-ernor on his behalf. When Bustamante was released from prison, there was a big crowd that cheered him; he got all the praise and according to Mardi, who always defended Pardi, even when he didn't seem to need defending, Pardi got pushed to one side and Bustamante never even mentioned who had got him out of jail. Mardi would always finish the story sadly: "and we just left that massive crowd who were in love with Busta, and in the darkness made our way to the car unnoticed, and drove quietly home."

And that was really the start of the first big mass-based union in Jamaica, though there were smaller ones for more specific groups of workers before. It was named after Bustamante, the Bustamante Industrial Trade Union. By September 1938, the first Jamaican political party to survive in modern Jamaica was launched, at the Ward Theatre. People said it was for the cause of freedom. They called it the People's National Party and Pardi was its unopposed leader. Bustamante was on the platform too that day, as a founding member. So was Sir Stafford Cripps, a lofty Englishman who represented the British Labour Party.

Two years later, according to family legend, Busta got jealous of Pardi. Pardi had not only kept Busta's namesake union alive while Busta was in jail, but had got them an increase of a penny in the shilling. People said that Busta thought Pardi was trying to take over his union.

"Imagine Norman Manley thinks you're only worth a penny," Busta told the workers. He was the most canny and street-smart politician.

"The antennae of a cat and the ethics of the alley," remarked Aunt Vera, Pardi's sometimes acerbic sister.

And away Busta went and formed his own party, the Jamaica Labour Party, of which he was president. The JLP supporters said it was because the PNP had just declared itself for socialism, which in fact it had. Whatever the reason, there was a big eruption and Busta went his own way.

That, as far as I knew, was the start of our two-party system. These were the facts I knew, the facts I was brought up on, though clearly they were biased by my family's point of view.

We didn't then have "universal adult suffrage". I relished reciting this term to my friends, who were as bewildered by it as I pretended not to be; I had a vague notion of a world where grown-ups were somehow entitled to their pain. That advance didn't come until 1944. Pardi fought for it without, he said, any particular help from his cousin Busta. And when we did get it, it was ironic that it proved to be the very factor that soundly defeated Pardi at the polls. His party lost again in 1949, but this time, I was told, he at least kept his own seat. I assumed this was a type of chair, as he had become an "Emaychar"—my interpretation of the initials MHR, which stood for "Member of the House of Representatives", the House still being fully answerable to His Majesty the King of England.

At first I thought "nation building" was a job in construction. I imagined that Pardi built all the big buildings I saw going up in the city. Since he had a workroom with a carpenter's table and saws and planes and sandpaper and spirit levels, and he made big, stable pieces of furniture that we all had to try for size and assist in varnishing afterwards, I imagined he was a sort of head carpenter who would sit astride a roof under construction and finish the building. I was sure that finishing anything was the most important thing one could do.

Then I was reminded that houses were only a small part of development, and that the roads and dams and markets had to be built too, and then there were all the schools that had to be not only built but made to work. Money had to be somehow extracted from rich people and shared out to poor people so they didn't starve, and robbers and madmen had to have special places to go, and natural disasters like hurricanes had to be coped with—no, not during the rain and wind, never during the rain and wind—you just have to sit that out. I could never understand the point of coping with a hurricane after it was over and done with, but grown-ups were like that.

And before one could do any of this, one had to own one's own country. And the first step towards this was something Pardi was struggling for all the time, which he called "internal self-government".

It was clear to me that nation building was a very big responsibility, and now I adjusted my sights and placed Pardi on some not clearly defined roof over the whole island, where he was finishing the job. But I could never get anyone to answer the simplest questions: when would the nation be built, when would we own it, and would Pardi then have to find a new job? Mardi said that first he would have to get a good rest.

If I believed it was Pardi who wrote the script of our country's story, then I believed equally that Mardi somehow illustrated the text. Her sculptures seemed to coincide with these watersheds that redefined us. *The Prophet, Strike, Negro Aroused.* If anyone suggested that Mardi's illustrations came first, Miss Boyd would close her eyes to dismiss such heresy, and say, "Sshh," as though to soothe such a thought to sleep. Mardi's name might be there under "illustrations by", but as far as either Mardi or Miss Boyd was concerned, Pardi was the great "written by" author in the sky.

But I had my very own relationship with Pardi, which had nothing to do with history.

I got to know Pardi best up in the hills, "in the middle of nowhere", as Mardi called it, where he was also a builder of sorts, and where, by the time I arrived, they had a small wooden house which they called "Nomdmi". We spent many weekends and holidays there.

A long, long time ago, Mardi had ridden off the bridle track on one of her freedom trails, and ended up high in the Blue Mountains, where the skies met the clouds and the altitude made her ears pop, and where the sturdy mountain population was not even registered at birth.

"So much for adult suffrage!" He would shake his head at the irony.

"Pack of Labourites," Mardi would say. "Good thing they don't register!"

Labourites were supporters of the JLP, Busta's party, which was then in power, though that just meant they had more seats in the elected legislature through which, as I said, we were ruled by the British. Supporters of the People's National Party were called comrades.

Pardi swore Mardi was mad, but he accompanied her on her adventure as she had so often accompanied him on his. The mounds of shale from the landslides, the patches of torn hillside and brutal black burns on the bodies of his mountains were more than Pardi could bear to see, and resurrected the "bush man" he had been in his youth, when he had grown up on his mother's farm in the country, cleaning pastures and chipping logwood for pocket money.

"They must learn to terrace. They burn the land to get a quick crop next season, but in the long run they will diminish these hills, and the very earth will die!"

So by the time he got to the top of the mountain, where she had already purchased her site of refuge at little cost, he had committed himself, on his own terms, to her new cosmos.

The view from those hills was startling, and threw back an unforgiving image of the island's gnarled and sporadic survival. Kingston, a city created to serve a great natural harbour, nestled in a side pocket of a distant plain, where it looked oddly practical beneath the virgin mountains. In the distance the encircling sea stretched like the island's imagination.

Most of the land in the mountains belonged legally to no one, and those who laid claim to it expected little for this arid hilltop that had no agricultural value; the valleys collected the fertile soil, and a view was not a priority for these farmers. A small payment usually ensured that one's squatter's rights would go unmolested. But Mardi discovered that this piece of land was actually the edge of a property that was accounted for, and bought it for a modest price.

It was Mardi's idea to build a house. She planned two rooms, one on top of the other, a small kitchen at the back and at the front a veranda.

"Why not side by side? It would be easier to build."

"No, dear, I must have a dormer window upstairs where I can peep through the trees in the morning and look across at the mountains."

Pardi soon appropriated her dream-house, deciding on a carpenter he knew from nearby Mavis Bank who could help him to build it. He would return to his first love, the land, and his agricultural exploits would, he felt sure, set an example for the hill farmers.

The dormer window became the focal point around which the house was built. The tree that Pardi decided she should peep through was identified; it was a juniper and became the marker for the window, and the two rooms followed, stacked one on top of the other to accommodate the view. But the rooms were built beneath the brow of the hill, facing its descent. The mountains, including Blue Mountain and Lady Peak, actually climbed up behind them and out of view. This was never mentioned. Instead of trying to rectify the problem by asking that the window be put in another wall, Mardi made a point of exclaiming about the view of the sky, clouded or cloudless, so as never to alert Pardi to the awkward fact that he had chosen the wrong tree and therefore the wrong view.

They then discovered that they had forgotten a staircase, so it had to be tacked on, and for many years it ran up the outside of the cottage as a cheerful afterthought.

The house became known as Nomdmi through a misadventure. Mike Smith, who in his youth had lived with the family like a son, was then spending a weekend at the cottage. Mike was a poet—at least until shortly after the Second World War, when, from a vantage point in the English countryside, he gazed over an industrial valley and decided in a fit of pique that poetry was useless in the faceless world of modern progress. He claimed that he never wrote another line of verse, proceeding instead to arm himself with anthropology, becoming a professor and writing through the course of his life many highly acclaimed books on the Hausa—books with which those who loved him persevered, and none of which any of our family members ever claimed to fully understand.

Pardi and my father had painstakingly constructed a small bridge over a waterway that crossed the entrance, erecting gateposts which would wait a long time for an actual gate. Mike was asked to paint a "No Admittance" sign on the new gatepost. While he painted, Pardi and Mike and my father were deep in some philosophical meandering. Whether distracted by this conversation or by his earlier longings, or maybe by a rum too many, or just victim to the absent-mindedness of his new-found profession, he got as far as

"No Mdmi" and realized his mistake: the M should have been an A. Mike, greatly irritated with himself, would have corrected the mistake if Mardi had not ventured along the path and been delighted with the semantic consequence of his error. On discovering this, he packed in the project. So the letters remained in orange paint over the years, and people started trying to pronounce them, which bestowed on it the full authority of a name.

To journey through the house meant weaving in and out of the elements, for you had to cross a muddy path to get to the kitchen built separately at the back. On their first weekend there they discovered that the chimmey, an enamelled chamber-pot, was not adequate for their needs, so a pit toilet was constructed at quite some distance, which was a constant reminder to Mardi of the evolution of the artist. She was haunted by the story of a fierce and tender writer she knew who, as a child, had accidentally dropped a roll of toilet paper down the subterranean belly of a pit toilet; his father, as punishment, had made him retrieve it.

"He could have become a murderer. He might simply have become a civil servant and tried to forget it. Instead he became a writer."

"I'm not sure I follow your reasoning on that one, my dear."

The thoughtful lawyer in Pardi was perpetually challenged by the intuitive shorthand of his wife's conclusions. He had learned to follow her trail and not to dismiss what he could not logically recognize. Within the turbulence of her being, insights flashed with the whimsy of sheet lightning. This made her a shrewd politician.

"After an experience like that, one is never a nice person," she reasoned.

"But who says he was a nice person in the first place? I believe the Freudians blame a lot of genetic traits on the retrieval of toilet rolls from pit lavatories!"

"So you believe he was just born a very difficult man? You think it's congenital?"

He could always lure her into the labyrinth of his mind, where she tiptoed through a million traps. She felt silly entering at all, but had long since learnt that on these expeditions her company delighted and amused him.

"I did not say congenital. I said genetic."

"Oh, don't be so tiresome! What difference does it make whether it's congenital or genetic?"

"There is a lot of difference. Congenital is from birth. But genetic comes from one's chromosomes, and so is handed down through heredity. If the Freudians are right, and they may be, partially, then I suppose one could argue that it is possible that personality traits develop after birth, as a response to a child's stimuli and environment."

"So you are saying that he was conceived a difficult man, and no matter what happens in his life, that's what he is. And nothing can change that."

"I did not say that," he countered. "Of course he can behave differently if he chooses to. But however he may alter his behaviour, it will be a reaction to what he ultimately knows himself to be, and in this case you described that as not a nice person!"

"I can't believe you could be so ungenerous," she said petulantly, beginning to feel trapped. In court, the cool of his logic unravelled even the most conscientious witnesses.

"Generosity has nothing to do with it." He was getting an ox-blood tinge in his cheeks from repressing a smile as his mind sprinted from one marker to the next, down the trail that his reasoning prepared for him. Her frustration reminded him of the moment when a witness discovered the inevitability of his own destruction.

"You are genetically ungenerous, then," she said triumphantly.

"Has it occurred to you"—and now he was trying to tame the words that arrived in spurts on his laughter—"that the father was not himself a nice person, judging from what he did to his son over the toilet-paper roll? So it would be logical to assume that his son inherited his chromosomes and therefore was genetically predisposed to being not a nice person too. Now, you could argue that if the father hadn't sent the son into that hell-hole of a pit, maybe the son would have done more to temper his natural inclinations!"

She didn't sulk. Sulking was too negative and persistent for her mercurial nature. She might pretend to sulk if it suited her, but only as a ploy. He would always beat her at the minutiae.

"Maybe so," she sighed, "but that still brings me back to my point. Having to endure such an unjust act of cruelty, he was faced with options. He could have felt enough outrage to become a murderer. He might have hidden his outrage by submerging the memory in his subconscious and filling his life with the day-to-dayness of the civil service. Or he could do what he did, which was to face the horror of evil headlong, and commit himself to his demons. He harnessed all that pain, damned to hell the loss of his innocence and became a writer! Amen."

She might very well be right. Maybe you couldn't be an artist worth a damn and be a nice person too. Being a nice person was a sort of refuge from the darker side of life. To be an artist one had to be able to make the extremes of human experience speak and be real. Maybe to be good at anything you had to be able to understand evil in a visceral way, as he did in his courtroom. Once again she had flashed illumination on a horizon that would have passed him unseen, had he not been travelling with her.

And when the young writer, lit by liquor or memory, stood on the table at Drumblair urinating at Mardi's alarmed guests, as he once did at a party, or uncharacteristically goaded her by defending the painting of daffodils, or writing about daffodils, in a land where daffodils were only a colonial rumour, she forgave him for being provocative and contradictory, remembering his dark journey into the fouled earth, and his father's evil.

"And he never once wrote of daffodils or of anything that didn't belong to his beloved Jamaica! He hated his father, but he forgave the earth!" she announced with satisfaction.

And Pardi understood. He understood because he had watched her battle over the daffodil syndrome as she struggled against the neatly but firmly imposed images of snowy Christmas cards in a land without winter, blond Christs in a country of black congregations, daffodils and tulips in a land of ram-goat roses and poinciana trees.

A quarter of a century earlier she had found her land legs after a grim passage from England on a banana boat, crossing from one limb of her ancestry to the other, her pale grey eyes adjusting to the brilliance of colour under a sun that few clouds dared to challenge. She was coming to Jamaica for the first time, with her husband and their infant son, Douglas. Mardi was born in England, but although her father was a Yorkshireman, her mother was a Jamaican, the sister of Pardi's mother, Margaret. Although she had grown up abroad, she always claimed to have a deep sense of being Jamaican and—

what seemed incongruous, as she was very fair—a deep sense of being coloured, as she was of mixed blood.

"We are not a mixed marriage," she'd insist, "but a marriage of mixtures!"

In Jamaica she found a people who were more massive than the English, and yet who moved with ebullience through their lives, though the majority had little to share among themselves. The English had managed to subdue only a small fringe of this island's leaves; the rest of the tree, biding its time, swayed above its own deepening roots.

So she began her work: goats instead of the basic British lion; buxom bodies and Caribbean life with pain and rum and laughter, the local revivalist cult of pocomania; women whose heavy loads swayed for balance and not, as the British expatriates neatly patronized, because while they worked their bodies were happy dancing to some imaginary music that kept them besotted and unsuspicious of the ravages taking place.

She taught young artists, and then writers as well started to wander into Drumblair, with their poems and short stories. It was here that the young writer would have brooded over the incongruity of daffodils, irritated by a growing enthusiasm that was collecting itself into anthologies of Jamaican literature. These early publications were called *Focus*, and by the time Mardi had edited two issues, he had contributed Jamaican white-wings, Jamaican dumplings and Jamaicans talking Jamaican, his short stories picking their way through the human seasons and the contradictions of the island's landscape.

Both Pardi and Mardi relished the rustic deprivation of their modest mountain cabin with a cussed determination. They kept life arduous even after the addition to Nomdmi,

one at a time, of a dining-room and living-room and more
bedrooms, which all squatted on the ground floor, leaving the
upstairs dormer window as the visionary eye of the house.

A bench was built where Mardi would sit to face the pro-
cession of peaks which she could not see from her bed, and
their ruling gods as they triumphed across the sky from
Catherine's Peak to Blue Mountain Peak. Mardi named the
mountains, met the gods who were there and made up some
more. They had their very own names, I suppose, but also
names Mardi gave them, like Kablan and Hooman. Catherine's Peak we always called Dillmoon because Mardi said
she was a mystic mountain and passed through the dawn as
only a memory.

She discovered her very own cosmos. It all began very
early when she sat on that very same bench at the edge of
this world, facing the reopening sky to watch the dawn.
There, incredibly, as if in slow motion, she saw the ascen-
sion of a single, golden, majestic horse, its mane coming up
first behind the mountains, flooding the sky with light; then
the forelock beneath which the lidless wide-open orbs
charged the world to life; and then a single lifted foreleg. She
recognized it. It was the Horse of the Morning.

"I've seen the Horse of the Morning," she announced to
Pardi.

"That's good," he said, but she always felt he didn't
believe her.

She never was sure that Blue Mountain Peak was really
the highest point in Jamaica. From certain directions Lady
Peak beside him looked higher, and there were days when
they both looked the same, so she didn't see why he should
be known as the major peak of the Blue Mountain Range.
She decided to call them the August Pair. When Pardi said

that they had found ice on the Peak, or that he had seen Cuba from the Peak because it was a clear day, she would always ask, "Blue Mountain or Lady Peak, dear? It could have been either!"

Then there was the tiny, unmarked grave in the pines behind the house. It looked like a child's. No, Mardi said, it was not a child's. She said the grave belonged to the little old lady who had built Bellevue, the great house which stood on the adjacent hill, and of whose property the Nomdmi land had once been a part. In her youth she had fallen in love with a visiting sailor. She sat in the upstairs window, also a dormer, and waited for the rest of her life for his return. He never came, and she lost first her youth, then her weight, and finally even her height, as she never stood up to stretch or exercise, but just sat gazing out at Kingston harbour, where she thought his ship would come in. Who this was I do not know, as the original owners were in fact Governor James Swettenham and his wife, Lady Swettenham. Lady Swettenham brought tree tomatoes from England, tasting more of fruit than of vegetable, along with lupins and lavender and hydrangeas, cottage flowers that could grow in the mountain cool all year round. There was even a nearby path to a spring called the Lady Swettenham walk.

After that another English couple came to Bellevue. She was loved by her husband and loved by her friends, and loved by the women in the village, whom she taught to plait the dry leaves of the watsonia Easter lily into long tresses which they wound tightly and sewed into mats and sold in Kingston. And then the husband died and it is said that she went quite mad, and had to be taken from her Bellevue on the hilltop to its namesake in Kingston, which was an asylum for lunatics. It was rumoured that finally, in a gross act of frustration, she set herself alight, leaving her mountain home and its ghosts as a gift in perpetuity to the newly created West Indian university.

Mardi built a studio in which to carve the mythical gods of her cosmos, a shingle shack with a concrete floor among the pine trees on the way to the gate. She called it Mini, short for Minimus.

Lurking behind every summer of weekends that he spent in the hills was Pardi's hurricane vigil. Nomdmi had no electricity, no running water except from the old oil-drums used to collect rainwater, no postal service and no telephone, and no driving road above the bottom of the hill. Any news came slowly up the hill by bearer in a letter or telegram, or by radio with the advent of the battery-powered transistor. The latter carried the meteorological bulletins which supplied Pardi with information to plot the course of each storm. He used a large blue and white map of the region, which he would spread out over his home-made dining-table. The map was already well worn from the leanings of anticipatory elbows and the pencilled journeys of each storm when, in those hottest of months, the weather could no longer keep its temper.

It would be unfair to say that he wished for a hurricane, for he was conscious of the devastation it would wreak on the island. But if a hurricane should come, an arbitrary act of God beyond any man's control, he would be able to prove the worth of Nomdmi's construction; insofar as he had supervised it with a pencil over his ear each weekend, he felt himself in large part responsible for it.

The map became a family tree. He would show me the sporadic progression of islands that formed the Caribbean like footprints across the sea. His stories swept the map.

There was British Guiana, on the South American continent, where Cheddi Jagan struggled to achieve a perpetually noble but often illusive socialist dream; his activist wife, Janet, sent logs of purple-heart wood like lovers for Mardi's desires. We travelled through Williams' Trinidad (and don't forget Tobago), where I heard of pitch lakes, steel drums and hearing aids; through the mountains and patois of St. Lucia, and Dominica, and Marryshow's Grenada. We lingered in Adams' Barbados, where I heard of the superb batting styles of the three great W's of West Indies cricket—Worrell, Walcott and Weeks—ninety-seven per cent literacy and a society unofficially divided by the colour of people's skin. On to Muñoz Marín's Puerto Rico, shaking its fist at the mighty States while toe to toe in a cha-cha-cha; across Bird's flat Antigua and the donkeys of Barbuda, past Dutch and Spanish and French possessions and Haiti, the betrayed land of Toussaint L'Ouverture, till beneath Cuba we came to rest at our heartland, Jamaica.

It seemed to me that our English-speaking brothers and sisters on the family tree were comparatively very small; I was, however, mesmerized by our fat foreign cousins, huge islands with exotic names and bloody revolutions from which emerged wicked "desk-pots", as I thought they were called, whose balletic names—Machado, Trujillo, Batista, Duvalier—curled with difficulty off my grandfather's lips and spun around in my head.

It came in 1951. Its name was Hurricane Charlie.

We were up there for the summer, Mardi carving a massive woman called Papine, the name of a mountain range,

Pardi building a trunk for the Nomdmi linen and blankets. Mardi encouraged me to bring friends along, and so Milton and Juanita, the great-nephew and great-niece of Miss Boyd, were there, and we were all painting the water-drums. Miss Boyd was recovering the cushions and making new curtains. We all had projects.

Mardi spent her mornings submerged in her studio, Mini, wearing pants, chewing her tongue and smelling of turpentine. The rat-tat-tat of her tools echoed all over the valley. It must have confused the woodpeckers tapping away at their trees, to hear these echoes that didn't tally—as though someone was poking fun at them.

Pardi's workbench was under the mahoe trees at the back, beside a woodshed. He planed the planks of wood for hours on end, rubbing them with his fingertips from time to time to sense his progress. We were not allowed to disturb Mardi, but this was the best time to talk to him. The water-tanks, the smaller of which were just oil-drums opened and emptied, were alongside the kitchen at the back, within sight of the workbench. In this way Pardi kept an eye on our artistic adventures, with a possibly more critical response than Mardi's predictable encouragements.

Only up here would he take off his three-piece suit and wear either his soft red or his ox-blood shirt with his Nomdmi khaki pants. His pants were both too wide and too long for him, and he dragged them in and up at the waist with an old leather belt that was sometimes used as a luggage strap. He would shout to ask the time. He never wore a wristwatch, but had a fob watch which, because it fell out of his shirt pocket every time he bent over, he left beside his bed. Miss Boyd would answer from where she whirred away on her hand sewing machine in the dining-room, which by now had been erected as a strategic link between the bottom room and the kitchen.

"Only ten to, sir, not time for the broadcast yet!"

At twelve he hurried into the house for the weather bulletin put out by the Met office. We dashed in behind him, and Mardi appeared at the doorway ready for a drink before lunch.

"You children haven't cleaned the brushes or put away the paints, have you?"

Miss Boyd tidily folded her world of threads and fabric away from intrusion. Her "greats", as she sometimes fondly called Milton and Juanita—she had mothered them since they lost their own mother in infancy—were perched with me at the edge of Pardi's disaster map. We awaited his proclamation as he extended the red-crayon trail by its three-hour inch.

"Lord-oh!" he exclaimed, as he always did when astonished, but this was pronounced "Luddo" and I thought as a child that he was calling the name of my uncle Ludlow, who had married his oldest sister, my aunt Vera, and I could never understand why. "Lord-oh, I think it's coming. Look! It's headed straight our way. Unless it veers north it'll be here by tomorrow evening!"

"Oh my God," Mardi gasped, her familiar theatrical gesture covering her mouth with her hand. Her eyes, wide with alarm and excitement, met our astonished gazes.

"Oh dear, we'll just have to lock up and go down." She looked at us grimly.

"What a terrible shame, eh?" Miss Boyd consoled us; she had patiently rounded up the last of her knicks and knacks and fastened them more carefully than usual into the sewing-basket, as though preparing them for a long, rough passage.

The storm had been upgraded to a hurricane, the reports upgraded to warnings; they would be repeated hourly from now on. The excitement of our childhood innocence was as fierce as the gale-force winds.

Pardi finished his calculations and looked up through his ever-greasy bifocals. "No. We don't have to go anywhere. I've been waiting for years to test the strength of this house. She's as safe as anywhere. Maybe even safer than Drumblair."

"Oh, really, Norman dear...isn't this a little drastic?" Mardi protested with dutiful caution, but her eyes were shining with anticipation.

Miss Boyd seemed for the first time to lift her head from a thirty-year reverie of uninterrupted trust. "But sir, can you be absolutely sure?"

"Of course I'm sure. I built it, for God's sake! I should know. I am more certain of this little house than I am of Drumblair. I didn't build Drumblair."

Miss Boyd apologetically hustled us out of the house to clean the brushes and put away the paints.

Mardi fixed gin and tonics and cut small squares of cheese which she placed in a saucer. She liked cheese; she said its taste always replied to her. Then she came out to inspect our artwork.

Milton was cleaning his brush next to his three-layered drum. He had started at the bottom layer, working his way around the circumference with a neat pattern of squares to the section adjacent to the wall. But his earnest round face frowned with too-easy frustration.

"I couldn't reach the very back, so it's all spoilt!"

"His fingers are too fat!" jeered Juanita, whose constant high spirits spat like cold water on the slow, smouldering fire of her brother's soul.

"Shut up, you stupid...," he yelled, hurling the paint-brush at her and nearly falling over his plump little self. She easily escaped on legs three years longer and more agile, cackling with delight.

"Oh now, this is awful! You girls really tease Milton," intervened Mardi when she saw him on the ground next to his drum, sobbing in despair. "But what a wonderful pattern! Your hands are so steady... you have an eye for design, Mil. Why do you worry so over that little bit at the back? No one can see it."

"But it isn't finished!"

"Oh Milton, it's not the Sistine Chapel! Not everything that begins has an end! Life is full of unfinished thoughts that are lovely; they don't have to be complete! What is *finished*, anyway? You can even think you've finished a thing and find the next day that you've changed your mind, and then you start all over again!"

He didn't understand but reluctantly allowed himself to be comforted, though we all knew he would sulk.

Pardi appeared on the step and looked across at Milton's drum.

"If you need to finish it, I'll turn it around for you in the morning, son. There isn't much water in it, so it won't be too difficult."

Milton's face unwound from its anger, except for the hurt that was always in his eyes. Did his father blame him for his mother's death in childbirth? He seemed to be a boy whose world had already made the odds too great against him. He had a handsome face when he let go, with black, thoughtful eyes that shone like lakes against the sombre horizon of his dark skin. Juanita was a lighter, golden brown, and her resemblance to her mother could only have solidified her favoured status in their father's eyes. Most of the time Milton was on guard, his face fretted with anxiety. But he was open and caring to those he trusted—and he trusted Pardi, who understood his principles and respected that what one started, one finished. He retrieved his dignity and the paintbrush.

"I think we're all hungry, and it's time for some lunch. Blanchie!" called Mardi, as though Blanche were not in the kitchen but over on the next hillside, where she lived.

The silence from the kitchen was replaced by Blanche's nervous clatters, bangs and bumping. She was fine while making preparations, but panicked when any occasion actually arrived, resorting to a muttered monologue that seemed to bolster her courage.

Over lunch the master plan was carefully worked out, and responsibilities were delegated for the following day. Pardi would go down after lunch to see to Drumblair, his sister Muriel, who was a spinster and lived alone, and his constituency, and then he'd bring up provisions of canned food and kerosene and candles and whatever else we might need for at least two weeks if the roads were blocked and we couldn't get down. He'd try to be up before dark, and tomorrow we'd all batten down Nomdmi for the storm.

Ivan the caretaker saddled Doris the mule, and was told to have the pack donkeys wait where the car was usually parked at the forest ranger's house, at around six. Pardi would speak to the ranger about sending out warnings over the hillsides so people could make themselves and their livestock safe.

"Blanchie, you know a hurricane is coming straight for us?" Mardi said gently. "It will probably strike tomorrow night."

Blanche's tall, thin frame bent not at the shoulders but at the waist, giving her the permanent aspect of hovering. She stood stock-still with a plate extending from her hand. Her face, with its old beauty, was always framed by a halo of black cotton-woolly tufts held in place by a colourful headscarf.

"You must go home and tell everybody to get prepared. Just come and cook a little supper for us later. We'll ride this out up here, but you will want to go home."

Behind their cataracts her eyes settled into a stare of disbelief.

"You goin' to stay 'ere so?" She shuffled her feet for support.

"Yes, Blanchie, Barrister says the house is safe. You don't think so?"

"Well...." She appeared hesitant, looking around the room at the rest of us, then over at the needles of sunlight thumbing their noses at the walls as they squeezed through the slats and knotholes. She looked back at Mardi.

"Well, missus," she said as she attempted to sort out her misgivings, "me cyan seh...but it doan look so! De house 'pon top a hill, an' it h'expose an' will lif' up in a breeze-blow, you no t'ink so, Miss B?"

Miss Boyd, who held her own quietly conceived reservations, took refuge in both her faiths: "Well, Blanchie, you know Barrister knows best, and if we pray the Lord will protect us and see us through."

So Blanche lurched off in disbelief to boil water and fill containers, order a good pile of wood cut for the Dover stove by Len, the simple village giant said to have water on the brain, and send her querulous messages of despair through the country grapevine.

Mardi was organizing the help for tomorrow, not only to bolt down all she could, but also to transfer *Papine* to the house, for it was felt that the studio was bound to be destroyed; it would be our offering to the stormy gods.

"No!" said Milton. "If you leave the carving in Mini, she's so big and heavy she'll hold it down and stop it blowing away!"

But nobody paid any attention and we were sent off to rest.

"Pardi is a desert island man," Mardi announced as she settled into a cozy embrace of the earth cushioned by brown pine needles.

We were under the pine trees by the gate, waiting for Pardi. Milton had left supper at least six times to peer from the look-out over the lily valley behind the house, from which he could see the red peaked roof that covered the forest ranger's house. Everything was toy-sized, like a crèche, but with the binoculars he could just make out the tiny bundles of baskets moving with the restless donkeys, and he could hear faint phrases that were perishing by the time they reached the top of the hill.

Papine seemed smaller lying in a mound on Nomdmi's floor, her nurturing contours wrapped with plastic raincoats to keep her dry. At least she was clothed, I thought, for I used to get quite upset when Mardi's carvings were of naked people, and I'd often take a piece of white chalk and draw lines to indicate the end of a sleeve, a trouser leg or a skirt.

That was the night we caught Blanchie smoking ganja. We peeped through her bedroom window to investigate an argument that we heard her having with herself, though we had been told to ignore it. She had thrown herself onto the bed and lay supine with a now bald head against the wall, smoking her pipe of "sweet sensie". Black tufts were escaping from her discarded scarf, whose tied shape lay on the bed beside her, and her blouse gaped open with what seemed like stuffing from the haberdashery of secrets that all mountain women kept in their bosoms.

We reported this odd event to Mardi. Apparently unsurprised by the darker side of mountain custom, she distracted us with a game of cards in which tempers flared as Juanita agitated and won, and Milton took revenge in outbursts in which he called everyone except Mardi a cheat. The game lacked the flourish of Pardi's deal, the terror of his predictions as he scrutinized his hand and that of anyone else inattentive enough to let him. "A peep is worth two finesses," he'd say, but we wouldn't know what he meant till we graduated to bridge.

By now it was dark. The Tilley lamp was sighing above our heads and casting huge shadows of our hands on the walls. Already the mice were patrolling the ceiling, and the rat-bats were squeaking their way through the crevices in the walls where they slept all day. I had hated the mice since the time I'd woken up to find one staring at me from the bottom of the bed, but I loved the bats as they dived towards me and missed, for Pardi had explained about their radar and how they could sweep through a room without touching anything even when they couldn't see.

And then we heard the car horn a long way down in the valley, and ran outside to the look-out. Beneath us the dry Easter-lily leaves had disappeared into the dark with the valley. We felt we might be upside-down, until our eyes caught the distant glints of the storm lanterns where the animals were tied at the foot of the hill to wait for the Jaguar's head-lights searching out the final bends of the road.

Once the convoy started swinging in single file up the string of path, we took turns to shout, "Coo-eee," over the valley. I have no idea why; we just did, over and over. "Coo-eee, you are coming," "Coo-eee, we are waiting," "Coo-eee, come faster, don't forget we are here," or whatever it meant to each of us as we called, and occasionally we got an indulgent "coo-eee" back.

It would be a while before they climbed the steep, narrow hill past Grannum's plateau, the halfway mark where a BOAC pilot lived with his Scottish wife in a well-ventilated house whose hurricane shutters were already closed. Mrs. Grannum taught her two blooming-cheeked daughters herself as she waited for her husband's returns. She couldn't stand the heat in Kingston, she told us one day, while sharing out home-baked tarts to us and her plump, pink children; Ivan said they reminded him of Mass' Clinton's pigs.

So we settled in the pinewood next to the gate to wait. Around us the wind kept stroking the pine trees, as though reminding them over and over to grieve. They sighed slowly in response, reliving some ancient sorrow that had withered their leaves to splinters. There must have been a little moonlight through the trees, for Juanita kept finding pine-cones and plaiting pine needles. Every now and then a desolate solitaire tested the dark, repeating its lonely note like a piano tuner.

"Why won't that bird go to sleep?" I asked Mardi, who knew every secret of the universe.

"How can he? He's a solitaire! He is always alone looking for his mate. Could you sleep if you were always alone?"

The pine trees had lost their husbands, the solitaires their wives, and though the moon was the soft wife of the sun, she and her husband were rarely together. Bellevue's old lady had never found her sailor, then the mad lady had lost her husband, Mrs. Grannum was waiting for Mr. Grannum, Blanche was tearing her hair off her head, Nomdmi shone through its lone eye in the attic and we waited for Pardi to come home.

Milton was the first to the gate when we heard the hoofs picking their way through the putta-putta path, which the summer had baked to clay: clip, clop, not very even, for the animals were carrying great weight and they had to be careful. First came the lovely smell of the earth and the night, and then the men with huge boxes balancing on the cottas on their heads, and the mules and the faithful donkeys, who kept their sense of humour. And then we saw Pardi, Mardi's desert island man, home with the provisions, home to brace himself and the house for the fury of tomorrow's storm.

3

STORIES
IN
THE WIND

Red sky in the morning,
Sailors, take warning!
Red sky at night,
Sailor's delight.

MARDI HAD LEARNED these lines in her youth in Cornwall where the Methodist Ministry had sent her father. There she could walk the moors, saddle a horse or play in the hayricks as a child, and later courted her heart's first beau; there she preferred braving the fierce waves of the English Channel to coming home for supper and eight siblings and the chores of communal well-being.

"Red sky in the morning...," she announced at the dormer window, where the monolithic juniper was still standing blackly on guard against the night. The sky was blushing ominously and the air felt still and full of trouble.

Pardi, with the softest brown skin that always had the sweet grassy smell of khus khus, clean cupboards and woody nuts wore his blue pyjamas. He was almost upright on his stack of four pillows, which held his nose at a dignified angle. He was looking across the room at her from his dissolving sleep. Mardi seemed to disappear above her long legs where she leaned through the window.

Mardi believed, always, in the delicate offering of a sensuous nightie, having picked up only those bits she found useful from the options of the suffragette movement early in the century. She knew the fragile fabric set off the generous figure it clothed. It was fortunate for Pardi that, though his Aunt Ellie had married a white Methodist missionary, Mardi, a quadroon, had inherited the ample proportions of her bottom from the Shearer side of the family, her West Indian heritage.

He liked a bottom. There was something profoundly reassuring about a woman's bottom that weighed like a ballast as it swayed to and fro through life. It seemed to him to be an assurance of competence and resourcefulness, of continuity and permanence. He could not have loved a woman with no bottom, he said.

There was a tribe in Africa, he told us, who suffered from a disease called steatopygia. The bottoms of those who endured this affliction grew and grew, until the cheeks hung behind their legs like mammoth udders almost to the backs of their knees. Mardi had an African carving she had bought in London as an art student, and he felt certain it showed steatopygia.

It was good to see her there with her short mane of white, unruly hair which she tossed like a horse. She was always an impatient person trying to learn patience. She loved horses and liked to think she had a temperament a little like a horse's. Her passions were never spent, nor was her ability to commit herself. When she was carving he woke like a cuckold to see her empty bed in the corner, with the guilty look of linen folded back in stealth, and the room withholding the secrets of her departure.

He knew that she was secretly annoyed at not being able to work in Mini this morning. He would get up now and do his daily exercises of leg-raises, sit-ups and press-ups, his legs still those of a runner with their hard and powerful cords. Discipline was natural to him, for he had learned that it filled the spaces human loss had left. First his father when he was seven—he just slumped forward in the barber's chair as if to say *why bother?*, and was gone. Then his valiant mother when he was sixteen. Later, in the carnage of the Somme— where Norman was known by the Cockney foot-soldiers as "Gunner", for he was said to be the fastest gun-layer alive— a tiny piece of shrapnel took refuge in his brother Roy's heart, and so Roy too was gone (having exaggerated his age to join his brother at the front), wrapped in blankets and buried in a grave already dug and waiting nearby.

Shell-shocked by the rumble of machine-gun fire and exploding howitzers, the shells that sucked the air out of lungs, his soul bleeding from the wound left where his brother had been torn away, he returned to London to mend the pieces of his self.

"I think he's suffering from a complete nervous breakdown," confided his Aunt Ellie to her daughter Edna when he arrived on their doorstep in London. He was glued back together by his aunt's tender and constructive attention, and by the simple routines of work; hour by hour his concentration tightened the screws of his mind and filled the spaces of his grief.

That was when Pardi and Mardi fell in love. They had met in 1914 when Mardi was only fourteen. Aunt Ellie, a widow, was living with her nine children in Cornwall. The newly arrived cousin had been asked whom he liked best among them. "I rather think that little plain one...with the spirit," he had said. And then he went off to war and wrote her a letter from the front. She received it breathlessly, proud and bewildered, and slept with it under her pillow. By the time he returned, a gaunt and unsmiling man, the family had moved to Neasden in north-west London. Mardi worked in London at a remount depot, tending the supply of horses to make her contribution to a war that would cost her family dearly. One sister lost a husband of only six months, and another lost her fiancé. Worst of all for Edna was the loss of her favourite, ardent brother Leslie, only seventeen years old, a great reader who once announced proudly, "See, Edna, now I have one hundred books!" Leslie, like his cousin Roy, had lied about his age to fight an honourable war.

For a long time the walls of the home in Neasden would reflect the ghostly shadows of Pardi's hands at night as he recounted the unheroic tedium of living *en masse* and staying alive. And that was when Mardi discovered that time was a river, and that all things pass, for after a while he was able to return to his work at Oxford. She was in London at art school, and they would meet on the weekends in her tiny digs over a fish shop. Soon the mind that had carried Browning and the Bible through the war reopened itself to peace. They shared D.H. Lawrence and George Moore, and fought over H.G. Wells, whom he liked and she hated for "his egocentric bolstering of himself" as his mind "drove all emotion away before him". He explained to her Einstein's pamphlet on the theory of relativity. She would remember this time as their beginning. She called it "the apple trees, the singing and the gold."

As for Roy, Pardi seldom spoke of him, or of the loneliness and bitterness caused by that senseless loss; but for the rest of his life he wore only black ties knotted against that once terrible lump in his throat.

From the window, now, his wife was beckoning to the hours of the day, to hold and control them with deft fingers so that every minute fitted somewhere in the scaffolding with which she surrounded herself. It kept her imaginings contained, gave her access to her self and kept everything within reach. Within reach, or she might fall into the abyss or fly away into the illusions of her own head.

She turned and saw him looking at her.

"Ah," she said, "you're up! Now let us plan the day."

I remember that upstairs room with the raincoats somehow strung from bedpost to bedpost, as an improvised canopy. The world became very dark, and everything was hushed and still except for the animals and livestock all over the hills; their calls had become off-key and ludicrous, and they howled as they did before an earthquake.

We were almost sealed off in the little room, with the dormer window boarded up from the outside. It was cozy with the storm lanterns shielding their unsteady lights within.

Miss Boyd sat, minutely sceptical, her hands lost without their sewing. Confined by the sparsity of her Methodist faith, her fingers fiddled as if for a rosary's comfort. She had tidied everything away into neat bundles and tight corners, and her face had only the faintest evidence of disapproval, so fleeting that it would disappear if challenged. She kept leaning out through the door, which opened over the precarious outside staircase, looking for either the hurricane or my grandparents, who were still banging things about downstairs.

The beds were pulled together and Juanita lay in the corner looking unconcerned, one ankle crossed over the thigh of the other leg, reading her Enid Blyton. Milton sat bolt upright beside her with his fingers clutching the shirt over his tummy, prepared to wait the whole night through, if necessary, for the moment when he could finish the job of being brave. He had completed his water-tank that morning and had spent the rest of the day looking vaguely smug. But the day had not passed quite as smoothly for everybody else.

At about ten in the morning we had all been surprised when Leslie Clerk strolled in. We called him Uncle Leslie. He was not a real uncle, but a Caribbean uncle of family affection. Pardi didn't have a lot of friends. His originality of mind and behaviour tended to isolate him. Those friends he did have were the type of people who relaxed rather than excited him. Leslie was the only "best friend" Pardi had ever had. They had been friends from their youth, though one would hardly have known how tender and enduring was their mutual affection, as they mostly ignored each other, like a pair of small children who make no connection until they find a game to play.

They would immerse themselves in deep philosophical conversation about anything, significant or insignificant—except politics; on that subject they could never agree ("The masses are illiterate, Harry man, so how can you give them the vote!") so they had decided never to speak.

Uncle Leslie always called Pardi "Harry". We never knew why.

We had not heard him coming; he just walked through the door, a small man, pale, white-haired and unassuming as ever. He was a piano tuner, and his disposition—aptly enough—never seemed to add background noise, which might confuse the purity of diagnosis within his ears.

"Morning." He stood there waiting to be told where to find Pardi.

"Leslie!" Mardi had always loved him. She felt he was, like Pardi, vulnerable. She welcomed the gentler world that he offered Pardi. Though their shyness made each of them almost an island, the two men relaxed with each other.

But Leslie, to her utter astonishment, had lately become her own soul-mate. From the simplicity of striving for the perfection of a musical note, he suddenly emerged, late in life, as a sculptor. He did powerful work in stone—huge grey pieces, smooth and bold, with confident lines and a striking clarity of vision.

He had come to warn Pardi of the hurricane. He shrugged when he heard that we knew and were remaining put, for Pardi's decisions, no matter how reckless, had never surprised him. He understood that his friend would go to any extreme to prove or defend or realize his conviction, whether it involved a principle, an ideal or a house. That was Harry.

Mardi ushered him out to the back, where Pardi was dragging Milton's drum away from the kitchen wall. If he saw Leslie, he made no acknowledgement of his presence; he continued with what he was doing and then turned on his heel and walked over towards the tool shed. Leslie followed him wordlessly up the path.

Soon Pardi emerged from the shack with his saw, and again Leslie traipsed behind him, to a huge tree. Pardi had decided to limb it as it was so near the house. He stopped and looked up at it, handing Leslie the saw. At fifty-nine he found ascending it more of a challenge than it once had been, so after two great jump-and-heaves failed to establish him aloft, he resorted to calling for Ivan with the ladder.

After a lot of rustling and cracking he sat on the bottom branch, carefully facing the juncture where he must sever it from the trunk of the tree. When he had balanced himself, he reached down for the saw. Leslie took his pew on the doorstep nearby.

They settled without ceremony into a deep conversation on extrasensory perception, as Pardi kept up a steady rhythm with the saw.

Uncle Leslie was psychic, and fascinated by the world of metaphysics and the occult. He could hold an object, any-thing solid—a brooch or a tie-clip—and, having no idea whose it was, could sense many things about the person.

"Vera believes all this is a lot of hocus-pocus," said Uncle Leslie, the topic of ESP pulling at a troubled memory thread which dangled from something Pardi's severe sister had said.

Aunt Vera was the eldest of the four Manleys. There was also Aunt Muriel, then Pardi, then Roy, who had died in the war, in that order. Pardi just went on sawing, but Leslie knew he was listening and continued: "She has never believed that I'm psychic." He sounded like a hurt child.

"Well, she doesn't believe in psychic power, period. But I know Ludlow is very interested and he is, after all, a doctor."

Pardi's offer of his brother-in-law was significant, as he had great regard for Ludlow: for his mind and his medical capabilities as much as for his endurance of Vera. He pulled some small branches out of his way, and then settled back into the mechanical rowing of the saw. Leslie did not seem consoled, and looked out at a line of low bilberry shrubs whose berries were still not ripe. The shrubs stood there sturdily year after year, intent on outlasting each drought.

"She made an appointment to see me and said she was bringing an object for me to read. Said I didn't know the owner. It was a pen. I held it and closed my eyes, and Vera said, "Well, Leslie...," and she dragged out the "well" in that disapproving voice of hers, because you know she was just waiting to catch me, sure I was going to talk a pile of foolishness."

He chuckled at the memory. The sweat was pouring down Pardi's forehead from where his soft steel-grey hair was thinning. He rested a bit in the tree, blowing and watching Milton engrossed with painting the drum; then he looked down at Leslie as though signalling for the rest of the story.

"I held this pen, and in seconds I sensed the wood chips flying all over the room. I opened my eyes and I said, "Vera, you must think I'm a fool! This is Edna's pen.""

"I'll be damned!" Pardi said, beaming with satisfaction at the success of his friend's sorcery and his sister's temporary comeuppance. She had irritated him sorely by sending a telegram that expressed her views on his planned whereabouts during the storm. He had received it early that morning. It read: "Utter folly!"

The gnashing of the saw back and forth had taken on a new burst of energy.

"Vera doesn't like anything she can't logically understand, she has no imagination. She likes... Lord-ohhhh!"

His sentence was lost in a grating noise as the huge limb cracked and tore, the last strings of bark unable to bear the weight any more. Leslie looked up at the tree for the first time, shielding his eyes from the sun, as Pardi tumbled, his thighs bracing the limb like the sides of a bronco. He landed on a mulch heap of branches and leaves which mercifully broke his fall.

Leslie remained sitting on the doorstep. "Harry, man, looks like you sawed yourself off the tree," he observed.

Pardi continued to speak as smoothly as he could while clambering out of the mess, brushing off leaves and twigs and his dishevelment.

"...she likes to be able to control everything."

He tried to escape his humiliation by simply walking away, then glancing back at the mishap with mere neighbourly curiosity. "Pity you weren't clairvoyant a few moments ago," he muttered as he passed his friend on the step.

The rest of the day was spent carefully avoiding any mention of the unfortunate fall, as we all busied ourselves with securing our ark.

By the time the first winds came we were all huddled on the bed upstairs, except for Pardi, who sat in a slatted wooden chair he had made himself. It leaned backwards at an awkward angle for everyone else, but it gave him the distant objectivity of a judge. His thin lips were never ungenerous, and tonight they were full of mischief.

"Miss B.," he said, "you are looking like a smug Methodist!"

The pines had been moaning steadily, but now the wind blew one hard gust that slapped the side of the house, and then another. The rain came either with the wind or on its own, for sometimes it pummelled the walls and sometimes it tumbled straight down. We were no stronger than the skill of a single Mavis Bank carpenter, and we shook and rocked and leaked, and the wind had long since found the spaces between the roofing shingles and through the walls.

For us the hurricane was contained in that small attic, our endurance the only measure of its ferocity. Pardi's face became our touchstone. In the flamboyance of the light its lean angles were enthusiastic, his substantial brow unfurrowed as he manned our little ship through its journey. He stopped up holes we'd never known existed with bits of putty or rag; moved a dresser in front of the door; emptied the raincoats into buckets on the floor when they were awash, and replaced them over our heads.

I think we children were too busy to feel afraid. Our job was the catchment detail. We were each allotted pots and pans and basins, containers of any sort, which we shuttled back and forth over the floor to catch the leaks, but soon there were so many that we just tried to catch the biggest, and with all the trickles and tinkles around me I kept having to use the chimmey pot.

Mardi was repeating a cant over and over: "Rocked in the belly of the deep, Now I lay me down to sleep." And she kept shutting her eyes and lifting her chin in defiance of her own keen imagination. On her Atlantic crossing with Pardi and the infant Douglas, going to meet her Jamaica for the first time, they were caught in a storm at sea and she was desperately seasick. Forcing herself to stay on deck at first, the monstrous bladders of waves towered above her, their bulk surging up out of the water as she remembered it in Cornwall, where her nightmares of being stranded by the engulfing sea first began. Later as she lay in her cabin, battered by the ocean's retching and her own, she remembered the little lines from her missionary father in her childhood.

And so now, once again, she had trusted her life to an adventure with Pardi, and she rocked to and fro with her arms hugging her knees, at the bottom of the bed, smiling at us when she opened her eyes as though to convince us that all was very, very well.

We lurched along till Pardi seemed to have got the edge on the storm, and our ears had grown used to the violence and we had begun to believe that the roof would stay on, and the walls, though they leaked continuously, would stay upright. There was just the fretting of the door, batter, batter, batter against the frame, and finally Pardi sat on top of the dresser and leaned against the door to subdue it.

Our initial diffidence had become curiosity through Pardi's alchemy, and as he pioneered our survival we all became intoxicated by his enthusiasm, though now and then we had to push away the drift of sleepiness. Juanita's arm was around the little ball of her brother in a rare moment of truce, Miss Boyd remained chided and Mardi had calmed herself down, and I can't remember anything about myself except what I was living through.

The raincoats over our heads kept drooping lower and lower. Juanita liked them because she felt no croaking lizard could fall on her and get tangled in her hair. That prospect terrified her far more than the tempest, despite the fact that Mardi had assured her Nomdmi was too cold for lizards.

Then someone moved on the bed, and the raincoats shifted and spilled their pools down onto us, so Pardi gathered each one up as best he could and emptied them into the buckets, and strung them up again. He repeated this routine several times during the night. When the containers of every description were full, Mardi said, "But dear, why didn't we settle downstairs?..."

"What's that?" he shouted.

Miss Boyd made a clucking noise that sounded mildly disapproving and Mardi changed the subject.

"Let's each tell a story," she suggested over the bellow of the storm.

We all grabbed at the diversion, and Mardi was nominated to start.

"What kind of story do you want to hear?"

"A story about a hurricane!"

"I don't know a story about a hurricane, but I can tell you a story about a high wind." She looked at me as she began her tale. "When your daddy and Uncle Douglas were small, we used to take them for summer holidays to Arthur's Seat, a wonderful old Jamaican country house in the hills of St. Ann. They had a big lake at the bottom of the hill...well, it wasn't really a lake," she admitted, as Miss Boyd had that troubled look she got when Mardi exaggerated. "It was just a pond, right, Miss B.?"

Miss Boyd, who had been there for all the boys' holidays at Arthur's Seat, looked relieved at the correction. "Yes, Mrs. Manley, I would more say a pond." She chuckled fondly over the memory. "In fact, it wasn't even as big as the one at Drumblair!"

"Oh, Miss B., really! That was just a big pool of mud we had at Drumblair!"

But Miss Boyd had started to laugh so hard I don't think she heard Mardi. "Do you remember when the boys...I think it was Michael and someone...went out one evening before they were to go to boxing with you? All dressed in their little suits and ties, and they decided to have a quick row in that old tree trunk they had hollowed out...and Vivian the driver blew the horn to call them, as you were so anxious you were late, Mr. Manley, and Michael started to laugh and couldn't stop, and they capsized and fell in the pond, and when they arrived back at the house they were covered in mud! Mr. Manley, you were so hopping mad! You sent them to bed...."

Mardi prepared to settle back into her own story. "Anyway...where was I? All the villagers thought we were a little strange, because I had my log of wood I brought, and we had our little wind-up gramophone and played classical music at full tilt, and we took along Biggums!"

"Who's Biggums?" Juanita asked.

"Biggums was Daddy's dog who made him eat too fast," I explained.

"No, no, that was Skittles, a long time after Biggums! That was a tiny little dog that your Daddy insisted on eating beside on the veranda, and he could never gobble as fast as Skittles, though God knows he's still trying! No, Biggums was a huge mastiff. He loved people and he would place his great head on your lap and slobber all over it. They were such big dogs that the breed died out during the war, because people couldn't get enough meat to feed them. He was like a massive pony! And he was white. And all the villagers were terrified of him because of his size, and also because he used to attack and kill their goats. So we used to keep him chained to the leg of a big, sturdy kitchen table so he couldn't get out and frighten people and hunt the goats."

As the story seeped into our consciousness, the battering of the storm became no more than a hum that our senses were learning to accommodate. The world had shrunk to this exhausted room which had taken its gulp of air, held its nose and submerged itself beneath the water, and we wouldn't know what had gone on in the world, what had been dragged away and what had survived, until we came back up.

"Well, it was a night of bright moonlight, and the most terrific breeze was howling over the St. Ann hills. Even the little pond, as Miss B. so ungenerously would have me call it, was lapping at its edges. And we were all playing a game of rummy at the dining table, just as we do here with you kids, and suddenly there was the most tremendous smashing noise and then a clattering and banging down the path outside, and we looked, and Biggums had got away! Would you believe he had torn the leg clean off the table, jumped out the window, and was galloping off, dragging the table leg on the chain through the moonlight and the high breeze!

"The villagers talk about it to this day...the night the moon was full and the winds were high and the famous Jamaican Rolling Calf, which hadn't been seen in those parts for a century, came out to play with evil and sin, came from the Devil with his eyes rolling with hell's fire and all his chains from Hades rattling away, as Biggums tugged the table leg farther and farther up the hill looking for his very own curry-goat feed under a full blooming moon!"

We were trying to laugh, our tired beings resting against her story, when there was a thunderous tearing and splintering sound in the night, and the house shuddered and we thought Biggums was back or the world had simply broken in two. We clutched at each other and looked around, but nothing seemed to have happened: the room still stood around us; the little lights soldiered on; the roof leaked but, braced by its eaves, bravely withstood the battering over our heads.

"A tree has come down on the house, I fear." Pardi had dismounted from the dresser but found there was nowhere to go, no way to check, so he emptied the raincoats again and respread them, dragged a few pots to new positions and reluctantly climbed back onto his perch.

One of us had started to cry; it may have been me, for I remember Mardi hugging and reassuring me with a little bit of D.H. Lawrence that I loved: "It is not easy to fall out of the hands of the living God: They are so large, and they cradle so much of a man." I snuggled into the crook of her arm. Underneath her open cardigan, I could peep through the sleeveless blouse at her underarm, which reminded me of the goosebumpy skin of chicken breast, my favourite meat.

She drew us purposefully back into her story.

"And the villagers never realized that it was dear old Big-gums stretching his legs!"

"Aunta, your turn to tell a story."

"Well now," Aunta said with her comfortable, creaking voice like an old basket, "let's see . . . did I ever tell you about the time the boys were waging their war with the toy soldiers, and they had a mighty battle planned upstairs in the back room? And Michael had to have a whole new battalion and they pooled all their pocket money and got a drive down to Cross Roads with Dossie in the back of the car? Well, they sent Dossie in to buy two dozen soldiers. Poor Dossie emerged ten minutes later with a porter pushing a crate of two dozen sodas! When Dossie realized his mistake, they said he just sat there smiling in the back of the car. Michael was so mad, but Doug kept giggling, he laughed and laughed so hard for days . . . every time he thought about it. And then another time they were all going swimming and Michael kept asking Dossie if he could swim, and Dossie said oh yes he could, he had learned in the holidays. They went to Bournemouth, and Dossie jumped straight in the deep end and almost drowned." Again she was chuckling. "And Michael always said Dossie had that same smile on his face as they dragged him to the side of the pool."

We fidgeted through Aunta's stories as we had heard them all before.

"It's Pardi's turn to tell us a story... tell us a story about a hurricane!"

"When I think of a hurricane, I can't tell you why but I think of my cousin Alex," Pardi said thoughtfully. "Do you want to hear a story about him?"

"Yes, tell us a story about Bustamante!"

Alexander Bustamante was the best-known man in Jamaica. We knew his story. He was chief minister of our "government still in embryo", as I used to hear it called, for we had not yet achieved self-government. As leader of the Labourites, he kept winning more seats than Pardi in elections. We knew that Pardi had all the brains, but that Busta often outwitted Pardi and got praise for things Pardi had really thought of or done.

Comrade children like us proudly recited, "Bustamante, wet 'im panty." But if Pardi was one safe arm of our island, somehow in my mind Busta was the other, even if it wasn't the one that embraced me. And he was Pardi's cousin, and we loved to hear stories about him.

"Cousin Alex. He wasn't called Bustamante then. He was the son of my mother's half-sister, for my grandmother was formerly married to a man named Clarke, so his name was Alexander Clarke. He later changed it to Bustamante when he went abroad and met a lot of colour prejudice, and wanted to appear to be a Spanish grandee, for he thought this would explain his swarthiness and wavy hair! He was quite a character from when he used to come and stay with us at Belmont, our family home. He was older than me, maybe Vera's or Muriel's age. An absolute charmer, very dapper, but his hair was always flying all over the place. He would pass through there on his visits like this hurricane, and then he'd be gone, just like that, and we wouldn't see him again for ages.

"So on one of these visits—I was maybe nine or so, and he would have been a teenager—we used to have great romps. If we played robbers, Alex always had the only gun, a big old twelve-bore that we kept in the house unloaded. We were tearing around and Alex had the gun, "Stick 'em up, stick 'em up," and he was pointing at Aunt Muriel, and out of the blue Vera yelled at her, "Duck, Muriel, duck!" and she did, behind the couch, and the gun went off, "Baddaay!"

We had forgotten the storm.

"But who loaded the gun?"

"We never ever knew how that damn gun got loaded, but it was. And if Vera hadn't been her bossy self, your Aunt Mu would have been blown to smithereens."

"What did Busta do?" we asked.

"He ran," he said thoughtfully, his dark, deep-set eyes with their irises circled in grey looking beyond us, as though his past were facing him and he were trying to retrieve from it some small bit of evidence he had misplaced.

"He was so damned frightened he just dropped the gun, leapt through the window and ran, and we couldn't find him for hours, he must have gone to get a drink in the village. He had made great friends in the village, everybody loved him. He told the most fantastic stories. He didn't come back till night when we were all sleeping."

The story apparently troubled Pardi. A momentary anguish frustrated his face; there seemed to be more he might say, but he didn't.

Mardi started to speak and stopped, swallowing hard instead, as though pressing down a thought that rose in her. Maybe the story of the young cousins reminded her of how distant they had become, of the endless struggle wasted now against themselves, their own people, the other side of the same coin, when the fight against colonial rule would have been so much more effective had they remained united. They were locked in an ideological war that had split a common past into two tribes. It was this past that was the enemy, not themselves. Where had this divide begun? Had there been a moment in that living-room at Belmont years ago when, by some quite unrelated mischance, a natural trust, an assumption of innocence, had been broken?

"Yup. That is that. Story done."

The storm had stopped while he was telling his story. The world outside had changed. The drips were still plunking in the pots, but otherwise no sound was left in the world but what we made ourselves. Mardi looked over at us, but we too had let go and were falling into sleep, as though we were part of the storm.

Pardi climbed off his perch.

"I think it has stopped!" he said tentatively and, after waiting a while to be sure, Mardi and Miss Boyd helped him pull the chest of drawers away from the door, and he unlatched this and that and opened us up to the night. And very carefully he crept down the stairs, which were still intact.

"What a funny colour the sky is," observed Mardi. "It's sort of navy blue...how can that be? It looks like it's rising like a funnel into the heavens!" She couldn't see in the dark, yet that is the one thing she always remembered the same way in a tale that was to change in each telling over the years. She said it was like entering a cathedral and looking up at the great ocean wave of her youth hoisted on high, navy blue and made of air.

Apparently Pardi had not noticed the sky. We could hear him thrashing at branches and leaves and whistling his appraisals before he said his "Lord-oh's" and "Jesus wept's" as he rummaged through the chaos until an attack so ferocious blasted the other side of the house, and the wind which had kept us leaning one way now came from the opposite direction, as if answering its own argument.

God knows how he got back, but Mardi and Miss Boyd knotted themselves together with their arms and somehow managed to drag him up again, and had to pull so hard to close the door that everyone fell down when it was finally clenched shut.

They said we seemed to have reached the other side of the storm, which we then rode out; it sucked where it had blown before, and Pardi changed places as the door seemed to want to run away now, off into the night.

That's the last I remember before falling asleep. I didn't wake up till morning.

We never knew which winds took Mini away, leaving her little concrete floor in her memory, with the slain trunk of a giant tree lying beside it, or at what point the pines and mahoes were torn down. But by morning the bracken's young green frills on the hillside were the tallest trees in a ruined forest, and the view was so naked that the island seemed looted, and not even a child's cry could be heard from the valleys. In a world where every footstep had taken us deeper into mystery, leaving us each with our own interpretation, not a single secret was left.

All we knew for sure was that the crunching and thud we heard was a huge mahoe coming down and breaking the kitchen's back, leaving its red, waxy flowers mangled amid the debris like the lips of an ageing whore, and that it must have been *Papine* who held us down, for the house was all that was left on the hillside, looking like a grim Cyclops through its single eye across at Grannum's plateau, the juniper perched before it like a club in its clenched fist.

4

THE
GUAVA STICK

Two years after Hurricane Charlie, in late 1953, Pardi suffered a mild heart attack. I learned to pronounce "coronary" and "thrombosis", new words which I found very grand and thought befitted a grandfather, especially mine.

He woke up one morning with "indigestion".

Mardi heard him pacing up and down in the room next door and wondered what made him so restless. Was it his nightmares again? He got them when he was worried, and at the moment there was a lot of tension in his party, the PNP. An election was due in two years. They were squabbling over the question of ideological direction. When she got up and saw his newspaper, *The Daily Gleaner*, lying untouched in front of the door, she went over to check on him.

She found him standing in front of his medicine cabinet over the basin, distressed and preoccupied. No amount of Bisodol had brought him relief.

He was searching for something more peppermint, turning the labels around to face him, extracting a few potions to look at them closely through the thumb-print of magnification in the centre of his spectacles, then returning each to its circle of dust.

He settled on a bottle of Bayer Aspirin, opened it and took two.

"Do you have a headache?" she asked.

"No. Not really. Just in case," he explained.

It felt like his old ulcer. He had awakened in the grip of an acid tourniquet in his chest, knowing it was the result of tension and worry. If it was a nervous duodenum, why hadn't his usual triple dose of Bisodol worked? He thought he could feel a pain in his left shoulder, but it must be psychosomatic. He had once read about tetanus and developed such a stiff jaw that he was almost unable to finish arguing a case in court. It had been his imagination.

This too must be his imagination. Mind over matter. But he was fighting the knowledge that something basic was broken, that the quiet metronome that kept his life in the surety of its beat had somehow faltered. And no matter how he frowned his mind into service, a deep and inevitable flow of time and consequence was pulling his spirit into an awareness he could not resist.

"That's silly, dear. Aspirin is the worst thing to take for a stomach. Why not take off the day, and curl up in bed with a good book?"

Mardi loved to designate members of her family sick and place them in bed. It was the safest place to be, really, and when she was working she loved the thought that those for whom she felt responsible were out of harm's way, so that she could concentrate totally on the studio. It was the gentlest form of control, and provided us all with an abiding nostalgia for days when we woke with a cold or a queasy stomach, rewarded by her affection, dry toast and soft-boiled eggs with fresh squeezed and honeyed orange juice, and a sense of honour bestowed on the proud bearer of the affliction.

No. He would go and see Moodie.

But Ludlow Moodie was out doing his hospital rounds. Pardi declined the nurse's invitation to wait and, slipping into Moodie's office under the pretext of using the phone, helped himself to some medicine he found in a dark brown bottle in the cupboard. He took the foul-tasting liquid and worked through the day but it didn't help. When he came home that evening he still felt unwell.

The phone rang and Mardi was relieved to hear Moodie.

"How is Norman?" he asked, in a mildly testy voice.

"Still feeling lousy, I'm afraid, Moodie. He got some medicine from your office, but it hasn't worked, though he says it tasted so awful it must be good for him."

"But *what* did he take?"

"I'm not sure..."

"Edna, one of these days your husband is going to end up swallowing someone's urine sample by mistake."

"Oh, dear...."

"Exactly," he said, and after a pause, "Well, I'd better come and see him."

Moodie came, and he sent for Dr. Aub, and after some tests and probing they said he needed complete rest. He had suffered a mild coronary thrombosis.

He was home for weeks, learning to bowl dozens of small white pills from his fingers onto his tongue with great dexterity. He hated Mardi's bed-baths, and was relieved when the drought brought water lock-offs which saved him the indignity of the ritual. He had read everything he could find to read, and we could hear the powder-soft trails of his tiptoeing all through the upstairs of the house, its wooden bones cracking under his feet as he prowled through his recuperation.

Mardi received the news with such intensity that she felt it had happened to her own heart. As a young man Pardi had nearly died of typhoid fever. Maybe it had weakened his heart. It was always lungs or heart in our family. It had been lungs that afflicted her own father, Harvey Swithenbank, a frail Methodist minister with plumbago-blue eyes and skin so pale it seemed to have light instead of blood travelling beneath it. He used to sit and listen to her play the piano, and for a little while Edna, the middle child of the nine siblings, could find her differences, the differences that made her spirit unique and her self special to him. He was her greatest friend. The loss of him when she was only nine years old had been her life's heartbreak. He had gone out in a howling winter storm to visit a sick parishioner and as a result, a few days later was lying in bed with pneumonia. Halley's comet appeared that night at its brightest. Her mother let her kiss him goodbye. Mardi always said he had looked like a sculpture in white marble.

Men and storms. For weeks after the hurricane her husband had walked those hills, and for months the broken area of the Kingston constituency he represented in Parliament, finding solutions for each little roofless shack, each waterless stand-pipe, the homeless, the hungry, the roadless. He even used the Drumblair studio as a hurricane relief centre; he was like her father, lovingly driven by duty. The strain was terrific.

Keep the ones you love at home, safe from sickness, she believed. Service empties a good man till all he has left are his lungs parched in drought, and his flawed heart losing the rhythm of life.

Despite her concern, Pardi's condition brought certain benefits to my life. He was now house-bound. At first he had to stay in bed, but soon he was able to "potter around", as Mardi called it. His period of convalescence, which happened to coincide with a serious all-island drought, provided me with two of my most memorable adventures in Drumblair, and a glimpse into the maverick heart of my illustrious relative.

The first adventure took place soon after he was allowed downstairs. Pardi and I went on one of our long, meandering walks, each treated as a major expedition. This one began, as always, with us finding appropriate sticks for our height, just as we did when we were at Nomdmi. In the hills the sticks came in handy for climbing steep slopes, but on these flat lands we just dragged them along out of custom.

The gully behind Drumblair had a life of its own. Children from the nearby community of Four Roads played up and down its baked, cracked mud-bed. In some places sand washed down by the floods had gathered into dunes that men in trucks took away to mix with cement. The sides of the gully were reinforced with huge wire sausages of stones to protect the land from erosion when the rains came and the gully flooded. When these floods came, within ten minutes a car could not travel the road where it crossed the flow, for it would be swept away. Sometimes from Drumblair you could hear rumour of the weather from the stones' rumbling chatter before even a drizzle had started, and the darkened skies told you that the rain had already begun in the hills.

But the drought made it dry that day, and Pardi decided to cross to the other side, beyond the boundaries of Batiste's jurisdiction, where the land was wilful and orphaned. The tall trees stood nobly on acres of long grass which the wind would comb this way and that. We parted the beige, sometimes scratchy grass with our sticks and pulled our way through a hostile silence as the land watched our intrusion.

"I believe people think nobler thoughts under tall trees," Pardi observed, and I nodded.

We were covered in burrs, and the grass was up to my head and his waist.

"Even a piece of broken glass in the sun could start a fire in this grass, it's so dry! Have you ever seen a real fire?" he asked me.

I thought for a moment as I pulled some sticky nodules off my sleeve.

"Yes, Par. The time you lit the candles on the Christmas tree at Nomdmi." The tree had started to burn when we were having dinner.

"That wasn't a real fire. That was just a small accident. Fire is one of the great forces of nature. It can spread as fast as water can run in that gully, and it can be equally devastating. Fire shows us the majesty of creation, and reminds us how fragile and unimportant we are as mere humans in the sight of the universe."

"Yes, Par."

We walked on a little farther. Way over on the right we could hear the occasional drone of a car where the main road crossed the gully.

"I'll show you," he suddenly said as, dropping his stick, he searched in his pocket and retrieved a box of matches. On the second strike the match lit, and he shrouded it with the cupped hands of an old smoker. I stared in wonder. When the flame had caught and was steady, he gently placed it against a long straw of grass. In a second the dry blade singed, and then an orange tongue of flame leapt joyfully along it.

I don't remember the details, but I can still see his face shining, either from the heat or from elation at his own mischief, as he stood in the high grass, his hands on his hips, his gaze transfixed by the blaze of energy. To me he seemed as grand and fierce as the young flames that struggled in the wind for supremacy. I felt so honoured to be near his exhilaration that I didn't even think to be afraid.

Suddenly he reacted to the danger. With a "Lord-oh!" he grabbed me and tossed me over his shoulder and ran like hell through the high grass with its rising smoke. We made it to the main road and stopped so Pardi could catch his breath. A group of excited passers-by had gathered to watch the advancing army of flames, the bones of the underbrush cracking and crunching in the unexpected cremation.

"Lawd, me Jesus, Barrista land bu'n down!" said a toothless old man leaning on his bicycle, his cap tipped back on his head. He was too intent on the spectacle of his bad news to notice the rumpled Barrister beside him on the road.

We walked the long way back to Drumblair, along Old Church Road and up through the front gate. By this time the sirens of fire engines were sounding all over the sky, and we had made a pact that this would be our secret. Mardi must never know what had happened.

On that short walk home I experienced a feeling of awe, a wonder at the mischief and audacity of both the fire and my impetuous grandfather. Was he, as Mardi put it, a drastic man?

He did flirt with danger. He seemed fascinated by the macabre, and enjoyed other people's squeamishness at its manifestations. I remember how, in a mischievous mood, he would announce with a gleam in his eyes, "The days of our lives are three score years and ten," and then reduce me to screams by pretending suddenly to die; he'd grab his throat with a guttural, choking noise, then slump his head back with his tongue out.

Although he was a tease, behind all the humour of his pranks was a daring curiosity. His experiments were reckless in their innocence, as he staked everything on some notion he had, pushed some point to its limit. I think sometimes, because of his single-mindedness, the consequences took him by surprise.

Over the years I came to realize that he needed that fervour and courage, that whole-heartedness, to shake up the political system as he did. In the early days of our history, concepts like adult suffrage and national independence must have seemed as explosive and perilous as hurricanes and fires.

It was on a Sunday towards the end of Pardi's recuperation that the second notable adventure took place, one which would bring this period from drought and fire to what I considered an apt conclusion of water.

The family was invited to lunch. It was one of Mardi's structured "Let's have a nice time" occasions, which I suppose might have appeared self-conscious to others, although they were quite normal to us. She had begun to organize them because we now consisted of such a large cast of characters. These family occasions always included the great-aunts, Vera and Muriel. I loved the aunts, particularly the sterner one, Vera. They were like solid book-ends, safe and straightforward elements containing our lives. They seemed to me to be extensions of Pardi, ones he seldom noticed, rather the way houses have appendages such as a garage or a studio nearby that they don't have to look at. I sensed that they loved him dearly, especially Muriel, and with each moue it was clear to me that Mardi was someone they put up with. To a certain extent, too, Mardi was putting up with them.

As usual, the aunts arrived first, coming early to visit Pardi. They found him, Mardi and me poised at the brow of a slope behind the cow paddocks where Mardi kept a dairy. In the distance we could see a game of cricket being played by men lounging with lazy insolence in their formal whites, in a sport that seemed to afford any amount of time. There was suddenly a dash of movement, and the crack of a bat.

"Look, that's Nugget bowling." Mardi pointed to the subsequent burst of activity as two batsmen changed ends and the fielders hustled after the ball.

Behind us were stalls for the horses and paddocks with troughs for the cows. Two huge silos emerged from the earth with the smell of hay and molasses. The cows all had names like Moon and Day-Dream, and were listed alphabetically in Mardi's dairy books, where she entered their daily yield of milk by the pint. She had once announced to my father that her dairy made a profit, but Pardi quietly drew him aside to explain that since he paid all the expenses, and her figures did not take this into consideration, they were in fact misleading. We had an old black buggy in which Wright, a lean and agile herdmaster who buzzed efficiently around the listless cows like a persistent fly, drove to deliver the milk. The buggy was pulled by an elderly grey mare retired from an unsuccessful life as a racehorse. Her name was Harriet, and she was also used as a safe mount for children.

"Douglas, Carmen and Little Norman are coming to lunch, and Michael is bringing Thelma." Mardi listed the names carefully to the aunts and myself as though this information assured the family of continuity. She sat down nearby in the shade of a guango tree to worry over Pardi in comfort. These days she hovered in a mimed desperation which Pardi thought was caused by the drought; in fact what he saw was the containment of her horror at discovering that he had somehow damaged his heart.

The biggest addition to the house and my life was the arrival of my father, Michael. I had no memory of him in England. I don't remember seeing him there for a first time; the legend of him just became a presence in Drumblair that hadn't been there before. I became conscious of his tall frame on my horizon, a third statue against the skyline to join those of Pardi and Mardi.

My early impressions of my father had been vague, just stories I had heard from the family: the boy on the floor competing with Skittles to see who would finish his food first; the obsessed sixteen-year-old who drank every drop of liquor in the Drumblair cabinet and nearly died of alcohol poisoning when he fell in love for the first time and was rejected; the boy who stamped out bullying at his school with his characteristic loyalty to the underdog, a foible that inspired most of his life; the boy whose schoolmates called a strike against the teachers who expelled him, when he stuck to his guns on a matter of principle.

Whenever I found myself at odds with the world, I secretly believed he would arrive to champion my cause. I was told he missed me, and would be surprised if I had grown or put on any weight by the time he came home, so I was encouraged to eat more. This was part of a youth-long battle waged by the good people of Drumblair to get me to behave and to eat.

"These are all forms of protest," Mardi would explain sadly, "because you thought you were taken away from your mother."

"Well...was I?"

She said that it wasn't that simple, "but that's how you got it into that pretty little head of yours." But I knew only what I had been told, which was that Mummy had been sick and Daddy had had to sit his exams so I had to come to Jamaica, and then Daddy and Mummy had "broken up"—a disturbing image to my literal mind—and Daddy was coming home and Mummy "couldn't cope", so I would just stay here, and wouldn't I rather like that?

"Here" was Drumblair, the only home I knew. So for me there wasn't any alternative, and I never really thought about it much. But I liked it when my opinion was asked, and I loved the aura of concern that surrounded me when my "trauma" was discussed, as it was many times, and I especially enjoyed the stories of my tiny and exotic mother, who was said to be bubbly like champagne.

So at twenty-seven my father returned to Jamaica, with a degree in economics from London University, a few years' experience in journalism and a failed marriage. My earliest memory of him is watching this very large man, "six feet two and a half inches in my stockinged feet", fold himself with difficulty into his car, a tiny Standard 8.

My father, to me elusive and intangible, always had great power over my life, but I don't believe it was ever conscious on his part. I think the break in continuity when I left England resulted in the subsequent shyness between us.

I thought him the most exciting person in the world, and the second most handsome. I was very proud when everyone said I looked just like him. Although his features were not on their own outstanding, something in the way they shared his face was most attractive. He had the brightest glow of anyone I have ever known, and by contrast the most unsettling shadows. When he was happy, I knew. He would sing a simple tune—"Ba-de-di-du-du . . . pence-pence and tups-tups" —mimicking a lame man who used to sell peppermints and chewing-gum at his school, and he'd dance with a little lame shuffle, and if I wasn't in a good mood too, he'd put me in one. He was "the pence-pence and tups-tups man". He'd make everyone's troubles go away, find solutions for everything. Wherever he arrived, he lit up the room. Like yeast, he could always make the dough rise. In this sense he was very like Mardi.

I remember two silly things I loved about him. I thought he was ticklish on his calves because he had convinced me, toughing it out and not laughing, that he was not ticklish on the soles of his feet. But then once he forgot to laugh when I tickled his calves. That was how I found out. The other was that he'd call me when I wasn't looking. When I turned to answer him, his finger would jab my cheek where it pointed in wait, and he'd grin and say, "Caught you!"

He taught me to swim. He took me to Cable Hut Beach, where the south coast sand was grey and the sea had very big waves. He had become an excellent, strong swimmer as a schoolboy, when he had to stop playing football because of an injured knee and took up swimming instead; he became captain of the swimming team. He would take my friends and me, one at a time, into the battery of waves, screaming and gasping for air but always safe.

As far as I could determine, his two pet peeves were both related to our dining-table. One was any accidental spilling of rice grains on its surface, and the other was Percy the cat's cough, which usually hacked drily from underneath.

He taught me to catch a ball, and told me I had "extraordinary reflexes"—encouragement which was probably inspired by my poor showing, but which led me to persuade Milton to throw the ball to me repeatedly when my father was nearby, hoping to impress him. There was one rule he never compromised, and I learned it the hard way, being sent on one occasion to my bed: one had to be a good sport. Sometimes he would organize a ball-catching game of "broken bottle" with us, and his enthusiasm would be infectious, making magic of the lawn and an event of the day. There was never enough of him. No matter how much he gave, something in his nature made one hungry for more.

Then, like magic, the Michael I knew would be gone.

I never knew what caused his shadows. He kept his personal disappointments to himself. But he would change, and at these times I learned to be wary of him. It was not that his temper was out of the ordinary, for all the Manleys had bad tempers—none worse than Douglas', which Mardi said was "rare, but beware"; my father's always seemed by comparison more "managed". Nor was his irritability unusual in a very irritable family. But when he became preoccupied, the magic between us disappeared into some awful void. I would approach the "pence-pence and tups-tups man", and he would respond as though he had never seen me before, as though he had never heard of the pence-pence man, as though that man had never lived there. Each time it seemed to take away some important premise from me.

Miss Boyd, often frustrated by my misbehaviour, must have sensed this unease, for she used it with partial success to control me; there was always a list of my misdemeanours in progress which I was told would be presented to my father if it reached a total of twenty in a week. This did not help our relationship. I developed anxieties about him that he didn't deserve.

Michael lived in the downstairs annex of Pardi's study, which, like the dining-room and unlike the rest of the house, had a tiled floor; among his father's law books and papers and boxes and microphones and speakers, he had a small iron Vono bed from which his feet would protrude at the bottom. He smoked about eighty cigarettes a day, and his ashtrays were crammed with the maggots of his dead cigarettes, and the smell of nicotine and a cough not unlike Percy's followed him through the house.

He was seldom home, and when he was I mostly remember him either eating or typing, with a cigarette always burning beside him if it wasn't between his long yellow fingers. At first he was an associate editor for *Public Opinion*, a paper grandly referred to as the "official organ" of the People's National Party. He had an old black Olivetti he had pawned from time to time in England to get him through lean times. He ate with speed and desperation, always in a hurry, maybe still competing with Skittles in habit's memory. He was paying his dues, Mardi would explain, as, to my disappointment, he left for work.

I did not realize it then, but after the teachings of Harold Laski who would influence a generation of West Indian political thinkers, Michael must have found it an intriguing time to come home. There was a hard-working quartet of devout

Marxists in the PNP who wanted my grandfather and the moderates within the party to adopt that doctrine. They were called the Four H's because all four surnames began with the letter H. Their zealous refusal to compromise threatened to destroy the entire organization. Pardi, as party leader, swung the axe, and they were purged from the party. I don't know if Pardi necessarily disagreed with all of their views, for he was ideologically a Fabian Socialist, but his belief in the Western view of democratic process was profound, and in any case he was shrewd enough to know that there were tides against which one could not swim, and that the drift towards a radical left wing was one of them. Despite the purge in the early 1950s, this tug-of-war between centre left and radical left was to haunt the party for years to come.

The purge indirectly set off a course of events that would lead to my father's entry into trade unionism. Since the creation of Bustamante's union, the BITU, there had been a second important union formed called the Trade Union Congress. It had been affiliated with the PNP, but as it was in part founded and run by one of the Four H's, it promptly disaffiliated itself. That was how the National Workers' Union came into being in 1952. (As a child I thought the initials NW stood for Pardi's first and middle names, Norman Washington.) My father helped build this new trade union, later quitting his job at *Public Opinion* and joining the NWU, then one year old, as its sugar supervisor. The sugar industry had by far the largest workforce in Jamaica and the BITU had a monopoly on their bargaining rights. For what seemed like quite a long time I heard updates on the continuing inroads my father made on BITU territory to win representational rights for the younger union.

And then he met Thelma.

Thelma Verity was by an odd coincidence the adopted sister of my mother's first husband, Bob Verity. She lived in the Verity home, where my mother's eldest child, Jeremy, had grown up with his paternal grandparents. Her second child, a daughter Anita Verity, lived with my mother in England and I understood had been close to my father. As a child I knew I had important connections to the name Verity, but it was a riddle I didn't figure out till I was much older. The name just kept providing me with new relatives!

My father had fallen in love again—Mardi said this as though he had fallen down a well. Thelma was a dancer. She was beautiful and grown up but young, and she laughed a lot, and she had Chinese eyes and exotic curly black hair and smelled of gilded bottles of rare flowers, the perfumes of romance. She blew into the thoughtful, quiet world of Drumblair like a gust of summer wind, as impudent yet as lost as a severed petal. And she cooked with garlic.

Thelma worked at the airport with KLM (Dutch planes, dear, Mardi explained) and always had samples like miniature liquor bottles or tiny cups and saucers, and treasures of biscuits and sweets. She would have little dresses made for me out of the same fabric as her lovely summery frocks, and once she entered me in a costume competition as a dandelion, and she planned the costume and I won. It was a brand-new world for me.

Then there was Uncle Douglas, my father's only brother. He too had recently returned from England, where he had finished his doctorate. He brought with him his wife, Carmen, and their young son, Norman.

Douglas and Michael were said to be the antithesis of each other, although they did look somewhat alike. In some ways they seemed to be the genetic conclusion of what the family looked like, without actually looking very much like either parent. Their complexion was exactly the beige they would have been if their parents' shades had been mixed together on a palette. They were both men who entered a room and made others wonder who they were. They had presence. Their square faces were interesting, with strong jaws inherited from their grandmother Margaret, and candid, up-turned noses. Both had the family's thin lips, and well-spaced, intelligent eyes under an expressive forehead that displayed their thoughts. They had the family trait of ebullient hair with a natural wave that made me think of what I used to call "pinchy-combs", silver clips that salons used on ladies' heads to produce bounce.

Douglas was the elder by two years. He was an introverted man whose thoughtful grouchiness and lifelong myopia gave the impression that he was the serious son. Michael was by contrast taller and more charismatic; he had an energy and intensity that fuelled him and camouflaged his nervousness. Although Michael was individually intensely shy and self-conscious, he had a startling comfort with centre stage once he warmed up to it. Douglas always said Michael was no good with less than a thousand people.

Douglas loved a party. Michael could put on a social show when he had to, but would happily retreat into the recesses of his own world after that, and his own world was happiest for him when it included a woman. He had few male friends and they were, even if lifelong, merely occasional.

Douglas' great gift was that of friendship. If Michael's lens scanned the horizon for the size of a crowd, Douglas' by contrast zoomed in on individuals. Michael thought in concepts, huge visionary leaps, and left others to fill in the spaces for him. Douglas lingered with fascination on oddities of minutiae. The elder brother was more plodding—one thing at a time to its conclusion. He was never prone to crazes. Things he liked to do he continued doing. His hobby was growing orchids. He liked them because they were beautiful and he said not too demanding, growing slowly over a long period of time while being ignored. He was the phlegmatic one, wry, with a dry, witty sense of humour. He was unpredictable but, in what might appear to be surrounding disorder, always possessed a unique sense of order of his own.

They never attracted the same friends. They never attracted the same women. People usually liked one or the other.

Douglas had returned from writing a thesis on race relations in Liverpool. He submerged himself in academia. For him, university had provided a room where he could disappear, disconnecting himself from the world around him. The larger he made that room, the farther there was for him to prowl and the less he had to refer to anywhere else. The more detached he became, the more eccentric he appeared to be.

For Michael, ever the activist, university had been a passage through which he sprinted, hardly stopping to notice his grades, using it merely as a means to equip himself for re-entry into the practical world to which he was ultimately committed.

Douglas was a lecturer in sociology at the University of the West Indies on the Jamaican campus. At thirty his family trait of premature grey hair and his doctorate made him very distinguished despite the leather "Jesus sandals" whose buckles jingled along with his relaxed stride—so relaxed that it was hard to imagine he had once equalled his father's hundred-yard record, after which feat he stopped running, as though he had made his point.

By nature he was absent-minded and contrary, but the former was now thought to be professorial, and Mardi rationalized the latter as characteristic of both his ambidexterity and his birth sign, Gemini. "He's a maverick," she would explain. Beneath his reticence was an affable manner with which, at arm's length, he coped with the family, and which attracted a select group of, almost without exception, eccentric friends.

Carmen was a woman of exquisite ebony beauty who looked like a Spanish flamenco dancer in a black velvet picture I had seen somewhere. She wrote well. She was an actress. She had talent. Sometimes her black eyes looked cruel, sometimes they were daring. She was full of pantomime and wicked laughter, flashed like a lightning rod with impulse after impulse throughout the day, and would then strangely collapse at some time during the evening, usually at one of her dinner parties; she would just fall asleep and Douglas would at last get his chance to speak. He would wait for the ticking of her inner clock to run down, and would not rewind her.

My cousin Norman was two years younger than me, and the first companion of my generation within the family. I revealed to him the secrets of Drumblair. He was small, fast and wiry, with Pardi's capacity for complete detachment and preoccupation within his own thoughts. He was also Pardi's rich brown colour, and looked the most like him. He would enter the house with little regard for any of us, and head straight for an object or area of his interest. He had his father's ability to calculate a bee-line to wherever he needed to go without becoming embroiled in emotions along the way. He had great natural rhythm which, the moment he heard music, revealed him to be the only member of the family who could dance worth a damn.

Carmen called him by derogatory nicknames, such as "Stinker"; affectionately intended, she found this funny. But Mardi was alarmed. She found them unkind, inappropriate and unacceptable, but although she tried gently to stop Carmen on several occasions, it was to no avail; her daughter-in-law, who felt that our family took life far too seriously, persisted with the nicknames although they made everybody grimace.

"Gruesome!" was Aunt Muriel's verdict.

"Beneath contempt!" was Aunt Vera's.

"It's not amusing at all, it's vulgar," Mardi worried, "and God knows the effect it may have later on."

"Now, why do you think she does it?" mused Pardi.

But the family never found out why. That was just Carmen.

Mardi was much affected by her sons. She always seemed to make an effort when they appeared. She was proud of their achievements, but for some reason did not feel they were attributable to herself as a mother. She always felt guilty for the time she had taken from them to keep for herself. Especially Douglas—she felt he suffered from being first-born. He had borne the family's fears about the offspring of first cousins. Mardi and Pardi had read books to prepare themselves for parenting, and Mardi always regretted following some advice about leaving him to cry by himself. She also worried that their move to Jamaica had adversely affected him, as he had been only eleven weeks old and it had been a difficult adjustment for her. In fact the marriage had almost ended; within a short time she had lost her nerve and returned to England, taking Douglas.

If Douglas was the casualty of a bumpy start, Michael was the beneficiary of the couple's redefinition. He was the child of their reunion when Mardi returned five months later, having made up her mind to throw in her lot with her husband and Jamaica. Pardi bought Drumblair. They decided that they wanted a daughter called June Patricia. Michael was born into a new comfort and calm, and a pink nursery. When he came home from the hospital they couldn't be bothered with all the rules they had inflicted on their first child, and just slung the new baby into bed with them.

Mardi mustered a certain nobility to cope with her sons' attachments and her eventual daughters-in-law. I don't think she felt jealousy; she had, curiously, a male assumption of her place in the world, and an almost chauvinist assurance of her genetic and inalienable place as the matriarch of the family. Coquetry or plumage were incidental to the fixity of her status quo, and therefore the presence of either would never have caused her more than mild irritation. She was the sure, incorruptible centre of Drumblair, keeping it unspoiled by frivolity, maintaining its deeper purpose. Drumblair was the healing stream, the source of renewal and inspiration.

But she knew that her defence of this sanctuary in the face of her sons' wives might be mistaken for envy—of their youth, their glamour and flamboyance—so she willed her being to welcome their intrusion, fixing her enthusiasm on the creative talents she discovered in each woman. Sometimes her effort showed beyond the edge of her good will. But they seemed to enjoy the house, and this brought her sons home: Michael always waiting to connect with his father, Douglas, protected by his own moat, prowling a safe distance from everyone.

Mardi always said the tropics had their own seasons, so she didn't need to miss spring or winter or fall; she felt this hankering was an affectation of the British who came here. It was a put-down, she would say, they just wanted everyone to know that where they came from there were four seasons, and that they had fur coats and wool suits and grey sweaters, and fireplaces and heaters. They still loved to tell you something was over the hearth, in a country where there weren't any hearths. What they didn't tell you was that the only time they were ever happy was when the sun was shining. "Truth is," she would say, "the English are enough to make the weather grumble!"

Yes, the tropics had seasons. There was Bombay mango season, when Pardi could taste the poetry in the fruit, and the season of the subtle roseapple, which tempted us from the unreachable height of its tree; there was poui-blooming season, when the trees rejoiced with the ardour of a child's primary yellow, and the bitter compulsion of tamarind season. There was the season when the red plum trees bore fruit, and the season when the coolie plums gave every child bellyache. There was guinep season, when you had to pray that the children sucking the slippery, enfleshed seeds didn't choke. And there was the hungry season of the white-winged doves which Mardi called pea-doves, when she heard them calling to her early in the morning, "Put out the corn!" When they stopped, as the season stopped, she wondered where they went to.

But there were two seasons that affected Mardi the most. One was that of the night-blooming cereus, which came at midnight twice a year and lasted only a few hours. The cereus vine lived on the oak tree. Pardi and Mardi would sit out on the lawn in the moonlight—it always bloomed in moon-light—and a fragrance of tea and bark and lilacs and old shawls full of sorrow and musky closets with discreet secrets would assail them. In night's ghostly, altering depths which distort reason and make vision either false or too true, these opaque white flowers unfurled their huge blooms and fixed the darkness with their waxen gaze, and the air was full of sweet decadence for those fleeting funereal hours.

Pardi and Mardi seemed to love each other most for these hours, and pulled the strands of their years into the fierce aura, wrapped themselves, memory by memory, plan by plan, past with future into the vivid smell of this intimacy. It engulfed them, and all the weariness of routine and famil-iarity, the knowing too much and too well, dissipated as the tyranny of that first passion all those years ago overcame them. In those early days they had been cold and often hun-gry, surrounded by a lingering smell of fried food in her sin-gle room over the fish shop in London, but their union was fierce and inevitable, and quenched as surely as it generated, binding them in an unbreakable spell they cast on each other.

But these days they woke together in his bed by the far wall, middle aged and present again. Below them on the lawn, hanging along the trunk of the oak tree, the cereus' huge petals were yellowing, closed and stuck to each other in the flaccid grip of the long, pink sepals that held them like a sleeping claw, their spent weight dragging them down in exhaustion.

The other was the season of drought. This could be the longest season of all. The drought, Mardi would say, got into her hair. It was the blowing of the breeze that she dis-liked. She hated dust. Besides, the wind always made her feel caught in contradiction. The impertinence of its broadsides angered her. The seeds of the woman's-tongue trees rattled beige in their pods and reminded her of wood ants in dry walls. And yet, for all she hated this season, it occupied her like a victorious army, and she would outcarve the worrying wind, and chisel away like termites searching for the heart of the wood.

And now there was a drought, and I had my next great adventure with Pardi. He was looking for water, and he had summoned a diviner called Fish. It was his trail we were following—my grandparents, my two great-aunts and myself —in search of a source of water under the earth. I had no idea why, and when I asked Mardi she merely said that the Devil finds work for idle hands.

Pardi's search for water may have been inspired by a number of things. It could have been the bitterness of the bunches of grapes ripening on his arbour in gauze bags to keep them safe from the birds. Over each larger bunch he had marked the name of a beneficiary, but these chosen people came to dread the gift, which produced acid secretions in their jaws even before they tasted it. Oh that the birds had them instead!

Then there were the frustrations caused by the daily lock-offs by the Water Commission; no one could bathe, the cattle had to stand by the empty troughs and the clay in the studio waited to be drenched. Maybe he remembered our fire.

Whatever the reason, he was now following the trail of the water diviner, whose short legs bowed as though mimicking the forked guava stick that he carried aloft like a giant wishbone. It was said that if there was a subterranean tide, it would pull the end of the stick down towards the flow— sometimes so powerfully that it would break the diviner's arms if he did not give in. Then we would build a well to entice the water, Pardi said, and the cattle and land and house would be able to drink in abundance through any drought.

I jumped from pie to pie of cow dung, breaking the sunbaked surfaces and releasing the familiar smell of grassy excrement, which I found comforting as a child.

"My dear, what *are* you doing?" asked Aunt Vera, with her aura of severe reproach. She sat down on the severed stump of a tree and managed to remain immaculate and composed, her hair in its soft net resisting the breeze.

We all looked at her, wondering who was the object of her displeasure. Well, everyone did except Pardi, for he was lost in concentration as he watched the slow progress of Fish with his wand. The diviner's feet were now feeling their way; with each step he closed his eyes, and he seemed to be praying, or maybe intuiting through his extra sense; or perhaps he was just trying to avoid the cow dung.

"He's just watching the water diviner," Aunt Muriel hurried to explain. She had very hunched shoulders whose despair seemed to deepen from the strain of obliging her sister. Her response to Vera had no more substance than a timid habit. Vera had always daunted her. Vera didn't even have to make their life a competition, she just won. She dictated life from the total assurance of her posture, Victorian and humourless and upright.

Vera had gone to England bearing the notable beauty of her youth and a considerable musical talent. She had studied and become a concert pianist. Muriel—smaller, younger, with a more tentative nature—had taken refuge in science. She had followed Vera to England to study medicine. Moodie was studying medicine at the same time, and he and Muriel became acquainted. Moodie was tall, thin and brown-skinned, with a face of such ingrained sorrow that he reminded Muriel of a sad hound who couldn't lift his ears. Only a bemused smirk that skulked at the corners of his mouth betrayed his mischievous sense of humour. The pair formed a quiet friendship which seemed fated to become a permanent partnership—until the forceful Vera met him and swept him away.

"Not him," said Vera patiently. Her chin always tilted up, so she looked down her faintly retroussé nose at me; I was attempting to scrape the cow dung from my shoes. "I am wondering what you are doing, Rachel."

Muriel became a doctor at the children's crèche, and gave tireless service for a pittance of government salary. Maybe the years of spinsterhood spent caring for other people's children, many of whom were sorely neglected, made her impatient of the indulgence she witnessed in me, or just impatient of childhood. I always sensed that impatience. Muriel was everyone's favourite, with her rolling R's and musical laughter and the speed with which she politely agreed with everybody. But she wasn't mine. Though everyone dreaded Vera, I was certain I saw amusement and encouragement in her eyes when they softened, as though she had decided to discover some worth in me.

"I'm cleaning my shoes," I answered.

"And why is your grandfather looking for water?" she persisted.

"I think it's for the grapes," I suggested.

"I don't think so," Muriel said thoughtfully from her safe distance a few feet away. "I think it may be nitrogen they need. Do grapes need much water?"

"Um," said Vera indifferently, and turned her attention to the object of her visit, her sick brother.

He shouldn't be out of his bed, but there was no use telling him so. And there was no use speaking to her sister-in-law about it, for Mardi was entirely undisciplined and probably had some new-fangled idea that fresh air and exercise could help heal a heart attack. Indeed!

"Muriel!" She summoned the stooped figure of her sister. "Do you think it is wise for Norman to be up and around like this?"

Muriel, whose hands held her waist as though she was steadying herself, moved stealthily over to Vera.

"No. Not wise at all. But what can one do? One can't interfere!"

She shrugged her shoulders up and the corners of her mouth down, and in the subsequent disapproval of their raised eyebrows as they both glanced at Mardi, the conspiracy against her was again endorsed.

Vera turned to survey the farce in the pasture, the guava-piper leading her brilliant brother in ever-widening circles and exhausting his heart. She needed to sit quietly and talk to Pardi alone. Moodie had decided to leave her. He had found another woman, the matron of a hospital, a spinster, a woman older than herself and, by all accounts, extremely ill tempered.

"I'm not surprised," Mardi had commented sagely when she heard the rumour. Vera had mentioned to her that she and Moodie slept in separate rooms, and Mardi, who was greatly startled by this revelation, had asked why. Pardi and herself had separate rooms for their clothes and their habits, but they always slept in the same room, and sometimes in the same bed.

"Since Pamela was born," Vera had said matter-of-factly, as though Mardi had missed something very obvious, "there's been no reason not to!"

Where was home for people like Vera, people who were half one thing and half another? She loved Jamaica, it was where she'd been born and raised. But she ached for the pieces of England she had brought home in her heart: the theatre, the museums, the concert halls; the quiet dining-rooms and gentle manners of the middle classes, the discretion with which they spoke, the certainty of their pronunciation. Good books in the bookstores and libraries, fine stockings in a climate which permitted one to wear them comfortably. Sensible shoes. Recently she had even started a music school here to teach young people the classical music of Europe.

Her brother could not hide his contempt for her nostalgia. It separated them like a valley. Though he acknowledged her contribution to Jamaica, it was with the silent stride that accompanies duty.

He loved classical music, European art and literature, like the little book of Browning with its green cover that he carried in his knapsack all through the war, taking it out in the trenches at night when they dared to have firelight. He stole aspects of other cultures from his travels and kept them for himself, but he never longed for somewhere else to be home. These things he saw as ingredients with which to nourish Jamaican potential.

Some evenings Mardi and Pardi sat with the aunts after dinner, their eyes closed, and listened to music. Vera knew so much about music and technique that they waited with both interest and dread for what could be a censorial aftermath. On the rare occasion when she offered praise, this seemed to validate the musician's interpretation and the moment's joy.

By these very standards and her uncompromising approach, she was achieving wonders with the music school.

Pardi had called her "V" from when he was a child. And he called Muriel "Mu". He had always had difficulty pronouncing the letter "r", and when Roy was born, instead of calling him Woy, he stuck firmly to his middle name, Douglas. He had been plagued by a proximity of names bearing "r". He was fortunate to have married an Edna, and it may have been one of the reasons why he insisted on calling me Pie.

Not long ago, a matter of pronunciation had been a bitter embarrassment to Vera. In Jamaica the strictest rule of being middle class was to know when an initial "h" was pronounced and when it wasn't—and never to add one where it didn't belong.

Only a week before, she had been to court to give a character assessment of the gardener who had worked with her for twenty years. He was being sued for child support. He had given his name as "Hardman" when he first arrived, and so she had called him ever since. But when she started her prepared statement, the judge—who was a social acquaintance, and whose wife played bridge with many of her friends —interrupted her to ask whether they were speaking of the same person.

Vera peered at him over the rims of her glasses, as he likewise peered back at her.

"Do we speak of Mr. Neville Oddman, Mrs. Moodie?"

"Mr. Hardman, surely...." She started to feel embarrassed.

When he spelled out the name, it was clear that she had been adding this unforgivable "h" for twenty years.

The aunts moved towards the centre of the pasture, where Mardi had now joined Pardi; they watched with amazement as the stick trembled violently in the fighting hands of Fish. The veins pouted along his sturdy arms, his head was jerking and his clenched jaws seemed about to splinter.

"Jesus wept!" Pardi beamed with excitement and popped another pill under his tongue. "The damn place has water, can you believe it?"

Some of the cricket spectators had welcomed the diversion, climbing through the fence and wandering over to see what was happening. They watched the last tortured struggle of the stick to unite itself with the force that attracted it.

I wondered why a guava stick would yearn for water beneath the earth. Was it a longing to return to the eternity of its own river, or the truth of some other life that it had been searching for and could not forget? Was it the impulse to find the place where its first seed was planted centuries ago? How strong must be the instincts of its distant ancestors, if they still commanded the broken life of the stick.

For the first time in weeks Mardi looked elated, as she watched her husband's fad become both an art and a science before her eyes. For a moment she seemed to forget her worry over Pardi.

As soon as the branch touched the ground, the diviner let it go, and the stick seemed to let go too, losing its power and purpose. It just lay there on the ground, grey and weightless. Aunt Muriel looked astonished, her practical mind foraging for an element of plausible explanation. Vera, always angry in the face of magic, wished that her brother would desist from these meaningless diversions.

"Why did the stick pull down?" I asked Pardi.

"Because underneath the ground there is water."

"But why? Does the stick want water?"

"Yes. In a way. Tides are caused by needs, something's empty, something's full. Full needs the space of empty, empty needs the things that make it full."

He strode thoughtfully beside me, his hands clasped behind his back, his head forward, as he analysed the success of the morning. "Everything in life has something it needs to do. It's like the impulse of life. Imagine an ice-cream bucket. How do you think the ice-cream gets cold?"

I remembered the days when we'd make fresh nutmeg ice-cream.

"Because of the ice around it."

"Yes, in a way. But you have to understand the way. The cream doesn't get cold just because it lies next to the ice. The cream doesn't care if it's not cold. Some impulse must make the cream go cold, make it take the cold from the ice. That's where the salt comes in. Do you remember the salt? That we throw on the ice?"

I nodded.

"Well, the salt needs, by its nature, to melt the ice. And it has to have heat to do this. Where is the heat? The heat is in the cream. So the salt draws the heat from the cream in its impulse to melt the ice. A law of nature, a fact of its being. When it has drawn the heat, the cream is cold, so it freezes, and the ice melts.

"Well, believe it or not, Pie, the guava stick is following the trail of some impulse like that, some law of its nature. It isn't magic. There is never magic, just mystery to which we haven't found an answer."

Soon we all trailed back up the ennobled pasture with its underground glory: Fish, the successful soothsayer, looking relieved and messianic, the aunts hot and long-suffering, Pardi and I hand in hand carrying the secrets of the universe in our understanding, and Mardi now worrying about lunch, and firmly refusing the enhancement of garlic in the solid English format of Drumblair's menu.

5

My Mother
Who Makes
Puddings from
Yorkshire

THE FIRST REAL picture I have of my mother is, strangely enough, one of her before I was born; it was painted for me by my father.

I used to have a small red toy car; you sat in it and pumped the pedals back and forth and it would lurch along. Sometimes I got my father to push me, which was easier and a lot faster, and he would make roaring noises of the large engines he wished he owned. Milton had a young cousin from America called Joe Bush who came to live with Miss Boyd, and one day Joe and I were on the lawn squabbling over who should drive the car, and my father came over and sat beside us on the little curb at the edge of the lawn. He told us that if we went on quarrelling like that, we'd have to get Solomon from the Bible to cut the car in two. Then Joe said, no, he'd get Pardi as a lawyer to defend him instead.

"Indeed," said Michael, "you'd have the world's finest lawyer. He was truly legendary."

I wished I'd known my grandfather when he was in court. There seemed to be so many stories. Miss Boyd also said he was legendary, and I knew, by the way she groomed herself for the word as she whispered it, that it carried enormous significance. When I asked what it meant exactly, for I always liked a good word, she told me it was something or someone about whom there were many legends—that is, wonderful stories.

It was inside one of these legends that I was surprised to discover my mother—and my elder half-sister, Anita—tucked safely in there, busy and real, like a town that has laws and commerce and banks and a hairdresser and dentist, a flower shop and garbage day and even a fountain, but somehow a surveyor has forgotten to put it on the map.

"Tell us one of Pardi's legends," I asked him.

Probably glad not to have to push us in the car, he told us.

"It was in Nottingham. About 1947. Two groups, one white, one black, had a fight, and a young Englishman in the Royal Air Force was killed by a knife wound in the left side of his neck that severed the jugular vein. A young Jamaican at the scene was splattered with blood, so he was arrested and charged with murder. It was established by the coroner that the wound was inflicted by a right-handed person, and the accused was right-handed. There were two key elements to the case. One was a short, stocky English shopkeeper who had picked out the accused in an identification parade. The other was a diagonal bloodstain on the Jamaican's shirt which ran from the left hip up to the right shoulder. The stain matched the blood type of the victim. It was an open-and-shut case."

We had forgotten the car.

"Your mother and I were in England then, and Anita was a little girl...you weren't yet born. Pardi was retained to defend the man, and we met him at the airport; I think the Boeing Constellation had just started flying over the Atlantic. I remember him walking towards me; he looked gaunt and tired and there was egg on his tie, he had obviously spilled something while eating his breakfast...and typical Pardi, he was quite unconscious of it, and typical son, I hadn't the nerve to point it out to him."

"What about Mummy?" I asked. Up till then I had had odd snippets of information about myself as an infant in what I saw as a former life, but I had no cohesive impression of my mother. My mother yelling at my father to stop when he and Arthur Wint, an Olympic gold medallist at Helsinki, would throw me, laughing my head off, from one to the other. Amused reminiscences of my christening, when Errol Barrow from Barbados and Forbes "Odo" Burnham from British Guiana became my godparents. My father walking me in Hyde Park, where he said he used to show me off, and where he would collect old cigarette stubs for tobacco to put in his pipe. And my aunt called Madeleine, Mummy's sister, whom he seemed to like a lot.

"Well, wait," he said, "and I'll tell you. Pardi said there was a side to the case he wanted to probe very carefully...it was the bloodstains. Listen, Michael, he said, I'm going to come round to Clanricarde Gardens (that was where we lived). Ask Jacqueline to get a bottle of red ink...I take it she has flour in the house. And I said, yes Dad, she has flour in the house—I knew that because we used to make Yorkshire puddings, I would do the roast and she would do the Yorkshire pudding."

So she had an address. A place where she lived, with a stove in which she made puddings from the same place as Grandfather Swithenbank and Great Grandfather Manley.

"It was a Sunday. He arrived at our house with a paper-knife which was to play the role of the murder weapon. And there was a lot of preparation of the ink...your mother kept adding flour, putting in just a little, then too much, then saying, let's do another batch, then putting in some more till Pardi said, that's about right...Jacqueline, you have just the right viscosity!"

Fancy, I had a mother who produced the right viscosity for Pardi.

"Now, I want a sheet, he said. What do you want one of my sheets for, asked your mother, who was very fastidious and didn't like a mess. I'm going to treat that bottle of ink like the victim's jugular, Pardi explained. I'll stick the paper-knife in here at the neck and I'll pull it out, and we'll just see what sort of blood patterns we create on the sheet. Your mother could never say no to your grandfather, so out came an old sheet. I'll never forget that scene. Jacqueline stood with the open bottle, and I was positioned opposite as if I were the one who had done the crime—you could see from the wound that the victim must have been almost opposite the assailant, for it was a clean wound that went downward into the side of the neck, and there was no tearing when it came back out. It was established very precisely from the coroner's report that the knife went in and came straight back out. So I was standing there with the sheet, with my arms out to hold it like a big screen, and there was the diagonal spray of blood. *But*—nowhere near the victim! The splash pattern, from low to high, from left to right, was a good couple of feet to the right, and splashing beyond the sheet to your mother's consternation as she witnessed the splattered floor. And in a flash Pardi said, I've solved the case! The accused was obviously standing *next* to the man who did the killing. And it's all proved by the shirt, which is the Crown's star piece of physical evidence!"

My father was really excited. And so was I, for at last I had placed my mother; there in a room in Clanricarde Gardens, during a complex experiment, she was busy making blood for Pardi.

"Did Anita help too?"

"Yes, she would have been an eye witness." He then returned to his story.

"All right, let's probe it some more, Dad said, and he proceeded to try to see if there was any other way to get that pattern of drops, consistent with a clean exit wound. He was able to demonstrate physically, by the laws of physics, that it was impossible to reproduce that bloodstain in that position. He was triumphant!

"So...time for the case. I go with him to Nottingham to keep him company, and we stay in a hotel. But he can only afford one room, and I can afford no room at all, so we have to sleep in the same room...and there's only a double bed! It was the first time in history that we were sleeping in the same bed. Both of us take up our positions on the very edges of the bed—I tell you, how nobody ever fell out of that bed I don't know—and I'm just about settling, recovering from the sheer shy shock of being in the same bed with my father..."

And he says "father" so grandly that I know that he means "paterfamilias", a phrase I am particularly proud of having learned from my grandfather, and I wonder if my mother would be surprised to discover all the good words I know.

"...when I suddenly hear him get out of the bed and fumble around in the dark, because he's very nice, he doesn't want to wake me. He opens the door and I realize he's put his shoes out to be cleaned, but he hears me awake and he suddenly says, you know, Michael, I'm not taking any chances, it's the only pair of shoes I have here. Suppose in the morning they haven't come back with my shoes—anything could happen—they could be stolen—they could be mislaid—how could I walk into court to represent my client in my stockinged feet?

"We go into court. The Crown presents the case. The knife, the arrest, the bloodstained shirt, the blood type... the facts of the fight are established, the nature of the wound described. Comes now the end of their case: the star witness who saw it all. And he's taken through his evidence by the Crown, and it soon becomes obvious that this is the day of his life! He's the star, and he's full of his own importance. He proceeds to paint the picture in spades, hearts, diamonds and clubs. I remember Dad just listening and watching him... making the odd note. So the fellow is finished, having established that he saw the two groups advancing, and the knife flash in the accused's hand. Is this person in the court? Yes, and he points to the accused.

I'm sorry my mother has left the story.

"Dad gets up to cross-examine. He is almost meek... just a little brown man come from Jamaica to go through the formalities before the poor man hang. He takes the witness back through the story, and the man likes to chat. He says, I noticed up a side street so and so was going on.... Anything else, asks Dad. Yes, as a matter of fact I remember there was.... So Dad has him literally like God, seeing everything —and the guy was quite patronizing.

"And then you notice just a touch of steel entering Dad's voice as he walks him more closely through the story: now as I recall where you were standing, the black group was walking away from you. Of course, the shopkeeper replies.... And you had no particular reason to notice them *before* it became evident a fight was about to start? Of course not; nothing to notice....So when you first became aware of them, they were advancing on the white group (he doesn't put it the other way)? Yes.... And that meant going away from you? Yes....So presumably their backs were to you? Of course....I see, says Dad. Pause. And then you saw the knife flash. Had that person suddenly got in among the white crowd, and turned his back to them? Of course not, says the witness, he wouldn't have dared do that....

"So when the knife flashed, all the backs would still have been turned to you?

"The first tremor of doubt enters the witness' voice. Of course, he says.

"So they were going away from you, and the knife flashed, and whoever had that knife had his back to you.

"Well—maybe they were side on....

"Oh! When did they suddenly become side on? Did you tell the police that?

"No. I didn't think of it....

"So when did you think of it? Silence. Pardi looks at him with contempt. Come on—when did you think of it? Perhaps you just thought of it at this minute? And Pardi looks at the judge.

"Of course not. I'm under oath. I've been telling the truth the whole way through....

"So Dad says, oh I see. And he finally draws the noose, and what I will never forget till the day I die is that all of a sudden there emerged from hiding—the hiding of a great cross-examiner—the *true* Norman Washington Manley, and with the whole force of his personality he said to the man, I put it to you, Mr. Smith, that you never saw anybody's face at all. There was silence.

"Let me put it to you one last time—you are under oath, you know. And finally he just spat the words at him: you saw nothing, did you?

"No, sir.

"M'Lord, I suspect there's no case to answer.

"And the funny thing was this. There was jubilation in the court, which was packed with Jamaicans, and we're walking out after all the congratulations, and I notice Pardi looks quite dejected. He says to me, you know, Michael, I really am a little disappointed. I know, Dad, I said, you never gave your little demonstration. He had with him the sheet, the bottle of ink with the right viscosity, his paper-knife. He had hoped they might even lend him the real knife for the demonstration—it would be far more dramatic in court, he said, if I had the real knife. And he said, when you think of all the trouble we went to—me, you, Jacqueline...."

So Mummy was there, right to the end of the story, her contribution bottled and waiting to be called to its civic duty; meanwhile, in that safe world called Clanricarde Gardens, she presumably tidied up everything, for she was fastidious, and then returned to her kitchen, where in my mind she continued making puddings from Yorkshire for the rest of my childhood.

6

ANANCY AND
THE BROOM

BROOMS WERE EVERYWHERE at Drumblair. Not just the basic, everyday brooms that lived in the broom closet and came out for sweeping. Not just the tallest cobweb brooms on their awkward stilts, which were kept behind the pantry door because they couldn't fit in the cupboard. Nor just the neat little dusting broom that Mardi turned up behind the living-room door, its bloom of bristles sprinkled with salt, when guests wouldn't go home at the appropriate time.

For a long time there were bunches of cut brooms everywhere: leaning on the walls of the garage with their beige, stiff fringes not yet broken in, or lying on their sides, tied together in a huddle along the front veranda, awaiting their fortune. The Spanish jar in the living-room had once boasted magnificent peacock feathers, but when Mardi's friend Rose, a canny journalist with glorious red hair and a profound hospitality for horoscopes—hesitating as she did before any utterance—informed the deeply superstitious sculptress that peacock feathers in a house were unlucky, the contents were removed, and the jar now stood crowned with a bouquet of brooms.

There was a broom salesman who frequently visited Drumblair over the years. One day, striding slowly up the path with his straight back and uplifted head under a majestic cotta upon which he balanced the brooms, one arm steadying the sticks like a prophet, he was almost unbalanced as he was hailed with applause and cheers from every aperture on the face of the house. We all happened to be near a door or a window when he appeared, and Mardi became so excited by what she saw as a good omen that she led an exuberant chorus of appreciation.

Why the brooms?

The broom had become the mascot of the People's National Party. It had swept itself into place following a random whim of fortune's dust.

I would come to understand that in Jamaica a party mascot was a very important thing. I sometimes wondered if this was the element for which people in fact voted. I suppose it was unusual for a child to think about such things, but with my family embroiled in political life, it was simply my reality.

Voting was to create a basic cycle in my life. National general elections were due every five years. If I thought of the past, I saw it in strides of five years. I had been born almost exactly halfway between the 1944 elections and the 1949 elections, both of which the PNP lost. If I thought of the future, I saw it unfolding in five-year steps, from election to election. I still think like that today. It's the basic rhythm of my life, the seasonal change my life has grown to expect.

Back at the time of the brooms, we were facing the 1955 election. It was the first one I would be conscious of, and I was very sorry I didn't have a vote; I would have to wait thirteen years, which meant missing two more elections. I told Pardi I hoped he would fight for child suffrage.

Let me explain how the broom came to be the party symbol.

The back veranda, beside the dining-room, was the place where the PNP's executive met on Monday nights. Week after week throughout the years, these ardent Jamaicans designed through ideological debate what was to become Jamaica's path to nationhood, from adult suffrage to self-determination. They were a disparate group with differing backgrounds, professions, biases and personalities. This often caused fierce rivalries and factions, but their differences, inspired as they were by a somewhat Utopian dream they shared of Jamaica's future, were protected by the iron democracy in which the party was clad. And ultimately, to achieve any of their goals, they had to plot together to outwit the wily Bustamante, who had been chief minister for a decade.

To many, the tug of war between the two parties resembled a family feud; the fact that Pardi and Busta were cousins made the dissension seem less threatening, and lent it a comfortable air of romance. People, especially those nervous about change, convinced themselves that Busta and Pardi really loved each other, and that in private moments they sat together at Drumblair with a drink and laughed at the world.

"To believe there were close personal bonds of friendship between these two men is to completely misunderstand Jamaican history," Mardi once said.

I never ever saw Busta at Drumblair. If he came, it was obviously not to sit and be familial, or I think I would have been aware of his avuncular presence.

Mardi came to realize that their differences were the differences of Jamaica, the polarities pleached into the island's texture by the events of its history. They were the differences between the status quo and progress, between old fears and new ideas, between policing the colony for the British and braving the inexhaustible potential of freedom and statehood.

I had heard people say that the upper class and the rural working class supported Busta, and the middle class and the urban working class supported Pardi. I was told that the reasons for Busta's mass appeal were his charisma, his work in the union and the fact that he didn't really threaten the status quo. Pardi, on the other hand, was a symbol for the middle class, who had grown frustrated and angry with British domination; after years of Bustamante's leadership, many of them considered him a friend and instrument of the colonial status quo. The earthy, unsophisticated style that attracted the masses to Busta was an irritant to some of the middle class, who dismissed him as a ragamuffin.

For Pardi and me, the Monday-night executive meeting was a weekly battle for muffins. A large and ill-tempered cook called Iris baked them, with malice aforethought, to meet the exact numerical needs of the party gathering. She would leave the muffins in a biscuit tin on a trolley near the doorway to the back veranda, with mugs and a Thermos of coffee.

Vernon Arnett, a mild-mannered man who would one day be minister of Finance, did not have a sweet tooth. So there was always one spare muffin. But Sydney Veitch, the jolly, rotund general secretary—who had big irises, or maybe his spectacles magnified them, and a gutter under his nose which I thought must be useful when he had a cold—would always want two. So I had to get there before him.

Even if I did, Pardi and I were then left foraging for a second muffin. A lot depended on the element of absenteeism. In the event that all members were present, we needed a co-conspirator. I found one in the large and flat-footed Crab Nethersole, who I'd heard was a Rhodes Scholar like Pardi. He seldom spoke to me, but I liked him anyway. Perhaps I sensed tolerance in the benign resignation that myopia brought to his face. Or maybe it was because I knew Pardi loved and trusted him, and because, unlike most of the politicians, he never patronized me or tried to impress my grandparents by patting the top of my head. Or maybe I just liked Rhodes Scholars.

One Monday night we caught each other casing the trolley. After that, by tacit agreement, Crab would sit behind the door on guard duty while we raided the tin for the three of us. He used to come back at the end of the coffee break to retrieve the loose raisins from the empty tin; he would jab them with his finger and stick them in his mouth. Then, in keeping with his nickname, he would shuffle off to his place at the meeting.

One night they had a meeting while Pardi as an opposition leader was away in England, once again discussing a new constitution with the Colonial Office. For ten years and two elections all their combined resources of intellect and ideology had failed to dislodge Bustamante, but another election was coming soon. In a discussion that weighed the benefits of various airport welcomes, someone had the temerity to suggest that as soon as he got off the plane Pardi should be handed a broom. It would be his mandate, his instrument to sweep the Labourites out. The meeting collectively choked on the gimmickry of this suggestion amid such august planning, and the idea was set aside as an amusing impulse.

But someone leaked it. The party's weekly, *Public Opinion*, immediately cartooned the travelling leader with a broom, and in no time the rank and file of stalwarts were chanting the slogan "Sweep them out!"

Pardi heard the news in England with dismay. He, Mardi, Aunt Muriel and I were at the old Howard Hotel; both Mardi and Pardi liked the unpretentious comfort of its tired rooms with their high off-white ceilings, with ornate borders like elaborate upside-down serving dishes over their heads, and the dusty wallpaper with its reassuring flowers on the damp walls. Even the balding carpets with their deep red interweaves of exotic patterns from the far reaches of the empire made a strange hotel room somehow familiar and accommodating. In a country designed to exclude, it was good to both know and have one's place.

Paddy, the elevator man, who told us with pride that he used to be a taxi driver, brought us the *Guardian* every morning, and Smithy, whom Pardi and Mardi insisted on calling Mr. Smith, was the butler in charge of their floor and brought us our breakfast of kippers. If he found it unusual that the occupants had a mixed marriage, he showed not a shred of dismay at having to serve a brown man from Jamaica. After a week of corseted British pleasantries, on the last morning he suddenly remarked, in an awkward moment of courage which reddened his bleach-white face, "Sir, you are the first Jamaican with whom I have made an acquaintance. I have found you to be a gentleman and a scholar, and it has been my honour this week to serve you."

Then he reversed through the door without waiting to collect the usual tip.

I was seven, and Pardi and Mardi had decided it was a good time to bring me with them on this trip so that I could meet my mother, for whom I often asked. They made the decision partly in light of my "troubled" behaviour. (The label "troubled" was permanently attached after I gave my grandmother a huge bite on her bottom, because her attention strayed from me to a policeman on a motorbike who was delivering an invitation from the governor's house. That was the last straw.) Aunt Muriel came along with us, ostensibly to keep me company, but probably as a means of keeping me in check.

It's strange that I don't remember meeting my mother when she came with my elder half-sister, Anita, to visit me at the hotel. We had heard she was remarried, to a handsome British unionist, but in my mind she just continued making her puddings of Yorkshire in that warm kitchen in Clanricarde Gardens. I do remember locking Anita in the hotel bathroom and watching the handle of the door bend and return, bend and return. Anita seemed disappointed that my father wasn't there. I remember the walks down the cool city streets, the clean smell of Boots the Chemists, the hot vaporous smell of a small shop where Aunt Muriel took me when she went to have her stockings mended. I remember going up and down the elevator for numerous trips with Paddy, on whom I had a crush, but I do not remember meeting my mother.

Mardi said I did meet her, though at first I thought my sister was my mother. But she said that after my mother left the hotel I sat proprietorially on her lap for a change, with my arms round her neck, for a long time refusing to let go. I stopped asking to go to my mother after that, and the incident went down as another mysterious and alluring traumatic experience in my life. I wouldn't see my English family again for nine years.

The papers delivered to Pardi on Her Majesty's service were strewn over one side of a bruised but elegant oak table. Whether by nature or by sloth, Mardi could never understand the intricate structure or concept of legislation. She had a profound belief in the natural order of life, and little interest in just how it came about. The universe spilled through her quite unconsciously. Order was the rising of the morning in the sky, and the magical nymph-light of the moon between the trees at night. Order was the yin and yang of the rain and the wind, of woman and man. Order was the inevitable arabesque of the years and the lifelong journey of the soul through the skins of time, selving and unselving, being or only watching, watching or only being. Order was her Piscean world of dreams under the sea, tides which interpret but never define us.

This was the wonder of her man: he was able to comprehend the world in which he lived, and to know how it worked. He could build, piece by piece, the order of the life he traversed. And by doing so, he made such a conscious sense of existence that it was in his power to change it. She wondered at this almost as much as she did at the majesty of the universe.

"Goddamn, blasted, bloody fools!"

He was spitting his worst invective, all four of his curse words, his total thesaurus of abuse. A damn fool was the mildest of annoyances, a damn blasted fool the source of serious displeasure, and when he added "bloody" everyone kept very still so as not to irritate him further. But when he resorted to "God", everyone knew it was time to scatter. His irritability, like Mardi's, found its genesis in a long bloodline of prickly impatience, unsettling but fleeting, lacking the obduracy and ill-will for malice.

He was pacing in front of the fireplace; he turned and slumped into the chair beside her.

"They want to reduce my work to a campaign of brooms."

"Brooms?" she repeated, mystified.

"Brooms as a party mascot, I suppose. Brooms for sweeping out the JLP."

As many voters could neither read nor write, symbols were used to distinguish the parties on the ballot. The JLP used a bell, and the PNP had used the profile of a head. Pardi thought it symbolized everything in which the party believed and for which it fought. But Busta had easily finessed that high-minded concept with the clamour and distraction of ringing his bell. Even the comrades' silent fist raised in its salute of solidarity in struggle was no match for the turmoil the noisy bell created; although innocent of the more radical post-war political connections of the clenched fist and the term "comrade", Busta soon linked both PNP features to their wider, more sinister modern association with communism.

"I won't run a campaign this way," Pardi said. "I cannot do this. How can people inherit the responsibility of history if they do not understand the issues?"

"I like brooms," Mardi said thoughtfully. "They're cheerful."

She knew he hated gimmickry. He honestly, fervently believed that, if he had a duty in life, it was to teach the Jamaican people what had really happened through history so that they would become the guardians of the future. That was the reason for the meetings night after night, with handfuls of people in little street-corner shops, setting up groups across the length and breadth of Jamaica. "Each one teach one." That was why he taught at these little gatherings, not in dialect, which he couldn't convincingly speak; maybe some of the time they didn't even understand him, but they could hear the rhythms, and sense from the cadences when to nod and when to disapprove. Even at large campaign meetings, people always sensed when to listen quietly and when to applaud. They knew he was erudite, and were proud of him. Pardi represented the possibility of their potential.

Mardi always said this was the problem. She felt that Busta was what we are, broken and flawed by history; that like Busta we had survived by evolving flamboyant, cunning and opportunistic.

"It is like cheating," Pardi insisted. "This is gimcrack politics. You might as well steal the votes from the people, as win by grabbing an election because you have taken advantage...."

He paused and rose from the chair, and stood looking around the room as though for further explanation. Then he resumed his protest, measuring his thoughts against the strides of his pacing: "tapped in on their emotions, got them geared up, drunk with some pleasure. It's just another form of exploitation. I won't have any part of it."

But Mardi had the blood of both her cousins running through her being. She could see both sides, and intuit both perspectives.

"But dear, if the people are moved by an image, let them be moved. And a broom is a perfect symbol for sweeping change. Sometimes a person feels safer with an image that represents something that would be difficult to define. History is full of symbols."

"Well, history has often been wrong," he said moodily. "And our history has always cheated the people. Sold them down the river. Brooms are just another lot of nonsense."

He stood at the window, looking out at the city.

"Why do we expect so little of ourselves? We are worth more, we are owed more...we are capable of more." He turned abruptly away from the window and faced his wife. "Why should Jamaicans be no more than Anancy?"

Anancy, a mythical spider, could take on human shapes and characteristics. Mardi loved Anancy stories.

He turned to look at Mardi when she did not answer. She looked politely back at him.

"I like Anancy," she said.

"Yes, but Anancy was probably a tactical device to survive the Middle Passage. Chameleon trickery as our only weapon. It may be whimsical, but you can't keep fighting history with a school child's prank."

"You don't have the time to teach everyone," Mardi said firmly. "Think of an alternative. A way must be found to beat Busta, or *he* will be the alternative. If it takes a broom to get Anancy down off that wall, then stop being so damn noble and use a broom!"

He looked contemptuous, and she knew he didn't understand. He just didn't think like that. His was a serious mind, and in all things he was ethical, shadowed by the grim Protestant principles of integrity and the imperative sacrifice of service. Hard work without shortcuts. At times she felt that Jamaicans found his traits a burden they didn't wish to bear. He asked too much *of* them by believing so much *in* them. Because he was brilliant and shy, austere and even acerbic in

his public persona, he was never the object of mass adula-
tion, like Busta. Yet she believed that he was revered and
loved by many, in that deeper way one reserves for people
who we know represent the best of our possibilities.

She had always thought it amazing that he had as much
support as he did, as people did not naturally gravitate to
him. He was almost foreign in his own country. And yet he
was so Jamaican, so deeply committed to Jamaica. Pardi
would carry the name of Jamaica wherever he went, and by
his excellence take that name a little nearer greatness.

But now he was being humourless and a little tiresome.
They couldn't keep losing elections. Busta was so Jamaican
in temperament, and Jamaicans were comfortable with him.
He didn't make them strain to understand concepts, or alter
themselves to work towards some distant vision. With Busta
they could deal with life and its problems as they recognized
them: jobs, food, clothes, money. And Busta knew how to
work on a weakness and use it to his advantage. He knew
Jamaicans could be "got around". Just distract and amuse
them, get them in a good mood, and their defences would
drop and they would give you what you wanted, for basically
they were loving and large-hearted. They'd go a long way
with you if they'd had a belly laugh, a square meal and a good
time in the process.

"Let them have their brooms, dear, if that's what they
want," she said firmly. "I think you take it all a little too seriously sometimes. Why don't you just trust life?"

They spent their last evening in the city where they had
fallen in love. They walked through Hyde Park, with its
leaves turning amber and that oddly wilful red-rust; the
change in seasons seemed to exhort the lone anarchist on his
box at Speaker's Corner. The intermittent benches waited

benignly to offer their simple care and accommodation to passersby.

"Look at those silly ducks! You'd think they'd try to walk a little more gracefully over the centuries," she said as she suddenly stopped them both and snuggled nearer to him. For all her youth England had been too cold, and it was still the same, though her husband would say it was "mind over matter".

Hands in his pockets, he gazed over at the prim lake where the ducks, on entering the water, ceased to be ungainly. A young couple still nestled together in a rowboat where he had the impression he had seen them almost half a century ago. Whenever he came back to England, whether to argue for the Vicks Vaporub trademark case in an appeal to the Privy Council, or to haggle for one more inch of local autonomy at home, it was like returning to an orphanage. The place made otherness self-conscious and clumsy. There were so many immigrants from home. He wondered as they sauntered down the streets with their brave West Indian gait, ever the outsiders, whether they too felt orphaned in this city.

"I want to go home and feed my pea-doves!" she said as she turned him around to go back to the hotel. "I feel homesick."

She was there beside him as ever, with her long legs and impatient stride. She always seemed to be parting the leaves of the woods, letting in the sunshine, adjusting her pace every time she was plucked by birdsong. She opened windows, aired out the room of his soul with all its dark thoughts. He had called her Sunny Jim when they were young. She had called him Kid. She remained his Sunny. He still loved her so.

❋

We arrived on the squat double-decker Stratocruiser, watching the whipping propellers, almost transparent, pull us down the avenue of water with its embankment of mountains. In the distance the Palisadoes peninsula beckoned like the island's index finger.

Aunt Muriel and I, having learned how to accommodate our differences, now sat together in harmonious silence. In front, Mardi was leaning on Pardi's shoulder watching our descent.

I saw my land in the morning
And oh but she was fair!

Mardi recited Mike Smith's poem feelingly in her soft, breathless voice. The comforting drone of the engines made the familiar words hum. "Home to the beloved Jamaica!"

"That's Mike's," Pardi said absently. "Do you think you can get him to write poetry again?"

"Mike." She lifted her head off his shoulder. "I wonder." It was seven years since they had last produced an issue of the literary anthology *Focus*. The issues had been a great success, lifting national spirits with vibrant, authentic Jamaican voices. And now she had got them started again. They would have a new issue out by next year. Their meetings had resumed at Drumblair, but she missed Mike dragging sideways at his pipe from the salute of his hand; missed his impatience when no one could understand the shorthand he used even when his intention was to amplify the points he made; missed his irascible Leo nature. But she had a few good poems from his exile in England, before his apocalypse, his excuse for ignoring his muse.

We were making a wide circle, as though signing the sky before landing.

"Has George sent you any work yet?"

George Campbell was one of our most famous literary contributors. He now lived in New York, but yes, he had sent some new poems. Pardi was fond of George. He was Miss Boyd's nephew, a nervous, highly strung thread of a man who could snap in two at any time. He never stopped talking. Like Mike, he had grown up with Douglas and Michael as boys. Also Dossie Carberry. Dear old Dossie, fervent and slow, with a face like a full brown moon. In those days there were long summer holidays near the sea, on-going cricket matches and efforts to teach George the long jump in spite of his endless complaints that his knees hurt.

"Yes, he sent me some new ones. All our good writers are going away," she muttered despairingly.

"Not all, surely! But you can't make a living out of writing here." He returned to his window.

As we taxied to the ramp, Pardi saw an astonishing sight. It looked like giant sea-eggs waving in the distance, but as he focused his eyes beyond the boundary of the tarmac he realized it was a sea of supporters crested with gaudy banners, palm fronds and—brooms. The leader of the delegation that welcomed him at the foot of the steps handed him, in complete solemnity, a broom.

"With this broom, Comrade Leader, sweep them out!"

"Why the hell are you doing this?" Pardi muttered angrily.

He walked with us slowly towards the terminal building, awkwardly saddled with his broom. He had no idea how to be dignified holding such an object. Through the distortion of the fuel vapour streaking the air, he could see a large crowd breaking through a quite unprepared smattering of airport guards. People were running towards him with their lunatic fringe of brooms, dancing, shouting, "Sweep dem out!" "Sweep dem out!" Pardi stood still and stiffened when the branch of a coconut tree was thrown at his feet for us to cross. Then they surrounded us, pushing us forward, and formed a phalanx which separated him from us and propelled him towards the building.

Their voices lifted into the high eaves of a familiar hymn, "There were ninety and nine," and their droning and wailing lured him into their communion. As the crowd swayed, pulled slowly by each phrase from side to side, it seemed to grow in strength with its voice, and he knew before it came the moment when they would hoist him on their shoulders to carry him the rest of the way. It always embarrassed him, and it was even worse with the bloody broom.

Their leader aloft, the crowd reached the gate to the building. They arranged him gently, straightening his grey jacket, after setting him down on the step. Then they moved back, circling him like a coast as they waited for his words.

Who had started this carnival of brooms, this distraction from the many serious challenges facing them in this election? Year after year he had tried to teach people a concept; were they now to be given a broom as the answer to a cruel tradition of exploitation, or as a tool to fight a clever rival?

He looked out at the faithful soldiers of so many lost battles. Now they stood still, the brooms at ease in their command. He had watched this and every other faithful crowd barter its time in exchange for hope as speaker after speaker offered the simple promise of victory without explaining why this would be a good thing.

He started to speak.

He talked of history, and of the country at that time. He spoke of perils and solutions and the process of change. Mardi watched the crowds once again struggling with his erudite words and ideas. They clapped because they were aroused by the cadence of his oratory—not, as he thought, persuaded by reason. But their patience was proof of their faith and affection, and she found herself calling to him silently from her heart, "Meet them halfway."

As he spoke to them, he could feel their loyalty. Their brooms stopped tilting like the lance of Don Quixote, and they fixed their eyes on him, determined to wait forever if they had to. He thought of their joy a few moments ago, their simple faith that he would bring them a better deal in life.

"Trust life," his intuitive wife would always say. The broom was a strong tide pulling many waters and he didn't know why. "Trust life," he found his heart saying, without knowing why. And then—without any affectation at dialect, rising to the baffling moment with his most dignified voice —he stunned the crowd with his proclamation:

"Bell-tongue drop out."

Mardi was jarred from her reverie.

"Bell-tongue drop out!" he repeated less tentatively.

The crowd went wild. Their hero had met them halfway, with a simple point of humour to which they could relate. He swayed gently forwards and backwards on his heels with the courtroom action he used when he was satisfied he had won a point; but here there was no menace, only the ballast of the broomstick in his hand as it bore a message across acres of difference in experience and understanding. At last he had found an answer to the adroit strategies of his cousin, whose ambushes had undermined the dedication and ideals of his movement.

As the cheers died down, he repeated each word with renewed determination:

"Yes, comrades, this time the bell-tongue just drop out! And we shall sweep them away!"

※

So the days became full of brooms.

The comrades were rushing up and down Jamaica with loudspeakers on the roofs of their cars, rustling their brooms through the windows at mystified onlookers as shouts of "Sweep them away! Sweep them out!" blared through the streets. They had discovered that the broom was more versatile than the head in putting across their point of view, a more forthright answer to the banging and ringing of the JLP's various bells. For all Pardi's intellectual advantage, Busta's answer—clamour, noise and as little reason as possible—had been more than a match for intangible concepts. But now the crowds were huge and enthusiastic. And after the meetings they could be seen sweeping the roads, which was a nice way, Pardi said, to express the tough side of politics.

Mardi carried a neat little broom tied at the neck with a bow, but because the ribbon was red she eventually had to dispose of it, as she might be accused of having communist leanings. The party was still raw from the recent Four-H purge, and was sensitive to continuing suspicion.

After the epiphany of the brooms at the airport, even Pardi had a long broom strapped like a bayonet to the roof of his black Humber Super Snipe. There it led the charge into the destinations of the hectic election campaign, its fronds gnashing in the breeze of Pardi's impatience as he spurred on the driver, Graham, ever faster. (It reminded me of the caricatures of Leandro's *Daily Gleaner* comic strips which sometimes depicted Busta or Pardi with their wilful, breeze-blown hair flying behind them.) Beneath it, on the bonnet, fluttered a party flag with a stylized yellow globe and rayed sun on a red background, which Mardi had designed and which was by now so familiar as the rising sun of new ideas that the red background—unlike the bow on her broom—did not inspire sinister associations.

Drumblair was filled with activity. I used to sit on the stairs, the hub that linked the many agendas of the house. One of my most lasting images remains that of my grandmother in the evenings with her long strides disappearing into a world of literature or social work or art. She seemed to mesmerize an entire room, dispensing recognition to the gathering who were mostly unknown to me; in the morning they'd be gone, no more lasting than the clinks of ice against glass, or the filmy smoke gauzing the living-room.

In addition to the party executive, the *Focus* group was meeting from time to time to work on the third edition. It seemed quite natural to me that the progress towards nationhood should be made culturally in one room and politically in another. But this literary crowd was a rowdy group, with writers and rebels, eccentrics and mavericks and drinkers. The editorial committee—an axle of quiet thinkers and doers—guided their direction, while the disparate parts of the bodywork rattled exuberantly along.

On Wednesday nights the St. Andrew Children's Christmas Treat Committee met to plan its major fund-raiser, the Annual Drumblair Dance. I vividly remember this committee's meetings because I often received the blessing of a peach pie from one of its members, called Mrs. T. She was the matriarch of the Tomlinson clan, who worked tirelessly for the PNP cause. They were a joyous family who laughed with all their hearts and had the most colourful tempers, particularly with each other, which would erupt at different points during the meetings.

But the writers' group was of no benefit to me whatsoever. They drank steadily into the night and they seemed to cause endless trouble about anything at all, their personalities bumping into each other and Mardi, the puppeteer, trying to untangle their strings and keep each one separate.

"But they're all in love with you," someone said to her.

"Nonsense," she snapped irritably—maybe at the comment, or maybe at all the young men who were. "Anyway, I'm twice their age."

But somehow, since the advent of the brooms, the three groups had merged, and they were all coming and going in each other's times and voicing opinions on each other's subjects. Though the cause was common to the artists, reformers and charitable hearts alike, the joining of their forces often proved volatile.

The dance committee members got roped into much of the legwork for the campaign. The gentle-mannered electrical genius who made a fairyland of Drumblair's lawns once a year found himself battling the derelict equipment used to relay music and speeches at the meetings, and for his efforts was often cursed by the hurly-burly party organizers. The writers offended the politicians with their abstruse meanderings into symbol and motive regarding subjects that had hitherto been pigeon-holed according to conventional "isms". The executive annoyed everybody by behaving as though the popular mandate was already theirs. And on top of all that, the rapprochement of the (predominantly male) executive and writers' groups with the (predominantly female) charity group fostered quite a few brief romances, which spurred campaign contributions from the smitten, and added interesting contours to this feverish time.

In the last days of the campaign, each group's effort became indistinguishable from the others', as they emptied their purposes into one common cause: to outwit Bustamante and beat the JLP.

The family had one significant diversion: my father decided to marry Thelma. Michael had had a good year in 1954. The National Workers' Union had now moved into the bauxite industry, where it had gained exclusive bargaining rights. He had won significant victories for the union in the sugar industry. Two members of this industry were the biggest sugar estates in Jamaica: Frome, where the 1938 uprisings had started, and Moneymusk. Both were owned by the English firm Tate and Lyle. Since Thelma's adoptive father, D.J. Verity, was the manager of the Sugar Manufacturers' Association, the JLP promptly adopted the propaganda slogan "Michael marry Tate and Lyle daughter."

The wedding took place soon after the Drumblair Dance, on Boxing Day, 1954. The small ceremony was held up in the hills where Aunt Muriel lived with two joyful corgis called Dylan and Gayla. In her cottage was a desk with what I thought were a million drawers, covered by a wooden shell that disappeared right into the walls of the desk, and a cubist wooden monkey carved by Mardi that stood on guard by the door. Aunt Muriel's garden was planted between the rocks on the hillside, with the tiniest flowers I had ever seen.

I remember little of the wedding except that Thelma, in her off-white dress, was a beautiful sight. She had always reminded me of a girl on a beach in a Gauguin print that hung in Drumblair, and after the wedding I wanted to see the Tahitian wearing Thelma's wedding dress. I also have a recollection of the cake; as its rich, black fermentations reached the back of my throat, I discovered something hard in my mouth. I thought it was a sixpence, like those placed in our Christmas puddings. But instead I retrieved a tooth that had been shaking in anticipation of Pardi threading it and attaching it to the bedroom door. "I'll get a florin!" I said as I presented my treasure, shattering the sentimental mood which was watering Thelma's eyes and making my father fidget. Despite a childhood devoid of storks and Santa Clauses (you can't give children myths that you have later to take away, said Mardi), I defiantly installed my own tooth fairy.

"Of course you will," said Mardi; being a great fan of Freud, she was probably relieved that the focus had shifted to me lest my father's remarriage cause me further insecurity.

And so it was that the family—armed with one more member, a new controversy, a florin and a plethora of brooms—prepared to meet the new year and the general election.

The polls closed late in the afternoon on that January election day in 1955. That was when Drumblair came alive as the weary warriors made their way back to the house, their headquarters, to listen to the election results. In those days the process was a long one. The votes were counted by hand by the polling officer, under strict supervision and the vigilance of two representatives from each party. The urban areas would come in first, the rural counts later in the evening.

The airwaves carried the lone station, Radio Jamaica and Rediffusion. The Rediffusion network brought the messages of empire into the homes of all those who could afford to rent Rediffusion's sets. In addition to the BBC news, Rediffusion's perfect accents brought a diet of thought and attitude through daily soap operas and children's stories, musical appreciations and whatever else was expected to bring comfort to the colonizer far from home, and entertainment and information to Jamaicans; local programming content was predictably inadequate.

The large, ornate wooden radio was brought into the living-room and placed on top of the closed grand piano. The evening was arranged around it. All the Rediffusion sets in the house were also turned on, each like a sideshow encircled by a small audience.

An open bar on the veranda welcomed the guests as they entered on that cool January night, to warm the cockles of their hearts, Mardi would say, though I never knew what these cockles were. The smell of jasmine and frangipani lingered over the lawn like a memory of the ladies at the Drumblair Dance a fortnight before, when Pardi had gyrated so vigorously with Aunt Carmen and myself that he had to include the popping of heart pills in his choreography.

By ten o'clock the announcements were coming in fairly regularly, and the ballot boxes were showing a large PNP lead in the majority of urban constituencies. Each favourable piece of news was met with wild cheers from the company of comrades, and their elation grew with their confidence and liquor intake as the night wore on.

"It's not time to cheer yet," Pardi mumbled cautiously, leaning his chin on his long, thin hand and slumping over his space at the dining-table as his transistor radio's crackling pronouncements dealt themselves to him like so many cards of fate. He preferred to be alone, and had withdrawn to the dining-room where he listened from an inner sanctum.

"But it looks like you're winning, Par!"

I could not understand why he did not appear happy.

"These are city results. We always win in the cities, with the urban votes. We have to wait and see what happens with the rural areas. They won't start coming in till midnight."

Iris brought him a bowl of hot red pea soup.

" 'Ave some soup now, chief!"

If he heard the transfer of title, he ignored it. I positioned myself beside him, pretending to understand the source of such great suspense and relishing the excitement around me. The soup steamed up his glasses as he slurped it down rudely, without Mardi nearby to correct him. He stopped only to give a sharp blow of his nose into a rumpled white hanky which he then stuffed back into a pocket.

"Will you win, Par?"

"I don't know yet, Pie."

"If you do, will you be chief like Busta?"

"Well, I'll be the chief minister instead of him. But I won't be like him, no."

"But will everyone call you 'chief'?"

"No. I don't think so."

"After tonight, will everything be over?" I asked him, in the hope that they would sometimes be home at night again.

"Well, it depends. If we lose, yes, everything will be over. If we win it will be the beginning of a whole new thing. A whole new Jamaica."

He was wiping the empty bowl with a piece of bread.

"If you win, will the whole new Jamaica belong to you, Par?"

"No, my dear. It will more likely belong to you."

I was flattered by my inclusion, but didn't really understand what he meant.

The evening was enlivened from time to time by the arrival of supporters announcing bogus voting, or stolen ballot boxes, or stuffed ones. The comrades pitched easily from crisis to crisis, railing out at "the damned Labourites, wicked ol' tiefs" and threatening blood, thunderclaps, and divine and finally political retribution, as the night and its continuing good news wore on.

By midnight, from my tightening harness of exhaustion, I could feel the optimism in the house reeling with round after round of reinforcement. The atmosphere ached from too much joy, too much laughing in the soul's belly. The rural areas had challenged their own darkness. From ignorance and illiteracy they had mustered their X's and made their bid for a new beginning.

"Oh, Kid, we have slain the dragon!" Mardi said as she hugged him.

But as the house became louder, Pardi seemed to withdraw deeper and deeper into himself. He must have been struck, then, by the full realization of this commitment. There were not, as the hymn said, ninety and nine safe, and one to be saved. There was maybe one safe, and ninety and nine to be saved.

Where on earth could he begin? What promise had he meant to keep by achieving victory? Where was the line of light he had followed years ago from that moment on the wharf in Kingston when he had secured his cousin's release?

Here at the familiar table, with victory glaring at him, where was the line of light from 1938, the promise beyond the locked door?

I climbed into his lap. Something stabbed my cheek from the place where I could hear the racing of his heart. I raised my head and saw a small silver broom pinned where he usually wore a rose in his lapel.

SAMSON'S
HEAD

AFTER PARDI BECAME chief minister, Drumblair lumbered along as usual, showing not the least inclination to become the first house of the land. Mardi asked Miss Boyd to replace the curtains and recover the sofa, and Nugget from the Youth Club sanded and revarnished the furniture, suggesting an air of limited respectability for the old house. But it still kept its cobwebs and secrets, muttered to itself in the creak of its old stairs, had windows that wouldn't latch when the rain waterlogged the frames and toilets that flushed on any tug they felt like flushing on. It was temperamental, and seemed to resent the prominence that threatened its disorder.

Mardi said she had to make many what she alternately called "adjustments" or "sacrifices". She was learning to tie her creativity behind her back, and do the things she felt she should do. More and more she was having to make time for a long list of social functions and political obligations. Her work suffered. She had started to make appointments with a perplexed hairdresser, who watched her shake her head vigorously before leaving each week, until she looked very much as she had when she arrived. Her cupboards now featured hats and long white gloves.

"The Rastas have taken Samson."

Mardi made the declaration matter-of-factly one morning as she used the smaller teeth of Pardi's long silver comb to flatten the soft, steel-coloured curls against the nape of his neck. She always cut his hair. She held the scissors awkwardly in her other hand. The blades had been sharpened till they appeared to be thinning like the hair on the top of his head, as though in a show of support.

"What do you mean?" Pardi asked absently, his chin cooperatively tucked in and his mind dreamy from an activity he always found soporific.

"Just what I said, dear. The Rastas have taken off with my big head of Samson which was sitting in the studio."

Years earlier, Mardi had separated Delilah's head, which everyone preferred, and given it to Leslie Clerk. The huge head of Samson with all his hair had become a studio prop over which the coverings for clay models were strewn between uses, or against which Mardi would lean to appraise a morning's work at a distance, steady her spent self or sometimes just sharpen a tool against the whetstone in the grip of her hand.

Mardi was giving Pardi his fortnightly trim just as the long, wayward strands of hair reached that spot on his neck, her low-water mark, where she had decided they must be stopped, no matter what the fashion. The procedure usually took place upstairs at his bedroom window, but today they were down on the back veranda, far from the familiar view of the gate. For there were new and powerful presences on Old Church Road.

From his bedroom window each morning, sitting at his old wooden swivel stool and shaving his face, Pardi had ruefully watched months of dusty construction on the opposite side of the road. A modern flat-roofed bungalow had slowly emerged. It faced him squarely with open candour, a veranda the width of the house and glass doors whose diaphanous quality in sunlight faintly suggested coquetry.

Before this, the only neighbours had been a habitually quiet couple: a swimming instructor and his wife, a petite American beauty who, like Mardi, was an artist and valued the secret spaces of solitude. Not even their pool could be seen from Drumblair, as their life was built far back from the road in a twist of trees. Only the cars that ambled along to drop and pick up the aquatic students interrupted the sacred hush of Old Church Road.

Then *they* came. They moved in with a flourish, showing not the slightest breath of self-consciousness at the dislocation they caused with their trucks and boxes and battery of noise. They came as *conquistadores*, assuming their place and our acceptance of it, and treating us to their undisguised curiosity and amusement: four unabashed female presences who, from stage entrances left and right, crossed and recrossed their living-room in an assortment of bras and slips, bras and panties, towels and what appeared to be plastic bonnets, and sometimes nothing but a delighted yell as they clutched their bosoms and dashed across the scene visible from Drumblair's second-storey.

Pardi called them "the Gaggle". He wondered at their abandon. It was their irreverence, not so much to the world as to themselves, which he found perplexing.

"They're dreadfully brash," Mardi commented.

"They must be Americans," Pardi concluded.

But they were not Americans, as he soon found out, for they arrived to introduce themselves. Ga Ga, Queen of the Gaggle, was a vibrant migrant from Santo Domingo, a distant relative of the Spanish Duke of Alva, she explained. She had three winning daughters whose cheerful dispositions could be heard from the grass-piece at one end of Old Church Road to the plum tree in the pasture at the other. They had lustrous, healthy hair and even white teeth, fine postures and dark, vivacious eyes, very like their mother.

They had brought along their goose-pecked gander, a mild-mannered entrepreneur who got little said but his name and the means by which he supported this evidently matriarchal tribe.

Pardi now cringed every time he passed through the gate, as enthusiastic greetings were extended to him from the vantage point of their veranda, and after he honked his horn and offered a faint-hearted nod of acknowledgement he could hear their laughter following him down the road; they revelled in this formal, solemn, waistcoated anachronism appearing live before them.

He had thought until recently that his eye on the world was hidden within the darkened eyelid of his shaving window, that he could see out but nobody else could see in—as though the old house were shuttered by cataracts. But the arrivals soon located the window where he sat, and began waving brightly at him, startling him out of the morning musing induced by the buzz of the Philips. Although he still shaved at that window, he now pulled the mirror to one side and sat in the safety of the shadows. He had even planned to exchange his room for the one above the kitchen, overlooking the back yard, but relinquished the idea at the thought of the turkey's gobbling disturbing his quiet time.

Drumblair felt under siege.

For most things he stuck to his room and his window, but he wouldn't risk sharing such a tender and intimate ritual as his haircut, and relocated the procedure downstairs. Next to them, in the dining-room, Zethilda, the cook, was coming and going as she set the table for breakfast at seven sharp.

Zethilda had come to replace Iris, the bad-tempered cook, who fortunately had found a sponsor and gone overseas. Tildy, as she came to be called, was short and very black, with what Mardi decided was a moody Maroon nature which she seemed to bring from the eastern part of Jamaica, where she had been born. Like the ancestors of her region, who were runaway slaves, she found life a continuing battle.

"De end o' de worl' soon come!" she would say, not so much as a threat as in recognition of omens that confirmed her basic premise. Whatever she witnessed, she assured us, "Dese are truly de signs." She was a doomsday chorus of one.

But if what Tildy extracted from life was unharmonious, what she gave back, filtered through her every expectation of gloom, had a radiance of being, as though she had refined it to the purest carat. Whatever she gave of herself must have been total, to have survived her own mistrust.

Her cooking was subtle rather than bland, with interesting twists in small portions, each little bowl adding a dimension to both the meal and the abundant potential of tropical variety, a feat the British had never achieved. No matter the extra mouths to feed, she would feed them, glaring at the serving dishes she offered with enough disapproval to make sure the unexpected diners took no more than the allotted one piece of plantain or three slices of oranged beet.

She was loyal and, despite her own reluctance, deeply caring. And she never overcooked meat.

"Dose Rastas shudda neber be dere in de firs' place," she announced stoutly, fixing a plate firmly in front of Mardi's place at the table and releasing the shutter of her jaw to an odd, unlocked position, so that her chin dropped and her mouth hung open like the old-lady face of a nutcracker. She was referring to the other new presence, the Rastafarians. Their occupation of Mardi's studio was the cause of serious unease in Zethilda. She disapproved of the Rastas as much as she approved of the bungalow-dwellers. If Pardi viewed the Gaggle as an intrusion, Zethilda welcomed them as "decent white people wid tall 'air."

The smell of breakfast was accompanied by another irritable grumble as her bleak figure left the room. "Betta come an' 'ave you breakfas' 'fore it get col', Barrister."

"Coming," Mardi called as though across the mountains, finishing off the coiffure by ad-libbing what she believed to be a barber's flourish. "There," she said in satisfaction, removing the towel from around his now limp shoulders.

Pardi uncurled from his trance like a cat pulled from sleep in a sunny spot. Peering into the unmagnified side of his shaving mirror, which he always brought along as part of the ritual but never used till it was over, he passed his brown hand over his skull as though to make sure he still had a forehead. He did, high and magnificent; his retreating hairline was making the sweep of his brow even more majestic.

"Thank you, my dear," he said graciously as he followed her to the table, resting the mirror on the sideboard by the large table clock which seemed to be Drumblair's heart, if not its coat of arms.

He finished his grapefruit and turned his attention to the oily surface of the plate that collected the oozings produced by his latest fad, a deep-fat fryer he had discovered on his last trip through New York.

"It's Freudian," Mardi reasoned, "this preoccupation with oil. It's because he really wants Jamaica to discover oil underground, like Trinidad."

Now almost everything he ate was submerged in the deep pot, which hissed like Tildy's disapproval at the entry of each morsel, and then surrounded it with a frenzy of liquid fat. His brief-lived culinary persuasions tended to put a strain on the running of the house; Mardi always kept a safe distance from the kitchen for fear of becoming embroiled in an area of life which, like mathematics, she had long since sworn off.

After a good many mouthfuls, he pulled the starched white napkin across his lips impatiently and reached for the salt dish and its tiny, silver spoon. "Why?" he asked.

"Why what, dear?" she answered absently as she tidily married her fork to the knife on her plate.

"Why have the Rastas taken Samson?"

"Oh, the Rastas. I don't know why," she said dismissively, as though trying to close a door she wished she hadn't opened.

The Rastafarians had become the dread of Jamaica. Members of an entirely original movement, these disciples of Ethiopia's Haile Selassie had decided to grow their hair into long, matted locks, smoke the potent local marijuana plant, which they grew themselves and called "ganja", and amble through the realities of Jamaican life, its heat and its squalor, rejecting its customs and vanities, beating their drums and dreaming of Zion, of Africa and of their Lion of Judah, the unwitting Emperor.

Or so it seemed to nearly everyone else in Jamaica, who decided that they were simply dirty and lazy. The poorer people, among whom they lived, thought they were mad and laughed at them. The more well-to-do, who were at the time further removed from the problem, resorted to their customary bigotry. When they could find no plausible reason for their fear and hatred, they made one up.

At school I had heard they were dangerous, so I watched them from the safe distance of the car's passenger window as they walked down the road in their dusty robes, with their matted fronds that reminded me of Bellevue's watsonia lily plaits when they aged and started to fray, and their eyes wild and red with the effects of ganja, which I mistook for bloody intent.

When with high drama I was informed by the spellbinding Gaggle across the fence that there were Rastas living in Mardi's studio, which for a while she had been too busy to visit, I fled to the house in alarm and announced to Mardi, "Ga Ga says there are dangerous Rastas in the studio!"

"Nonsense," she said, "there's nobody dangerous in anybody's studio. The things you pick up!"

She explained that with all the politics in her life she had not been able to do any work, and so the Rastas had come along and squatted in her studio, and that that was all right for a while but they would soon have to move, for she planned to go back to work. '

"If they squat for seven years you can't move them any more." Pardi warned her of this as though he were offering a formal legal opinion on the matter.

"I have a big piece in my head," she announced, quite unconcerned by either his omen or the maverick zealots she would have to remove. "A totem pole."

That was the first I had ever heard of a totem pole, and it was probably the first time the Rastafarians had heard of one too. The very next day, Mardi walked over to the studio and explained to them with great courtesy that she had to create this icon for her mythology, and so she must ask them, please, to vacate her studio so she could begin work.

There were three of them there that morning. One was sitting on the step at the front of the studio, gazing towards the sound of a late rooster whose crowing mixed awkwardly with the distant sound of traffic. In the studio behind, the other two shuffled in the safety of their chosen corners, which may have added acuity to a vision only they could see. One was on the floor on a bed of flattened cardboard boxes, and the other was propped up against Samson's head, with a pillow of cloths and rags which were kept in the studio for wrapping the clay. Their quiet assurance seemed to her not so much defiance as a glimpse of an unfamiliar world whose customs would have to be explored to be understood.

She suddenly thought of Roger Mais, powerful and delinquent, who had written of a Jamaica she realized she scarcely knew except from the outside. He had written of this Jamaica from the inside, she felt. He had died in the year of all the brooms, leaving three landmark novels that she felt the need to read again.

Now they sensed her sympathy, and the placid presence of Batiste in the high grass posed no threat to them. If they absorbed anything from her firm but gentle lecture, they gave no sign; their movements were few and totally unrelated to her presence. It was as if they could not see her from their world.

As she prepared to leave, formally offering her hand to the presence guarding the door, a deep voice struggled out of the gloom behind him.

"I man like 'im lacks!"

She was relieved to hear the voice, for the figure on the steps still showed no sign of response.

"What is it you like?" she called to the man leaning against the huge head. She had never been able to speak dialect, and the Rastas had further modified the language. She presumed that by "I man" he referred to himself.

The large frame sat forward, and the bundles against which he rested fell to the floor. He gestured to the wooden head he had appropriated. "De lacks 'pan 'im 'ead. I man sey me like dese lacks. Man mus' nat cut 'im 'air, so Jah seh."

He was stroking the long gouges in the wood, his huge hands moving over the ropes of Samson's hair.

Moved by his show of appreciation, she asked, as though she were speaking to a small child whose concentration she wanted to keep, "Why mustn't man cut his hair?"

" 'Im strength wi' sap. A man's strength is in 'im 'air."

As though some evangelical purpose had now been achieved, the guardian of the steps reached out and took her hand in both of his, and looked at her conspiratorially.

"One love, daughter."

The meeting was over. By the next morning they had left. The place was neatly swept, a couple of large sheets of her paper from the cupboard were filled with small, infantile drawings and there was a round, blackened patch with stones outside the door where they had cooked their food and smoked out the mosquitoes.

And the head of Samson was gone.

"So they took it! I'll be damned," he said thoughtfully, pinching up some spilled salt with his right hand and tossing it over his left shoulder once, twice, three times, to counteract any bad luck. "Maybe they liked it!"

"Then I think I should be flattered," she said, as she looked over at me where I was still playing with the sour sections of a halved grapefruit. "No one else liked my Samson."

She often said she wondered why people were always critical of her work when she used a larger, bolder style, as she had done with Samson. She found that the bigger tools seemed to release the wood more quickly to its nature, chasing away the orderly epidermis, the years and years of stratification, each knot knowing its place more deeply after each season.

Wood was always old; people didn't understand that. You had to challenge it, for it already had its habits. You asked a piece of wood to go back through the journey of its growth, to reclaim the flexibility of its youth when it was facetious and nubile. Then you asked it to interpret itself, and accept another face. It was a story in the telling, a mound of clay in the rough. If you could only free it, fight your way through to its independence, its origin, then it could begin. But how could you reflect the turbulence, the sheer impatience of a young country, with small tools and fine, tidy outlines?

"I'm afraid of Rastas. I'm glad they are gone," I blurted.

"Silly girl," chided Mardi.

"Why are you afraid?" Pardi stopped short; he even stopped chewing. This made me nervous.

"Because their eyes are red and I don't like their hair. It's like tree roots. It frightens me."

"Well now." Mardi lifted her torso to the height of her surprise, which she dramatized for Pardi in that conspiratorial way adults have when they create parables for children.

"Good, Lord! They shouldn't frighten anyone! They are deeply religious people, Pie," he said with genuine bewilderment.

I took refuge in the source of my information: "Well, that's not what they say at school."

"They are talking a lot of middle-class bunk," he spat.

"You know, dear, their hair is spotlessly clean," Mardi said thoughtfully. "They created quite a putta-putta out there at the side of the studio, where they bathed with my hose and washed their long hair. Batiste saw them!"

"'Im shudda chase dem down de gully! Batiste too fraidy-fraidy," Tildy muttered contemptuously as she circled the table to collect Pardi's plate.

Mardi looked disapproving and hurt. I had got used to Pardi and Mardi re-evaluating most of the things I heard in school. I liked their legend of the world; it was inclusive. There was always enough room for the things no one else seemed able to accommodate . . . white mice or ducks, Easter chicks dyed pink and blue and yellow, even Rastafarians no one else seemed to want, and sometimes things as big as small islands. It made life more harmonious, more capable of surprise.

"You know, I get so sick and tired of this hysteria in middle-class Jamaicans. The minute a person takes off the traditional dress and habit of Britain, we all go into a state of shock. Year after year we are struggling, we say, for independence, and yet the minute a Jamaican wears his hair in his own way, or dresses the way he wants to dress, or believes in God the way he wants to believe in Him, or even smokes his own damn tobacco, there's all this big hullabaloo!" Pardi said this in his "winding up the argument" voice as he prepared to leave the table.

The middle class, of which I was then unaware of being a part, became for me a baffling phenomenon.

"But they all want to go back to Africa," said Mardi.

Pardi gave a stout blow of his nose into his handkerchief and buried it again in his pocket.

"Yes, but that's nonsense. They will find they can't be Jamaican in Africa; they can best be Jamaican right here."

"And I'm not so sure about that tobacco, dear," Mardi added mildly.

"What do you think Blanche smokes in her pipe, for God's sake?" he asked as he rose from the table, scraping the wooden legs of the chair over the squawking tiles. "When I was a small boy in Guanaboa Vale, I can remember all the countrymen smoking their ganja. Nothing new about that. The Jamaican has his white rum and smokes his ganja, and why not? An Englishman has his whisky or his port and his Virginia or his South African tobacco. I say it's about time Jamaicans unshackle themselves and do whatever it is that comes more naturally to them or we'll never have true independence." He punctuated the word "independence" with a kiss on each of our foreheads, open quotation, close quotation, as he set off for work, bracing himself for his exit past the neighbours' gate.

"Amen, and a fine Jamaican three-piece suit you are wearing, too!" mocked Mardi. She loved him in this mood. She seemed to love everything for the first time in a long time that morning.

Now that she had her studio back, Batiste hoisted a tall plank in the centre. Purple-heart from Janet Jagan in British Guiana. Cheddi Jagan had been in Jamaica, foraging for a structure for his newly formed political party; he wanted to base it on the People's National Party constitution. Everyone wanted to use it as the basis for new political parties, or at least borrow bits and pieces of it. As a democratic structure it worked. It had an elaborate infrastructure of small groups that could exist anywhere. Each group had its own chairman and secretary. All these groups were represented at the constituency level, and again at the national level. All party policy had to pass through this system; even the president and vice-presidents were elected that way. Many of the islands were watching Jamaica as it slowly gained ground towards internal self-government, and it was now the performance of the PNP that they were noticing. Mardi found it remarkable the way Pardi managed to ground everything he touched in a set of rules and principles.

"It's the only way to make anything last," he would say. And he would give whatever it was a set of rules, a system; a constitution. Mardi had to admit that sometimes the rules worked; as in the party, or Jamaica Welfare or the Boxing Board of Control. But sometimes they didn't. His system of growing grapes, enshrined forever in its set of rules, was misguided, so she supposed the grapes would remain sour and acid in perpetuity.

He was in fact creating his own cosmos in perpetuity. This would go on for ever and ever, making each innovation concrete, stone on stone, brick on brick. He was building. In the meantime, she was running his constituency for him, opening schools and making the right speeches, cutting ribbons and more ribbons that stretched their bright throats against the blade of the scissors.

"Mr. Howler and Mr. Fart," she had said last week in a speech, by mistake; oh dear, she winced at the memory. Poor Mr. Fowler, poor Mr. Hart. Poor her!

"I must get back to work," she muttered to herself as Pardi and I were leaving. Standing beside the rosebeds, Batiste shaded his eyes and watched the car circle him on the driveway, and Mardi fled down the overgrown path towards the studio, giving a furtive look behind as though checking to see if she had escaped unnoticed. Batiste smiled peacefully in the bright sunshine.

8

TOO MANY
HORSES

IT WAS THE end of 1956. Mardi was expecting her totem pole, Thelma was expecting a baby; Nellie, a common brown dog whose cheerful disposition made up for her woeful lack of pedigree but made her inept as a watchdog, was expecting puppies.

And Pardi was expecting a tribe of islands. These were smaller territories of the British Caribbean with which he hoped Jamaica would form a political union.

It seemed to me at nine years old that the whole of my world was fecund, gestating and waiting; as though with my imminent entry into double digits everything in my life had started to multiply.

Since becoming its chief minister, Mardi said, Pardi "challenged the government that he led, continuing to confront it, but now more effectively from within." I heard terms like "widespread change and development", "the building of institutions", "introduction of new concepts". And from the appearance at Drumblair, late at night, of the frazzled permanent secretaries, it seemed to me that Pardi was exhausting the well-intentioned directors of what was reputed to be a lethargic civil service.

Even within Drumblair the benefits of the PNP government were tangible. Batiste was now free to ride his bicycle without having to pay for a licence. Since being exempt from the tariff, he had managed to get himself badly scraped in his first two road accidents—a statistic that led Tildy to comment, "Same 'ting I tell you, mus' neber give black people nuttin' fe free. Dem 'ave bad mine."

"Bad mind" was a condition Jamaicans blamed on each other.

Milton was in the first crop of students to win free places in secondary school. He set off proudly in his khaki uniform for the largest boys' school in Kingston, where life would continue to bully him, but now by different means. I was more diffident about the prospect of my own success, as the JLP opposition had already been prompted to suggest that a free place in school for his granddaughter had been the motivating factor behind Pardi's educational reform.

There was a certain dislocation of our family life, as Mardi and Pardi were away more. Sometimes Miss Boyd would stay with me at Drumblair, and less frequently I would stay with my father and Thelma. I was hardly mollified by the knowledge that we were somehow "holding the fort" for the good of a larger family unit elsewhere. Even when they were on the island, they were mostly away from home. Sometimes when they were out they were also in, for news of them would come floating in through the radio. Sometimes the rest of us gathered around and listened to Pardi's recorded voice making his address to the island, or read his ardent postcards from the ports where he had docked during his exploration.

Most of their trips were "down the islands", as Miss Boyd would say. During her sojourns at Drumblair, her manner was sweetly disgruntled. She seemed to search for some reprieve while keeping me company, lurking by the windows, whispering to herself and, through the long evenings, waiting for a return to her home and her own routine.

"Down the islands" was really a journey east, but the phrase conveyed a tacit contempt among Jamaicans for the smaller islands which were now the subject of such great attention.

The idea of a West Indian federation was not a new one. Attempts at grouping the islands for financial and administrative purposes had been made almost from the beginning of English settlement. The Leeward Islands had federated in the previous century. In the 1930s there had been a proposal to unite the Windward Islands and the Leeward Islands with Trinidad, but this had been abandoned as unlikely to succeed.

After repeated turbulence in many of the islands in the 1930s, the English more than ever thought it a good idea to combine the government of all their Caribbean possessions into one central headquarters. But poor communications and rivalry for the same markets had resulted in insularity, and the islands were deeply suspicious of each other.

It wasn't till after the Second World War that the idea resurfaced, and this time it originated in the islands themselves. By 1948 the University College of the West Indies was created, its initial campus in Jamaica, in special relationship with London University; communication between the islands was by now improving, and producers had come to realize that they were no longer competitors. England, which had always felt federation would be cheaper and easier to organize, remained supportive of the idea. The Colonial Office proposed a conference which was held in Montego Bay, in the north-west of Jamaica, in 1947. The Montego Bay Conference, as it became known, passed a resolution which recommended a political federation, and by 1950 the committee's official report included a provisional scheme. Many of the Caribbean leaders who would become the actors in this unfolding drama were first heard at that conference and, ironic as this would later prove to be, perhaps the most memorable and passionate speech in favour of federation was made by Bustamante, who suggested that future generations would never forgive us if we failed to federate.

So the concept of combining all the British possessions into an independent and sovereign Caribbean was now the obsession of the region's politicians and intellectuals. The new West Indies Federation would include Jamaica, Trinidad and Tobago, Barbados, St. Lucia, Antigua and Barbuda, Grenada, St. Vincent and the Grenadines, Montserrat, and St. Kitts and Nevis.

But the question that dominated the region's thoughts for quite a long time was, where should the capital be? Every Jamaican was certain it could only be in Jamaica; it was the largest island, and surely the easterly islands realized that Jamaica was doing them a favour. Any travelling should be done by the smaller islands, causing no inconvenience to us. After all, Jamaicans had much grander places to visit—like London or New York or Miami. The American mainland was only an hour's flight away.

It took many trips to sort out this question, but in the end it was agreed that Trinidad would be the site of the new capital. It was the largest of the islands in the eastern Caribbean, and Trinidad and Jamaica would bear the overwhelming share of the economic burden. Their combined population was eighty per cent of the region. Jamaica was considered to be too inaccessible to the smaller units, being separated from them by several hundreds of miles and many intervening islands that were not part of the British West Indies.

This was a setback for Jamaica. It was felt by many that the island had earned its seniority by more than just its size; Jamaica walked its own road, neither accommodating the British with what was perceived by some to be embarrassing obedience, as Barbados had done, nor playing possum like Trinidad. Until the advent of its great nationalist Eric Williams, Trinidad had appeared to dose itself with the opiate of humour; Trinidadians seemed to laugh at everything, most of all themselves. About the only thing they took seriously was the masque of Carnival once a year, which they were always either preparing for, submerged in or recovering from.

For better or worse, Jamaicans took themselves and their politics very seriously, and were proud of this. Although Trinidad was actually the first island to erupt in the upheavals of the 1930s, Jamaicans had remained in the vanguard of struggle once they embarked on the journey, and felt justified in their claim to be leading the way towards modern nationhood.

Mardi wasn't sure what to think of it all.

"Mother, you are too near," Michael told her. "You see, when you get as far as England, it's hard to see Jamaica. It's easier to see the West Indies as a whole. As an artist you know what I mean…as one moves away from the object, one's vision takes more in." It reminded her of the way she had leant on the head of Samson to gain perspective. With distance one could indeed see more in the round: psychologically, emotionally and symbolically. But Pardi, through his formidable intellect, had grasped all that from the beginning.

And Michael had been far enough away. As a student in London, where the West Indian Student's Union was incubating nearly the entire leadership of the next Caribbean generation, he had seen the archipelago as the necklace of the imperial parure. As expatriates, the students found comfort and consolation in each other. They burned with the visceral commitment of youth joined in common cause. They fought the Colonial Office not as Jamaicans or Barbadians, St. Lucians or Guianese. Sitting round the table together, planning a strike to protest conditions, they were all West Indians. At that distance, Michael insisted, they needed each other so that strength would come with sovereignty.

"As a region we have shared a common violation," he explained.

"The original malady may have been the same, dear ardent Michael, but the survival has been individual."

But while Mardi felt Pardi was off on one of his tangents, Michael insisted that the union would be a source of strength for the relatively tiny islands. They could combine their forces, regionalize their needs, share their bills and increase their trade markets. He had followed the path of powerful logic on which his father had based his vision. It was neither a tangent nor an emotional response to the traumas of the past. It was a pragmatic judgement. It made sense.

And for once Norman Manley and Alexander Bustamante seemed to share the same goal. Jamaica loved the idea of the cousins agreeing; it was reassuring. But every time Mardi thought of this accord, she had to fight a sense of foreboding.

As for Pardi, he reminded her over and over of the West Indian cricket team, a combined force of the best of the region. So was the university, where for the first time young people from the various islands were getting to know one another and to understand their commonality.

Pardi could see the marvellous sweep of the islands as a crescent paling from blue to beige on the map, reaching across the years where a flick of history's whimsy had tossed a people like a handful of toy jacks. He could see the bright sea dotted with ships carrying oil from Trinidad, bauxite from Jamaica, spices from Grenada, every chemical mystery the profound subterranean life of British Guiana secreted in her chest. He could see students travelling to their choice of campus for their own specific talent, medical staff journeying to their faculties, patients ambulanced to the "ology" of their need. And for the time being Mardi moved from this terrain of doubt, away from the needling reminders of her own intuition to the higher ground of her husband's convictions, where she entertained only those positive thoughts that sustained his effort.

When she was asked to design a flag for the region, she devised a symmetrical series of waves, aqua and white, undulating but even, pierced by the central orange eye of a sun that neither cast a shadow nor spilled its reflection. This now fluttered over the federal capital in Port of Spain.

Their trips to England, from which I had received Clark's sandals, a chemistry set, Playbox biscuits and sturdy clothes from Marks and Spencer, were replaced by trips to the eastern Caribbean. Now I received a wonderful feathered headdress and a beaded mask from Trinidad, land of the Carnival, said Mardi; a pair of calabash chac-chacs from Barbados which looked like the ones I remembered seeing on the north coast at home but had the word "Barbados" prominently painted on them. There was even a little black cloth doll from St. Lucia, with a red plaid dress and a bright bandanna to match, that sat incongruously next to my polar bear, Brumus, on the bed.

"Dem stick pins in dese dolls," Tildy admonished, "dem 'ave all kin' o' voodoo in dat Lucia hiland, an' dem nuh shudda call it h'afta' no saint, fo' it no Christian place, dat...it full up a all a dem French voodoo people. You no can believe in voodoo an' God at the same time, you hear?"

Best of all were the stamps on the envelopes of their letters, foreign and rare. The empty pages of these islands took on new life in my stamp book.

And with their return from these trips a new word entered my vocabulary; it was "federation". It was a good word, something to be believed in, a concept ennobling, far-reaching and visionary. It was a word that people big of heart and courageous of soul believed in. It was a Pardi word.

At first I was not quite sure what it meant. Then I discovered that it concerned those islands on the hurricane map. Pardi spoke about them with renewed fervour, and it reminded me of the efforts being made by my father and Thelma to prepare me for the entry of my sibling into our world—except that it seemed to be the whole of Jamaica that Pardi was soothing and cajoling, and there were a lot more babies, nine islands or island groups, in fact, being brought into that bigger family. That would make us ten.

Soon I felt a common cause with the struggle to bring us all together, seeing my own personal sacrifice in the long periods of time I spent at home without them.

New leaders came to visit. They spoke with singsong accents, and laughed more readily than Jamaicans. They were always drinking and eating and posing for photographs, and seemed to bring a glamour of distant places with them. I thought they made the solemn members of the PNP seem dull by comparison.

My autograph book was filled with the names of people who adorned the front pages of *The Daily Gleaner*. From Trinidad there was the small and irritable figure of Eric Williams with his hearing aid, the doctor of thought, not deeds (Zethilda described him as "dat a dacta weh nuh cyan 'elp you!") who was said to like "strong central government" and whose obvious impatience led me to plead with Mardi to get the signature for me.

Then there was Grantley Adams—a Barbadian, not a barbarian, Mardi corrected me; I liked his large head and his heavily lidded eyes. He reminded me of Pardi. I considered him most noble, and became very agitated when Mardi insisted she thought he was furtive and insecure.

The tall and hearty V.C. Bird from Antigua I thought was generous because he smiled at me even when no one else was watching, and gave me coins I had never seen before. His signature was simple and readable, with two uncomplicated full stops, just like those under the N and W of Pardi's. And Marryshow of Grenada I remember as excitable with a lot of bouncing hair.

Best of all was C.L.R. James, who wasn't a leader of anywhere, but a writer and philosopher. He was the first West Indian writer who seemed to confer with Pardi instead of Mardi, a fact of which Pardi was proud. James was a man of ideas, and his ideas were often quoted by Pardi to those he thought deserved to hear them, like Mardi and my father. His autograph was so scratchy and unruly that I asked Pardi if this was what was called writer's cramp. He explained that

James had a disease called Parkinson's. I noticed that James, like Crab Nethersole of the muffin chase, became one of the rare people Pardi kept in mind. He would say "I must tell C.L.R." or "I must show C.L.R." or "C.L.R. told me...."

The dénouement of life's promises began with the birth of my brother on January 2, 1957. He was called Joseph. "The biblical Joseph," said Michael. We thought at first he meant Joseph the carpenter from Nazareth.

"Not *that* Joseph. The other one, the one with the coat of many colours. He was a unionist! He was the first person I've heard of who used collective bargaining."

We were all intrigued by his gangly long legs, and large, unsteady head. Mardi always insisted that the Shearer line common to our family through herself and Pardi featured a sink at the base of the back of the skull. This she checked solemnly on Joseph, and seemed pleased with the results of her investigation. "There it is," she said with satisfaction.

My father had built a small house on the only hillock of land when Pardi subdivided the backlands of Drumblair into what would be sold as residential lots. Pardi was broke, having spent on the party most of the money he'd made from the ludicrously modest fees of his legal career, so he had to sell part of the land. Along with Drumblair, he kept a spot for himself, and gave Michael this piece beside it, which was covered in ebony trees. Michael and Thelma had gone to great trouble to build the house between the trees, so as not to uproot them. They called their home Ebony Hill.

Threatened by the likelihood of a miscarriage, Thelma had spent many months in bed. Whenever I visited the house I anticipated the baby suddenly falling out, pitched from some unsafe carriage in which it slept. But Joseph's survival had been cradled by a wise and gentle nurse whose enduring calm and benevolence made even her withered arm seem an instrument of safety. She too was called Edna. She steadied the havoc within her patient, and calmed whatever was making the gestation unsafe. Even the quagmire of ambivalence that now surrounded their marriage, making the relationship a series of bad habits as unbreakable as they were obsessive, seemed to thin in her presence.

Although I didn't live at Ebony Hill, I still saw a lot of my father. He often came to visit me at Drumblair, where he would peruse his mother's work and discuss politics with his father. The union had become his life, and his commitment to the federation was drawing him closer to the party; he valiantly endorsed their cause on every platform and every occasion.

I thought of Ebony Hill as braata, a little extra, like the thirteenth sweet the grocer gives you in the bag with a wink. It was there if I needed it, but home and my centre remained Drumblair. And there was the added attraction of those neighbours, the Gaggle. It had taken me time to pluck up the courage to visit, but after a while they became the high point of my afternoons. I would approach their home cautiously, tree by tree, as I fought my instinctive shyness. They introduced me to bobby socks and rock-and-roll, and *arroz con pollo* with olives, and gave me beautiful new frilly dresses from Florida which were said to be too small for the youngest daughter. There was an exciting abundance about their lives after the ordered austerity of Drumblair.

What did Jamaica feel about becoming part of a wider focus? And the other islands? Federal elections, soon to be held all over the Caribbean, would provide an answer.

And this was what I found confusing. Instead of one predictable cycle of national general elections every five years, there was now a second stream of elections as well—federal elections. And two different contesting federal parties, the West Indies Federal Labour Party, of which Pardi was leader, and the Democratic Labour Party of the West Indies, which was led by Bustamante. For the time being the cousins served as leaders of both national and federal parties, but when the time came for elections they would have to make a choice. Both faced the same dilemma: whether to run in the federal elections, or stay and contest the national elections at home. They could not do both.

The general elections to be held in 1959 were suddenly no longer my next marker. The rhythm was broken. The federation formally came into existence in Trinidad in 1958, and federal elections were announced for March of that year.

Before this election was called, Pardi had to decide whether or not he was going to contest a federal seat. Should he leave Jamaica and join the federal party? If he did, he knew that he would most likely become the first prime minister of the federation. Or should he stay and lead the local parliament, ensuring Jamaica's co-operation and support of a federal government far away in Trinidad? Being chief minister he had the harder decision, for he had more to lose than Bustamante.

The heavy financial responsibility of such a union lay largely on Jamaica's shoulders. The economy was booming with bauxite and tourism, but what if things were not well managed at home? Could he be sure of anything if he was not there himself? Though more glorious, running the federation was probably the less arduous task.

Even the new neighbours were less ebullient and more curious as he passed in his car, and they watched the sphinx-like exterior of the house looking for signs.

Everyone was waiting for the answer.

✖

It was late afternoon. Pardi found Mardi in the studio, gazing up at the beginnings of the wooden totem pole, which she had decided to call *Growth*. She was sitting on the floor, with her mallet beside her, and chewing defiantly on a piece of straw. Her hair was damp and lay limply over her ear. The studio was hot. A circular Japanese fan, with its unfolded garden of miniature trees under statuesque women in kimonos, lay on the arm of the only chair.

He had made his decision. He had come to share this news with his wife. He seldom interrupted her work, so now his approach was cautious, and he stopped at the doorway where he could see the rough outline of the new carving.

"They seem to be taking a journey," he said.

Where the base had shown only chalk marks, figures were now moving up the totem pole like flames in a fire: two men leading the way, leaning towards the left and reaching up to follow their gaze, and a woman following and looking back. Above this, as though travelling onward, the same three figures leaned towards the right and bowed their heads in their crooked arms, the first man as though the bent limb might part the wind, the second and third figures still following but now looking down, their arms shielding their faces.

The rest was chalk on the roughed-out flat surface, a soft pink that blushed through the wood from the fresh chipping.

In the flurry of white markings, like abandoned edges of clouds, he saw the outlines of horses—three horses, or was it two? It might be two, the horses of the night and of the morning. Above these the wood curved into what he thought was a head, maybe because there was a suggestion of eyes in a whim of the chalk.

"What do you think?" She patted the floor beside her as if inviting him to sit.

"Their bodies move beautifully in unison, and yet each head is reacting differently," he noted. "Maybe they are not all taking the same journey in their thoughts."

She frowned and looked farther up to the horses.

"And there are your horses...." He followed her eyes to where it appeared she had last been carving, for the wood had stopped in its tracks. A few shavings, not totally disconnected, curled to an abrupt standstill amid their own amputation, homeless and unsure.

"How many horses?"

"Too many...." She said this so quietly and incidentally that he felt that her gentle response had somehow exonerated him. He came in and sat in the chair. "I remember during the war at the remount depot, you couldn't put them together in the same stable. Oh dear, it's awful when I think of it...we trained those poor horses to send them to almost certain death."

Now she looked at the carving as if she could see the frantic horses bolting and rearing up in the unbridled strokes of frenzied chalk; as though she imagined them trying to escape over and over again.

"Where are they going, my love...these too many horses?"

She looked surprised by the softness with which he sent those words into the afternoon, as though they were private messages, or scribbled notes from the war front. He had somehow moved, like pronouns in a foreign language, from the formal to the familiar.

"I'm not sure," she faltered, and then she steadied herself on her elbow and looked at the figures surging inexorably upwards in front of the rays of a sun he had not noticed before at the base. "But the figures...now I don't think they are journeying so much as evolving."

She said this last word deliberately, as though first weighing and then placing each syllable as if it had its own correct historical place.

"The woman is looking back. She is like Lot's wife," he said thoughtfully.

"Well, that's what women do," she said defensively. When he didn't answer, she seemed to relent. "They have to, I suppose. Men tend to start afresh every day, whereas women unwind from yesterday, and they are still holding yesterday's hand. They are more introspective, which leads them back to the past. Their living is more internal, I think."

He wasn't sure that was true.

"Oh, we remember the past all right."

"Yes, but you don't hold hands with it and bring it along with you into the next day."

"You better mind she doesn't turn into a pillar of salt!"

"She won't. There she is"—she got to her feet and stood looking at the second row in the wood—"and she's not salt at all, she's moving forward, she's just afraid to look. Maybe she's afraid of change."

Pardi walked to the back of the studio, where the open windows let in steamy air filled with the insistent argument of flies. He pushed open the narrow door at the back, which she seldom used, as she felt that somehow her energy would leak out of the room if it could simply come in one way and leave by the other.

"Or maybe she'd just rather be alone," she added thoughtfully, cocking her head sympathetically at the reluctant figure. "It will need to be oiled when it's finished."

"I will do that for you," he said, and he leaned against the door frame, looking out at the guango trees idling high above the long grass.

"I don't know how we shall manage, my dear. You know we have the federal election this year, and then the general election after that. Whatever choice I make, it's still going to cost me to keep the party going."

"Maybe I'll sell this carving," she soothed him, but she knew he had more to say. He never worried particularly about money, speeding through it as one would travel down a road towards a vital destination. But he knew money bothered other people, so this was a signal that he meant to talk seriously.

The mention of the federal election, coming when his back was turned, reminded her of how little they faced each other to talk about the federation. He looked away to tell her things, because he didn't want to have to interpret her face. And she did the same, so that what she said was said easily and by itself, like writing a letter or a list.

"We'll have to campaign both here and through the islands."

"You are *so* Cancerian. You carry your home with you on your back—it's your shell. Sometimes I think you love all this scuttling up and down. You see, the crab has two elements . . . land and sea."

"I can't think what this has to do with it, but may I remind you that you are Piscean . . . two fish swimming, and

your element is the sea. And you should love all this travelling up and down of boats and planes and people and ideas.
And anyway your two fish swim in opposite directions, so
you should enjoy the conflict!"

"Well, I have only one element, so my conflicts have to be
contained to that—two fishes in the same sea."

But his face had become suddenly solemn.

"Norman?"

"I have decided to stay," he said.

The afternoon locked, still and deliberate, as if it were a
painting.

It was unusual for them that the pros and cons of this
decision should have been weighed only on the scales of his
thought. They pulled at his attention late at night, the recurring sheep of his insomnia, the meaning disguised in his
dreams. For her, the dilemma became a flavour, singular and
undiminishing, that she could taste behind all her activities.

Mardi had always been ambivalent about federation. She
had come to see the good sense of pooling resources, the
additional strength of being a region. Her reservations were
emotional, and seemed to involve her lifelong wish to be a
Jamaican as well as something more nebulous: an intuition
that, in the whole complicated conundrum of the federal
issue, her husband was left vulnerable on too many fronts.
But she was certain of one thing. If there was going to be a
federation at all, it had to be led by him. Pardi was the magnet that would pull the region together.

"Why?" She asked the question very softly.

The room enshrined the afternoon as if Pardi and Mardi
were statues. The totem pole in the slanting light looking
maimed in its prematurity.

Later, walking along the path towards the house, he returned to her question, which he had been mulling over in his head.

"How can I leave Jamaica?"

"Busta," she said almost involuntarily, as though Pardi's question stirred in her a machiavellian response to her other cousin.

"Busta only on one front...." He sounded tentative.

"What do you mean?"

"I might have fiercer opposition from inside my own party. If I did and I wasn't here it might split us in two and smash up the party."

"Oh, that's not possible...." She stopped mid-sentence.

Mardi was always reluctant to concede that anyone from within her own ranks, be it a friend, one of her children, a member of her political party, could pose a threat, or even be mistaken. The prospect of disloyalty made her defensive of those close to her, as though she were defending them against her own guilty thought. If she recognized the danger, she sheltered it with excuses.

Pardi stopped on the path at a place where the late and tenacious Wog had once dug a deep hole in the earth; it had remained as a monument to a life that was remembered with more celebration than grief.

He stooped in the grass, pulling aside the long, itchy shafts that made delicious-smelling silage for the cows.

"Here. I have a surprise to show you."

He looked up at Mardi, who was standing with her hands on her hips, trying to make out what it was in the fading light. There in Wog's dugout was an unexpected crèche. Five parasitic puppies were tearing blindly at Nellie's swollen teats, wriggling like fat little worms in an Edgar Allan Poe nightmare. She gave a little shudder, pulling in her chin, and the gesture reminded Pardi of the girl he had first seen when she was thirteen, in his Aunt Ellie's living-room in Cornwall. She had been summoned from a joyous romp in the haystacks, and she had come in tall, angular and tousled, her body hard and boyishly busy. She did not want to be drawn away from a game outside and told to go and wash her hands to be presented to her cousin, and had displayed an irritated reluctance, just as she did now.

He had watched her from where he leaned on the mantelpiece over the unlit fireplace. His mother had died, and he had brought the final bits of news for his surviving aunt to complete the shroud of her sister's memory. For a moment the young girl had stared at him intently. She had an unusual face, it had a searching quality that swept like a beacon. Her features were sharp, her expression was fierce and wary of containment, as though she had to ensure her escape from the clutter of eight siblings.

That was when he decided that she was the one he liked, as though she were the pick of the litter.

"She will never survive, you know." Mardi's voice brought him back to Nellie. "We will have to give them away as soon as we can. They'll suck the life out of you, little dog," she addressed Nellie, as though she had told her so before.

Nellie looked back at her and, panting under the siege, gave her mistress a brief salute with the blink of her eyes.

"Nonsense," said Pardi and set off to and fro, gathering straw and leaves for the manger, while Mardi sat on the mound of earth displaced by Wog's tunneling. Nellie was cleaning the puppies indulgently while they fought each other for supremacy. Already one of them, a brown one with black markings, was getting the better of the others.

"We are too young to cope with all this," she said as she stared at the nativity.

"What, with the puppies?" He didn't look up, but continued stuffing the cave with straw.

"No, with the islands...."

Mardi sensed that the party had never been behind the idea of a federation. Like most of Jamaica, the members had just gone along with a leader they believed in almost absolutely. Where they felt reservation, they substituted faith. He had carried them through each phase of his reasoning, and inferred from their acquiescence that they shared his conviction. He hated blind faith, because he thought it a danger to thoughtful democracy.

Most Jamaicans were high on the expectation of independence, and the promise of prosperity that his years in government had created. Pardi had thrown out the concept of independence like a challenge, a goal. People had been inspired by this. Pardi had provided a road map and Jamaicans were following it.

"She'll have to go for water." He said this like an instruction to the dog, as he tried to push a handful of leaves under her shoulder, and retreated when she snapped at him.

"Oh, she can't. Not now. They wouldn't know what to do without her. You'll have to bring her back a bowl from the house."

"Are you glad I'm staying?" He made the question personal.

"I don't know what I am, dear. Except that I'm very confused. I mean, what will happen to this federal thing if you don't go?"

She had said "federal thing" as though relegating it to the realm of his hobbies. Seeing his face suddenly disappointed, she tried to explain. "Look, Norman, you have to face one thing. *You* are the glue. You are the one factor in this whole federal business that can make the thing stick!"

"You know, it may work even better without me. I've been thinking that maybe I am too closely identified with Jamaica to lead a federal government with credibility. The other islands are so suspicious of our size and our distance. They will accept a leader from one of the other islands much more easily. No matter what Jamaica does, remember we are still a geographic entity. But as a group of islands we are held together by something far more sophisticated and vulnerable than geography."

"But what about Jamaica?" she argued. "How will Jamaica take it? She is just as suspicious as they are! They have already got the capital, and now...this."

"Sometimes I think you really don't care for federation," he said—without rancour, just as an observation.

"It's not as simple as that, dear. You see, you move at a great speed; you are a sprinter. And as soon as you have laid the plans for one event, got all this in our heads and given us starting orders, you tear off on a new track, careering along and badgering us all to follow. In the meantime, we have just grasped your original idea, and while you plan the Olympics the rest of us are trying to...to"—she searched the ground for the right words, and grabbed at the best she could find—"to finish the hundred yards, so to speak!"

"But this is all one movement towards freedom...it's a play with more than one act. Regionalism is inevitable, whether it's now or fifty years away."

"Follow my logic, Norman. When we stood on the back of a truck during the general strike, waiting for Busta's release from prison after you negotiated it, and Miss Aggie and I were passing down soup to the hungry dock workers, I got the notion in my head—and so did the thousands on that march for freedom—that we had begun a fight against the British, against colonization—that we were embarking on a journey to independence. We were going to struggle as much as we had to, to achieve this."

As he paced, Pardi's steps had become less measured, and he had an almost chastened demeanour. Sometimes he was astonished by just how little he understood of what people were thinking. He remembered his first revelation of this in 1944. He had fought an election against someone he considered a charlatan. He had concentrated on the issues, trying to enlighten the minds of an almost uneducated electorate, and they had listened like obedient children in Sunday School. And then—maybe only for the promise of bread, or swayed by some rumour, who knew why—they had voted for the other man.

"Greed and fear. They voted for the familiar." Mardi had shrugged at the simplicity of the explanation.

He had leaned on his wife, asking her for explanations of a simple, but idiosyncratic world which seldom conspired to be logical. It was not losing the election that broke his confidence; he was too committed a democrat for that. It was the fact that he could not comprehend the reasons for his defeat, reasons which his wife easily intuited.

Until then, Pardi had never known defeat. His life had been full of challenge and daunting odds. Whether it was his hundred-yard record, or coming from far behind to win the Rhodes; surmounting typhoid fever or surviving the Great War; acting on one side of the copyright law for the Vicks Corporation, which claimed that its name had been appropriated, and on the other side for Pepsi Cola when

Coca Cola tried to monopolize the term "cola"—invariably and consistently he won. And every single murder case he defended, he won.

But that time he had lost, and because defeat was new to him he felt it more profoundly than any of his victories.

She noticed the slight drag of his heels now. Mardi tried again to explain. "So we are all pursuing this goal, inch by inch. The writers are writing like Jamaicans, the painters are painting Jamaican themes, the musicians are making Jamaican music...even the Rastas are busy being what they feel is Jamaican, searching for a Jamaican spirituality.

"But then we wake up one day and the rules are changed. We are going to be West Indians, and here is a new how-to manual. And I find I am asking myself, when did the independence movement mysteriously mutate into the federal movement? I feel...here I am trying to make myself known as one thing, and suddenly I'm supposed to be another. It's like a derailment. It's confusing. First things first."

Light flees like a thief in the tropics. It just turns on its heel and slips away. Where before the landscape had made sense, now there were only dark shapes like shoulders in a crowd. She could no longer see his face. But he had stopped his restless meander, and it seemed that the distant monosyllabic throb of the Four Roads jukebox grew out of the dark.

"How close the rest of the world is coming," he said.

He thought of the stealthy erosion of Drumblair's privacy: the committees and constituents, the music from Four Roads, the Rastafarians in the studio, even the Gaggle.

"Drums," she said, as though to establish herself in the world again. She hugged her knees and lifted her head to listen. "It's so insistent. Instead of flutes and pianos and violins, we've gone back to our drums."

"It's a bit umpy-umpy," he said with distaste.

He wasn't prepared to be philosophical about a sound system that was keeping him awake every night. He had called the police, who had made the offenders lower the volume, but the following day he had been besieged by wounded messages from the area—which was a stalwart political ally.

They retrieved each other from the darkness, and walked arm in arm back towards the house. At the steps she stopped and hugged him. Behind them the arms of the circular path surrounded the lawn.

"I am glad we're staying," she said.

"I am staying," he said to the large crowd assembled around the old clock-tower at Half Way Tree Square, near Kingston. The clock—like every other town-centre clock in Jamaica— was a polite reminder from the British to a native population who had so far declined any invitation to punctuality. During the days the market women yelled above the disciplined chimes, and at night the beggars and homeless gathered on its steps to sleep through each hourly pronouncement.

"I am staying," he said again, in response to the quiet with which his news was greeted.

Standing near him, Mardi recognized the pause—it was the same uncertainty she had felt in herself. It was neither of relief nor of despair. It was a pause of disjointment, a circumstance for which the heart had learned no reflex. It was a moment of dislocation.

He was the one who had plotted and planned this trek to federation. He understood the new terrain, and urged the Jamaicans on from the preoccupation of his exploration. They only knew for sure that he had called to them before and never failed them. He had already led them through one

successful term of office, and he had headed the government with imagination and distinction. They were marching
with him to independence—whatever he chose to call it,
and by whichever route he chose to take.

If he led the way, they would follow him, even blindly,
for they knew they could trust him. But if he did not go,
federation made no sense. He was their only solid link to
that nebulous concept. And so they paused, until he made
his announcement the second time.

First the relief came, as a stampede of applause charged
through the air from the majority of the audience crowded
before the platform. If "the Father of the Nation" was staying, then everything must be all right. He would be there
with them, whatever happened with that leaky federal ship.

Mardi watched the party's hierarchy, tired from standing
in ovation on the platform, settle one by one into the
scooped iron chairs provided. They looked pleased but
somewhat noncommittal, as though the crowd might at any
moment change its mind. And some of it did. The boos
came shortly after. There were fewer of them, and they came
from farther away, their distance lending a sinister quality,
and an air of trouble which was short-lived, either drowned
out by the reinforcements of more applause with which it
was met, or maybe by the abrupt departure of the dissen-
ters. It sounded to Mardi as though the crowd was having its
own argument.

Sitting beside her, Crab Nethersole looked mildly smug,
and this she knew was because the threads of his intricate,
tireless weft crossed her husband's warp day by day, plan
by plan, in the minute details of their weave. As minister
of Finance he had been Pardi's alter ego, transforming his
vision into workable reality.

It wasn't that they both started from some rock-hard point of conviction, or had some irrefutable preconception of where they must go. It was more that they had the ability to spark thought in each other; they both had minds that could travel to or away from a premise, fast and flexible minds that were neither muscle-bound by bigotry nor confined by the arrogance of opinion. They could take an idea and run with it as far as it could go. The trouble was that they often thought years ahead of everyone else.

Pardi's decision to stay relieved his party—at least for the time being—of a daunting question: who would be the heirs to these two men? The younger, fervent ones like Vivian Blake and David Coore—lawyers and friends who, along with Michael, worked so hard for the party— appeared idealistic and gauche to its rank and file; and there were so few of them. Like all establishments, the party valued the promise of adolescence at a safe distance. And, like most innovators or revolutionaries, the senior members never entertained the thought that they, and their ideas, could be getting old. So tonight the majority rose once more and applauded a decision they found reassuring, and the people clapped to the beat of their own relief.

Mardi watched from the platform behind Pardi. In the lights rigged above their heads, she could see myriad tiny flies and moths struggling towards the luminescence. Soon there would be the federal elections, and they would see which way these fantastic crowds voted when put to the test.

"Me glad!" a man near the platform gloated. "Dem nat gwine get we leader. Dem na deserve a man like 'im. A fe we leader. Mek dem find dem own, dem fool-fool likle h'iland dem. We na go' give dem we food, and we na give dem fe we leader!"

No, we will not give them our food and we will not give them our leader, Mardi echoed in the recess of her mind, which blinked at the facile logic. But now the whole crowd was becoming unstuck.

Davidson, the party's song-leader, a tall, thin man with a larynx that warbled with the longing of gospel music, had started singing to try to focus the evening. His enormous eyes seemed to bulge with the effort, as though his fervour might burst out of his sockets. On how many campaign trails, she wondered, had he whipped the crowd into a frenzy, or distracted them from an outburst that threatened their solidarity. He and so many other stalwarts, earning scarcely any pay, but supported by their profound faith in the movement.

Even Davidson was having difficulty getting their attention tonight. He resorted to "Ninety and Nine", whose hypnotic effect started the crowd rocking from side to side, leaning against each other in the tender, joyous rendering of their song of redemption.

Her eyes moved from the anonymity of the crowd to the figure of her husband. Pardi stood there waiting and watching. His hands in his pockets made him look tentative, as though he was cautioning himself not to take success too seriously, for danger and disappointment were always near at hand. "Chicken merry, hawk de near," he would say.

As though they were her misgivings, she brushed away a few tiny dead rain flies which had fallen from the light onto her shoulders, and they joined a small cemetery of their fellows between the feet on the platform.

By now, Davidson had captured the crowd's attention and handed back the microphone to his leader. "I did not come into politics for honours or glory...," Pardi explained.

His voice rocked her like the sound of the sea, and she was back in Green Island, in the far west of the island, where they had taken the children on long holidays. The sea was not frightening as it was in Cornwall. Here it was only melodic or petulant.

"I am probably facing the last job of my life..."

He was a man with a boat, oaring his way across the horizon on a mission. Always on a mission, sixty minutes of each hour of each day. A life must never be wasted, he'd say.

"I am not afraid of hard roads..."

The children would dive and swim and row and plan fishing trips with their father at dawn. Children were by nature creatures of the sea, who disappeared leaving a ball floating, or the struggling head of a dog.

"...the maintenance of Jamaica's support of federation..."

Her mind strained for their young faces: Douglas' serious and Michael's smiling, and the faces of their friends coming and going. She swallowed as if to return a familiar pang to its rest.

"...the two things I believe in most and am resolved to support to the end of my days..."

Norman would leave his boat stranded on the sand and be done. With his brown skin and green mind, he had no use for a beach. She would gather shells and listen to the voice of the sea lamenting, each wave advocating its argument with equal conviction. She knew the same things had been said from the beginning of time.

❋

I can never forget the fateful afternoon when *Growth* became as dark as it did.

I am not sure why Pardi didn't think of discussing his promise to oil the carving before he kept it. I think he wanted to surprise Mardi. He was an impetuous man, and I think he wanted to please her. I know it wasn't mischief, though it is possible that the well-meant gesture may have extended from Pardi's present preoccupation with oil.

We all knew that the carving was finished.

Pardi came skulking home round the side of the house in a new routine he had developed to avoid sightings by the neighbours. He had been working on a plan to avoid passing the bungalow at all. He had thought of opening up a driveway into the grass-piece from the corner at Old Church Road, as an escape route, but his wife had vetoed the suggestion as "a little too drastic, dear." He reminded her that they had moved the studio from beside the garage to the grass-piece, and that had been to avoid people, but the court of the law was easier than that of the heart. She hadn't admitted the precedent. Life was like that.

There was havoc behind the kitchen. Tildy had met her match. She was held hostage by Eric, a huge black turkey gobbler who made it his duty to charge at everybody who wandered into his sphere of influence.

"Lard, God," she screamed mightily, and Batiste laughed toothlessly from the step overlooking the backyard.

I watched from an upstairs window in the back room, where Pardi and I had organized a lab around a chemistry set he had discovered on one of his trips. It had provided our Cancerian hearts with a purpose, according to Mardi, though mine more resembled an obsession as I took to collecting and stacking spare bottles and jars, often throwing away usable contents in my impatience. For his part, Pardi conducted experiments with enthusiasm; but, like an intuitive chef who seldom follows a recipe, he gave little more than a cursory glance at the handbook, so most of them failed, and a few exploded.

"Barrista shudda neber spare you. 'Im shudda gobble you up fe Christmas dinna!"

The word "gobble" seemed to set Eric off again, and with a renewed surge he ran after her, looking like a fat woman flouncing, hands on hips, neck straight and immobile as though balancing something aloft.

"Yobble, yobble, yobble," he crowed at Zethilda defiantly, stopping just short of her, and she crashed backwards onto the sheets of zinc where the white laundry lay bleaching, and the ducks and geese squawked and flapped in surprise and outrage, and the fowl coop overhead shook with a beating of wings and alarmed cluck-clucking.

"Batiste!" she yelled, "save me from dis damn buzzard!" It sounded more like a command than like a plea, but Batiste only heaved and gasped like a drowning man coming up for air, revealing his blackened gums.

On the turkey's next lunge, Zethilda stumbled into the miniature duckpond. "Now me wet up me shoes, you ole h'ugly land crow you!" And she lifted her skirt as though to save it from getting wet, though the catchment was no more than six inches deep.

"Why you no cook 'im dinna, Miss Tildy?" cackled Batiste, glad to see the warlike old Maroon under attack for a change. "After 'im no 'ab nu teet, 'im cyan bite you, an 'im wing cyan beat you. What 'im can do, eh Miss Tildy?" he chided.

"'Im we butt me down," she said, taking advantage of a brief lull to step out of the cemented puddle and compose herself with more elegance in front of the chicken coop.

"After 'im doan 'ave no horn, an 'im na peck you cos im a 'ole back im 'ead like 'im doan eben wan' kiss you!"

"Yobble, yobble, yobble," asserted the bird unconditionally.

Pardi watched the standoff with pride.

He was very fond of that turkey. We asked him if he had named the bird after Eric Williams, the Trinidadian leader, and he just smiled as though the comparison was appropriate, and said that good turkeys, like good politicians, should be able to stand their ground and pontificate.

Eric had a great deal of pluck. He had fought the family since he had arrived as a young chick to be fattened for Christmas. He had sensed the abattoir of intention from the generosity of feed-time, and though he fell on the grain with alacrity, he made it his business to challenge everyone, attacking the first sign of a shadow that fell across the path between the kitchen and the staff quarters.

In November Pardi had decided to save the stout-hearted bird, and Christmas dinner had been reduced to a vengeful ham that, as though resentful of its understudy role, turned out to be tainted.

Now, in his three-piece suit, Pardi strode into the fray.

"Stop it at once," he yelled to the recalcitrant bird, who stalked the area grimly, defending its borders from insubordination. The turkey flapped backwards for a few surprised steps, regrouped, and stood his ground with somewhat less certainty. "Yobble, yobble," he sulked.

His saviour set off at a pace towards him, charging the fat bird with the fierce familiarity of a friend who has paid his dues and earned the right to be critical.

"You're god-damn facety, how dare you hold Tildy to ransom?"

Eric retreated in haste towards the pineapple patch, and Zethilda sauntered with renewed bravado back towards the kitchen. "Saucy one," Pardi muttered affectionately to the retreating bird.

"Sauce!" Tildy grabbed the word from Pardi. "Me will mek a sauce fe dat dere bird when me bake 'im!" She delivered her ultimatum as she disappeared up the stairs: "De foolish fowl bad-lucky, Barrista! I tell you, sah, is h'ider dat turkey go or me!"

Ignoring her threat, he looked up and beckoned to me to join him. "I promised your Mardi I'd oil the carving."

Victorious from one mission, he set off more furtively on another, with me in tow.

At the studio, the completed totem pole lay flat where Batiste had balanced it between a log and the arms of the Pardi chair. Pardi hovered along its length, stroking the uneven shades with the awe of fingers capable only of carpentry.

"Look at him," he said, as though giving the piece gender did it necessary honour. Then his eyes settled above the figures, fixed on the powerful forelegs, the resolute movement of the head of a single brave horse, neck arched to face eventuality and mane standing in the air of a last gallop. It seemed to startle him.

"Only one horse! I'll be damned," he muttered.

With its neck reared back, the horse made him think of Eric. Stubborn, intractable, delinquent Eric. Eric who had survived.

Above the horse stood the mask of a godhead: resolute, single-minded, irrevocable, a large hand resting beside its face the way one blinkers one's eyes in the mountains to see beyond the nearest hilltop.

"Too many horses." He repeated the words as softly as they had returned to him from a moment he had once neglected. It seemed very long ago.

He felt his wife's presence in the room.

"Too many horses." He said it again, but now more as if to convince himself of how little sense such a premise made. The single horse, as it reared up defiantly, now seemed insular and isolationist.

He walked over to the cupboard and after rummaging through some tins and bottles, produced the oil and two brushes, one larger than the other, and set us to work: Cover up all the uneven blotches where the wood is fading.

Was he sure, I asked. I thought it seemed a little too dark.

He was sure, and we worked tirelessly until with the smaller brush we had covered the in-betweens, the hollows that punctuated the legend; and with the boldly splayed bristles of the wider brush we had done the faces and bodies.

When we were finished, the carving was sleek and dark, lurking broodily under the oil as though it had found a place to hide. It said less and absorbed more, bringing the dusk of afternoon into the studio as though darkness were not just a single state but something to be collected, like the depth of a well with its seepings, or the deep undergrowth of a forest whose secrets are perpetually covering themselves.

"I will never see it as it was again..." Mardi burst into tears and fled from the room.

Pardi and I were left staring at the doorway through which she disappeared.

"The road to hell...." Pardi said sadly from the depth of his Spanish chair in the living-room from where we witnessed her distraught return from the studio. She said we had used the wrong tin, and had stained the totem pole impossibly dark and that the eye could not separate one figure from another; oh why hadn't we *asked* her?

"But *she* asked me to," he said to me weakly, lifting his hands in a frail gesture that seemed to leave a semicolon after what he had said.

The wood would lighten over the years, but by that time it would not matter. Not so the mood. In her own unique way she never forgave us. The more indignant she became, the more she forgot that she had asked Pardi; the more firmly forgotten the request, the more outrageous our crime appeared to be. Perhaps to make amends, we let her tell the story the way she pleased, and she did, unburdening herself until it became apocrypha.

9

THE ENIGMA

As a result of a short conversation with my Aunt Vera, soon after my scholarship exam I volunteered to go to boarding-school.

"Don't you think you are spoilt?" she had said in her "now let's do something about it" voice. I didn't like not to agree. I took no umbrage, suspecting that the criticism was intended more for Mardi than for myself. In any case it was true.

"You know, boarding-school would fix all that. There is that fine Presbyterian school named after the church's Scottish founder, John Knox. It teaches self-sufficiency and resourcefulness. You would have to learn discipline. It's a pity it's co-educational, but I'm sure your Mardi will approve of that!"

She made it seem like a rescue; I wasn't sure from what, but with Aunt Vera one was always anxious to please.

I thought of boarding-school the way one imagines summer camp when one has never been to one of those homesick, hungry, inconvenient reversals of civilization. Arriving

there, I found that it was in fact a beautiful site in the heart
of red clay mountains in the centre of the island. The climate was cool and it rained a lot in that area, so the lawns
and football field were a startling green against the terra-
cotta pathways and embankments. The school's buildings
were staggered up a hill, and I would discover that the farms
with produce and livestock that we drove past provided our
food and were all manned by my fellow students.

But from the moment I climbed the hostel steps I wanted
to leave, and the sound of the car crunching back down the
drive, taking away my father and grandmother, became the
saddest, most unforgettable sound in the world. Waking up
that first morning was as unbearable as anything I can ever
remember. I survived life at school through the discovery of
letter writing. At first my letters were like a lonely solitaire's
calls, but when answers started to come back they became
conversations that would last for ever, and with my best think-
twice words, which I could never manage in conversations.

I would send poems. Mardi declared me a poet.

"Edit," Pardi advised.

Pardi's letters were the best. It was through these that I
discovered the origin of my nickname. When I asked about
the way he addressed me, with what seemed to be a small
doorway with the letter "r" and the number 2, he revealed
the existence of Pythagoras' theorem. I was pi R squared,
the sum of his affection for me, he said. In each missive he
enclosed at least one stamp for my next letter, which he
stuck at the top of a page by the thin strip beyond its per-
forations, and I wondered how he always secured an edge
stamp from the postage sheets. He sent me news of each and
every person, useful, practical news that situated them for
me, even the dog and the cats and the current livestock.

Mardi's letters, in her round, curly hand, were longer by comparison, and full of views and opinions on maybe only one thing, not necessarily a person; and if the subject was a person, then it might be not what he or she did but only what was felt, or what Mardi thought was felt. Sometimes her affection filled me with even more tears.

My father's writing always made his letters look busy, as though his handwriting had started at the bottom of a hill and moved steadily up the slope. In a way our correspondence was like the beginning of our first real conversation. "My darling Ra-Ra, Every time I fly to Trinidad without Kelly [the president of the NWU] I arrive on time and without mishap. Every time I fly with Kelly, we break down in San Juan. Last night was no exception. We broke down in San Juan!" "I am delighted to hear you have joined the Guides.... Have you found out the precise meaning of 'penny wise and pound foolish'? I thought your guess was a very intelligent guess and involved the essence of the meaning of the saying. Glad you dig that volleyball stuff. I hear it's a good game, like crazy. (Is that OK as jive talk?)" Or, from the Santa Maria Hotel in Grenada, "Here I am in a hotel on a steep hill overlooking the bay and town of St. George's, capital of Grenada. There is a lovely sea breeze pouring in through the window as the dusk gathers suddenly around the hotel. The music of a steel band floats in like a windborne echo through the window. It is quite enchantingly beautiful as the whole town is built on steep slopes that run straight up from the bay so that the effect is of a thousand lanterns suspended from the dark night sky."

Thelma wrote too, the warmest of letters, with vibrant capitals. And also the aunts, each keeping to the appropriate two pages. I had the feeling I had become their project.

I started a list. On the left were the names, and beside them a row of columns in which I entered each letter received and each I answered. Once I had answered, that was that until they wrote again and re-entered the list. Although in some cases it became a record of grudge scores, my list was to be a way of pinning people down so I wouldn't lose them.

Fix your purpose clearly in sight, Pardi wrote to me. Life is like walking a tightrope across a deep abyss. You need to look at your point of purpose on the horizon in front of you. You are not going down into the abyss, so don't concern yourself with it. Go carefully towards that purpose, step by step, so you keep your balance. And never lose your nerve ... no one can tell you how to do it, he said, it's a question of guts, something you have to find within yourself.

And this was how, step by step, I made my journey across those weeks of the first term, with his letters held like a balancing stick in my hands.

Late in the Easter term of 1959, I was home for a few days. I found that my homesickness was worse at Drumblair, exacerbated by my dread of returning to school.

But one afternoon I found a greater sorrow in the room across the hall.

Pardi sat at his shaving window staring sadly out at the oak tree, oblivious of the house beyond. I found it unusual that he should be there in the afternoon.

"What's wrong?" I asked.

After a long silence, and as though he were talking to himself, he said thoughtfully, "A stitch has dropped."

I recognized that this was a cryptic message, potent with meaning, and although I didn't know its significance I nodded sagely at him.

"I know what you mean, Par," I said, for Miss Boyd had taught me to knit, and I certainly felt many stitches had dropped in my own life since my departure to school. I waited while he seemed to scan the tree for something missing beyond the brow of this present dismay, but he said no more for a while, returning to his thoughts. There were tears in his eyes.

"Crab's dead." The words, though simple, seemed difficult for him to say.

"I'm so sorry, Par." I hugged him.

"Life is like that," he said, returning, I suppose, to the familiar comfort of his own philosophy. I assumed that his friend's death was the misstep in the fabric of life of which he spoke.

"Remember not to look down," I said.

But he still appeared to be searching for something, as though carefully retracing his own steps for the source of a fundamental unease from which the pieces of his life seemed to diverge, and upon which floated this immediate sorrow.

What was it Mardi would say? The letter that slips under the mat . . . the small incident of fortune that changes the landscape . . . she, like Thomas Hardy, believed we were only shadows of landscapes, victims of fate. Although Pardi had a more participatory and practical view of destiny, there were times when he could make sense of his life only through his wife's notions. Maybe he needed them now. He kept remembering three relatively insignificant and unrelated incidents; a question posed as a mathematical problem, an evening of music, and Mardi's dream.

※

The mathematical question was posed in Crab's handwriting and read: "Find the amount of pounds, shillings, and pence which when written as a single number gives the total farthings in the amount."

"It's a mathematical problem," Crab called out to him from the four o'clock position in the circle of the driveway as he leaned through the car window. Crab was the only person who drove into Drumblair clockwise. That wasn't strange in itself since, being a British colony, the island drove on the left. What was strange was that everyone else swept up on the right, counter-clockwise—maybe because the garage was on the right, or because that slope looked easier to climb. Only Crab took the logical route.

He had driven over early one morning to deliver this numerical enigma. He looked tired and rumpled, overwrung by too many hours of yesterday.

"Slow down, Crab," Pardi admonished through the car window. "Give yourself a rest."

"See what you can do with that. I'll be damned if I can figure it out."

It was so like Crab to push himself too hard. This was the man who had also won the Rhodes, but had almost flunked out of Oxford because he was so busy playing cricket. By nature capable of joyous abandon and sloth, he now drove himself harder than anyone, for there was so much at stake.

The West Indies Federal Labour Party, the regional federal party to which the PNP and Pardi were ideologically and politically aligned, had not done well in the first vote to elect members for the new Federal House of Representatives. Although it had narrowly won in the islands, it had lost heavily at home in the constituency of Jamaica, a fact which for Mardi regrettably fitted neatly into the shape of her sense of foreboding on the federal issue.

Grantley Adams of Barbados became the prime minister of the first federal government. The WIFLP were under extreme pressure from Trinidad to make the central federal government in Port of Spain more powerful. Why bother with the union of islands at all if you didn't have a strong central government, the other islands argued.

Meanwhile, the Jamaican politicians jealously guarded the power of local government at home. And like it or not, Pardi had to support this view; he realized that the only way he could keep Jamaica on board the federation was by ensuring undiminished power at home. Unlike Eric Williams in Trinidad and the other leaders in the Caribbean at the time, he had a significant opposition around which dissenting voices could coalesce. If he gave Bustamante half an excuse, Busta would topple the PNP and, worse yet, remove Jamaica from the federal equation.

And at six in the morning, amid all this, Crab arrived with what he called a mathematical problem, as though it were a test in the midst of all these imponderables. The certainty of farthings, expressed one way, or another, somehow authenticated the world and therefore the times—as though perspective and objectivity could only be trusted if one could verify, by the number of farthings in an equation, that the world was based on fact, and therefore logical.

The aunts came to spend an evening listening to music. It was shortly after I promised Aunt Vera I'd go to boarding-school. The organ lifted its throat and piped its argument up the walls of the living-room. The sound travelled assiduously upward, the notes stretching from the waist of the body of music, one way and then another around each premise, each flicker of the invisible conductor's command. If you closed your eyes you could imagine a lofty roof with criss-crossing eaves, and a steepling darkness musty with bats and the remnants of prayers that had floated up into its cobwebs and crevices and been forgotten.

But this was Drumblair, and the new high-fidelity gramophone was playing Bach's Toccata and Fugue. As children growing up in rural Jamaica, the young Manleys must have been very much what they were here tonight: just the family, lamplight flickering over a book, and a stand-up piano which their mother, Margaret, and the girls would play—maybe discussing books or classical music, interrupted by Norman or Roy's local gossip or some sensibility gleaned from a visit to the village, or the local mento music and calypso brought into the home by the filibuster of Norman's mouth-organ.

As a family they all had this quiet introversion, and a nineteenth-century formality of good manners with appropriate behaviour. Cut off from the middle-class society that held Margaret in disfavour for marrying a black man, they grew up suspended in the format of a life to whose mainstream they had no access.

"A gathering of the clan," proclaimed Mardi as I led my Aunt Vera inside. This was what she always said grandly when two or more family members visited. Vera had long since resigned herself to her sister-in-law's bewildering tendency to exaggerate.

From the moment she arrived Vera seemed somewhat distracted. We wondered if she was still in a fret about the tapeworm they had found to be the cause of her recent discomfort. Muriel, who dealt with this condition daily at her clinic, confided the base revelation to Mardi in a moment of mischief. She said that her sister, who had assumed it was a complaint limited to the barefoot among the poor, was mortified.

Vera now lived by herself in a small, modern bungalow in a smart residential area of the suburbs. Though Pardi remained close to his delinquent friend—who by now had married his new love, the matron—in consideration of the family, Moodie no longer visited Drumblair. And no one mentioned his name in front of Vera.

"I hear Douglas is down in the southern Caribbean," Vera said conversationally as they waited for the next piece of music.

"Um." Mardi's acknowledgement rose like an old discomfort at Vera's mention of her son. As a small child, Douglas had gone to live with his Aunt Vera for a while before going to the country with Miss Boyd and then on to boarding-school. The reason why remains one of the mysteries in the family. I have heard it said that he was a nervous child and that the doctors thought he would do better in a calmer environment, away from his father and mother. If this was the reason, it seems that Mardi had accepted the advice as though it were a verdict. But she was still distressed by the memory of his absence.

"Surely he's not on any federal business?" Muriel asked in surprise, for her older nephew had so far stayed out of politics.

Pardi was perusing each record as he pulled it from the carefully filed positions in the cabinet.

The aunts were waiting for Mardi's answer.

"Oh no, just work he's doing for the university," she said, and she looked at her feet, their bunions covered by bright

Guatemalan alpargatas, as though the aunts would understand it to be as simple as that, and expect no more on the subject.

"Carmen has been so busy with the pantomime," she continued quickly, as a diversion.

"She's a delightful actress, isn't she?" Muriel's face beamed at the memory of the pantomime.

"Just wonderful! And when it's over, she'll be off to Trinidad for Carnival!" Mardi's buoyant flourish was meant to conclude the subject.

"I see." Vera lifted her brow disapprovingly, and no one could tell if it was Carnival, the islands, trips abroad, or just simply having fun that aroused her disapproval.

Since her marital upheavals, Vera's more frequent visits to Drumblair made Mardi uncomfortable. It was not that Vera was exactly a conscience, for such a graft between them could never take successfully; they played by different rules. Mardi's fierce obedience to the senses made her indifferent to the more structured principles that guided her sister-in-law. But there was something about Vera that always left Mardi with a feeling of shame. It was nothing she actually said; rather an involuntary presumption of her own guilt when judged from Vera's perspective.

News of Norman and Edna's marriage, a simple signing of a contract in a registrar's office, had not been popular with the sisters. Any relatives might be reasonably forgiven their doubts over the marital prospect of a nervy and passionate artist in the 1920s. But the more sinister reason for their uneasiness lay in the fact that Norman's mother and Edna's mother were sisters.

An abhorrence of incest is a common response that, because it is reasonable, cannot be lifted by fashion from ultimate taboo. On the outer edge of this most fanatical and binding of civilization's laws is the grey area of cousins. The fact that Norman and Edna had grown up worlds apart, and that the contrasts of their colour were a vivid endorsement of their differences, was quite irrelevant. They were therefore never safe from this verge of doubt.

This worry presented itself less subtly after their marriage. Searching eyes looked at their firstborn son for any evidence of genetic overlap. And Vera's genuine concern over Douglas was a constant if unintentional reminder. She offered practical solutions to situations, otherwise undefined, that she identified as problems. When Douglas was a boy, Mardi saw in him a quiet child with an inner world and a thoughtful reticence of nature. He was nervous, "highly strung", they called it, and deeply introverted. His eyes seemed dazzled by light, giving him a perpetually puzzled expression. But Vera viewed him as troubled and, although she left her opinion unstated, it was nevertheless clear that in her view Mardi's unconventionality as a mother was, if not the cause, certainly not the solution.

It was not just a fear of nature's fury—or, for that matter, of Vera's—that made Mardi retreat. In truth, she was never sure of herself as a mother. Maternal quality was then judged strictly by domesticity, a virtue that Mardi avoided because she could. Maybe art and children, evolving as they both do from the creative process, are inevitably in a tug-of-war. Mardi was already an artist when she became a mother, so, for her, art had literally come first. In this form her creativity felt more familiar and compelling. She had mastered it, and it gave her an assurance she never felt about motherhood.

Her hunger to create was not entirely satisfied by the birth of her sons, so she was often pulled away from her children by a competing drive. Initially she felt relieved when she was free of them "for a little while . . . just long enough to do a morning's work," she would say. But then she would feel guilty.

Finally the time came when Douglas was gone. It seems to have been around the time Mardi developed adhesions from an earlier operation, an appendectomy. She had to go to England, and it may have been then that Douglas went to Aunt Vera. My father doesn't remember him being at Drumblair, but has many memories of being with him by the sea on their long family holidays.

Even Mardi couldn't remember the details. She had blocked them out as completely as she had relinquished her right to mother him. She remembered odd things: Michael asking for his big brother, "D, D, Dougie," in his fervent little childhood stutter just like his father's. And the anguish she felt when she saw Miss Boyd's painstaking handwriting on the envelopes on the hall table at Drumblair when she returned. But she couldn't remember what the letters from St. Ann had said.

Douglas had lived with his Aunt Vera. Douglas, accompanied by Miss Boyd, had lived in St. Ann. Douglas had gone to boarding-school. These had simply been things which "should be done". They were facts that surprised her when she occasionally bumped into them; or she would slip into them, as though into sleep, to be saved from their depths only by a lurch of self-preservation.

Michael had escaped such grim appraisals, either by the accidental virtue of being second-born, or because the sheer buoyancy of his nature distracted his aunt and vouchsafed his normalcy. He was an open child, fetching a rose for his aunt, or dashing out to escort her from her car with astonishing tales of adventure. When he was a child his introspective moments were sporadic, as though he briefly needed to situate himself by reference to an inner compass. Though much of his time at home was spent alone, he had a gift for entertaining himself. He would spend hours on the roof planning military battles or living adventures in his head. It was difficult to dwell on someone who appeared to be without secrets. His youth belonged, unchallenged, to the family, even when he went to a Kingston boarding-school. But Douglas became a summer tourist in their lives.

Now Pardi had filled the room with Bach's third Brandenburg concerto; with intricate things that spin around their own axis to eternity, shrinking in the distance like an ever-diminishing ship.

This was not unusual. The living-room had a way of offering a small central area for the family's use, and lending just sufficient air and light to keep the fringe of activity sustained while still holding the people intangibly subservient to the room.

Pardi had discovered that only Bartók subdued every corner and depth of the large room, commandeered every clandestine rendezvous of the walls, every reluctance of space. It was the only music of which Drumblair stood in awe, as though its sheer eccentricity was a challenge that took the house by surprise, arresting it from years of wilful self-absorption.

But now, though accompanied by Bach, Pardi still was struggling with Crab's equation; it had got stuck in his head like the bars of a simpler song. Let the amount be x pounds and y shillings and z pence . . . this was how the premise began.

Trial had shown him that either y or z must be greater than nine.

Vera sat slightly apart, her legs gracefully crossed, as were her elegant hands in her lap. She was gazing at a point beneath the piano with the proprietorial manner of the only trained musician in the room. Her eyes, whose stare could be so intimidating, now settled into quiet circles of grey, deep wells that contained her thoughts and opinions. Though by clasping her hands she appeared to be grounding them from any involuntary enthusiasm, her free ankle was rotating gently to the sound, nudged by the music's phrasing, and her face had a soft expression that slackened the imperious clench of her jaw.

"It's the only time she relents," Mardi would say to Pardi.

Muriel was perched on a Queen Anne chair, at the edge of the music, unable to take the plunge. She was looking politely down the centre of the room as though trying not to venture into the area of her sister's competence on one hand, or intrude upon the rapture of her brother and his wife on the other.

I was used to the routine. Pardi and Mardi would sit back in their chairs and close their eyes. Pardi's face remained quiet and serene, sometimes thoughtful; his attention was passive. As for Mardi, a sweet pain seemed to press against her face, her brow lifted in quiet ecstasy above the storm of sound, her mouth, with a twitch, indulged some tenderness in the movement as she deftly arranged her feelings.

On these occasions I sometimes brushed Pardi's hair with his blue Addis brush, and sometimes attempted to dance. Now I offered a clumsy but energetic rendering of leaps, bounds and jetés mischoreographed from my recent ballet class, which Mardi had been advised would improve my fallen arches.

"AGM," Vera said quietly but very clearly.

"What's that?" Muriel leaned forward for an explanation.

"Attention-Getting Mechanism," explained Vera, and Muriel repeated it co-operatively in case the rest of the room had not heard.

"That will all stop at boarding-school," Aunt Vera added firmly, and I felt the reproach guide me back to my chair.

"Don't be so discouraging, Vera," Mardi lifted her voice in exasperation. She was also needled by the fact that, with my going to boarding-school, once again Vera had interfered and prevailed.

Pardi, who already knew that my ballet was unlikely to come to anything, looked at me fondly and pulled a prim face, unseen by the aunts, which made me giggle. He thought boarding-school a good idea. He felt I needed the discipline and routine. He would miss me, but they were away so often, and Kingston was so full of distractions. He thought I was bright but restless and needed a framework of purpose to my life.

Everyone returned to the music except Mardi, who now looked preoccupied.

Usually, when the record came to an end, Mardi and Pardi would wait until the needle tripped on the cracks of the last grooves before lifting their heads as though out of prayer, their eyes finding each other's to measure their fulfilment and acknowledge the magic. Then came the post-mortem— a discussion of each piece of music as though they could hear stories in the notes the way Mardi saw forms in uncarved wood.

But not tonight; not with the aunts.

As Bach receded, a cacophony of sound stormed in from the neighbours' equipment across the street, taking possession of every possibility of silence. This was rock-and-roll, and not even the throb of Four Roads could be heard to strive below its jubilation. The house seemed to bristle.

Mardi was poised at the brim of the box, waiting to wrest the needle delicately from the track before the threat of a scratched record could excite Vera's disapproval. But the noisy intrusion provided more immediate bait.

"That's how it is nowadays," Pardi explained to his perplexed sisters. "If it's not the umpy-umpy over in Four Roads, it's this tiresome wailing and yelling from next door."

"I prefer the umpy-umpy, quite frankly," said Mardi. "Somehow it's more reassuring. Like the beat of a heart."

"How ghastly," pronounced Muriel, whose sweetness could dissolve in the shift of a note.

Vera appeared to be evaluating the rotation of her ankle, under attack from this violation, intent on maintaining its movement sacred to the memory of Bach's now silent metronome.

Pardi looked sadly at the large mahogany record cabinet, which enshrined many years of 78 r.p.m. records.

"Well, life can't stand still," he sighed. "You know by the beat of this new music at every streetcorner that the face of Jamaica is changing."

"It's Jamaica asserting itself," Mardi said bravely.

"But not with *this* racket." Vera's ankle stopped short in its exercise on the word "this", and she turned her head towards her brother as though to verify his wife's mistake.

He gave a little gesture of irritation towards the house over the road: "That nonsense! That's just some foreign fashion. But Jamaicans are forgetting who they are."

Muriel's ready acquiescence clove to her brother's contempt: "Indeed."

"Some of our people have even suggested that we become a ward of the United States, like Puerto Rico," Pardi continued, outraged by this sudden memory.

"Well"—Mardi turned from the hi-fi set—"Jamaicans of all classes have been migrating for years. Why, we literally run the transport system in London, for heaven's sake! And now the Rastafarians are agitating to go back to Africa! We are always going somewhere."

"Africa! Why on earth would they want to go there?" Muriel asked in surprise.

"They are trying to find themselves ... or to be themselves, I suppose," Mardi offered.

"Well there's no use trying to be somebody, by going somewhere else," Pardi addressed this subject with customary irritability.

"But the Rastafarians are in search of their roots, dear. Jamaicans are in diaspora ... they are trying to discover themselves by retracing the steps of the Middle Passage," explained Mardi grandly.

"I can't think why they called that the 'Middle' Passage ..." she went on dreamily. "I mean, 'middle' is such a transition word ... its like a link ... but this was a tearing ... a routing of souls. A drowning," she concluded, this last phrase said more emphatically.

Vera appeared to be uncomfortable. Maybe it was the tapeworm again.

"Well, it's all a protest of one sort or another, isn't it?" Muriel rolled the "r" in the word "protest" and looked at her sister, who had distanced herself.

"Your brother is just being argumentative!" Mardi gave Pardi a swift, sharp look. "What do you think, Vera?" She was trying to draw Vera back into the discussion.

"I think whoever they are, and whatever their purpose, they should get basic training before they attempt to perform music," Vera said flatly, then seemed to be calming herself with a purposely slow and strong ankle rotation. Muriel had to look away, for it reminded her of an angry cat's tail.

"You can't learn to be born, Vera," Mardi said almost fiercely, with an exasperation at many larger irritations which had collided with a smaller one that happened to be in the way.

Vera had that grim look of displeasure that Mardi supposed she had developed from the responsibilities thrust on her when her mother died and she was responsible for the others, especially the two boys still in school.

The tumult next door subsided into a piteous love song warbling sentimentally to the twang of a guitar. The neutrality of the voice caused Muriel to ask:

"Is it a male or female voice singing?"

"It's the voice of a young America," said Mardi, leaving Muriel looking perplexed.

Vera was facing the night framed in the window whose stillness was unaffected by the whinnying love song.

Mardi looked guarded but powerless, afraid to lose control of the threads of harmony. She looked over at Pardi who had shifted into some inner gear. His forehead seemed to have snatched a new concentration, and though he withdrew, there was something alert and immediate about his preoccupation, like someone counting money, or memorizing the lines of a poem. Recently Mardi kept finding bits of paper with letters of the alphabet and numbers and symbols littering the house. In between governing the country, at this the most glorious time of his life, these hieroglyphics seemed to be wandering out from his head through his hands.

She believed in the sanctity of the written word on paper as private, and it would be discourteous to ask him about it. He needed distraction, whatever it was; it relaxed him. He needed his secrets and his foibles. She painted them as enchantments in her mental picture of him.

He looked at the sum in his head. He knew he was piecing together a puzzle that must have an answer, after one had eliminated all but one turning in the maze of alternatives. But elimination was ad hoc. He needed to find that key which was unique to the logic of this problem, and what was unique was, paradoxically, its common factor.

Let y be greater than nine, he reasoned, and z be less than ten.

Mardi saw the members of her family beginning to form into separate clouds. "Let's have a little more music, shall we?" she suggested. She was about to ask what they would like to hear when Vera spoke.

"Since you are all here, there's something I have to tell you." She said this carefully, as though reading it from a cue card.

The response was an intake of air that we all sensed rather than heard, and it made Mardi look around the room as though the lungs of the old house had given an asthmatic wheeze.

We all stared at Vera without moving our heads. A little while passed, and then we shuffled around to face her, thinking she was waiting for fuller attention.

"I have decided I'm going. That is, going back to England to live."

I was jolted by a fleeting memory of the dog Biggums breaking away with the leg of the table.

"How can you?" Mardi spat the words out before she

weighed their meaning. They were projectiles of her indignation.

Vera looked at her as though Mardi had once again said a very odd and inappropriate thing. Pardi winced as though Mardi's reaction was a barb aimed at him which he felt he deserved.

Vera was calmly explaining the obvious. Since the breakdown of her marriage her life seemed to be slowly shrinking. Any social life she had enjoyed had been shared with Moodie. When she retired from the art school, what would be left for her?

Mardi appeared to think about this. Already Vera's world had become one of quiet routine; she wandered from one correct place to another, expressing herself by tending her heart's carefully filed souvenirs. Her daughter and grandchildren were in England. And though she had given much to her birthplace, England was the source of all the things she cherished.

Mardi watched Muriel feign surprise at what she must already know, for her sister told her everything, and then mime expressions of suitable accompaniment to what Vera said.

With Vera's announcement, Pardi was thrown back to the beginning of his own life, that inextricable nest. His mother and his two sisters had been like pillars that loomed from his first breath, before Roy or the sight of logwood, before the ring of an axe or the smell of pimento. Everything he did was appraised by these three women. Even the things on which they could not agree were alternates of a world they supported. Somewhere in the gut of his intention his mother had buried an acorn of responsibility for his sisters.

His motivation had long since faded to the drone of habit, but deep inside him was a profoundly heartfelt duty to the memory of his mother, and the assumption of the presence of his sisters in his life.

The thought that Vera would leave Jamaica in an instant threw doubt on everything he had worked to achieve. It was not a logical doubt—more a massive short circuit of every thought he had ever had, leaving his mind a blank and his soul in that empty place where it sensed he had made a great mistake. If one of his sisters had to leave beloved Jamaica, he felt that in some way he must have failed to uphold their world.

The imminent withdrawal of Mardi's nemesis from her life seemed to leave her too in the lurch. It was as though all things finally unwound to their end, whether they were sustaining or contentious.

And in this case, for Mardi, the issue unwound to Douglas. As their elder son breast-stroked through his life in a desperation so quiet that he was often sucked in, unaware, by his own slip-stream, she would be forever weighing the gravity of her mistakes, Vera having already left her pincers of doubt gripping Mardi.

But Vera had always been there as her excuse not to cope. Vera's opinion had validated the premise upon which Mardi's freedom was based: if she was unsuitable as a mother, others would have to pick up the pieces. Though the children were now men, there remained a time in Douglas' childhood for which Mardi would now be solely accountable. And with Vera's departure went any hope of absolution.

Mardi recovered a sense of the moment, and was offering encouragement and assistance. Pardi watched her tidying up the far-flung pieces of herself displaced by her surprise. She hated surprises.

Later that evening, after he had walked the aunts to their cars, Pardi joined us on the steps to meditate at the edge of a world where the moon wandered over the night-dead faces of flowers. The peenie-wallies flashed their Morse code, but the sky ignored them. The stars were very far away, small and mean-looking.

Listen, Moon,
Last night you died too soon . . .

Mardi was reciting a George Campbell poem.

Pardi surveyed the quiet hedge of Chinese hat shrubs that stood on guard before him, keeping the neighbours at bay. He addressed it as though the dense mass, and not Mardi lost in her poetry, were his company.

"It was the use of the word 'going'."

He said this with satisfaction, as though he had retrieved some small piece of vital evidence.

"Does he say 'going'?" she asked.

Mardi turned back from the verse to her husband's contemplation of a word which he had apparently retrieved not from George's poem, but from the bottom of the garden.

"No dear. It's nothing. Just something Vera said."

I looked for you
and you had fled . . .

For a moment he thought she meant him, but then he realized she was reliving some ghosted moment through the familiar lines of the poem. George, the nephew of Miss Boyd who had spent summers with their sons; the most erratic of their young friends, with the mind of a mattoid, part genius, part fool. The greatest Jamaican poet, according to Mardi.

The word "going" was not about the place of departure, but about the destination. In any mention of a journey somewhere is honoured, and that honour falls to the country of the heart. If Jamaica were that country, he thought to himself, then Vera would have said she was "leaving".

The world was dead
And residue of nothingness
In my head.

Mardi had moved onto the lawn and was waltzing in her deliberate way, nodding her head as though to recapture the beat with her motions. Reduced to glimpses and phrases by the moonlight, one might not realize what a bad dancer she was.

I held my lover in my arms, Pardi continued with a line later in the poem, his voice full of mischief.

And you were dead. She lifted her voice to meet him. *And you were dead.*

Her long legs had reached him, and she searched for the next line in his face. He laced his hands in hers as though to join their voices.

I will never see her face again
I will never see her face again.

The hedge hid them staunchly from view, its eyes averted from a silliness inappropriate to its tenure.

"Do you think one day Muriel will go too?" Mardi asked.

"No," he said with certainty. "I think she's decided she's a Jamaican."

Going or leaving. Perhaps the moon in her coquetry couldn't care less. But he knew there was a difference. He knew that life would not be quite the same again.

※

Then there was Mardi's dream.

Normally it was Mardi who retrieved her moaning husband from his dreams. But that night she was whimpering, making a little fluted sound driven by a progression of shudders, like a dog in a prairie dream. Both her arms disappeared under the pillow as she squeezed it to her face. She was sweating, and her grey hair clung to her temples, which were webbed with tiny blue veins that seemed to have lost direction. Her eyelids were fiercely gripping their inner panorama.

This is how she related it.

She said it was one of those No-days, proclaimed inauspicious by her friend Rose, who studied the horoscopes. She was at the sea, on the rough side of the Palisadoes peninsula, which extended to the airport and what remained of Port Royal. She had picked this side of the road, rather than the safe harbour on the opposite side where far-out ships moored and leaked their bowels into the sea.

On the coarse, hostile sand, which felt like tiny broken rocks under her feet, there were pieces of grey driftwood with their antlers rocking in the wind. She hitched up her skirt, tucking the sides into her waist so that her bare, long legs felt free and ready, as if she were preparing to mount a horse. She was walking along the sand to collect pieces of driftwood for Thelma, who loved them as sculptures. But every time she came close to them, she realized that they were really the skeletons of animals, and that the bones were almost threads from the sawing of the salt wind.

The air made her feel hot and thirsty, and she turned towards the sea. Where it had been pounding on the shore like a family quarrel, it now appeared to have stacked its waves one on top of another, and she remembered that while she had been combing the sand she had noticed the coast hold

(above) Margaret and Thomas
Albert Manley, Norman's parents

(left) Harvey and Ellie
Swithenbank, Edna's parents

Edna, posed at thirtyish (she really never inhaled)

(above) Norman and Edna, a handsome couple

(above left) Norman Manley, The Queen's Council
(above right) Douglas (standing) and Michael Manley

(left) Pardi picks a rose—"I should have been a farmer"

(below) Norman addressing a group on the docks

(Left to right) Norman, Edna, Lady Sylvia Foote, HRH Princess Margaret, Sir Hugh Foote, then Governor of Jamaica, during a Royal Visit to Jamaica in 1960. Mardi always thought Princess Margaret "quite fancied" her Norman

Norman with John F. Kennedy in Washington in 1961

Norman with Canadian Prime Minister John Diefenbaker
on his official visit to Jamaica in 1961

Norman and N. N. "Crab" Nethersole watching
Douglas equal his father's 100 yard record

Norman touring West Kingston

Mardi in her public role

Norman in his seventies—always a black tie

(left) Rachel's great aunt Vera Moodie, Norman's eldest sister
(right) Dr. Muriel Manley, Rachel's great aunt and Norman's sister

(left) Nomdmi, "in the middle of nowhere", with Edna and Leslie Clark on the verandah

(below) "Negro Aroused" (back view)—Edna's 1935 icon: mahogany; National Gallery of Jamaica; Dennis Gick photo

(above) Douglas, Norman and Michael at Drumblair

(left) Michael and Jacqueline, Rachel's parents, pushing her in a pram in Hyde Park

(above) Edna and Rachel
(first photograph together)

(left) Rachel at five

"How I first remember my father"

Carmen and Douglas (standing), Edna and Norman with
Norman Junior and Rachel on their laps, at Drumblair

(above) Michael's second wife, the dancer Thelma

(left) Barbara, Michael's third wife, in her sharkskin suit

Michael from "young boy" to "Joshua"

Michael at fortyish

its breath, but had put it out of her mind. Now the old terror of Cornwall was real—the water had gathered in a force against her—and she wanted to run to the other side of the road, to the dead still harbour.

But then the prow of a ship came slowly creeping up over the tidal furor, growing steeper in the sky. The tiny figurehead of a man was crying out for help as he was hoisted higher and higher. She knew what she saw was all going to fall on her. She dropped onto her knees and covered her head with her arms and waited to die, waited for the crashing of her childhood thunderclap over her head.

Then it was suddenly very cold, and steady ropes of water were beating down on her bowed head and shoulders. She realized she no longer had any arms.

"I am stranded," called the man's voice, which she recognized as her husband's.

He shouldn't be up there, she thought incongruously, for today we are accident-prone. But she couldn't look up because of the force of the water.

"Why don't you love me?" came a voice, but this time she thought she heard the staccato tone of George, the poet, and she remembered with shock that she was no longer young.

Then she felt a thudding coming through the sand into her being, and she knew it was horses. She felt a great joy, and pressed her head up, and there she was at the foot of the waterfall at Dunn's River, braced against its torrent. She looked around and there were hundreds of horses coming down the beach and veering at the falls to plunge into the cold water where it entered the sea. House of Cards, her first horse in Jamaica; and Roysterer was there, her Derby winner, and Gay Lady and Harriet—every horse she had groomed and cared for, and some more she did not know.

Each horse carried a rider, and each rider carried a flag—all they had in common—but she couldn't see their faces, and the flags were just blurs on poles that they threw like javelins into the sand before they headed out to sea.

She watched them disappearing one by one beneath the water, which snapped shut over their heads as though it were no longer liquid, but made of metal. She wished she had hands so that she could shield her eyes from the bright light where the sun glinted on the pewter surface.

The falls had stopped. She looked around her on the now soft, white St. Ann sand of the north coast, and she saw bubbles of blue man-of-wars strewn in the distance. As she approached each one it popped like an egg, leaving aqua albumen and orange yolk. But on coming even closer she realized that they were the horsemen's dead flags, toppled over as though their staffs were broken on the sand.

Each was the federal flag she had designed.

When she woke, Pardi was tenderly cajoling her back to his world, his arms offering that odd forgiveness that comes to refugees of nightmares. But she wanted her book of Jung, and wanted to shake out her arms, for they had fallen asleep where they were pinned under the dread of her sleep.

He was sitting in his room at his shaving window when I came in.

His things were pushed to one side, the small tortoiseshell mirror unable to either magnify or verify his mood. He sat on his revolving backless stool with his shoulders slumped forward, and his chin resting in his hands, helping to hold the weight of his grief.

It was just the way I had once seen Mardi look, but she had been standing uncertainly at the edge of the window in her room. She was holding the curtain, and gazing out over the paddock, beyond the hills. She looked as though she had borrowed the room, the window and the view. She turned back for a moment to blink at the scorch-marks her sunlit eyes brought into the gloom, faltering as though outraged, as though something really must be done, and then returned to the clear sky; perhaps she hoped to see infinity and the departed.

It was the morning she learned that her mother had died.

Now once again Pardi must enter the stark inner room of human loss. He was crying, for the only time I can remember. Long tears had formed a riverbed down to his chin. His eyes blinked not a single apology for them, but stared at a distance between the tops of the trees, as though looking between the lines of life for a soul, a ghostly presence to intercept his human fall into inconceivable endlessness.

Crab had died of a heart attack that afternoon.

The loss was so much greater than a man's tears, but he had only a man's tears to shed. There would be a big hullabaloo, and everyone would be sorry, but beyond all that emotion, and one's sense of betrayal at being left behind, at losing the other side of a rare conversation, was the monumental loss this would be for Jamaica.

A stitch had dropped. A stitch essential to the continuity, whose lapse would start things untwining. A flaw in the fabric that would multiply as he moved along. This was not prescience, but a grim realization that whatever he did after this rift would surely unravel.

We start a thing and wish we hadn't, but we have to finish. Looking around at the papers scattered over the sparse furniture, the vivid yellow pineapples grinning like masks from the pattern of leaves on the curtains and bedspread, he felt more surprise than comfort at finding his things the same. He was searching for some clue, some answer, in the rubble of his experience.

On the desk was a carefully concluded equation, reasoning line by line in x's and y's and z's, pounds, shillings and pence, and amounts that could be expressed as a number thus, and things *ex hypothesi*, and things that were evident; and the amount, signed by a neat *N.W.M.* underlined as though this were the leg it stood on, was finally twelve pounds, twelve shillings and eightpence, which was 12,128 farthings, Crab, and the abrupt rejoinder "Note: This is an intelligence test—not a mathematical problem!" It was written on a piece of paper with the last words Crab had written to him. It was the ultimate clue. It was nothing, but it was everything. Out of the darkness, Crab's intention floated beyond the relationship of politics and nations and the vanity of human effort. It moved up there, half a shift above the white notes, a shade off-key and random, rhymeless, holding no tune of its own, intangible as shadows hiding from the sun.

He searched for the ever-elusive relevance in the minor keys; was it in Crab's postscript, Vera's departure, or his wife's apparent prophecy? Was it not so much the question that was posed, but the irrelevance of finding an answer which was there sewn into the lining of life, whether one found it or not?

The numbers and letters lay on the page like bones in an X-ray, lean and matter-of-fact.

He had identified the enigma, but Crab had taken that answer with him.

10

THE INK
STAIN

On July 4, 1959, Jamaica achieved full self-government. Due to the coincidence of the date, Pardi surrendered the title of chief minister and became the island's first, and incidentally only, premier on his sixty-sixth birthday. This new constitution gave the island full autonomy except for defence and international relations; these bills were to be kept for the special assent of the Queen. It was ironic that in April 1958, the same month in which the report for these constitutional reforms was tabled by a special committee of the Jamaican House, the Federation of the West Indies was formally established.

Despite the crushing defeat of the WIFLP in the federal elections a year before, with a certain audacity Pardi called a snap election for July 28 that year, and the PNP won by a massive landslide, with a popular vote of 54.8 per cent. It was then the biggest electoral triumph in Jamaican history, validating Pardi as a leader and endorsing his national policies. The Jamaican people trusted him. In Michael's eyes it gave his father an earned magnificence, and he sounded almost light-hearted when he talked about it.

As for Michael, his work in the union had extended to the other islands. He had persuaded other unions in the Caribbean to form the Caribbean Bauxite and Mineworkers' Federation, which would give them all greater bargaining power.

But another contribution had captured the hearts and imaginations of the Jamaican workers. I used to think it was called "The Golden Commission". There had been a deadlock with the sugar manufacturers over wages. Both the big unions were involved. A strike was called and eventually Pardi set up an independent Commission of Inquiry with a Canadian chairman, Carl Goldenberg, a Queen's Council who would later be a Liberal senator. Michael prepared the case meticulously over several weeks with help from his counterpart, Hugh Shearer, the island supervisor of the Bustamante Industrial Trade Union. The Goldenberg Commission awarded the workers half the undisclosed profits uncovered by the commission. It was an astonishing victory, and earned Michael, who already enjoyed the fond nickname "Young Boy" among the workers, the reputation that he could "make figures whisper and talk!" He reminded some people of Bustamante, who, having no son of his own, was rumoured to be proud of the young Manley.

As far as I could tell things in the world of the adults around me were going well. But circumstances had a way of changing in our family. Before success could become too familiar, we were forced to brace ourselves for another political din.

In late May of 1960 I happened to be home for a few days at half-term. Though Kingston seemed very hot in comparison with the mountain weather at my school, its mornings are cool, coming off the mountains for the island's first shift. I could hear Mardi moving around in her room on the other side of the upstairs landing. I knew she liked to sort out her thoughts into some order in the morning, or untangle problems left from the day before. This was when she would write her letters or notes, or make sporadic entries in her diaries. It was probably a habit from the days when she ran the dairy which she had to close when she found that she no longer had the time after Pardi became chief minister.

"Bustamante has done the unthinkable," she wrote to Michael in one of her more cryptic early morning notes.

Bustamante, the man who spoke out loudest in favour of federation at the Montego Bay conference in 1947, now demanded that Jamaica secede from the federation. He had announced his resignation from the federal party he led, the Democratic Labour Party of the West Indies.

I don't remember what day of the week it was, though I do remember that Pardi had on his red shirt. Maybe it was Sunday. But Drumblair was equally crisis-prone any day of the week. For me, weaving between my world and theirs, it would be a day of huddled conversations.

My father came to see Pardi. When he entered Drumblair the living-room was empty but the rest of the house was never quiet. It always had an energy that exhilarated him. The drone of voices came from the back of the house. From the gramophone came a chorus of voices: *Miya sama, miya sama . . .*

My school was preparing a production of Gilbert and Sullivan's *Mikado*. It was to be staged in July first in Christiana and later in Kingston. My minor role in this venture was to sing in the chorus, dressed in a kimono, as part of a Japanese crowd scene. It became my *raison d'être*. Waiting for me at home had been Pardi's gift of a record of the production.

As Michael's long legs moved over the large straw mat with its hopscotch of squares, the sliding doors of Mardi's study clattered open, and he turned to see his mother beckoning in conspiracy.

"Ah, thank God you've come." She held the door as though signalling him to enter, but he gestured towards his father's study.

"He's in there?"

But Mardi wanted to speak to him first. "Come and see my little commission, it's all finished."

Michael flinched at the sound of her favourite diminutive. He said that the use of the word "little" had become her ploy, a cuteness which at her age did not become her, and that it was the only aspect in which she had met the years without dignity. (I did not agree, since I had the same foible and I was only twelve.) He couldn't quite explain why it affected him so, but he seemed to sense the adjective before it came, and tensed in the way that an animal expecting abuse or unwelcome affection flattens its ears.

"I've got a little problem", "here's a little gift", "they had a little meeting", "she's a little bit upset"; she even spoke from time to time of "N's little heart attack."

The other day he had seemed to have difficulty containing himself after he complained to her that trespassing cows had eaten the only colourful thing in his garden, a rhapsodic hedge of red, green and gold crotons. With a sharp intake of breath she had uttered tenderly, "They are naughty, those little cows"... cows as fat as the unlimited prairies of their desires.

Now he turned back, attempting to hide the irritation he felt at having to change the mental gear he had arrived in.

"But I thought...never mind...okay," he said in resignation, leaning down to kiss the cheek offered him as she mimed her reciprocation into the air.

He expected to be led outside to the studio, but she returned instead to her study. When Michael was a child this had been part of a longer living-room, and the narrow addition, now an enclosed waiting-room, had been the end of a childhood racetrack that extended as a veranda halfway around the house. Long ago they had each lopped off an end of the veranda for themselves, and her study was where she dealt on a daily basis with the consequences of her husband's political career.

"I brought this up from the studio." She turned to the carving. "It's to be delivered this week. I've got a young student down there, learning to carve."

He nearly bumped into her when an unforeseen spin of worry turned her around.

"I've discovered he hasn't got a lifeline."

"A what?"

"Lifeline."

"Who hasn't? You mean Dad?"

"No! This young student..."

"Clearly he has a life, though." He smiled indulgently, relieved that this was not about his father and wondering why she always needed to play the sorceress. She was holding out a strong, freckled, once elegant hand.

"His hand, it's quite smooth...no lifeline at all....I hope gripping the mallet and tools, you know"—stroking the fold of her thumb in reply to his perplexity—"may encourage one."

As though life were simply a muscle that one developed. Having apparently dealt with the student's problem, she moved smoothly on.

"See, I've had it all nicely polished," she was saying. "It's a silly little piece, really... very minor...."

She looked at him hopefully, and he knew she was needing reassurance on a quite separate matter.

He leaned his large frame slightly forward, and stared at the glowing mahogany piece that Batiste had placed on a stool in front of the bookcase. In the indirect light it took him a moment to make out the tender, joyful figure of a young girl embracing a goat.

The carving was already living its own narration. Out of the wood came a human moment from the blueing distance of mountains one passed too swiftly day after day. A child's trusting head leaned towards the eager figure of a kid standing on its hind legs. Such uncomplicated pleasure. The girl's face held a familiar fragment from every childhood.

"Jesus!" he whispered, as though not so much to her as to his own disbelief.

"Maybe you don't like it." She sounded childlike, and then added almost like an inducement, "It's a little bit like Ray, don't you think?"

Michael straightened his back and shifted his head as though to get a clearer view.

"Maybe." He sounded tentative, but his shrug suggested that it didn't remind him of me at all, or no more than it did of any young girl. It was as if she didn't trust the independent viability of her creation, young and forever tender, revealing a glimpse of nature's intimacy.

Sometimes it was difficult to equate the compelling substance of Mardi's work with her self-doubts. Although she appeared straightforward, she was never self-explanatory; one had to search for her meaning through the clues of her coming and going, for the various parts of her spirit never seemed to surface at the same time. In a way she was as inviolate and contained as one of her pieces.

In the last half-dozen years she had felt it necessary to revise herself for a public role she secretly dreaded. She imagined she owed it to her husband, but it was also a response to her belief that she had failed her overburdened mother, or a disappointed headmistress, or her noble sister, Nora, shaking less from Parkinson's disease than from the chill of Mardi's neglect; a response to the Old Testament God, a ghost of her father, who drove her so many times to hide from His sporadic anger, refusing, though she feared Him well enough, simply to love Him.

This was how she justified the recent taming of her presence, which she could perform like a parlour trick as her soul hovered between the leaves of her mind, a startled faun in the forest, her artist's eye glaring at the ordered life her husband's universe determined for her.

Michael looked away to relieve a crick in his neck, and the desk slid conveniently into his peripheral view, a judicious sobriety to ground him. He sat on it. The carving, no longer on show, appeared to breathe again.

"Dougie says it's uncharacteristic..."

"Uncharacteristic of what?"

"Well, I asked him. He said, of girls and of goats. He came to take away my orchid."

Douglas had dropped by that morning with his son Norman and a gang of young friends who quickly disappeared into the life of the old house. When he had last visited, he had recognized his orchid somewhere in the garden, but he could not remember where. So now he had come to retrieve his treasure from Mardi. As he approached the house he looked around him at a haberdashery of images; a hedge that had shed its leaves to cover its feet, interruptions of June roses like pink and white sheep, and the back of the fat, black Jaguar stuck in the garage door. But no orchid. Where had he seen it?

When he entered Drumblair, the energy of the house seemed to make him nervous. Sometimes he would forget why he had come. He always found it easier to make his assault by bee-lines, point to point, his buckles seeming to part the way for him, avoiding the quicksand of both the temperamental house and his own emotions. Not that it didn't have answers for him, but to find them he would have to become embroiled. This way, the house remained at arm's length in his mind, a postponement, a distant birthright.

So he usually waited until he had a specific reason to justify a visit to Drumblair. Today his excuse was the orchid. But he had also been drawn by an impulse to arrive and simply shed the weight of his burden. Roy, his younger son, was not well. He was out of school due to heavy sedation, hovered over by Carmen and Gertie the nanny. These were the facts. If he brought along his preoccupation, his mother might recognize it and know what to do.

"What's that?" he had asked.

"What's what, dear?"

"Oh, it's one of your carvings," he observed. He looked at the carving as though faced with a tree that had fallen and blocked his path. "What is it . . . a goat?" he asked, temporarily distracted from his problems.

"It's a girl holding a little kid," Mardi said in her careful, oh-but-you-should-know voice.

He looked for a moment, lifting his chin and searching as though he might find something more definitive with which to field his mother's hovering question. He leaned over the tip of its perked ear which seemed to him trapped against the wide, complacent human face, to pull a book from the shelf behind it. He peered at its cover which he then opened and, being startled by a cloud of insecticide powder which Miss Boyd had recently sprinkled into tell-tale holes, banged the book shut and replaced it awkwardly on the shelf.

"I like the goat," he answered. "It's idyllic, but rather uncharacteristic...."

"Of what?" asked his mother, moving nearer to the carving as though in loyalty.

"Well, of girls and of goats, of course!"

He looked at Mardi, wishing he hadn't bothered to come at all. He had been relying on her intuition, her insight, but the goat had got in the way of his purpose. It was always like that at Drumblair; there was always some unforeseen distraction in which everyone was engrossed.

Mardi looked at her Gemini son and sensed that he was abandoning some purpose, some intent. Was he really absent-minded, or did he just lack resolve? Maybe he was lost between the twin souls of his sign. At times Mardi saw her two sons as products of her own alternatives. She knew Douglas was born of unresolved love from an unresolved time. Maybe Michael's determination was born of their renewed commitment. Because she was strongly influenced by Freud, it had not occurred to her that she might have no influence over what they were, or what they would become. Her instinctive guilt was part of her assumption that, as a mother, she held the trump card that would triumph over whatever suit they held. Now she felt an awful regret that she had taken so little advantage of their impressionable years.

"How's Carmen?" she asked.

Douglas grunted. He looked jaded, as though he were starting to feel a blight, a browning like over-ripe fruit—a sensation he got whenever he was with his family.

He started the Manley pace, and his buckles reasserted themselves merrily with each step. All the Manley men paced, and Mardi was always amazed by how Michael would defer to his elder brother's habit by leaving floor space available to him if they were in the room together. She assumed that was nature's pecking order.

Now he slowed, and his trail which had been oval tightened till it was just a small circle. He had named his second son Roy. "An unlucky name for the family," Mardi observed, but that was all. It was his Aunt Vera who then took charge of the judgements. But the more the indomitable lady advised to the contrary, the more determined Carmen became to perpetuate Roy's dependency.

He stopped abruptly in front of the carving and blinked. He suddenly remembered where he had seen his plant. He glared at his mother.

"You have my orchid."

"Your what, dear?" She looked confused.

"That yellow and white orchid you have hanging on the oak out there is *my* plant!"

It was a single plume of yellow and white, an impeccable flower, precise, self-sustaining and memorable. And it was Douglas' bloom. He looked triumphant.

"I'm taking it," he said. Its singularity, his certainty of ownership, his simple victory of recognition—just its sheer recollection seemed to fill the void of his morning's other aborted mission.

"Well! Excuse me, dear, I bought it at vast expense from Ras Tundy."

"I'm sure you did!" He had the perfect timing of a comedian. "That's just the point. Tundy is my gardener, Mother!"

"Are you saying that Tundy is selling *your* orchids?"

"Exactly!"

"But that's outrageous! Why don't you fire him?"

Douglas shrugged. "I can't, he's a good gardener."

There was the determined sound of idea-bright children, a change of many minds toppling down the descent of stairs. They scattered in around Mardi and Douglas like stones from the gully's tide, and disappeared around the corner, banging the louvers shut as they passed. Douglas winced. He had quite forgotten that he had brought children.

"Better go," he muttered, like an instruction to himself.

On his way out he recaptured his orchid.

Douglas had a point: girls and goats rarely hug. But then, Douglas was unable to think in metaphors. As for Michael he was able to think in more than one way; he just had to be sure which language he was in, which grammar to use.

He made a bracing motion with his arms, his hands gripping the edge of the desk, a signal to his mother that he was about to leave. But she had not forgotten why she had summoned him.

"Did you get my note?" she asked.

He nodded. "That's why I came."

She stared at him from the corner of some invisible ring of combat. The large blue amoebas on her loose cotton blouse seemed to focus on him, so that for the first time he noticed what she was wearing.

"He can't!" Her cry was resolute and short, her voice high but contained but not within her—as though in a box that withheld the echoes. But her eyes that were usually soft and grey like amiable entry-points for light, now amassed their colour, blue, steel, green, as though making one of their rare assertions. Michael tensed at what he thought was the sound of glass breaking. The potter's windbells outside the study were gossiping in her aftermath.

"Who can't...?"

"Do something, Michael. Oh, that Busta! This could break up everything!"

"I know. Don't worry yet...let me talk to Dad." He moved to the door, then paused as if hovering between decisions.

"Here we go, then," she said, mustering strength. "I suppose we will all survive—somehow."

But her son had already gone.

As Michael stood at the open doorway to his father's study, the familiar cool of the room lifted itself off the tiled floor to meet him. Other than the basement, it was the only dark room in the house. The walls were cluttered with pigeon holes filled with papers and books. A large table sprawled in the centre of the extension at the far end, which had once served as Michael's bedroom. There were the familiar batteries and microphones, piles of pamphlets and boxes of wires and cords, and a huge speaker lying on the table, waiting for another election.

It was only when his eyes had adjusted to the quiet light that he saw his father at the desk.

"Dad! Are you busy...?"

His father did not look up. His face was lean and narrow again, the way it had been when Michael was a boy. It must be his new eating fad: on another journey through the States he had discovered Teflon, and when he returned home he had thrown away the grimy deep-fat fryer and instituted a purge of all forms of grease. His weight loss was swift and noticeable, but he was saved from dwindling away when he developed a severe rash on his back which Moodie declared was an allergy to this new-fangled substance.

"Son, wait...," he said, with a gesture of his free hand, but he continued writing smoothly with his lips moving as though prompting his fountain pen, a reluctant old silver Parker that drank quantities of black Quink ink and leaked onto the hand-held green blotter at every pause.

Michael slipped into the room and closed the door behind him. He began a quiet pace up and down the tiles, passing law books and government gazettes, his father's legal opinions and pink official files. They all slouched as though they had fallen asleep where they lay. All Michael's life he had watched these piles grow. Sometimes even their dust was recognizable, maybe the only thing that stood still in his father's life.

"You know," Pardi began, but when Michael looked at him he was still deep in his missive, only signalling his intention to have a talk. As though his pacing might be mistaken for impatience, Michael freed a chair from a pile of "On Her Majesty's Service" files and sat down facing the desk. His father seemed to settle deeper into his preoccupation, and Michael grew peaceful as he watched the familiar figure lifting his brow to meet his thoughts and muttering them to his hands.

This room was so much his father's. Even when he had slept in here, Michael had always been wedged between the elements of his father's interests. The old man and the contents of the room had a direct relationship with each other, so much taken for granted that neither appeared to pay the least attention to the other. The man and each inanimate thing knew their places in the room, and what was expected of them. They held each other's secrets.

It was a room that worked best in its darkness, which could intensify almost imperceptibly, willing a profound concentration. And one could draw all sorts of intelligence out of its hidden cells, so it was often used by Pardi for thrashing out problems and determining strategy.

It had not changed much in the years since Pardi had worked on his murder cases. It had often witnessed the solution of tangled mysteries by deft detective work. Sometimes the whole family had got involved, reconstructing murder scenes with family hands master-minded by Pardi. Mardi once had to provide a clay body for the repeated infliction of a wound. In another famous case Uncle Moodie had to round up Colt .38 calibre guns so that Pardi could check the marks made on the bullets when they were fired; then Moodie was asked to produce a Bunsen burner to heat the barrels of the guns in an effort to reproduce an idiosyncratic mark that would solve the case and free the accused. Pardi, a normally impatient man, would go to infinite pains to trace such details.

Michael was often asked how it felt to be in the shadow of such a father, and he said the question always surprised him.

He had found the world the way it was, with his father and mother and a big brother who, whether at home or away, were facts in his life. Whatever shadow they cast, it was a shade of his life, a depth of existence that he never questioned any more than he would the clarity of air or the ponderous heads of the mountains leaning over Kingston's shoulders. To ask the question would be to lay blame, to make excuses.

Still, his father's presence had indeed filled his sky. He could remember as a boy of ten first going into Jamaica College, his father's Alma Mater. He was in the hall on the first day of term, and there on the walls above him loomed long wooden plaques engraved with the names of the school's heroes... cricket, track and field, rifle shooting, football. The Rhodes Scholars. Those who had gone on to distinguish themselves with military medals in the Great War. On each was his father's name, sometimes over and over.

At four years old Michael had prepared his first rebellion. He planned to challenge his father, who had given him a sound thrashing, a punishment that Michael considered unreasonable. He hid behind the door with a cricket bat, waiting for his father to come home. To his relief, his father entered through another door; the issue was never settled, and the question never again raised. Michael's rebellion appeared to be over.

Perhaps Douglas had shaken off that shadow when he equalled his father's hundred-yard dash. As for Michael, with the convenient truth of an injured knee he resorted to swimming, a sport whose tablet of tributes was free of the family name. Later on, he firmly refused the notion of law, a subject in which many felt he would have excelled, and studied economics instead. After university he leaned towards the safe distance that journalism would ensure, and for a while planned a career as an art critic. Finally, unable to resist his interest in public life, he chose the trade union as his profession rather than seeking a seat in Parliament through his father's party.

Recently he had become more self-confident through his work in the union. He stopped seeing his family tree as a burden of overhanging leaves, and began to feel its presence as a huge network of roots beneath him, driving his inevitable growth towards his own space of sunlight. He altered the question: how does it feel to spring from such a root?

He had grown up not so much by his father's example as the man of the house, for he was seldom home except for the long holidays by the sea; it was more that he grew up in a world that was growing up with him at the same time. And everything around him seemed to be another child of his father's intellect.

His father's world always had purpose. It always looked out from himself and moved towards a vision that Michael as a child imagined to be the Jerusalem of Blake's hymn, since his father sang it with such fervour. Despite his influence, his father's life never seemed to be about himself, and its movement seemed to offer a distance and objectivity that made his son's attachment to him anything but umbilical. Maybe that was why he had never felt an urge to rebel after that early untried skirmish. It had never been necessary.

A closeness had developed between them through the union and politics, quite separate from the family unit and his mother.

Sometimes he felt as though his blood and his feelings were aspects of his mother, but that in the centre of himself, climbing step by step, were the quiet vertebrae of his father, one at a time, logical and balanced, and that when her elements were battering him, he could always return to the rungs of this paternal ladder and climb the consequential ascent of his rational self.

Depending on which route he took to his head, his thoughts could be either his mother's or his father's.

Pardi was now halfway out of the page in front of him. He nodded at what he had written, blotted the surface with finality and cleared his throat. "So! The battle is joined," he said, and looked squarely at his son.

Michael was pulling at his Albany cigarette, which never seemed to have enough smoke to satisfy him. His long, yellowing fingers hovered watchfully over the inhalation and then retrieved the recoiling paper cylinder from his lips.

"This thing with Busta," Michael prompted.

"Yes." Pardi nodded firmly, settling back against the carved circular posts of his wooden desk chair, his hands clasped except for the index fingers touching and pointing like a spotlight. "I can't be sure what really happened, but I hear on the grapevine..."

It all started in Trinidad, when the federal government made an unexpected announcement.

Grantley Adams, the first prime minister of the West Indies, was at the federal capital in Port of Spain. Many felt he was like the restless ghost of the disembodied federation. It had formally come into existence in January 1958, and by April 1963 it was due to take its place as a self-governing dominion within the British Commonwealth. But now, just over two years old, and with neither Pardi nor Williams at the helm, it was plagued by disputes. Locked in a continuing argument with Jamaica over taxation, Adams made an impromptu declaration to the press that the federal government intended to introduce retroactive tax legislation.

The result was catastrophic.

After the 1959 PNP victory, Bustamante knew that he must content himself with nit-picking on minor issues. Jamaican politics had shown a pattern of a ten-year swing to each party. Unless fate intervened, he must wait till the opposing momentum lost its strength. Two terms. That was the pattern.

But Adams' announcement about retroactive taxation was just the kind of opportunity Busta and the JLP needed. He saw his chance. Now was the time to lead Jamaica out of the federation, and become the hero of a truly independent Jamaica. He resigned from the federal Democratic Labour Party and declared that Jamaica should secede from the federation.

Within hours the pendulum started its swing.

In the Jamaican parish of St. Thomas, a by-election was due to fill a seat for the federal parliament. The JLP leadership were all gathered in a private house in the area. Bustamante was expected to present the candidate they had selected, a teacher from outside the area, at a public meeting later that evening; the man had been defeated in the 1959 national general election, and was now mending his dreams with the hope of serving the federal government instead.

"I hear that Busta said to the federal candidate he was supposed to be nominating, 'You're not going to any meeting. We're not nominating you for it!' Just like that." Pardi nodded as though he expected his son to be surprised. "Can't you just see the startled JLP members looking up at their chief as he leaned back in his chair and smirked into his champagne?"

"I just can't believe...." Michael heaved himself out of the chair to speak, as though his thoughts had left a track on the floor that he must follow. "The utter, incredible irresponsibility...the shameless opportunism....Busta can't oppose federation simply because of the threat of a tax...he's just using this to whip up feelings and win a general election. If Jamaica pulls out, that will be that...it will smash up the federation."

"Oh, I can believe it," Pardi stated simply, and he gazed at the queue of smoke dispersing behind his peripatetic son. "I can believe it, but even after all these years I was still not able to predict it. I leave predictions to your mother!"

His son looked at him and then lowered his head with a small, dismissive suck on his teeth, so slight and sudden that it could be mistaken for punctuation.

They heard the sound of voices and footsteps in the hall outside.

The two men went silent, and Michael stood still as they watched shadows cutting the light beneath the door. They both shared a dislike of intrusion. They both hated surprises, and the Caribbean delight in dropping in on friends, on colleagues, on houses. They had a winter instinct of hibernation and sanctuary at home, of privacy and the formality of visits by invitation. No matter what the traffic within Drumblair, or what commitment to public service, they would cleave to their secret hiding-places.

As the footsteps ambled towards the front door, the two men breathed again. Pardi blew his nose and Michael resumed his prowl and hacked a passage through the nicotine in his throat.

"What on earth possessed Grantley?" Michael asked, as though by starting at the beginning of the story they could somehow rearrange the facts.

"God knows," Pardi sighed. "I hear he's not happy there...."

Adams was said to be lonely for home, as are all absent islanders—the more profoundly so, the smaller the land mass, as though each native son carried a larger share of patriotism because there were fewer to bear the load. According to Mardi, he was missing his wife, Grace, a teacher, who remained behind in Barbados. With characteristic embellishment Mardi surmised that Grace probably spent long holidays leaning over the eastern coast's savage sea at Bathsheba where, from that confining space, she said that one's mind could drift unimpeded, free in the certainty that nothing lay between the churning coast and the continent of Africa but the ghosts of the past and the occasional Sahara dust.

"I suppose you have to feel a little sorry for him," Michael said. "I mean, he's in a federation which needs to have autonomy"—his face lit up with amusement as his hands mimed holding an imaginary ball—"but each territory is either fighting for, or has just got, its own internal self-government, so they are all busy guarding their new individual powers . . . just look at us. . . ."

He had started one of those uncontrollable laughs that assailed him on occasion. "Here we are, all flexing our muscles and lifting the dumb-bells of our own egos," he pointed out, when he could get his breath. "I suppose by keeping the centre weak the periphery feels consoled! Ah God . . . it's just a gigantic, insoluble jigsaw at times. So what does Adams do? He says, 'A tax on all your houses!'"

The older man picked up a letter opener from the desk.

"I'm going to take the case to the people," he said. "I'm going to settle the question once and for all. I'm calling a referendum. Simple as that!" He twisted the slim object between his fingers and sent it spinning with a flick.

"A referendum! But Dad . . . do you dare?"

"I don't have a choice."

"I'm not sure I agree with you. I mean, you just won the most spectacular landslide. You don't have to stretch democracy that far! All you have to do is use their good will and keep selling them the new deal. Busta can't do anything till the next election, and that buys you enough time."

"We will just have to hope that this present goodwill carries the 'yes' vote in the referendum."

"But Dad, think of the federal election, the way you were beaten in Jamaica. That shows the local unease on the federal issue."

His father was staring at a pile of files where a small house lizard unfurled his yellow tongue and then withdrew it again. Michael was touched by the notion that, without his glasses, his father's eyes seemed more at ease with thinking than with seeing. He seemed to have lost interest, but when he spoke his son discovered that he had just changed his viewpoint.

"Your mother thinks me reckless."

He said this sadly, with a sigh that drooped his shoulders. Michael noticed the thinning hair on the top of his father's head, reflexively patted his own thick waves, wondering how soon his hair would start thinning too.

He thought of his mother's note dropped off at his house that morning in her conspiratorial way. His father was about to do something quixotic, would he pop in and have a word with him? So she had known. Now he feigned surprise as simply as he could, irritated by the subterfuge. "Does she?" he asked.

His father was often reckless in his personal actions: cutting corners to finish a task swiftly, going off on a sudden tangent of mischief. But he was ultimately disciplined and rational. And because of that, he was never fanatical. Not even about being democratic. In areas where he held any form of public trust, he was always responsible. Michael knew that while his father was idealistic, he was not driven by some romantic notion of democracy at every turn, at any cost. He wouldn't trust history to the whim of a moment because of an idealistic preoccupation.

"She feels I'm about to toss the federation into the hands of an illiterate and unpredictable electorate in a highly charged political situation." He looked straight at his son. "And of course she's right."

"Then why are you doing it?" Michael was playing devil's advocate, but he knew he was being taken step by step through a process of reasoning, like a captive jury.

Pardi sat up, replaced his glasses and pulled himself to attention at his desk, straightening the papers and notes in front of him, capping his pen and ink bottle as though tidying his mind and arranging his thoughts. He pressed an already flat piece of paper before him, removed his glasses again and stared up at the ceiling.

"Follow my dilemma. Before my next term is up, the West Indies Federation is due to adopt an independent constitution. And no matter the timing, there are bound to be gaps between when the various islands achieve their federal constitution... they will be ratified... and when I have to go back to face the Jamaican people in a national general election."

He turned his attention to the far side of his desk and leaned across to flip up a piece of paper in one of his stacked trays, looked marginally surprised at what he saw, and pulled it towards him. The pen came out of his pocket again, and his son noticed the beginning of a black stain leaking across the red sports shirt. He stared at it with fastidious discomfort, and leaned forward to draw his father's attention to it.

"Um, Dad...the pen is leaking, you know...your shirt ...."

His father wrote a hurried scrawl at the edge of the paper, and was about to cap the pen again when he followed his son's disgruntled gaze to the offending blemish, and then to the source of the mischief.

"Oh, chut," he added the prim 't' which made the expression of Jamaican exasperation so much more conclusive, "bloody pen dribbles like a baby," he said fondly and started cleaning it's cap against the blotter. "I cannot abolish that duty," he blew into the cap, then added emphatically, "that requirement," as if this last word were better.

"If I rest upon my albeit comfortable majority in Parliament, and go ahead with what has been agreed on, I can keep the process from bogging down. I'll see the West Indies home to its joint independence, see it take its place in the United Nations...see us fly our flag and have a West Indian national anthem."

He seemed on the verge of indulging his imagination further, then he quickly reclaimed his face and became businesslike again: "But I can't avoid facing Busta in an election. In five years—or maybe I bring it forward—I have to face him at the polls."

"But surely you'd be stronger. I mean, with federal independence already a *fait accompli*...a reality in the Caribbean consciousness, not just the vision of a small group of idealists..."

"That's just the trouble, son. That's the whole problem. You see, if Busta is going to fight federation, it makes no difference if it's now or later. If I wait, every damn pinprick of difficulty—and we're bound to have them in the early days of a federal experiment, for it's a damn difficult system to run, I don't have to tell you that—every difficulty will present itself like a gift to him." He waved his hand in an exaggerated gesture of presentation. "He'll exaggerate and exploit each problem...oh Lord, I can just hear him!"

Looking down at his hands, with their fingertips carefully castled together, Michael could indeed imagine Busta's possible jabs in his high staccato voice, *You see wha' happen, you cost of living? Is Manley federation cause it. You see the problem you have buying you baby milk? Is Manley federation cause it!*

"I would have given him the very weapons to fight me with! Not only would he defeat me, but because of his anti-federal campaign he would then have no choice but to withdraw Jamaica and smash up the federation." These words spilled out of Pardi as the last few grains of salt spill through an egg-timer, and he leaned wearily back in his chair.

But Michael was not persuaded. "I see what you're saying, but as long as you are the government and you are in there building—where there was only a concept, now they see a system, institutions...there's nothing like reality! And you'll teach the electorate as you go along. It's what you do best, Dad. If you have a referendum and you lose, it will smash up the federation that much earlier! Why tempt fate?"

The older man looked at him as though they had just completed a long climb up a hill, and were stopping to rest and consider the view.

"But there is another problem. As you say, if I wait till the next election is due, in 1964, the islands will be bound by the knot of institutionalized independence. But that is how the world will see us, too. Remember that we are not on the political map yet, we are not in the United Nations. We are still seen as a scattering of colonial fragments. But after April of 1963 we will be an international presence. Can you imagine the shame for us, the whole Caribbean people, if Busta breaks up our unity at *that* stage? If we handled our affairs with such inefficiency, with such incompetence, that we barely arrived before we fell apart? The humiliation! We would be the mockery of the world!"

Thin ropes of blood beneath the skin of his temples defined his passion.

Michael looked at the spent figure of his father, as Pardi popped a pill under his tongue; he looked too weary now for his own impatience. Framed by the corners of his simple room, he was now a portrait more of vulnerability than valour. Michael saw no bronzed horse, no monument, no statue, only a well-worn holiday shirt with an ink stain for a badge.

"Michael, the only thing I can do is flush Busta out and make him fight the battle now, when I think we have enough momentum. We must sell the federation as a dream for the future, before we get trapped by the tendency to swing away from the incumbent in the second term. I am going to let the people defeat him now, and once they find their voice in a referendum, he will be silenced *forever*."

Beneath the oratory, Michael heard the tough-minded pragmatism that always grounded his father. Although his Edwardian pride led him to revile the prospect of regional humiliation, and his commitment to democracy made him choose that process as the way to resolve the crisis, he presented his argument without a trace of idealism.

"If only the British empire would stop being so damned accommodating," Michael muttered.

"What's that?" He was looking down sadly at his shirt. It had become, and would remain, a shirt with a stain.

"Our trouble is, we haven't an outside enemy to make us stand together and fight!"

Pardi smiled wryly.

"Too true. Isn't it ironic that George III sending his troops to collect taxes was what started the American War of Independence!"

Pardi looked at his son, who now sat back with his arms slackly folded.

"Thank you, son," he said very softly, and before Michael could speak, he covered the naked moment with his next words. "I'll talk to both Cabinet and Executive."

"Will they...," Michael began, and stopped.

But his father knew the question, as he thought of the glazed eyes and polite tolerance with which his own caucus reacted to even the most cursory mention of matters federal. Although they stood by the party, he knew many of his colleagues were unconvinced about federation. The place they wanted power was right here at home, and each step they took nearer to political self-determination made them more potent as Jamaicans.

"Are they with you in spirit?"

"No, probably not all of them."

But I am, thought Michael.

On his way up to his bedroom, Pardi stopped at the door to the living-room and listened to the plonk, plonk as I searched out a tune on the piano.

"Pie?"

I tried again to find the note: *Was it weakness of intellect birdie, I cried...*

He moved behind me. He loved to finish a quote or a verse, to recall the words of some past moment, to hold the longest breath. So he sang: *Or a rather-tough worm in your little insiiiiiiiiide....* And he seemed to hold the last note forever, till I turned round and he was bauxite and earth-brown red and I thought he might burst.

By the time Mardi went up to have her four o'clock bath, he had made his intentions known to the Cabinet, and he now sat in his room, stripped to a vest and his blue boxers, getting upset for the second time that day over some politically hostile editorial in the *Daily Gleaner*.

He had taken off his Sunday shirt and left it lying in the tightly woven, square laundry basket under the lignum vitae lid, the ink stain dry and saved where it insinuated itself into the fate of the fibres.

11

AN
EXTRA-TOUGH
WORM

BOARDING-SCHOOL BECAME a waiting period, a weightless interim, a time to be endured before I rejoined the mainstream. In exile I felt like a fragment. I learned not to count time second by second, but ticked off the squares on my calendar before going to bed to confirm I had rid myself of another day. I honed my distraction into patience more through helplessness than through virtue.

My family also seemed distracted and at odds.

Pardi and Mardi, who had travelled "down the islands" on campaigns for federal elections, now journeyed across Jamaica on another trail. The predictable five-year cycle of elections which had given my life its comfortable structure was again interrupted, this time by the referendum campaign, to squeeze out a "yes" for federation. As far as I was concerned, "yes" became a comrade word and "no" a Labourite one.

My time with my grandparents was reduced to brief lunches in a nearby country hotel, the Villa Bella, when I was whisked away from school, or a few days at half-term, when we'd meet in St. Ann by the sea at Eaton Hall, or in a guest house with ninety-six steps; Pardi and I climbed and counted them as Mardi cried from the bottom of the hill, "Norman, your heart!" Then there were my school holidays at Nomdmi with Milton, Juanita and Miss Boyd, when Pardi and Mardi would actually come to "visit" when they could find a day or two to spare.

I have no clear recollection of the events at the time, just a sense of family undulation, of their rocking to and fro, into and out of my life, or me rocking into and out of theirs; a sense of oddments that became reality till the next visit.

Mardi described her life as having become one endless campaign. The seams which distinguish periods, one from another, had blurred in her mind, replaced by the more immediate markers which jarred, like the landing of a plane, the parking of a car, the identifying name on a piece of hotel stationery; sometimes just bracing herself for the next pothole on the current road.

My understanding of politics at home and outside the Caribbean was limited to their stories. Sometimes I had glimpses of the wider world, images that became vivid through splinters of news I could not relate to any wider landscape than the mood of their source. These vignettes I never forgot. My image of the Cuban Revolution and its aftermath was one of Fidel Castro in New York, holding fried chicken in his war-weary hands.

"Oh, it's too awful; they just don't understand," moaned Mardi, lifting her hands in a gesture of despair. To her, the fact that the American press focused on Castro's table manners showed a complete failure to recognize his role in history. He came straight from the hills of Cuba, with his fatigued warriors, she explained to me, and "the press", and America, misunderstood their noble cause to free their land from the wicked Batista.

For a long time I thought she had actually been there, seeing their rumpled green uniforms, the burning, magnificent sense of purpose that made them unable to eat with a knife and a fork. "They were in the hills, struggling to survive, fighting for cherished freedom, and the press dare to nitpick over table manners! The Americans of all people should be ashamed of themselves!"

Similarly, sitting out on a rock overlooking the little sloshing bay at Eaton Hall, Pardi recalled John Kennedy seated before him at his desk at the White House: how young and bright he was, how much he liked him; and the figure of his wife, Jackie (this image must have been separate, or on television), in a tennis outfit, racquet in hand, speaking in an incongruous voice that was too cute, too tiny, to emanate from such a deliberate jaw. That was all I knew of the Kennedy phenomenon.

And while black America fought for its civil rights, and Americans filled their basements with tinned food in case the Cold War suddenly heated up and engulfed the world in a nuclear holocaust—with the Bay of Pigs looming only one year and ninety miles away—we in Jamaica were grumbling about whether to say yes or no to federation, and Mardi was worried that this latest campaign might prove to be Pardi's Waterloo.

Jamaica too was living on hold. The more Pardi widened the island's dream through his prism of regional hope, the more Bustamante encouraged Jamaica to narrow and harden the focus of her heart on herself.

For me, ill health became a conduit home, one I chanced upon as a result of genuine chronic sinusitis. I repeated the symptoms with success on three occasions, resulting in two antrum wash-outs and the removal of my tonsils, the adenoids plucked out for good measure. It seemed a reasonable price to pay for a return to Drumblair, home food, Rediffusion plays in the mornings and the pleasure of waking without the smell of leaky-bladdered Mildred's wet sheets at the bottom of the dormitory.

Whereas Drumblair had become quite grumpy with its occupants often away, probably feeling itself neglected and used merely as a convenience, I found the Nuttall Hospital most welcoming. It was a sprawling, comfortable institution in Cross Roads, just above the city of Kingston and near my grandfather's office. I loved its smells of formaldehyde and disinfectant, its floor polish and powdered nurses, its stiff white sheets, green gowns and green corridors, the ice-cold theatre with its silver saucer of bright white lights and its hovering, masked faces, and someone always holding my hand. I basked in the sympathy and attention.

"Here I shall die, with a dry Martini in my hand, listening to the love stories of silly young nurses," Mardi would vow. She loved the Nuttall too.

Pardi dutifully carried away the bottles with my floating remnants of tonsils and adenoids from his hospital visits, and placed them in our chemistry lab in the back room at Drumblair.

At the hospital I stayed in a small room with high ceilings and tall, curtained windows. It was next to the nurses' station "so they can keep an eye on you," Mardi explained.

I could hear them chattering between shifts, and tried to discover if there had been any deaths or other disasters, information I would share with Pardi on his afternoon drop-ins before Cabinet. Along with each round of constitutional change there would be new names and titles. I was getting used to this.

Bustamante furnished the island with malaise and a sick-bay's worth of excuses. If Pardi provided purpose, Bustamante provided impediments. The more Jamaica felt it needed to get back home, the more Bustamante diagnosed conditions to justify this inclination. We would be ruled by the "little Doc", as he called Dr. Eric Williams, who was not a large man; we would have to share our prosperity with the smaller islands—he had a litany of phobias to feed what was becoming through the federal focus a time of increasing national homesickness.

Pardi was a man whose mind had no corridors. His thoughts lived in wide rooms where there were no places to hide, no lurking areas in which to form conspiracies. This was his nature. The campaign leading up to the referendum became as futile as his trips to my bedside. He felt he was not fighting a real enemy but a shadow, a rumour rather than a voice of rational argument; he was defending something he valued against a challenge he considered to be of merely machiavellian motivation.

Perhaps this was the most remote and isolated he ever felt from his own people, including all the years spent in England and during the Great War. His own party stalwarts continued to be unconvinced. They appeared to do what they should without any enthusiasm. It was not that they were antagonistic, or even stubborn. But they appeared to be without a brief, as though they were following guidelines for a mission as yet undisclosed. When they sat on the platform around him, he felt that his explanation had to convince the baffled faces of his own first phalanx before it could persuade the people gathered namelessly beyond the platform. "I feel like I am treading water with a body in my arms," he explained to Mardi.

"Have you ever thought, Kid, that perhaps its nationalism you're fighting? Theirs and ours in a strange way. The dead weight you feel is, well, like the contradiction in even your own self maybe? Add to that a cunning opponent who knows how to let your own weight defeat you...." She hesitated; he was looking at her intently, but his face betrayed no reaction. "And maybe you just have an idea before its time...."

Pardi took refuge in the crowds, and the large crowds took refuge in song to confirm their support. "Oh let the fire fall on them, my Lord," they invoked the heavenly cataclysm on the heads of their political foes.

"Manley you win de referendum," they affirmed. The lyrics demanded a thumping optimism which was easily assumed by a congregation glad to partake of something direct and familiar.

As the campaign wore on, Pardi found his speeches becoming more convoluted as he tried repeatedly to explain himself, and so what was at stake became steadily more obscure. In his days in court the jurors had often been simple people, but he had learned that if you led reasonable people through the consecution of facts, their logic would bring them to a rational conclusion. But now his arguments somehow left him stranded at the end of each day, each minute becoming more complicated as he fought against a tide of incomprehension. At night he felt a tightness in his chest, and though he swallowed various pills, he would remain clenched in its fist.

In her ambivalence over the federal issue, Mardi developed an annoying calm on her face and it was hard to read her mood as her eyes seemed indefinite as they wandered from colour to colour.

As though to assert his place in the world, Pardi had embarked on the addition of a bedroom and an indoor bathroom at Nomdmi. Before this, we had always bathed in a mobile bathtub which we had christened Norman Washingtub. Mardi had painted it black to absorb the sun's rays. Each day it would be left full of water in the sun, and by two o'clock the designated bather would sit upright in its warm water and perform his or her ablutions.

He was also growing ortaniques at Nomdmi. He would pick these bright yellow hybrids of oranges and tangerines and squeeze them into juice which he stored in the freezer at Drumblair, and which he claimed Mardi was drinking at the rate of three dozen bottles a week. She always lived as a woman with ailing kidneys, though the malady was never fully substantiated. She had generally drunk coconut water, but recently, in an effort to be supportive of Pardi, she had switched to his sour, homegrown juice, adding honey or brown sugar to the bottles when he wasn't looking.

One afternoon during the campaign, when he could not settle down to anything, he unexpectedly collected me from a convalescence at the house and took me for a drive up to Nomdmi to check on the builders and his ortanique grove.

I had pulled off what I considered to be my greatest coup. A friend at school who slept in the bed next to mine had returned from holidays late when she had her appendix removed. When she described to me the symptoms and her reactions to a diagnostic probe, I was able to simulate a convincing tenderness. A week later I was rushed to Kingston for an appendectomy. Afterwards, in tight stitches more of gas than of nylon, I wondered if this time I had gone too far.

When Pardi had come to see me in hospital after my surgery, he had stood at the door with his hands on his hips, looking intently at me. I had the feeling he saw straight through me.

"Well, now you know what a bad thing a real stomach-ache is, my dear. Not something one would ever wish on oneself."

I wondered if he knew.

But the beagle-faced doctor, his expression distorted between large ears that seemed to pull down his kindly features, had come in holding my grey and disintegrating appendage in its bottle of formaldehyde. If he knew of my deception he said nothing, perhaps not wanting to admit he had been duped. And Pardi had dutifully left with a new prize for our lab collection.

On the way up to Nomdmi, Pardi grew more cheerful as the air thinned and cooled, becoming subtly other. We plunged and heaved and lurched round the bends, and I could feel the stitches in my side.

The forest ranger lent us a mule, and I sat in front of Pardi holding onto the saddle-horn, trying not to bend at the waist. Pardi rode the mule for all it was worth, which was very little—no more than a saunter—as the animal's wide hips swayed dispassionately and the hoofs said hello and goodbye to each other with tiny clops beneath us. Perhaps the mule decided that its barren state required minimal ambition.

The extension was a clutter of house parts and the small, circular graves from remains of concrete mixings. The hammerings and sawings echoed from distant mountains. Pardi surveyed the progress and quarrelled hyperbolically over the mistakes of his workforce, who paused to listen with evident amusement.

He measured me with his pocket tape and added a new scratch with the date on the veranda wall where he kept a record of my height. This was always a cause for mild concern as Mardi, worried that I did not eat enough, felt I wouldn't grow to the height predicted by my feet. They were unusually long "Manley" feet. The Manleys were a tall family, but I was told that the Kamellards, my maternal tribe, were short, and my mother was a mere five feet in height.

We broke off some bamboo sticks which he trimmed with his pen-knife, and set off along the path behind the house that led to "the bench", a narrow promontory like an eyebrow of the mountain under which we would "sit and be still and peruse like Mrs. Brown Cow," according to Mardi. There was a Mrs. White Cow who would go straight to the river to have her drink, but Mrs. Brown Cow would meander slowly for she liked to stop and look at everything. Mardi insisted there was a profound and enduring lesson to be gained from this anecdote.

We passed a familiar crater in the hill planted with apple trees. On one of my long holidays I had believed it was the site of a Russian bomb-blast.

"We used to think Nursie was a Russian spy," I remembered, with the pride that comes of outgrowing one's own folly. Nursie had worked with us for a while, apparently to help Miss Boyd cope with me.

We could only walk single-file. Pardi moved along ahead

of me, his low, horizontal steps parting the nested pine needles. Mountains are very private. You cannot own them. When you walk through them, it's like walking through someone else's house.

"Well, she's gone now," he replied absently.

Nursie had left for America at the same time I left for boarding-school. Later we heard that she had married a California millionaire or a minister of religion, we were never quite sure which.

Rounding a corner, we suddenly faced a bare hilltop. It was a shock, as if we had walked in while the hills were changing their clothes. The land had been cleared by the forestry department for planting. About three acres stretched out stripped and desolate. Pardi stared at it gravely.

"One day when you are about twenty-five or thirty this will be a wonderful pinewood. Such is tree life and tree time!"

"If I live that long," I said, having recently seen to it that my lifespan appeared to hang in the balance.

"I daresay you will," he said flatly.

We reached the bench, which sloped sideways with the lay of the land. "It's cocking its head," Mardi used to explain. We sat.

"I wonder what I'll be doing then," I said.

"I never knew at your age what I would be doing. I'm not even sure what I am doing now, or what I'll be doing next year!"

"Mardi says I'm going to be a poet."

"Well, that's a good thing to be if that's what you are to be." The thin mountain air made him breathe more heavily.

We were sitting beside a faded sign that read, "Trespassers will be persecuted." It was always there, painted white and mounted on a tree, and none of us knew who had put it there or why.

"You know, I always loved maths." He said this with gently amused wonder. "I loved geometry. It opened up a new dimension in life for me that never closes or contracts."

"I like the arts stream, not the sciences," I asserted, for I lived in a system where you had to choose.

"Yes...like your Mardi. It's harder to be an artist, though I daresay a lot more exciting and satisfying," he conceded.

"Why is it harder?"

"Creativity can close up on you. How to live and keep that all alive is every artist's and writer's problem. It's Mardi's great problem." He shook his head. "Some people think it has to do with preserving tension in regard to the outside world. I'm not sure they're right. Sometimes I think that's just an excuse to be disagreeable."

"Well, I can't draw and paint like Mardi. And I can't dance like Thelma. And now I can't sing, without my tonsils," I said, and Pardi let it pass, though the truth was that I hadn't been able to sing even before they were removed. The continuing *Mikado* rehearsals were proof of that. "Maybe I'll be an actress...."

My mind was on my recent success as a dying swan.

"And Daddy says I could go to the method school in New York where Marlon Brando went."

Pardi was travelling his own thoughts, pacing his words across the valleys in front of him, so when he started speaking they came slowly, like journeying paths twining the hills, and his voice had that rare quality of gifting itself to you. It came from deep secrets within him, and left the sentences still moving, the ideas never closing.

"All young people worry about what they are going to do when they grow up. I know I did. But looking back I realize it's very hard to be sure when you are young. The fact is, you don't know enough about yourself. And you can't forecast opportunity." He suddenly looked irritable. "Lucky are the people who are born babbling, 'I am going to be a this or a that,'" he said, and whacked the ground with his bamboo stick.

I was in fact more worried about getting out of boarding-school than about later on, but I loved the proximity his advice brought, and his voice sharing its wise vowels and noble pauses, its brinks and its floodings.

"The way will open," he said decisively, and he looked at me swinging my legs on the edge of the bench. "What matters most is to live now with the full force of yourself, so that when the day comes that you know, the drive is there … it's a habit of being that will take you where you wish to go."

I felt guilty and lowered my head, eating the ends of my long hair to hide my face from his view.

"I know you are worried about going back to school," he said quietly. "It may always be a wrench to face the first few days. That's natural. I think I found it like that myself when I was young, and even now at my age, though your Mardi doesn't believe this, I feel upset when I leave home. That's life."

But he was always leaving home, I thought.

"Pie, I want to tell you something very important."

I could feel him turning towards me. I didn't move, but I felt awkward and chewed more hair.

"There is nothing more hurtful or harmful in life than to refuse to accept something that you know you have to do, and that is good and worth doing. It is bad because to swing to and fro from one side to the other is to split yourself open, it is self-inflicted torture...it drains your energy and confuses your soul."

He was sitting forward, his chin propped on his hands, which rested one on top of the other on the upright bamboo. He sounded like one of his radio speeches to the country as he addressed the gathering of peaks facing us.

"Once your course is set, hold it steady and keep your doubts and worries outside your real self. Do not allow them to cry too loud and never, never let them drown out the real music, which is found in purpose...and loyalty...and going forward."

He gave me a minute to absorb this and, side by side in our isolated intimacy, our birth dates one day apart, I felt his good will. I looked up at a brief intrusion of sunlight where the sky had opened its blinds. As though the shaft brought him revelation, Pardi related his abstractions through a familiar story.

"The Bible tells of a woman who, forced to go on a journey to save herself, looked back over her shoulder longing for what she was leaving. She turned into a pillar of salt. It's a wise story."

He was looking at the place where he assumed there would be a pinewood in thirty years. He reminded me of a picture in the newspaper I had cut out and saved many years before, in which he looked with overworn love at the carnage of Jamaica's famous Kendall train crash. He was watching the future as if it might not survive. He seemed to be summoning his own courage.

On the hill there was not a single tree. Pardi stood like a surgeon, addressing his mind to the raw clearing before him, and then seemed to stay his hands, as though lost in a fragment of heart-held poetry:

"Not to see the trees nor hear the young lambs crying in the frost..."

It was from a play on a record we had listened to the previous summer. A production about Joan of Arc.

I remembered.

"At the end, when Joan refused to go to prison for life...."

"Yes, Par." I swallowed, and now I could hardly see. Even for me this was an emotional afternoon. And I knew, although it wasn't mentioned, that he was very near an inner dilemma, and that my adolescent uncertainty had become part of a more complicated weave.

I was relieved when old Dixon came down the path. He was Ivan's father and had worked for years at Nomdmi. His retirement had been announced by the arrival of his son to do the handy work around the house one holiday, instead of Dixon.

Now he had a water-can on his head, and carried a cardboard box which he laid down on the path.

"Barrista!" He grinned from gums as fleshy as his eyes. He was already part of his own rubble, as though over time he was moving stealthily back into the mountain.

"What's good, Dixon?"

"Not so bad, sah! Weh de missis?"

"Fine, fine," Pardi misanswered. "What a helluva pine forest you will have here!"

"Not pine, sah. Dem clear dis fe eucalyptus."

Pardi, whose hearing was becoming less acute, again missed what Dixon said, and returned down the path as we retraced our steps.

"Eucalyptus," reiterated Dixon stubbornly, even less likely to be heard as he followed us down.

We stopped beyond the house to check Pardi's latest hobby. The birds had already gouged many of the ortaniques. Pardi picked some and produced his knife again and proceeded to peel the thin skins, releasing the juice from below the vicious rind.

"Dem fruit can't sweet, Barrista!" Dixon said ominously.

"Nonsense. They are just young," Pardi said as he automatically blinked at an acid squirt that splashed his glasses.

"Nobody doan wan' dem sour so." The old farmer, knowing what would sell in a market, looked at the fruit contemptuously.

"Damn sissies." Pardi sucked the fruit vehemently. It was a bit acid, but he liked it. He had his own notions about food. According to Mardi, he liked drastic extremes of flavour. She always said fish was good for the brain; Pardi believed it was actually the salt in the fish that fed the brain, that made you think. Like Bovril—he loved to spread its strong, brown, wet saltiness over a slice of bread. As for anything acid, it was a waking taste, clean, swift and penetrating, and therefore probably good.

Dixon watched till Pardi had finished his bitter cup and laughed as his thirst was quenched with a grimace.

"Dem is cross-breed like mule. Nuttin' cross can sweet!" And he looked without apology at Pardi, the famous hybrid mulatto savouring the fruit's shortcomings under its mother tree.

I sat nearby, leaning on Dixon's box, while the two men loosened the belt of earth around some of the trees and bedded them with pine needles.

"When I come up again I'll sprinkle salt for the slugs," said Pardi.

"Soon election again, sah," Dixon muttered into a compost of leaves.

Pardi didn't appear to hear him. "Mardi must really come up," he called to me, as though it were time to hail her across the valley.

I think we missed Mardi. The mountain seemed lonely with only his purpose. The rough little house looked less presentable without her interpreting its crude language. The possibility of her wanderings in the most unlikely places provided suspense; the discovery of myth in the otherwise ordinary landscape was her magical alchemy.

"We will come to live here soon," he said, as though making an arrangement with himself, and he was as surprised when Dixon answered him as he was at himself for saying this.

"You a retire, sah?"

Pardi swore irritably. He hated the word "retire", which sounded like a slow leak in a tire. There wasn't any such thing, one just lived and tried to be worthy until it was over. That was all.

Eventually there would be no money. There wasn't any money now. But they could live up here and she would work on her carving and he would plant coffee and citrus and make the place viable. They needed a driving road right up to the top, and a larger water-tank. He must build a tank, he thought.

"Then what would happen to Drumblair?" I asked.

"Well, it would be there. But you know, one day we may have to sell it. If we can't afford it any longer, you know...." His voice trailed off on gusts of effort as he tugged at an embedded stone.

"I would rather die than leave Drumblair," I asserted, tossing a mutilated ortanique into the distance.

"Oh, don't be silly, Pie. You can't die rather than leave a house. Houses are houses. Life is life."

"But Drumblair is not just any house."

"It's a nice house. But still, it's a house. When you say "Drumblair", you are talking about all that has happened there. All the good people, even the bad people, all the good things you have learned, all the growing up you have done. That's not a house. That's a way of living, a state of being... that you will carry with you all your years, house or no house!" He straightened and appeared to stretch his back. "You know, after the referendum..."

On hearing this last word, Dixon startled the afternoon with a raucous, cruel laugh:

"Federandum no!"

The *non sequitur* was a rude interruption. Pardi was appalled at the sheer lack of manners, and even of sensitivity, shown by the old countryman.

"What?" he snapped.

But Dixon refused to make any more of his prediction; he returned to tugging at the shoots of stray lilies from their tuberous bellies under the grass.

"No" was such an easy word, so without responsibility. It seemed to him nowadays to punctuate every list of ills and misfortunes. "No federation, no!" "No", the decree of a child who stamped his feet in mindless rejection. "No", a word whose pronunciation finished with its own energy; a facile way to settle questions that asked too much. And it was a natural word to a people evolved from a history that should never have been.

In any case it was easy to band people together in the momentum of iconoclasm. Easier to smash than to build. To tear down rules, inadequacies, laws, habits, status quos and the very empire itself. The harder job was to build from the wreckage.

"De li'ka docta nat gwan' rule we!"

"You get that damn rubbish from Busta."

Pardi looked ready to argue his federal case, but Dixon had retired into self-righteousness, his head nodding knowingly in agreement with himself. It was clearly time to go.

We walked to the gate and remounted the surly animal. As Pardi was about to kick-start the mule, he turned the animal around for a moment to face the old man who had now become an unharmonious companion.

"I should have been a farmer, you know."

"Shudda been a farmer, heh, heh, heh," Dixon laughed, repeating this as though savouring whatever flavour he tasted from the dry seed of Pardi's observation.

"Drumblair, dear, you know you are getting old."

That's what Mardi said. Pardi wasn't there when she said it, but she had a way of saying things that made events follow. She was a woman who made hasty decisions. And Pardi was a man who could make any decision irrevocable.

I am sure the house was doomed from that moment.

Mardi moved about the living-room rearranging the furniture, pulling the chairs first into clusters for conversation; then no, better into lines in front of the big radio. The walls looked speckled and in need of paint, the wood on the chairs looked battered. Miss Boyd's nice slipcovers were fading and soiled in spots. Mardi could see where one of the Queen Anne chairs caught the sun in the morning, and where the cat's coat had left a shadow on the other, its favourite sleeping-place.

Mardi saw this as an indifference on the part of the house, a cussed refusal to rise to a sense of occasion.

The house ignored her.

The car had taken the various members of the staff to their polling stations to vote. Pardi and Michael were out scouting. Only we were there, two women of Drumblair, waiting: Mardi, the political thoroughbred, for a confirmation that her lifted eyebrows and the resigned fixity of her lips had already inferred from omens, dreams or common sense; and I, the garron, simply for the thrill of a familiar turmoil with its compelling emotions.

Everywhere there were pamphlets whose messages had become obsolete when the polls opened that morning. The campaign paraphernalia sprawled over the discarded plannings of the most recent edition of *Focus*, the now disbanded committee's efforts eked out in slivered phases which lay in various manuscripts beneath the federal weight. "Man of Destiny" announced a blue cover with a profiled portrait of Pardi looking intensely over his nose at some purpose on the horizon that gave his face interest and satisfaction. Man of destiny, two shillings. That was an old pamphlet, from before their first electoral victory.

Against the wall, on a folded mahogany card table, there were newer, thinner offerings. Mardi's federal flag on a cover whose statement curiously ended with a question mark: "Federation, what it will really cost Jamaica?" Another announced "Great Sayings on Federation", with three gaudy gems outlined in blue, and the spliced rays of a sun radiating over the cover.

Here in the skin of their own world they could not count the cost. It was more than the bills piling up at the constituency office, or the frown of the party over what it considered sheer indulgence, or the wavering, frantic spirit of the country.

It was more recent, nearer by. It was more to do with bone and muscle and blood, and the blood's own blood and will, the soul. These were tired. These needed mending and pulling firm. She was seeing her home as a field of yams needing splints: torn stems, weariness, weights that slowly exposed the nucleus; splints for broken furniture legs, for sagging curtains.

That's when she said it. "Drumblair, dear, you know you are getting old."

"But Drumblair has always been old," I observed.

"Um," she said dreamily, the way she said it when I asked for Daffy the duck after eating her, unwittingly, for lunch; the way she said it when Wog had left for his last car ride to the vet.

And from then on that "Um" was like a distant drum roll announcing the fate of our dear house.

She was pulling the afternoon flat like tracing paper on which she would copy the details she needed. And so she continued to tidy and straighten the house.

It was September 19, 1961, the day of the referendum. If Pardi lost, he would have to re-examine his role in Jamaica's future; would he resign, or call an early election to ensure a vote of confidence from the electorate, a mandate to proceed? So much was on the line for him.

It was as though an examination, with all its preparation and endeavour, were over. Now people were quietly marking, finger after finger stained by the red voting ink which blued on brown skin but settled like blood on Mardi's own as she fidgeted throughout the day.

Dip your finger in the voting ink,
And Manley sure to win.

It was a day of hours in which her world stood still and she was left with only herself. There was never a need to have an opinion on election day... it was either too late or too presumptuous.

A truck delivered an order of assorted drinks for the evening, and left it stacked in boxes out by the gate. The drinks were not even missed till the following morning, and then only because they were found.

The night of the referendum defeat felt somehow threadbare to Pardi. By comparison to other election nights it was thin. There were fewer people in the house. Because of this the announcements from the radio were louder, and echoed mercilessly, as though they were hammering themselves into the Drumblair walls as well as his head. The early good news of urban support had dissolved with the rural results. No, the votes came rumbling in from the hills, from the plains east and west. "No, Federandum, no."

He felt vulnerable. He cocked his head at a memory: his court days. A policeman hitched a ride beside him in the car. He was late for court, and a comrade hailed him from the side of the road, making him look back at a corner, and the Humber scrambled over the bank and seemed to fly... my word! he thought, and his heart jerked. He started to fall, and remembered from his high-jump that the key to all falls is to keep relaxed, and he willed his limbs to land gently, no matter what the impact.

They fell, the horrified officer braced against misfortune and Pardi quietly calculating their chances as they landed in the riverbed below and the car hesitated, and then rolled over to try the landscape from a new perspective.

"I have to get to court," said the barrister, as he scrambled through the window and reached back for his leather satchel, which lay incongruously in the basin of the car's roof. The policeman also survived. He climbed out, following the driver up the side of the ravine towards the astonished comrade whose greeting had caused the distraction. The funny thing was, Pardi never felt his considerable bruises till later.

He was surprised now that his heart wasn't broken.

He merely wished to concede and be done. It was over. The people decided. One did one's best, but one must be satisfied with the will of democracy.

The stalwarts were in the house, bandaging their hearts with the hope of a miracle, the brief announcements of favourable boxes, the possibility of fraud, or the sometimes conflicting results between constituencies and the popular vote.

He wasn't concerned with any of that. It was over.

Then my father arrived. He wore a soft, rumpled short-sleeved shirt, auspicious only because it was worn that day. His pens had tired the pocket. His hair appeared to have freed itself from the strong resolve of its waves, making his entry seem a little frantic.

Mardi knew he was looking for his father, always looking for Dad. He stared at her as though only reading a direction. Dad was upstairs.

Sons and mothers indeed, she thought; so much for Dr. Freud. It is his father he loves!

Michael double-stepped the stairs, then slowed as he listened for the sound of his father. Pardi was in the bedroom, the room of his convalescence, where he was not compelled to see the piles of newspapers chronicling his repeated purposes, his imminent defeat. He was in the middle of the room, and suddenly stooped. He looked at his son with neither disappointment nor blame, without excuse and without thanks. It was an implicit comradeship. They had lost the war together.

Michael had been there before—in a different room. It had been on the back veranda, where his father held his meetings. It was 1944 and Pardi had just lost his seat. Michael had felt compelled to come home. He had hitchhiked, then scrounged an airfare from half a world away where he was in Montreal in the Royal Air Force on the last demands of the Second World War. He had witnessed his first heartbreak of public life then, and now he had come with only one instinct: to catch his falling father. But he was faced with nothing more than the older man's phlegmatic resignation. Michael tried to remember which poet had said a heart learns to break better each time. Maybe a heart can break only once, he thought.

Mardi called up from the tiled acoustics at the bottom of the stairs, "Better come to the phone, my dear," and the sound of her voice was alarming and clear, and sharp enough to break through the concentration of any despair.

Pardi automatically followed her voice to the phone downstairs.

"I am finished," his son heard him say. "I don't want to go on. There is nothing to go on for... the people have spoken, they've rejected it, they've rejected me."

Michael would remember the words forever.

Later, he couldn't remember whether it was that night or afterwards, maybe the following day, that the party persuaded his father to go on. Only you can lead us back from this catastrophe, they said; we are sorry you lost, but you cannot leave us now.

And even if he shouldn't have, he stayed.

I can still see Pardi at the head of the table, in front of the Drumblair clock, his being supported by one elbow where it rested in the cup of a hand whose index finger formed a thoughtful axis along his cheek. Only his eyes stirred, their grey rings somehow indifferent, as they followed the small scorchings of sound that outlasted the announcements from the old radio.

The large federal flag Mardi had painted was neatly folded like an ended life on the table in front of him. The blue had been burnt by the sunlight, and only the white seemed intact, where the foam of the waves had no paint. The strings from the edges were frayed and filthy.

I was fourteen, old enough to recognize a watershed in our lives if not in history.

I hugged him. He stroked my long hair firmly, as if it belonged to a horse he was settling. He always liked my hair long.

"So we lost," he said matter-of-factly, and released me. He picked up the flag with concern, as though he had somehow failed the spirit of his wife, and unfolded it so we both saw the cracked sun. He wrapped it around me like a sarong and smiled, and then arranged it like a shawl over my shoulders and pulled me to him.

"*Was it weakness of intellect birdie, I cried?*" he muttered rather than sang in amused self-deprecation.

"*Or an extra-tough worm,*" I improvised the words as, leaning back, I tried to read him.

"Never, never forget this flag," his eyes implored; and although he said it incidentally, as if it were an eye appointment I must keep, he watched me like a man who throws a stone into the river and waits to see how wide the circle of the ripple will extend.

12

THE GATE

"ONE FROM TEN leaves nothing", observed Eric Williams when he heard the result of Jamaica's referendum. At midnight on the last day of May the following year, the West Indian Federation, like an obliging terminal patient, officially ceased to exist. There were in fact two electoral defeats in short succession. In my memory they have merged into an inseparable blur of family disappointment, except for a few defining features. If I remember the first, the referendum, for the federal flag, I remember the general election that followed, for little more than a slogan and the improbable berth of a Russian ship in a Jamaican harbour.

This national general election, not due constitutionally until 1964, Pardi called two years early to establish who should lead Jamaica into independence. After the "no" vote of the referendum, Pardi felt he needed an immediate mandate if he was to proceed.

"The Man with the Plan" went the slogan, as if to assure Jamaica that, after all was said and done, it was he who had brought them this far. The slogan centred on Pardi, as he symbolized the party and its leadership, but also on the head in which great plans were hatched, even if they could not be immediately fathomed. He was standing on his reputation as a leader and a visionary.

An independent country needs a man who can lead,
A man with a plan that is bound to succeed.

So went the new party song, which was available on a 45 r.p.m. record.

Pardi's face, in a rare moment of looking benign, approachable and benevolent, smiled down at comrades from a sepia photograph that adorned posters and pamphlets. It even appeared on ladies' fans, held by glued-on Popsicle sticks, so that the owners wafted their leader to and fro as they listened to all the compelling reasons why the architect of independence should be our first prime minister of independence .

Meanwhile, the JLP, who had successfully wrested Jamaica from what they portrayed as the dangerous jaws of federation, responded by calling themselves "The Party with the Programme".

Pardi had responded to the new reality and his comrades' insistence that he stay. He narrowed his view to the immediate future, and trimmed the panorama of his goals. It was not difficult for him as a Jamaican to be whole-hearted about independence; it was what his political work had been about. His disappointment over federation was soon overwhelmed by the momentum of the new campaign, and the practical details of establishing Jamaica's new constitution.

Mardi had developed a regular route which the car learned by heart. Turn left at the Drumblair gate, a quick charge to the fork at the end of Old Church Road, where both the car and Mardi seemed to squint their eyes shut, either to ignore the stop sign and blind corner to the right, or like a child bracing itself for a crash. Then an aggressive shaking and bumping through the familiar intestine, the mud-bed of the gully, and a scramble up the other side to make a sharp left, opposite the tobacco factory, onto Annette Crescent.

By now the engine had lost some momentum, and both Mardi and the car seemed to bow their heads like horses as she commanded the gas pedal with her long, thin foot; in the surge that followed, as her head snapped back, she would always wonder who this Annette was after whom the road was named—why Annette? Past the soft waist of Annette's crescent, bearing left up the straight stretch of Washington Drive, named for her husband's middle name. So she thought of it as her husband's road, which began with a push uphill, like all good journeys.

After another corner, she sped through a low sweep between tasteless cement bungalows saved from pretentiousness by lack of sufficient finances; she saw a certain irony in the subdivided plots of what had been their kingdom, now sold to the encroaching middle classes that her husband's politics had to a large extent created. She slowed at the loose gravel strewn around the paraphernalia of construction, and swung sharp left up a steep driveway. This was their lot, number four Washington Drive, which they had saved for themselves next to Ebony Hill, my father's home.

Mardi was building a house. I was not sure why, for Drumblair was very much there, and the rest of the family seemed only vaguely aware of the project—it was a "just in case" sort of house. "It's just a plain little cement box, really," Mardi would explain fondly and sympathetically, the way she

would pat a mongrel. Thelma would wander over with lemon-
ade or a gin and tonic for Mardi, depending on the time of
day. Her backyard became the province of the workmen,
who had built a shack on what they felt was the common
border, there being no fence, stationing themselves strategi-
cally nearer to Ebony Hill with its water pipes and the fridge
in its kitchen.

Thelma coped with good humour, but Mardi wondered
if she imagined in her daughter-in-law an increasing unhappiness, a desperation in those eyes that never smiled in a
smiling face, that seemed about to impart some secret sadness, but never did. It was as if Thelma had suspended her
life in a nervous hammock of carefully interwoven laughter
and gaiety. She swung in this safety net, soothed and cradled, for the time being safe from either painful memories
or subsequent insight.

Mardi would meet the architect. He was charged with
making the house cost as little as possible, and designing it
without corridors.

You couldn't say they chose the site. It had been self-
evident years ago, when Drumblair was whole; it was behind
the house, across the gully, in that wilderness of seymour
grass on the brow of the only slope, so that Drumblair
could, if it needed assurance, reach behind and touch the
spot like a back pocket. Here the evolving new house faced
the unseen town of Four Roads, whose presence was
nonetheless felt through the ceaselessly pounding heart of
its sound systems.

Rising behind it was a very different view of the hills
than that from Drumblair's windows. I don't know why, but
from here one tended to notice the nearer hills, although it
was not a new range. They seemed more alive. Though their

antlike activity was distant, it gave them a sense of immediacy. These were foothills, greener, brighter, closer, with an impoverished lifestyle strewn randomly up the slopes like the elements in a child's painting. Mardi thought them comforting, for though they were more exact, she found them less exhausting. Beyond were those sterner mountains, the blue-black ones of her original cosmos, like dour chiefs with whom vision dares not trifle.

Mardi was fond of the architect. He had recently fallen on his head from the considerable height of one of a cluster of modestly high-rise apartment blocks he was building. What was almost a tragedy turned out to be his turning-point. This slow-speaking champion of local arts, whose eyes and words had only drifted longingly after the things that captured his heart, had regained consciousness with new resolve. He changed his English wife for a Jamaican love, and his role of aficionado for that of artist. Mardi couldn't help thinking of Leslie Clerk, who in late middle age had decided that he was in fact a sculptor.

The architect's genuine affection for the sculptress and her husband may have somewhat mellowed the frustration he must have felt as a designer. The house was like a grave or a crib—it was hard to decide which. It was not so much its smallness as its confounding way of turning in upon itself. Drumblair was a creation of height and depth, a place that travelled outwards from itself, a place of more openings than closings. A place an outsider could see but not fully understand.

This was not such a place.

Mardi snapped shut each idea as he opened it. No doubt she wanted to be practical, but behind this lay a profound need to be matter-of-fact, a need not to dream dreams or, by softening corners or lines, create hope; it was as though she was reducing her world to Methodist simplicity to provide her spirit with the most arduous challenge.

The house was really just five rooms surrounding a long, unfulfilled space. Usually one could envisage a room long before it was finished, but when the workmen were building this, laying its tiles and installing its electrical needs—even when it was painted—the area only presented itself as a space. It came from nowhere, and seemed to have nowhere to go; it simply stood there and waited. On one side were two square bedrooms with an obligatory bathroom between, which all converged on a common exit. On the other side were a third room with neither a door nor a function, a kitchen and a smaller oblong room for staff whose only entrance was from the back.

As if to allow later correction of an error he could not yet define, or perhaps to accommodate the supposed probability of a woman changing her mind, the architect reinforced the low flat roof so that one day, if the need arose, they could add a second floor.

He must have been relieved when Mardi arrived one afternoon and tentatively announced that she wanted a patio.

"Only a very, very narrow little square of a patio, here between the two front rooms and a step lower, safely between these walls, and some sliding doors here to separate it from that long room...." She was indicating the mouth of the space. "Not a veranda, just a patio."

This was the single concession she made, the only time she breached the limits of her own austerity.

"We will lift up our eyes to the hills from whence cometh our help...." she intoned, raising her hands towards the

unsuspecting range to predict the expected benediction...
"our help cometh from there!" And she stood between the
raw cement walls girlishly balanced on a plank that lifted
itself across the mud towards a wide almond tree whose ample
leaves were now covered in cement dust.

Pardi would drive over to this site from another project.
The government was renovating a charming old wooden
house which was called Vale Royal. It had been decided that
with the advent of independence Jamaica would need an
official residence for prime ministers, and this had been chosen to be the house.

I understood that after the election on April 10, 1962,
if Pardi won, this would be our new home. There I was
promised walk-in closets and a room at the top of the house
where there was an attic window, if I wished, and the use of
a swimming pool with blue water and a modern filter system. If Pardi lost, well—Mardi and Pardi would tilt their
heads and lift their brows in a certain way, and yet not say
anything, as they sheepishly avoided the powerful indifference of Drumblair.

As for Drumblair, it bellowed its orders in the slam of a
door or the insistent rattling of a windowpane in the seasonal rains. It became like an old uncle in a sick-bed, muttering with unrelenting bitterness, a bile fierce enough to
keep him alive, an unforgiveness that sat without words, without repentance, in a once-a-day, he-needs-to-get-air chair,
causing the nieces to shake their heads in despair and whisper, "He's senile, it is sad...," and causing the lady of swift
decisions to say, "Drumblair, dear, you know you are getting
old."

I always blamed it on the Russian ship. Pardi lost.

"I haven't the energy," Pardi answered listlessly when, two days after the election, Mardi suggested that they move to Regardless. That was the name given to the just-in-case house. On the day she asked me, "Ray, dear, you are the poet...what shall we name the house?" I was planning to see the English comedy "Carry On Regardless". Considering the family's ups and downs, the title seemed an appropriate name to have. She nodded once, briefly, as though to swallow it, and by my next visit to the house the name "Regardless" was inscribed on a plaque at the gate in a facsimile of Mardi's curling handwriting.

Since this last electoral defeat, Mardi noticed that Pardi's voice was somehow thicker, giving the impression of fallibility. Maybe it was all the public speaking; she held to the thought hopefully, but released it as she faced his despair. It was not the effort of moving house that he dreaded, but the effort of moving sadness. He felt he could manage no more, despite her knocking at his windows. He was the wounded, shipwrecked flotsam of a finished day.

Her voice drifted in through his distraction and out again, extracting from him only this brief information: "I haven't the energy." He was pondering a single Russian ship. It had steamed into the harbour on polling day, soon enough to spur opposition propaganda and general panic, too late for the PNP to prevent the damage. The length and breadth of Jamaica was flooded with the rumour of a Communist takeover. This was not in itself the cause of the tide; by then public feeling had decided their fate. But it was a brief outline of foam on the last wave, that moment of curling surf which, before it fades, defines the legacy of a wave. It was the gesture of finesse by which future generations would remember the times.

Mardi could not sit for long in the blank aftermath of the electoral defeat. This second defeat was the irrevocable one. It was no use hearing that he had nearly pulled it off, that he had lost by less than .8 per cent of the popular vote, as Michael kept reminding her, "*and* after the federal defeat, *and* in a second term." She hated these borderline outcomes that seemed to weaken the truth.

There was no point pondering on how close they had come, or dwelling on the vagaries of fortune. The election was over, that was that. They had worked for independence and Jamaica would officially achieve that in another four months. Now they must gather up the new reality the way you gathered up the remains of anything—noting what was possible and what was not, accepting that tomorrow was another day and that when you reached it you started again, from scratch, if necessary.

In times of crisis Mardi, whose abiding sin Douglas always said was her sentimentality, could be surprisingly practical. She lived every day of her life with the rule "Never let the sun go down on your anger." No matter who she had quarrelled with, by the end of the day she would turn up to make amends, or just to forgive, or at least to write a note to be delivered first thing in the morning. And the point of this dictum had less to do with the ruins of the present day than with the need to ensure the advent of the following one, the world's capacity for renewal and the sun's return.

She thought of Regardless. It was ready for occupancy. And knowing that she could not sleep in Drumblair for the last time and know it was the last time, she made her decision.

She must move. She got in the car and left Drumblair.

As she drove, it was the years that moved, not her. She seemed to have been in the same place for a long time, watching the century move silently by, its articulation and life somehow lost on her as though she viewed it from a silent underwater world.

She drove to wherever it was necessary to inform those who must help her move that day. Miss Boyd and her friend John Burrow, a mathematics teacher who shared her love of horses, would stay at Drumblair and organize the filling of the trucks. Batiste and Tildy would help her at the other end. She would move into that house; the world would think it a hard and poky little place, but she knew she would clothe it with her dreams; it was the place where she would rejoin the years and rejoin the road. Pardi would be out all day clearing out his office. She would call him when everything was ready, for he had that dead still mood, like a settled shrub you had to transplant with its earth.

She sent for only those things that would fit in the small house. The grand piano went to the music school, but the large hanging cupboards, the bulky chests of drawers, the side tables and high tables and low tables, the years of Drumblair's silent and stubborn service, went with the ungladness of life's orphans to the ready hands of those whose fortune it was to be nearby.

Their desks, and their beds and mine, all came; and his bureau and hers, the latter being part of a unique set of metal bedroom furniture all of which came. And the better fridge and stove, and a bed and dresser for Tildy, and the veranda chairs to face the hills. All the household things carefully packed by Miss Boyd, all the pictures and sculptures and ceramics—they all came, in swaddlings of blankets and boxes.

And for "the space" there were the dining table and chairs, with the large old buffet and its loyal clock, and along the side the huge library of bookshelves over cupboards that held the family photographs and bulbs and glue and Christmas tree lights. These formed a square at one end. And at the other end, forming a second square, went the pretty, primly uncomfortable Drumblair recliner, the seat of which Miss Boyd had recently changed from its lumpy cotton filling to a modern sponge that defied her seams and seemed to pull faces at guests; the Queen Anne chairs and two lovely square wicker seats; Mike the poet's gift of leather hassocks from a Hausa tribe, and Pardi's Spanish chair; and one modern highbacked upholstered thing with a footstool that had been a gift to Mardi from a constituency group, and which she protected loyally from the scorn of its surroundings.

Even whole shrubs and young trees, and a dead lignum vitae trunk with orchids growing on it, they all came, and between Batiste, Zethilda and Mardi everything was settled into place, the pictures on the walls, the clothes in the cupboards, each piece of furniture, each plant in its new bed, smoothly and silently as though not to wake them.

By three that afternoon Mardi had buried the past and put the present in place. The new house was already learning how to dream. The bright green hills seemed suddenly self-conscious as they played to their new audience. Batiste was dragging the hose around his fledgling garden and encouraging the transplanted blooms to accept their fate as philosophically as he had. Zethilda, changed into a fresh blue uniform and with a bold geometric headscarf holding in her disbelief at such a wilful morning, was nudging the skins off the potatoes and vegetables with an accustomed articulation of her wrists, and Mardi got on the phone to Pardi:

"Pass by the little house, dear...I want us to plant a tree."

"I want us to plant a tree," she had said in her light, hopeful voice, as though nothing at all had happened, and one could just pass by anywhere in a world where being casual was still possible, and of all things on earth, of all the most noble, or hopeful, or life-affirming that she could pick at such a dead time, she chooses to plant a tree!

He stood at the door of Regardless, and for the first time he realized that the front was the back of the house, and the back facing the hills was the front. There was his place at the table, there were his books on the shelves; he would eat and read and rest and love and grieve right there in the familiar shapes before him.

"Nothing bad has happened to me here," he thought, and he moved into the world of his wife feeling as he had felt when his Aunt Ellie had taken him in after the war in England. He could hear the clumping sounds of utensils returning to drawers in the kitchen, and the hissy sound of water over the sink, and there was his stereo next to his chair and his records a little far away, where she'd put them against the wall of what he now saw was his dining-room, and the speakers a little too near. Never mind. What was far here would have been near in Drumblair; he must remember that. It was like living in a smaller country.

She watched him gingerly approach the chair as if he were afraid to slip on the unfamiliar tiles, and he sat down in silence. He reached for the cabinet that held the turntable, stroked it as if to make sure it was real and, reassured, patted it, and then gave himself up to his chair. His glasses were so filmy that she didn't see when his eyes closed, but he was there for a very long time without a movement, just a settling in, till he seemed more red leather than man, and the skin on his head peeped vulnerably through the thin, tired separations of hair. His arms in their red shirt-sleeves slumped trustingly. For a moment it crossed her mind to wonder whether he was held by the hand of life or of death; then he lifted his arms from their despondency and he said:

"I think I rather like this house."

※

Pardi watched Drumblair being torn down. He watched from the opposite side of the gully, from the irrevocable distance of migration. He stood on the verge of the sloping lawn at his new home and looked at the shingled roof that had covered so many years of his life. Now it looked as though it had been pecked by vultures, and there were dark strips where boards were missing. Then there was the drone of a bulldozer, and a shoulder was torn from the body of the house, and then a whole side crumbled.

He did not attempt to avert his gaze. It was no more torture to watch a thing than to know it. This thing he had done, this act of betrayal, had been done weeks before.

"The National Trust has asked me not to destroy the house," said the young entrepreneur who had purchased Drumblair. The doubt in his face was asking for either a thou-shalt-not commandment, or at least absolution. "They want to save it as a historic building."

"Save *what?*" asked Pardi. "Rubbish. There's nothing to save. Anyway, the house has termites. Just tear it down."

Well, if it has termites, shrugged the developer, and he comfortably proceeded to clear the way for his real-estate fortune. After all, he had been prepared to make the financial sacrifice.

Pardi gave witness. It was only a house, for God's sake, a

wood and concrete thing that you rebuild if it blows away, that you replace if it's gutted by fire.

He had built more than that, and how it had fallen! Not shingle by shingle or plank by plank; it had gone in the time it took to have dinner. A lifetime of commitment, simply gone. Like Roxborough, his first home; the house he was born in. Gone when he was only six. He was there and then he wasn't. It simply ceased to exist.

Roxborough, on a property near Mandeville in Manchester at the centre of the island, had been owned by his father, Thomas Albert Manley. Then his father had died and they had moved to Grandfather Shearer's property at Belmont. Although he knew in his child's heart that his father had gone for good, for a long time he waited to go home to Roxborough. After experience distilled its lessons from the loss and the change, one plain truth remained: houses are transient things and you cannot put your faith in them.

But this time he would watch the old boards tumbling down, and the dust of so many years rising up as though flying from blasphemy.

When the oak tree broke at the back of the house, behind the rubbled veranda, for a moment he squeezed his eyes shut, expecting that there would be blood. But the cracking noise was so bone-dry, so splitting in splinters, that he knew it to be a dry death.

And when it was all done, when Drumblair had all come down without a battle, Pardi could see through its pyre of mangled boards and tossed shingles, the broad, mocking grin flashing off the glass doors of the Gaggle's bungalow, and he was not surprised to see that it had survived us on Old Church Road.

Later on, when the story had become family lore, Mardi would say that there had been a family conference, that everyone had said, "Move." Maybe the sudden shift of gears, the sheer fury of her actions that day, made her believe that she must have had a family mandate. But nobody in the family had known, save her.

For a long time I blamed Mardi for building Regardless and therefore plotting Drumblair's demise. I do not remember leaving. I somehow postponed my grief, diverted from the loss by adolescence. Still, for a long time I avoided looking across to the old pasture and the void of Drumblair's ruin.

For me the new house was simply a stage set in my metamorphosis. Whenever I was there, and not next door at my father's house, I had the use of Pardi's room. Mardi had shortened his bureau by two drawers for fear it might overwhelm its surroundings, logic Pardi accepted but never understood as he coped with the overstuffed remaining four. The grey aluminum louvers blocked out the mornings in a way Drumblair never could, so I slept later, and thought this sophisticated. Being young, I liked the modernity of the house and found the old furniture incongruous, even mildly embarrassing in the presence of my friends.

Whatever this new life was, it seemed not to extend from the past but to spring from my own transformation as I entered the parentheses of puberty. Life was full of distractions, of ways of living and being that beckoned me from both an emergence within me and a newness without.

It's strange but, although it wasn't a finale, just an incident during that fluctuating time, when I try to conjure up a last memory of Drumblair it's always the night after the performance of *The Mikado* before the two consecutive electoral defeats. When the show was over, we all trooped back to Drumblair, where the lawn looked like a fairyland. I think it was probably the only time the place got dressed up in my honour. The huge spotlights in the oak trees borrowed some green light with which to diffuse the obvious. I was fourteen years old and my school had come to me, clattered up the driveway in the blue school bus and staff members' cars and spilled out over the wide lawn.

Concealed by an alamander bush, I was kissed by a boy from Aruba who was strong and stocky and bright, and who had always disturbed me. It was such a silent, commanding anointment, and gave me a curious, secret strength afterwards. I became one who had been kissed; the rest of me seemed to grow from that moment. That evening I was Drumblair's debutante.

I would not see the giver of that first kiss again, nor would I return to Knox College, my boarding-school, but I did not know then how many bends in my road I was approaching.

Somewhere at the university, Douglas raged. He had refused the gift of a pocket of Drumblair land, assuming his first-born right to a home whose welcome and sanctuary had always been postponed. His fury had nothing to do with greed or acquisition; it was a longing of his soul for home, a deal he had made with time when the promise that child-hood held was broken. And it was on this point that his life became unforgiving.

As far as Michael was concerned, this move was only logical, and he was perplexed by the surprise and range of emotions it engendered. Drumblair had to be sold, for his father was in debt. The new house had been built, he thought, for that reason. He had never asked to have this explained to him; he didn't need to. He was seldom nostalgic, for life was a set of circumstances that he lived fully, in the now. Now was what was here. He remembered and honoured the past but never missed it, refusing to romanticize its relevance.

He was simply glad to have his parents next door.

What was aching his heart was the small margin of his father's defeat, and the irony that his country would be led into independence by anyone but Norman Manley. He knew of no other colonial territory of that time where the man who led the fight for independence was not the acknowledged leader of the emerging nation, the runaway victor of its first election; Ghana's Nkrumah, Nigeria's Azikiwi, India's Nehru—the names would hammer in his head.

And Mardi had in a way made her peace, said her goodbye. The night before she left Drumblair, when she did not even know she was leaving, she chose a book of sheet music from inside the piano seat, then arranged it before her and haltingly played Beethoven's "Moonlight Sonata". She was honouring Drumblair, perpetuating its name in the repeating drifts of moonlight as they pose on a leaf until the wind moves; she was comforting Drumblair, the great heart that had kept time for her, for Norman, for the children. Drumblair had kept them safe in themselves.

"Don't look back," Ellie Swithenbank had said to Mardi as she left England for the last time in her mother's life, for Mardi had stopped at the gate, suddenly aware that she might never again see the dear figure seated in the rocker, watching the birds feeding on the windowsill where she always left bread.

No use to say goodbye, she seemed to say. Parting was just the marking of a book's page to which one would return. The story was the years they had all shared. The gate might be shut, but never locked against memory.

She fumbled a little each time she turned a page of music, and she made many mistakes, for she was rusty on the piano. But she went on playing the piece over and over till the beginning slid through the end, knowing that no journey could take her beyond the landscape this house and her family had painted with their lives. The edge of night surrounded her, but like the last line of each turning page it sheltered the music. She knew that boundaries do not kill, they just contain.

For a moment she stopped on a note, lifted her head and looked all around the room. There were tears in her eyes, for she thought she saw the house looking back at her.

PART TWO

13

"Each
Frustrate
Ghost"

It was Pardi's theory that a man knows when he owns his last dog. He does not know the date of his death, but he recognizes the dog who will grieve him.

When Uhuru came, Pardi knew.

Uhuru was a near-perfect Doberman, except that he was small for a male. He had those fierce black eyes whose menace is fixed in the obscurity of their darkness. His expression came from a carefully bred assumption that the world was to be mistrusted.

Zethilda swore he was colour-prejudiced, as he always greeted her with furious barking. To make matters worse, he embraced the diminutive figure of the comparatively fair Miss Boyd who now came only twice a week, and bestowed upon her lavish, overwhelming kisses. Pardi assured Zethilda that her theory was flawed, since he was coloured and Uhuru never barked at him. And anyway, Mardi pointed out, Uhuru himself was black.

Uhuru would bring gifts to Pardi: a shoe, a lizard, a bone and, up at Nomdmi, where he roamed his freedom joyously, a bird or a pine cone, or the seeds of roseapples, which he laid at Pardi's feet for approval.

He was highly strung and, according to Mardi and Pardi, highly intelligent—qualities which Mardi felt were related. He was expected to be the perfect watchdog. Despite the protest of Mardi's friend John, a man who truly loved and understood most animals, at the stipulated age Uhuru was taken to a dog-training school. There the perplexed dog spent six weeks locked in a coffin-like box, let out only for the few hours of his training. This was supposed to make him ferocious, but he returned home somewhat dispirited instead, and insisted on sleeping in the bathtub at first where he appeared to find the familiarity of enclosure comforting.

Pardi gave him his name. Uhuru was an African word for freedom. In a house where more and more he felt his wife inventing his surroundings, Pardi came to rely on Uhuru as a touchstone by which to measure life's spontaneity.

The intimacy of tragedy came to Pardi when the wake of his political defeats had subsided. Disaster is epic, grief is ceremonious; both have their own momentum. But real life stretched on after that, he discovered. Only then were elections really lost or houses gone—in the dead calm of afterwards, when neither tears nor loss nor the shock of destruction could move one.

Jamaica's birthday had come and gone. It was the sixth of August, 1962. Independence Day each year still leaves me with a feeling of sadness. Although the family attended all the public functions, it felt like somebody else's party. This was the realization of a dream for which Pardi had struggled for a quarter century, and it was incomprehensible to me that he should be only peripheral.

It was a further irony that the celebrations took place in a new national stadium which Pardi had insisted be built for the new nation despite loud and widespread opposition as the project was felt to be unnecessary and costly. It was some consolation that over the years there was always applause when he entered that stadium, even at times of great party unpopularity when he might be booed anywhere else by the same people. This was particularly poignant at boxing events which were held there, when the three Manley men attended, Douglas at ringside as a judge, Michael cheering a protégé, and Pardi watching raptly after his customary welcome.

As national leaders, both Bustamante and Pardi were offered knighthoods at Jamaica's independence. Busta accepted his, Pardi did not; within the context of his life, an honour from Westminster was unthinkable. But the title "Sir Alexander" came as an affirmation to the Labourites, and the absence of an official reward, for whatever reason, was subtly undermining and disheartening to the comrades, although by now in 1964 Bustamante was less in the public eye, as ill health had placed him in a state of semi-retirement. A political era was ending.

Pardi returned to Duke Street, the hub of Jamaican legal activity, where he rented a small office and offered his services as a consultant. But among the things he had forgotten about the law over a decade was the sheer boredom induced by the job. He had re-entered what was for him an arid plane. Many of the island's politicians were lawyers, and he wondered if the tedium of the first profession was at the root of this secondary ambition.

The only person he employed was a wise and competent secretary who sensed his lack of enthusiasm and tried to buoy him up with her warmth and valour, as if to say, life's like that but we must make the best of it.

"There is nothing in life less creative than opposition" was Mardi's new truism. She was frustrated by Pardi's decision to remain in politics. She had wanted him to make a clean break and get on with the rest of his life. She suggested alternatives. He ignored them. Losing the election did not alter his motive or purpose.

Every weekday afternoon Pardi went to Parliament. The gazetted records of debate chronicled a steady stream of accusation and invective at him, and there were times when he felt that the leader of what was, in the light of our dominion status, still Her Majesty's loyal opposition was more a recipient of abuse than a voice of constructive criticism. No matter what difficulty the government faced in this formative time of early independence, it was less concerned with implicating a history of colonial rule than with blaming the stewards of the previous government, and particularly, Pardi.

At first his life was simply a question of discipline. Sometimes just keeping faith in his own usefulness was his greatest challenge. He found that his return home in the evening had become like his nights in the trenches during the war, when one laid low to survive, and survived because one had to. And as in the war, he kept with him the things he considered essential to his soul, only now he carried them in his mind rather than in a knapsack: his program for an evening of music, his return to a good book, the plans for a piece of furniture he was working on at Nomdmi.

When he drove through the streets of Kingston on his way to Parliament or his law practice—even on his drives up to Nomdmi, when many of those walking the steep hill along the way hurled messages that he barely made out, as his hearing had definitely worsened—he could see that little of his country's progress, of its prosperity, had reached the people he most cared about, those who needed it most. The failure gave him a dull, disappointed ache.

By 1964 the landscape had settled at Washington Drive. Pardi and Mardi had lived there for almost two years. Ebony Hill and Regardless encompassed the limited sphere of the family's influence. It was not so much that life had shrunk; its elements were more concentrated, if not more intense. I remember it vividly as a happy time in my own life. For once that I can remember, we had the core of the family all in one place. All to ourselves. It was less wingspan but more bedrock. It was not that we clung together; more that being cocooned provided each of us with the means of a hibernation necessary for renewal.

Michael and Thelma's marriage ended. My brother, Joseph, seven years old, went to live with his mother. Thelma seemed to take a prettiness out of the place when she left, taking her dresses and exotic-smelling bottles, her bony memorabilia of dried branches, flowers and cones, and little else. There was little to take from my father's house, and anyway she was never by nature a taker.

Douglas came to live with us. His marriage had also ended, and Norman and Roy remained with their mother; Douglas got custody of the orchids. He moved into his brother's house, staying in what had been Joseph's room and relocating his orchids next door, on his parents' patio. My uncle's presence was to be a rare gift to me. His mischief and dry humour reminded me of Pardi, of that side of the public man that others failed to see. He became the butt of every joke around the house.

Aunt Muriel now lived in a small cottage at the bottom of Ebony Hill, with her two corgis, Dylan and Gayla. Her driveway faced the gully, and from a studio Mardi had built at the back of Regardless she could see Aunt Muriel's thoughtfully arranged garden of quaint cottage flowers.

I can't remember when Aunt Vera finally left; she remained for a while, becoming the registrar at the Jamaica School of Music after independence. But since her departure remained imminent, Aunt Muriel, who had lived alone at the top of a hill and depended on visits from her elder sister for company, thought of moving to Kingston to be nearer the family. When her small Austin tipped over the side of the mountain road for the second time, its pilot having once again fallen asleep at the wheel, a home was quickly built for her at the bottom of Michael's land.

It was a time when the family was not on show, and had no conjugal appendages. Maybe it was the only time I saw them all relaxed. On its own, the family had a capacity for resilience, a philosophical ability to shrug at what it understood to be inevitable. As a unit, that was its enduring strength.

There was no fence between the two houses. Where the lots met, there was a low retaining wall that edged the garage at Ebony Hill and indicated a border. The grass formed a natural cockscomb as it met at that line. Ebony Hill's was thin and high and lawless, like the eccentric strands of a dishevelled head. The grass of Regardless, though younger, seemed more settled, less parched, probably due to Batiste's careful tending of his now limited world.

Left to ourselves, we kept bumping into the reality of each other. We were not a family who knew the details of each other's lives. Only Douglas and I were any good at small talk. Douglas and I gossiped. Usually, family get-togethers were dinners or meetings on specified subjects that evoked rapt discussion. Even alone with each other on these occasions, we were self-conscious. We were seldom affectionate to each other, but always concerned and interested. News of each other usually came from outsiders, or from myself as a go-between.

Now that we were in close proximity, there were daily surprises.

"Fancy, Doug gets up several times a night to raid the fridge!"

"How do you know that, my dear?" Pardi peered at his wife over the newspaper.

"Ray told me. He prowls around all night. Says he has to keep feeding his ulcer."

Or Douglas, ever mystified by routine, despairing of his mother: "Does she bathe at the same time every goddamn day!" as she shouted from the bathroom when the water disappeared from her tap. Since the water pressure was low, bathing and garden-watering were mutually exclusive activities, and her four o'clock bath always coincided with his drop-around to water his orchids on his way home from the university. It didn't occur to him that this fact also established the fixity of his own routine.

I now lived with my father. I enjoyed my role as woman of the house, although in terms of domestic duty this was little more than a title bestowed on me by Mardi, who was still trying to encourage a closer bond between my father and me. It was to become a pattern: in the troughs between my father's marriages, I would get to know him, feeling for a time, as Mardi put it, as if "I had my daddy all to myself." We did become close, which was in some ways the start of a friendship, and in others the beginning of a war.

Although I lived at Ebony Hill, I wandered conveniently between the two houses. At Ebony Hill my freedom was usually unlimited, as my father was seldom at home and Douglas was either indifferent or a good sport. I could play Ben E. King as loud as I liked, and we could all smoke. Also I was spared the embarrassment of Pardi's oddly formal, hands-in-pockets interrogations of my friends. "And what do *you* think of television, young man?" he would ask.

As leader of the opposition, Pardi had received a smart twenty-seven-inch television set, a cabinet with doors. At least one could shut them, Mardi had remarked when it arrived. It was watched avidly but suspiciously by Pardi and Zethilda. Pardi's government had established the state-owned national radio station, the Jamaica Broadcasting Corporation in 1957. It was Pardi's brainchild, conceived to reflect Jamaican culture, promote public education and give Jamaicans their own voice. He intended it to be politically independent. Since independence the station ran a television service, and Pardi worried about its influence on the island. He turned up the volume full blast and considered the programming. He was concerned about its foreign content, and was wary of the political motivation behind the local material, much of which would be influenced by the opposing party who had placed their dynamic young minister of Culture and Development as head of its statutory board. Zethilda's objections were more fundamental: she considered all television depictions a giant hoax.

Batiste, on the few occasions when he peered in from the garage, was unable to stop laughing at the display, hailing whatever was on the screen with "Lard, what a poppy show!"

Mardi's attention to television never lasted longer than a few minutes because, according to Pardi, "she won't sit still long enough." She would have ignored its influence had she not been questioning her younger grandchildren one day about the Bible, among many other topics, in an effort to keep them quiet and see what they knew.

"Where was the garden of Eden?" she asked Joseph and Roy.

Blank silence.

"Well, who was Adam?"

Both together: "The son of Pa Cartwright!"

Like Pardi, she began to take a dim view of the new arrival.

If Mardi was content to have the whole family together and on its own, she made no smug show of it, settling naturally into matriarchal responsibility over her nest. She was saddened by the unhappiness the demise of her sons' marriages had caused them, but she was never one to fear change, and anyway the tension of both situations had been gruelling. But she liked these two women no less than before, and continued to relate to them as she always had, separate from their husbands.

"I am not a 'couple' person," she would say, extricating the person like a segment from an orange, just as she offered herself individually to her friendships.

As for Pardi, he probably missed the presence of his daughters-in-law who he found vivacious and provocative; they flirted with him. They would have seemed so unlike the stern sisters with whom he grew up, who had firmly drawn a veil over the potential of sexual difference. He liked the surprise of a woman's otherness which he had just discovered in Mardi, like a hitherto unknown flower blooming in his path.

Pardi was saddened by the wrecks of his sons' marriages. His own marriage was now a long partnership, one in which each had slowly moved back into the room of the self. Although there were seldom any new details and one knew the phrases and expressions almost without having to listen or see, there was comfort in the knowledge that what had once been the vital sketching of outline had long since become a familiar portrait in one's periphery, a fellow column holding up the logic of one's world.

Worn down by a combination of my endless carping and the stress of their political problems, my grandparents' resistance gave way during my summer holiday after *The Mikado*. I was allowed to remain in Kingston and was accepted as a day student at St. Andrew High School, an old and well-respected girls' school whose kindergarten I had attended.

By the time I left boarding-school, Miss Boyd's great-niece, Juanita, had married and moved to America, and her brother, Milton, was working towards a place in university. We kept in touch, but for the time being our lives had diverged, creating a void for me. This was filled by the discovery of two friends, Lem and Kik, whom I met at my new school. They were like yin and yang—opposites pulling me two different ways—but in my case no balance was achieved.

Lem was solid in build and nature, energetic, headstrong and opinionated, equal to any thought that was based on fact; practical, loyal and loving; and in trap and skeet shooting, a champion shot. She was a born conservative. She was from one of Jamaica's wealthiest families, and gave me a glimpse of an opulence I had never imagined; I remember being particularly struck by an electrical device that did nothing but produce ice. Lem sat like an example at the desk in front of me on my first day, and so she remained.

Kik was more nebulous, less sure of herself and comfortable only with things that were open to interpretation. Even her face could totally alter, depending on what she wore, how she fixed her hair. She loved art and was talented at drawing, but seemed to lack the resolve of either ambition or self-confidence. She had a knack for living through other people, and a complete disregard for time.

It was curiosity that brought Kik into my life. We were dating the same boy. I invited her home one afternoon so I could vet my competition. We became friends, and dumped the common suitor.

Mardi, who came from a large family, worried about the "only-child syndrome". She also knew from her own childhood that the dynamic of a family left to itself could be an ever-tightening circle. She liked throwing in a diversion and watching everyone regroup.

"It's like putting dry rice in the salt-cellar. Stops the salt grains from sticking together and making a muck," she observed. This process of "unsticking" had begun when Douglas and Michael were boys, and by now we had many adopted grains to show for it.

So Kik, whose parents had been transferred to another island, came to stay with us. She settled in with hardly a ripple. She was an Aquarian, which for Mardi was assurance of two admirable qualities, an empathetic nature and a fondness for the occult. Pardi referred to Kik as the dormouse; coming from a rural childhood, and belonging to a family of nervous and often insomniac early risers, he was bemused by her habit of sleeping till late in the day. But he found her comfort with silence restful.

In what was becoming an increasingly self-conscious relationship between my father and myself, due in part to Mardi's continuing obsession with it, and probably also because our family structure was somewhat unusual, Kik became a mediator between my father and me. While Kik and I were harmonious enablers of Douglas' meandering stream of consciousness, he was in turn good-naturedly indulgent. Sometimes we stole his dinners when we had to feed a friend, and replaced the dish in its customary place over a steaming pot with something as insubstantial as a raw egg that proceeded to poach, or a single green pea. On one occasion we acquired a life-sized poster of a blond pin-up girl from a downtown theatre, and this we attached to the ceiling over his bed with cellophane tape. We watched him late that night after he returned and quietly prepared for bed so as not to wake the household. He lay down on his back and was about to remove his glasses when he spotted the lady above him. He stared at the ceiling for a short while, shrugged, swallowed, closed his eyes, and in a major anticlimax to the event, proceeded to fall asleep with the light still on, his spectacles perched on his nose.

Ours was the middle room along a narrow, windowless corridor whose tiles, though the pattern matched, were in three distinct stages, from faded to bright, marking my father's summer renovations. His last improvement had been a large airy room that looked back over the gully. It was built over the slope of the descending hill, so he had room beneath for a study. I came to realize that Manley buildings spawned studies or studios the way dogs have puppies.

My father had designed a walk-in cupboard and dressing alcove for my room. I was extremely proud of these additions, and in the alcove I hung my pictures of famous ballerinas. Kik impressed Mardi by saving her allowance to buy a tasteful nude from her art teacher, which she hung starkly between my frilly, Slavic dancers. I resisted a prudish urge to draw in the outline of sleeves and a skirt hem; it would not have been "cool".

This had been Michael and Thelma's room, the place where Thelma lay in bed to save Joseph, and our bathroom across the corridor was the one from which I had so often heard the retching of morning sickness. The young house already had its ghosts. The firm thuds of the dancer's determined heels with which Thelma woke us were never totally gone from that place. They were a nagging memory of a time of distress.

I loved the precarious world of my father, with its jazz and boxing, its trade unionists and strikes, its battles for human rights, its struggles against injustice, its good guys and bad guys. And I loved his ability to create a legend out of sport or politics from the wealth of his generous enthusiasms. There was always some cause, some match, some game, some record, that prodded my consciousness up a notch.

My father was never a trivial fan of anything. If he was a fan, he was what he called "a *deep* fan". His was a world of heroes: Joe Louis, George Headley, Jessie Owens, Herb McKenley; the three W's, Harold Laski, Edward R. Murrow, Adlai Stevenson, Fidel Castro, Julius Nyerere, Nat King Cole. It was a world that smelled of stale cigarette smoke and coffee.

In the deep, bumpy Morris chairs there often waited trade unionists, or boxers and their trainers, for my father partially managed a Dixie and a Percy, local fighters whom, because they were basically nice men, he fed with steak and pep talk before each fight, as though either proteins or advice could nurture a killer instinct. I don't remember that either did.

Although I didn't like jazz then, the cool strains of Brubeck or Davis or Coltrane were like a musical score behind the lurchings of my father's life, and seemed to hold the daily script together as he paced the floor in wide circles, talking on a telephone at the end of a super-long cord. This had been installed by a union delegate at the telephone company who found my father's pacing at the end of a short cord too dizzying to watch.

It is strange how life can imitate landscape. Or maybe it was just my own longing for symbol and allegory, for the backdrops that place scenes in context for me. But I saw in the clustering of those two houses a slow and natural shift of my father's life towards politics. As though the proximity of his father made this inevitable, the trade union became closer to the party, and my father became closer to politics.

Pardi named him for the Senate as spokesman on labour affairs when he was forming the new opposition. Michael found this more title than substance; he attached greater significance to his work in the party. I thought "senator" a fine title for my handsome father. As far as I was concerned, it was small consolation after our many disappointments with the advent of independence.

For me, watching Pardi and all his work shrink into the margins of a strange new text, this was a heartbreaking experience; one for which, however illogically, I blamed Jamaica.

Over the intervening years, much of the drifting population of Drumblair had disappeared; the loyalists had gone
off to lick their wounds, the opportunists had crossed the
fence. With the diminished traffic in their lives came a certain peace and a quieter home. There were times when Mardi
sat on the veranda and her inviolate spirit, neither mellowed
nor tamed by age, would risk surfacing to peep out at the
mountains. There was a serene integrity to her life now that
it was partially free of the contortions of social obligation.

Pardi and Mardi seemed to have fewer friends now, with
treasured exceptions. One of these was a young, wiry Australian who taught music at the university, and knew her
subject with the vehemence of one who has had to fight for
it. In the "man's world" of rural Australia, where Pam had
grown up, a woman was expected to practise more useful
skills than music.

Pardi was deeply fond of Pam, who had listened to music
with them from their late Drumblair days. He was delighted
by her academic curiosity, which gave her a tolerance for the
local, unclassical strains. He would look at her for approval
during his new stereo's recitals, and sometimes offer one of
his rare jokes. "Have you ever considered what would happen if cows could fly?" And he waited mischievously at the
edge of what he thought a very risqué supposition, for the
penny (and hopefully nothing else) to drop.

Mardi felt it was good for Pardi to have his own evenings
—even if she invented them. To have interests without her.
He always had had in the past, but now it was up to her to
create them for him, as though he were some magnificent
being of the deep stranded in the shallows, whom she must
rescue, if she could only provide the tug of a great tide.

She tried to string the days smoothly across the week, so they reached the clasp of the weekend neatly and painlessly. The weekends usually took care of themselves. They would arrive at Nomdmi on Friday by two o'clock in the afternoon—the scratchy time according to Mardi, for which she had instituted a daily rest as a remedy. Even up there she sometimes gave him a bit of a prod with a visitor, or the family came for a meal and a game of bridge. They would stay till early Monday morning. In the last few years she had found that Pardi lived for the weekends "up the hill", a journey which she always referred to as "to the mountains".

She often invited Pam. Mardi liked Pam. "She's not fenky, fenky…," she'd explain. When asked what that meant, she'd only lift her arms and let her wrists drop flaccidly. Aunt Muriel, who liked to feel anchored by logic, once remarked that she thought the word came from "fenks", which was melted whale's blubber. And Mardi had decided that "a little crush" in Pardi's life would do him no harm.

Pardi enjoyed an evening with the young Australian. She was bright and sensitive, and had that unapologetic strength in her femininity that his wife had—the feeling of muscle under skin, of a mind in charge of beauty and charm. She had an unusual intellectual understanding of music which equalled her love of the art. And she had the audacity to confront the classics, a "piece of facetyness" common to cultures that have endured colonization, where self-respect longs to reject the traditional and accommodate fresh expression.

But Pardi noticed that Pam came into Regardless more softly nowadays, looking more gently at him, her eyes on sentry watch behind her glow. The last time she came he had seen her in a skirt for the first time, and she had spent the evening awkwardly arranging her knees beneath it. He missed her tomboyish shrug into a chair, and the toss of her chin while she appeared to listen from some Australian field of reminiscence, as if flat on her back in the outback with the stars spitting back at her. He sensed his wife's handiwork.

In fact he sensed Mardi's deft fingers everywhere, and her hegemony soon expanded to include the rest of her family. There were certain phrases she used that the family found very unsettling. "Now let us all be light-hearted," she would say, as though waving a wand for a band of clowns. Or "Now let's see what we can plan today...."

Pardi spent a lot of time trying to avoid this cheer. He missed the acreage of Drumblair, its alternate routes, its many chambers and shadows in which he could lose himself. But he still managed to disappear. One day, in search of cigarettes, which Mardi kept on a shelf in the clothes cupboard, Kik slid open the heavy door and found Pardi crouched among his long, black leather shoes, beneath the hems of his own jackets, which hung from a rail above. His face emerged from some sleeves with a single finger raised to his pursed lips. Kik replied with a similar gesture as she withdrew, taking with her the stolen pack of cigarettes. As she left, the house resounded with Mardi's voice calling, "Noooorrrr... maaaaaaan," from the veranda where his guests for that day were seated and waiting.

For quite some while Mardi had been suspecting that Pardi was avoiding his evenings of music because he had difficulty hearing. That was probably why he had stopped initiating them himself. It dawned on her that maybe his withdrawal was not altogether due to heartbreak caused by the loss of the referendum and the election. Maybe it also stemmed from his inability to hear. She was determined not to let him move into a world of silence.

And then Mardi had had one of her brainwaves, in the middle of smoothing clay across the back of a figure she was modelling. She was working on a government commission. It was probably the most important challenge she had ever faced. At independence Jamaica had partially redefined itself by naming its own national heroes. One of them was the deacon Paul Bogle, from Stony Gut, a legendary figure who had killed the Custos with a machete in the Morant Bay rebellion of 1865. Now the government wanted statues of the heroes, and she had been asked to do Bogle.

She had been thinking about up-coming changes that would end our harmonious era. Douglas was going away to start a UNESCO contract in Africa. Kik and I planned to go down to Barbados for the summer after our exams. With everyone gone, Michael planned to rent out his house and get a smaller place. Mardi was musing over how often life changed, and how people had to adapt.

That was when it struck her that the problem with Pardi was a failure to do just that—adapt. He must get a hearing aid. She knew he'd resist the idea, for she sensed that his deafness completed a wall behind which he had decided to retreat. Seeing this as her crusade for the day, she decided to convene a family conference behind Pardi's back.

Mardi always entered Ebony Hill through the front door. It was strange that she came that way, for it meant walking all the way around the house when she could easily enter through the kitchen door fifty yards from her own garage. But she didn't like entering anywhere through back doors, she said, not out of some misplaced notion of grandeur, but because she felt it was like sneaking up on people.

Besides, she loved coming around the driveway sprinkled with the joyous yellow overflow of the poui and ebony trees overhead which seemed more to interpret the sun than to interrupt it. A crude path ran up the side of a circular out-door patio intermittently shaded by sweet-smelling, floppy white flowers that were sibilant with bees. The rough, crazy-paved cement structure resembled the crown of a giant molar. Ascending its rim at its shallowest point, Mardi was careful to step across the wide crack where the earth beneath had settled and caused the centre to sink like a fallen cake.

As she approached the plywood front door, frayed at the bottom by sun and rain, she was overwhelmed by the rich sound of Mongo Santamaria. She drifted in, looking delib-erately temporary, and was taken aback by Michael, Kik and myself in a neat line doing quarter-turns of a cha-cha-cha.

The large, L-shaped room rallied around the surging "Horse of the Morning" the way a lawn does around a mag-nificent tree. This horse was perhaps Mardi's best-loved carving; this frustrated her for she felt she could never live it down. The visiting eyes' afterthought soon found a rich collection of Jamaican paintings by younger artists. The presence of a television set, though small and seldom used, gained its attention simply by the contrast of its glassy, pre-cise modernity in a room whose only permanence among the mild disorder of circumstances was art.

We finished a couple more steps, then my father led the way, still in a cha-cha-cha, to the dining table. He looked up at his mother sheepishly; he always felt guilty when his par-ents saw him enjoying himself too much.

"Oh, now I've gone and spoilt it...you all looked so happy doing that wonderful dance." She sat down.

"Not at all...in fact I must be off soon...I've got this strike at JBC." Michael looked instinctively toward the myopic curve of the television's void surface which seemed to challenge the cosmic significance of Mardi's horse. His interest in the new medium seemed limited to the employees of the station who were members of the NWU. They were now on strike in support of two wrongful-dismissal claims. It was dragging on, and Michael had stunned the island during a demonstration by lying in the streets of Kingston to block traffic. Wheels had rolled right up to his head. When he faced the walls of the station and addressed the structure as "Jericho", the workers rechristened him, changing his nickname from "Young Boy" to "Joshua", and the name stuck.

Mardi shrewdly recognized the significance of the episode in the development of Michael's public persona. Although he had so far failed to get the two workers reinstated, the incident brought him into focus; for too long there had been a blurred perception of him as just the selvage on his father's hem. Though the gesture was not as vivid as Busta's going to jail, it would place him indelibly on the side of the workers. She often felt that her husband's career had suffered for lack of just such a legitimizing moment.

Pardi too had been impressed by his son. "Passive resistance," he observed with pride, and to mark his disapproval of the station management's stand, he sent back his television set.

"How is it going, dear? You know your father sent back the TV set."

"I know. I spoke to him. It was such a deeply principled thing to do...but we won't win this one," he said, but brightened the expression on his face. "Not to worry, Mother."

She seemed to search the room for inspiration, but she was distracted by the sight of a Ouija board Kik and I had consulted the night before. "Something has to be done about Norman," she announced, picking up the plastic oracle. She rubbed it against her thigh as though summoning a genie, and then placed it on the lettered board so that it faced the corner marked "YES".

Hearing his son's name pronounced by his mother, Douglas struggled out to the living-room, crumpled and curious. "What's happened to Norman?" He paused for the answer, holding the back of a chair as though unable to arrange himself until he knew if it was worth sitting down.

"Not little Norman...big Norman." Mardi spread her hands incongruously, indicating obesity rather than height.

Douglas sat down squarely at the dining-room table amid the breakfast debris, the Ouija board, the homework books and newspapers, reached for a slice of cold buttered toast and looked mildly around him. The presence of his family always caused him to blink.

"Big Norman must get a hearing aid," she said.

Douglas stared suspiciously at the jug of orange juice while he chewed.

"It will bring your father back," she insisted.

"From where?" Douglas was being obtuse. We all knew Pardi's hearing was bad.

"You see, he has come through an awful depression. It's been so difficult, really. And he seems to have weathered the storm, and he's tackling the damned politics again, that's his choice. But he seems so—how shall I put it?—*unalive* around the house. Almost withdrawn." She thought about this for a bit, as she appeared to assess her thoughts by repeatedly stroking a fold in the napkin. Douglas watched intently as if she were performing a magical trick that might produce a bird or a rabbit. "And I have been trying to put my finger on it...what's at the bottom of it all. There is something a lot deeper than losing the election—some level at which he has refused to plug back in, one might say...." She looked at Michael for understanding. "I think it's because he can't *hear* any of us. Can't hear his music, even."

"Oh, dear." Douglas grunted as he reached for the marmalade. He had apparently decided to make the most of her visit.

"I think he needs some fun in his life. Not to be so serious. He needs to learn to flirt again and be mischievous. We have to take him *out* of himself. He's a terribly attractive man, you know. I'm trying to get Pam over more often, they used to have such lovely evenings...but it's no use without a hearing aid. Deafness can make one so lonely...." Her voice trailed off into some silent cavern she had created in her imagination.

"I'm very worried," my father confessed.

Michael too had been troubled by Pardi's gloom. His father's life was a less flexible journey than his mother's. It had dug its roots deeper in, so it presented fewer options. Mardi's life resembled a series of raids; her enthusiasms disappeared as soon as she was sated, and she could always start over again. Maybe this flexibility was the ultimate gift of her imagination. Pardi had to reach back to things to which he was unavoidably attached—like the law—or continue along the course already set for his political life. His purposes were more fundamental and consecutive, his goals predetermined, and he was bound to them.

"Are you okay?" Michael had asked his father recently, when he seemed very tired after a meeting of the party executive.

Pardi had looked at the night sky as if to judge the time.

"Son, I'm just getting old."

If his mother was mercury, his father was steel, Michael concluded, and was pleased with the analogy.

"I agree he needs a hearing aid. It's a question of how to convince him." Michael appeared to be taking over chairmanship of the meeting. Mardi relaxed; this was obviously what she had wanted.

Pressing her hands in a wider circle as though the napkin were Plasticine she was spreading, Mardi explained that she had talked to Moodie, and he had suggested a modern hearing aid that was smaller and didn't have the embarrassing line trailing from it. It was available in England.

"When are you actually going away, Doug?"

Her elder son pulled the newspaper towards him, creating a line of defense, and smudging round prints of butter onto its surface which my father stared at with predictable displeasure. Douglas looked uncomfortable at the reference made to his upcoming trip. He was plucking up the courage to take Roy to London with him. Roy needed an operation that was very risky, but without which he would always be sick. Douglas had wrestled with the idea of leaving things as they were, but watching his son one day, looking out on a world the youngster could only observe as a voyeur, he decided that the risk was worthwhile. As if this was all he could muster of fatherhood, he concentrated a lifetime's worth of responsibility into one fierce objective. He would live with an awful guilt if he lost the gamble.

Douglas had told no one about this added agenda, not even Carmen. As far as we knew, the London trip was a routine stop on his way to the new job in Africa. "I think the duty has been delegated..." he said distractedly, and looked questioningly at his brother.

"...to you," Michael answered, and they laughed gently, looking at each other in a rare moment of camaraderie.

To others, an uncomfortable silence always charged the space between the two brothers. But no one ever knew for sure if they themselves felt uncomfortable. At Ebony Hill they always sat firmly faced forward in their habitual places on adjacent sides of the table where they need not look at each other.

Michael related better to his elder brother as a concept, or a phenomenon. Up close, his brother seemed to bewilder him. It was like watching a child pushing at round holes with triangular blocks; things never seemed to fit. Mardi often contrived their relationship. Maybe she had always done this, leaving them stranded in an uncomfortable scenario of her invention.

Although Michael and Douglas had seen little of each other as children, except on their seaside holidays, there were brief interludes in New York, when Michael would visit him at Columbia University, and in London, when they were both married and briefly shared a flat. Michael, always intrigued by uncommon talent and struggle, removed his brother from a void and placed him firmly, and at safe distance, among his pantheon of heroes which he mentally counted and replaced like a child's regiment of toy soldiers.

His brother had progressed from being simply older, initially taller and therefore stronger than himself, to the mysterious sibling with an aura. Douglas who endured and survived a tough rural boarding school. Douglas who was a boxer and track star, emerging as the first sprinter to equal their father's hundred yards' record. The wry, unpredictable brother who graduated from school in a packed auditorium to the sound of discords from the chapel organ played by the music teacher, a humourless Hun alarmed by the lack of co-operation from the instrument's stops, because Douglas, the deeply mischievous firstborn, had rearranged them incorrectly beforehand.

And then there was Douglas' ambidexterity which Mardi referred to with odd semantic fascination. She spoke of it as though it were a parlour trick. One day, in what Mardi described as a churlish moment, Douglas announced that his mother had in fact concocted this condition to divert attention from her heinous crime in standing idly by whilst his teachers forced him to use the unnatural right hand, when he was in fact left-handed. But for Michael it was another talent which increased his awe of his brother, and it sailed endearingly along with the legend of him.

Since his return to Jamaica he was the brilliant brother with the doctorate.

Mardi looked across the table from one to the other in satisfaction, either at settling the problem, or at the harmonious way in which her sons had collaborated.

"There, that's settled then," she said, "you'll track it down, Doug, and we will have to find a way to get it back here." As she got up to go the phone rang. Michael went to the small alcove that was the nucleus of the haphazard house. He lowered his voice after the initial "Hallo", and went down to his room clutching the phone, the extra-long black cord disappearing under the door.

"That's a sure sign," I observed.

"A sign? A sign of what?" asked Mardi.

"He's talking to *the* girlfriend."

"Oh, you children!"

"The Ouija board says he'll get married again," said Kik.

Pardi watched Mardi crossing the lawn as she returned to the studio, and noticed how quickly she still moved. Above her tall frame, her head darted like a small bird. Age for her was merely another wild horse to break. He loved her for that, particularly since nowadays he could feel an indifference in his own physical self. It liked to be left alone. And yet his was not a state of settling fat, more the narrow determination of quiet ruin. He knew this was his final age. He felt capable of just one last surge of energy. He did not speak about it but it lurked behind all his thoughts, not as a spur but as a way out.

He had watched his wife's transplantations over the years the way he checked on the young grafts on his mountain farm. "It catch," as old Dixon would say at the sight of the pale green shoots of reaffirmation. She had done it again. The new studio was a more earthen place than the one at Drumblair, which had smelled of trees and wood shavings. Every niche was sealed with a seam of clay, and its smell, damp and poignant as though from the secret folds of the ground's body, seeped up out of the cement.

He had sat on the veranda for an hour this morning feeling excluded from Mardi's locked world in the studio. He used to find the drift of short, sharp phrases from her carving reassuring. But it was quiet in the studio, for now she worked in clay. He had lost his sense of her, and the silence was full of her idiosyncratic secrets. It wasn't till he saw her returning furtively from Ebony Hill, hurrying towards the studio, that he realized with surprise that she had not been in there at all.

She must have gone off on one of her "now let's get the day organized" swoops. Probably the next intrigue in the continuing drama of keeping the family afloat.

Pardi was proud that she was recreating a moment of Jamaican history with the statue of Bogle. He knew this would one day stare down over the passing years from the steps of the Morant Bay courthouse. He was reminded again that the lens of the artist's eye in its considered blink could have more impact on events than all the daily machinations of planning and building. As a politician he found the thought humbling.

Many people disagreed with Bogle being a national hero, but Pardi approved of the choice. Marcus Garvey was obvious; he had spoken to the concerns of the black world, especially in America. George William Gordon, like Paul Bogle, had played a role in the Morant Bay rebellion, a bright, self-educated mulatto who had been able to represent the emancipated Jamaican workers to the officials in desperate times. But it was Bogle who had been the ferocious hand of outrage hitting out from the body of unrest. Although the rebellion had been efficiently quashed and Bogle executed for his role in the uprising, he had become a symbol of change in the island, for he had expressed the will rather than the promise, the deed rather than the word.

Mardi was going to use fibreglass for the cast, a new substance which was said to be lighter and easier to use than plaster of Paris. She planned a monumental figure. It would be a hell of a job, and Pardi was planning to build a second studio for her, nearer the house, with a higher ceiling to accommodate the work.

"You'll have to raise the roof," he had suggested.

"I always do," she had quipped.

He heard the door scrape, and she stuck her head out of the studio. "Norman, come and see before I cover the clay," she called. "And be a dear... ask Tildy to bring us coffee." She withdrew again, leaving the door ajar.

Uhuru looked up at the interruption but opted for staying put.

Pardi was hungry. He was on a new diet designed to shock the body with proteins. He had several boiled eggs a day, which Zethilda prepared with less outrage than one might have expected. Even Zethilda grumbled less around him. Sometimes Uhuru was the only one in the house whose manner was truly natural.

When he entered the studio, Pardi stood for a while absorbing the progress of the clay figure before him, while Mardi dampened rags over the small sink in the corner. She had done a good morning's work. She was always reluctant to leave the peace of her studio. She valued this small wooden haven even though its solitude and defiance were modest statements compared to her studio at Drumblair. It was not lost in trees and high grass, but tucked into the edge of a lawn behind two large beds of ice-blue plumbago shrubs.

Beside the studio she had placed a grim-faced, cross-legged Aztec god who held a bird-bath aloft. The birds refused to use it, congregating with their usual squabbles around the more traditional stone bath that had been at Drumblair. "Well, they're used to it," she said, for they too had come from Drumblair. But she believed this savage deity protected her privacy, and on any occasion she deemed special, or to make a wish, she gave it an offering of an orange. The squat figure was intimidating, and we all took this ritual very seriously until one day, in a high wind, it blew off its plinth and we discovered that the god was made of plastic. The birds were very smug.

During the days leading up to what Mardi referred to as the "palaver of independence", a smart new hotel, the Sheraton Kingston, had commissioned one of her carvings. The work was a very large bas-relief in purple-heart which she had to carve at the site, not yet having a place to work at home.

The hotel was still under construction, and she used to pick her way carefully over rubble among the workers who averted their eyes as she passed, and pointedly refused to acknowledge her presence. Occasionally she saw a "cut eye" or heard the anonymous suck of teeth behind her, which she knew was a message to her husband. She had lived through years of political animosity, but this was different. It was more personal and painful, as though the electorate felt betrayed.

It took every ounce of determination for her to finish her work. The composition was unusually controlled for her, completely stylized, and its discipline almost stoic. The outlines were so precise that she seemed to be simplifying life for herself, telling the story with neither emotion nor opinion.

She would never forget the raw sensation of working in front of other people. The inner world she needed to draw on was trapped beneath her defensive shell. She had once carved the figure of Christ on the cross at a church, but there the silence had translated into aloneness. She had worked high up on scaffolding, and the movement of people beneath her had sounded like the tentative steps of mourners trying —oddly—not to disturb the dead.

One morning she looked down from her perch at the Sheraton to see a toothless mason gaping intently at her as she worked. He was balancing a trowel heaped with wet cement, and wearing a kerchief knotted at four corners on his head, presumably to protect him from falling paint and dust. For a startled moment she wondered if he was planning to hurl the wet cement at her or, worse yet, at the carving.

Assuming he was compelled by the figure she was working on, Mardi explained, "She is Mother Earth," and waited for his reaction.

He stared at the composition of man, woman and child amid the foliage that rose behind the emerging bulk of a woman. His arm relaxed, lowered by the weight of the trowel, and he lifted his chin and returned his bemused gaze to her. "Modor earth," he repeated

"Yes," she went on, "that's what I call her. You see, the man is responsible for so much...his woman, his child, even the things he grows on the land. But Mother Earth has even more to be responsible for. So she has to keep calm. For everything ultimately depends on her, and she can't lose her head, not even in the bad times."

He listened patiently to her sermon.

His name, he said, was Jeremiah. From then on there was a truce of sorts in the place, and although she never received a welcome, sometimes she caught a friendly glance when she arrived; if there was an argument, someone would whisper and look towards her and they would lower their voices, which demonstrated respect if not kinship. Now and then a worker would come and watch her for a while on his break, and the mason, Jeremiah, stopped every day after that first encounter.

One day when the carving was nearly completed, Jeremiah stood by its base, considering something he saw there. Mardi found him noticeably altered. He had changed his clothes to go home, and seemed much younger than before. He now had an overbearing row of large, even teeth that overwhelmed the frustrations of his face and gave him a stretched and awkward look.

"Who dis man response for, lady? De two woman?"

Mardi looked at the figures in the carving. "Oh, I see what you mean. No, no. The woman with the baby is his 'baby-mother'. Remember this other one is Mother Earth!"

Jeremiah frowned, though his mouth remained spread open over its bright new pearls.

Aware that Jamaicans know their Bible, Mardi embarked on a recitation with her most God-fearing voice:

Man that is born of a woman
Is of few days, and full of trouble.
He cometh forth like a flower,
and is cut down...

Jeremiah nodded with recognition, as he seemed to find the reference in his mind, and stated with satisfaction, "De Book of Job!"

She prowled on over the last phrase:
he fleeth also as a shadow,
and continueth not.

Jeremiah looked at her as though *she* finally made sense, if not the carving. Then he studied the work for a last, long time.

"Me t'ink me unnerstan', lady." He hesitated, and then moved his face nearer to hers and whispered, "He cometh forth...me know who de man is now."

She decided she'd call it *He Cometh Forth*.

Despite Jeremiah, she knew that she could never attempt to work in public again. That was why they built this small wooden studio on Regardless' hillward brow. She didn't know why, but the things she wanted to do, the things she felt she was meant to do, were much easier with her youth out of the way. Youth was like a too-tight skin which had encumbered her, and imposed expectations on her that always felt unnatural to fulfil. For the first time she felt peaceful...not like a motionless lake, but like a high tide swollen and brimming and secure in the moon's gravity; the creatures of the sea had lived and died in her, and she held beautiful formations of coral, and crabs would feel safe to come to her.... When she woke in the mornings she was happy.

And she was free of Drumblair too. She had lived every minute of the house, but had not mourned it. Through her window she could see all the small houses going up on its site; because the place was unrecognizable; it caused her less pain. She sidestepped mourning for the past by throwing her future into Regardless.

Either influenced by that last difficult work, the new studio, or in a mood for experimentation and change, she had turned to the less resistant medium of clay. It was quicker, she thought, and allowed freedom of movement. And it was lovely. She felt she was back at the beginning, starting over with the elements. She loved the concept of these elements working together. Clay had to be watered, and it had to be fired. Earth, water and fire.

She had a large silver kiln installed in the garage, which Batiste surreptitiously used to house seedlings, his going home clothes, or any secret he wished to keep safe from the ever intrusive Zethilda. Mardi regarded the kiln as a firmament, creation's ultimate challenge, "so like life, and what comes through has stood the test!" she averred.

Her studio was littered with newborn terracottas and unborn clay. Mardi was determined to keep things simple, to keep light of heart. A twist of fate had offered her a new dimension. Carmen had written a children's story called "Land of Wood and Water", and Mardi agreed to illustrate it with pictures of animals. These became working drawings for small terracottas: *Tyg the Tyger*, *Owlie the Owl* and *Goatie the Goat*. *Tyg*, spelled with deference to Blake's "Tyger, Tyger", she made for me. She said she was doing for me what she'd done for my father years ago with "Horse of the Morning." She was giving me something I would value, and something that was in a sense an expression of myself. She challenged me to get to the bottom of the tiger's nature, for she considered the tiger totally at one with the urges of his own being. She also said something about never wasting a movement, the significance of which I suspect I deliberately ignored.

The watchful *Bull*, whose horns kept his head safe from being touched, she made for Douglas. Pardi identified the animal as "a real meadow bull, sultry in the afternoon sun." Having thus rewarded the family for being family, she made the sure-footed survivor, the goat, for herself. When *Goatie the Goat* came safely out of the kiln in one piece, we each got a phone call with the announcement "Baee, baee."

Things seemed to be falling into place. The house, though small, was manageable. Pardi was broke from his years of politics, but their debts had been paid by the sale of Drumblair. He had a much smaller salary from the government now—even augmented by the fees from his legal briefs, it hardly covered the costs of his office and home. It was her steady flow of commissions that helped them pull through. And now this, a chance to do this vast statue of a national hero. She felt she had been validated by Jamaica.

Pardi had lowered himself into his customary seat. Tildy brought in the coffee with an indecipherable undertow of grumblings to do with Aunt Muriel's cook, Mae.

"What's the matter, Zethilda?" Pardi enquired, balancing his dripping cup over its saucer for a slurp of steaming coffee.

"Look like Mae gone off again, Barrista!"

"What did she say?" Pardi looked at Mardi for volume.

"Oh, dear, it's really so tiresome." Mae's employment was interrupted by spells in the mental home. Mardi turned round from the window and leaned against the ledge of the shelves as though bracing for another family ordeal. "What's happened now?" she shouted at Zethilda, who had no problem hearing her.

"Mae bay like a daag all night in the yard . . . look like it a full moon. Dat time she gone off 'er 'ead. Doctor send for the man dem wid de straitjacket."

Mardi took a deep breath, blinked profoundly and mouthed, "It's Mae," at Pardi.

"Why does Mu persist?" he asked quietly.

"Because she's a superb cook," Mardi said almost to herself, and her eyebrows lifted as though in salutation of Mae's gift. "There is something perverse about their relationship."

Zethilda hesitated by the door. Having no further bad news to offer, she mumbled something about at least being able to sweep out chips, which Mardi realized was a criticism of her use of clay, and left.

In the centre of the room a muddy grey figure, still just bulk and outline, grew from the modelling stand. Already Pardi could sense the sturdy presence of Bogle. The original maquette Mardi had been working on was up at Nomdmi. It was a figure standing very straight in a great pause, both elbows pressed to his sides, with his right forearm lifted to hold a machete flat against his torso, the blade pointing to the ground. That head was slightly inclined; he seemed to be looking down at what he had done.

Even in the rough this figure was different.

"This is new," Pardi said. "Both arms are up?"

This figure was astride, its arms extended like wings at shoulder height and bent at the elbows; the hands met at the centre of the chest and clutched the handle of a machete whose blade pointed towards the ground. She had worked on this only a few hours this morning, modelling clay with her thumbs and wire-tipped tools.

"Well, yes. You see, I felt the other was maybe a bit too" —she seemed to both pull and press the edges of the form, the way one would straighten clothes on the shoulders of a small child—"too tentative, really. You see, when I was down at Stony Gut, where he was born, I met this old woman who knew Bogle's son...she was fascinating. And I came away with one word she used...*bold*...she said Bogle was a *bold* man."

And she turned to look at Pardi as she said "bold," blowing the word out of her small mouth as though setting a bubble adrift.

"I like the symmetry," he said. "It is bold. The figure looks planted."

"He can't be apologetic, can he? He has to be so very sure. It's one of those moments, isn't it?"

"Indeed," he said and got up to circle the model stand. She stepped back, giving him room.

"I see you have almost transformed the machete into a sword—as a symbol of the act. And the way he holds it... it's more deliberate, more like a quest. I like that."

"Bold. That's what I want to capture. I was thinking, there are times when history cries out for a statement. Something irrevocable. Now Gordon, he was more a middle-class voice, wasn't he? I mean, he spoke on behalf of the masses with a rational voice. That's what we are still trying to do. Even Garvey... he was a psychological force. His was a great stone rolling, calling other stones. But this... this was just one brave moment, the sudden slamming down of a fist or a foot, saying, *Enough! Stop!* This was not conscious, but it expressed the will of the people. The blood of a dam that burst...."

She stopped and, in the ensuing silence, shrugged as if she was resigned to the certainty of detractors.

"One can say the act is just a bloody murder. I daresay a lot of people will feel that way. People say he's overrated; he was a simple hero. But the world is mostly made of the simplest people. The workers, the uneducated or the poor. And they may have the hardest time finding their voice, expressing their feelings, but when they do there are an awful lot of them, and you'd better listen to what they have to say!"

"Deacons are not necessarily simple people," Pardi said.

She looked sympathetically down at the figure and pressed some small bits of clay firmly but fondly onto its head. "He would have known that his own life was over... he had done a terrible deed chopping up the Custos. But this was his great sacrifice to fight a terrible system."

"The cross created by the arms aloft and the weapon perpendicular is reminiscent of the crucifixion," Pardi said, sketching a small cross in the air before him.

"Yes. This is his sacrifice. But his head will be upright, looking at the future—both his demise and his hope for change. This is what I told Ray...I said, look dear, he is a fighter, not a martyr. In his face you will see confrontation and the sort of bloody determination that is at the heart of human outrage. No other cheek to turn...no happy heaven of resurrection...no fairy tale. This is a man whose moment of truth is today. He has staked everything..."

"Yes." Pardi looked at the piece as though he could see the features there already. "You mean 'God's angels in the path to see'. It's no use seeing angels if you're not prepared to wrestle with them."

"That's it! Not whether he's done the deed or not done the deed. You've put it in a nutshell. He's prepared to wrestle those angels." She was lost in the hills of Stony Gut, fighting her way down treacherous winding paths towards a destiny in front of a country courthouse where the Custos of the parish would be slain.

And Pardi, letting himself be carried by the moment, fell into a half-forgotten recital of Browning:

And the sin I impute to each frustrate ghost
Is—the unlit lamp and the ungirt loin,
De-dah, de-dah, de-dah, de-de-dah
You of the virtue (we issue join)
How strive you? De te, fabula!

"Or something like that," he trailed off.

"Kid, that's 'The Statue and the Bust'!" She was full of their life together, suddenly one with journey and road. "That was little David. And here we have the mighty empire looming over poor Bogle, like Goliath in the figure of the Custos, with all his pomp and ceremony. And the other day I heard that in addition to Browning's wife being a Jamaican, his great-great-grandfather was a shoemaker and tavernkeeper in Port Royal. How it all comes round full circle in this life! Oh, Kid, we've got to get you *listening* again...."

14

A
MIDSUMMER-
NIGHT'S
DREAM

THE OUIJA WAS right. My father did marry again. Her name was Barbara, and he first saw her in 1964 during the JBC strike. She was a public relations writer for a local advertising agency. She arrived at the broadcasting station to make a commercial, but refused to cross the picket line, returning quickly to her car. She wore a bright yellow sharkskin suit and, long after he discovered who she was, Michael could retrace her quiet, certain steps, her long legs which were a little too thin and the gentle disagreement between her jacket and skirt as she walked away from him. That was all, and yet, romantic that he was, he felt the unmistakable tug in the pit of his stomach.

It was not till later that summer that he actually met her. It must have been premeditated for, as Mardi pointed out, it was unlikely that he would go by himself to an event that was primarily social unless he had good reason.

Often in summer the grounds of some elegant home would fall under the spell of Shakespeare. This was "garden theatre," and this production featured celebrities of the local dramatic world in *A Midsummer Night's Dream*. A who's who of Kingston was there. But whereas no Anglophile should set off without the ponderings of Othello or Hamlet, Julius Caesar or Macbeth, Michael could have done without the social paraphernalia of an evening "at the arts" for the sake of Puck. Shakespeare's comedies were not high on his list of cultural priorities.

Michael would travel far, and with huge curiosity, in pursuit of the areas in which he was interested, but he tended towards the untraditional in life. In dance he began with a brief childhood yearning to be a Nijinsky—one that his mother, ever kindly disposed towards the aspirations of youth, had tried to encourage by taking him to his first and only dance class. He stood at the bottom of a flight of stone steps where he had a view of little girls in pink slippers and white practice dresses, bobbing up and down in *pliés* and *relevés* at a barre to the tapping of the ballet mistress's stick, as an unseen piano irritably stopped and started. He hid under the steps for an hour, until he was rescued by his mother's return.

It was eventually modern dance that won his appreciation. In music his taste ripened to jazz, and in art he was drawn to the adventurous Post-Impressionists.

Yet, soon after he first saw the fleeting figure in the yellow suit, despite his cultural tastes and painful social shyness, and aching for a cigarette, Michael made his way alone across the floodlit lawn of the garden theatre and manoeuvred his frame into an iron seat to watch *A Midsummer Night's Dream*.

Barbara played Titania.

Barbara was the most amazing-looking woman I had ever seen, in magazines, movies or real life. She used to say that the endless attention paid to her looks made her feel like an object and was quick to admit that, if you dismantled her she was very far from perfect. Her face was an absolute square, with a jaw like Dick Tracy's, which made any expression seem too emphatic. Her forehead resembled the smooth contours of a calabash, and was as wide, she said, as Cable Hut Beach. Her nose was too small and pinched, her front teeth tipped out from an overbite, her eyebrows were intermittent and unruly and grew like thin scrub on a rock face, so she plucked them and pencilled on new ones. Yet all this together was, yes, beautiful.

"She certainly has a presence," said Mardi guardedly one day when the family asked her opinion. Mardi found all the fuss over Barbara off-putting. It made her somewhat cautious.

"Mardi is used to other women being shorter," surmised Douglas, for Mardi was five foot eight and Barbara, though five feet seven, was the same height for she wore higher heels. Mardi's other daughters-in-law had been short women.

Barbara's father was the town clerk, a gentle, old-fashioned man who loved and served his family, his God and his country, in that order. Her mother looked out from the years gathered thickly around her body with the serenity of one who had once been beautiful, worked only in the home and always knew herself to be righteous and respected, obeyed by a meek husband, well-trained staff and disciplined children who, despite the tropical heat, wore their vests and their socks without question.

But as so often the case in my father's life, there was a snag: Barbara was married to somebody else. She had abandoned university to wed an attractive Jamaican actor and they were thought by many to be the perfect couple.

Barbara was the eldest of three handsome sisters. She was an exemplary student who had once been chosen, because of her perfect diction and careful enunciation, to address the Queen and Prince Philip on a royal visit. Prince Philip had winked at her. Her affair with Michael was to be her only act of disobedience to her parents and to society.

She said her family always made her feel engulfed. As a child she used to have a recurring dream that she was in her big wooden house, the official residence of the town clerk, feeling surrounded by its light and shadows, its familiar features, the peculiarities that abound in old wooden houses. All of a sudden the house burst into flames and she was a helpless witness to the collapse of walls, bending, distorting, falling in on themselves as the house succumbed. She always felt guilt in the dream, as though she had been somehow dishonourable, but never knew how.

The dream became so frequent that sometimes, before the house started to burn, she would feel her body, her skin, begin to collapse instead.

Although she had separated from her husband, Barbara met Michael secretly for quite a while. He introduced her to his world, and she found it rich with ideas and art, philosophy and politics, music and sport. He took her to cricket. He explained the game, drew her a map of the field with tiny stick men and marked their positions. After five days of a test match with the British, she remarked to him, "I think cricket is really the Englishman's method of meditation."

Barbara's parents were at first horrified, especially after her father was told by a mutual friend that Michael had so disappointed a woman they all knew that she had been driven to slit her wrists in a futile attempt at suicide. Michael had only met the woman once, and very formally, but the damage was done. He was made to collect Barbara outside her parent's gate for a year.

Mardi worried for a while. Pardi made no judgement. Friends had their opinions, not all of them divisive. But when it was clear that the match was unshakable, and as the rumours and scandal settled, all who knew them found themselves mesmerized by the couple. They were superb together. They looked good; they sparked each other. They were happy.

"Barbara always says with two people the nubs have to fit," he explained to me one day, and he made two fists facing each other and let the knuckles find the opposite spaces in which to slot themselves. "We are like this...the nubs fit!"

Pardi and Mardi finally met Barbara when she was invited to join the family at Nomdmi for New Year's Eve. Mardi planned to have a few friends help her not so much drink in the new year, as drink out the old, which for one reason and another she had not considered a good one. Michael brought her up to the top of the hill bringing champagne and starlights. Barbara got them all to burn the small grey firesticks in the darkness, so the fiery, spitting starbursts traced the circling of their hands in the mountain darkness. It was a joyous, uncomplicated evening. Michael and the wife of a writer fell into the hydrangeas when the veranda rail collapsed with them. They laughed a lot and no one was hurt. Pardi subsequently rebuilt it—that was how Nomdmi got the larger veranda.

Because he was flat broke, in 1965 Pardi, who Mardi always maintained was unpredictable, decided to rent out Regardless. They would pack up their things and go to live at Nomdmi.

"But my wild unconventional God lives somewhere up amongst the pine trees at Nomdmi!" Mardi protested.

What on earth did she mean? Pardi frowned.

"Don't you see?" she implored, careful not to rant. "How can I live there permanently? It's awfully hard to share a house with God!"

But nothing Mardi could do or say would change his mind. He planned to commute every day, continuing both his law and his politics. He would do his party work, fulfil his constituency obligations and attend Parliament in the afternoons. It took workmen twenty days to carry jar pipes up the hill on mules and install a colossal cesspit which Pardi insisted was one of two additions they must have. The other was a small kerosene generator to which light outlets were connected in the dining-room, living-room and kitchen. (The bedrooms, bathroom and veranda remained dependent on Tilly gas or kerosene lamps, and there were candles and matches in every room.) And then they moved.

Zethilda was left behind as housekeeper to a large American lady who dressed her in Bermuda pink with a frilly white lace cap and apron, and introduced her to the joys of Betty Crocker. Batiste was retitled "landscaper" after attempts failed to transform him into a butler. He was provided with overalls which made him laugh heartily even after he put "de big baby drawers" out of sight in the kiln, which had become his cupboard.

And that was when a fence finally went up between the two properties on Washington Drive.

"They have closed the fence," Mardi said one day, in a tone so foreboding that it seemed to Pardi, who was quietly crunching away at cabbage and carrots, to indicate something more profound than the simple convenience of a boundary. Pardi was now on a salad diet in which he ate mostly raw, shredded vegetables.

"Sorry, I don't understand you." He offered the words after he made room in his mouth for his tongue to move, but she thought he had failed to hear due to the crunching of the uncooked greens. Horses were like that when they ate oats, she remembered. Even cows were blamed for inattention, and she suspected that it was simply that they could not hear. Grass could be very noisy.

She checked to see if he was wearing his hearing aid. There it was, a beige plastic, miniature kidney dish in place behind his ear. She knew he hated it, and often turned it off, just leaving it there to appease the family.

To Mardi, the fence was definitive. She considered the years without a boundary between the houses as an era. I saw it more as a hiatus. It had been a very happy time for me, likely for the selfish reason that it was between my father's marriages. Wives, I would discover, no matter how different, had a few things in common. They managed with deft fingers to extract the spirit of a home and the heart of my father for themselves. And they were afraid of lizards.

But the family era ended before the fence was built. Douglas was leaving for Africa. Kik and I had finished our exams and after our summer in Barbados we would be going to England to school. My father had decided to move into a small flat and rent Ebony Hill to help him financially, as he no longer needed such a big place.

The event that symbolized this for me was a family goodbye party that Douglas and Michael threw at Ebony Hill. We all invited our friends, each group unconnected to the others, only swept together by mutual friendships and a flow of brew from a contraption that spurted draft beer provided by my friend Lem's parents.

Late in the evening Pardi found himself facing one of Douglas' guests, who, arriving late, strode over to him draped in a black stole and, apropos of nothing, proceeded to let the fringed article slip down her shoulders to reveal the first topless dress worn in Jamaica.

What was memorable to most was not so much the lady's ample proportions as the steadfast gaze which Pardi kept unblinkingly at eye level, finishing the story he had been telling when she walked up to him.

For a time after the electoral defeats, the family's political compulsions had lain fallow. But that period was soon over.

Despite the fact that in 1952 Pardi had expelled the infamous "Four H's" for being communists, a new generation of the party's members now felt that only a left-wing agenda would ever redress the economic imbalance. Soon after his electoral defeat, Pardi had opened the debate at the party's annual conference with a speech stating flatly that the benefits from the island's economic growth were not being fairly shared. After much contemplation in 1964, he had formed a policy advisory committee chaired by David Coore which included Michael. By November that year, the PNP emerged from its period of review and announced a socialist program. It proposed the nationalization of "the most commanding heights" (I loved the oratorical way my grandfather said this, as if a mountain had blown a trumpet for attention) of the economy, and a five-hundred-acre limit on land ownership. It dropped like a bombshell into the island's consciousness. They would design a more socialist agenda. This was his radical new economic model.

Pardi had become revitalized by his "new platform". I remember the word "socialism" being retrieved from its banishment and bandied about again. For a while Mardi felt he'd got his bite back. This audacious heave to the left, which was causing such a stir, seemed to amuse the devil in him. She felt a rush of optimism.

Tensions were even greater between the two parties and in Western Kingston, gangs had become politicized and their disputes were being settled by the use of guns and Molotov cocktails.

Mardi's statue of Bogle was completed in 1965. The figure now stood in front of the courthouse in the Morant Bay square. At the dedication the crowded square and the public figures giving their speeches had seemed almost antlike beneath the towering figure of the hero. The government had decided to erect a second monument, a bust of Bogle's torso at National Heroes Park, which was formerly George VI Memorial Park in Kingston, and the dedication of this smaller piece had been a stormy event. The minister of Development and Welfare did not invite Pardi to sit with Mardi on the platform. Mardi felt that etiquette and simple good manners required that her husband be there, and given that he was leader of the opposition it was a national insult to leave him in the crowd.

So in dignified protest she made her way down off the platform and passed through the audience to join her husband. There were boos for the minister from the excited crowd, and two chairs were grabbed off the platform for Pardi and Mardi, but only she sat down—a portrait of hurt indignation under a wide-brimmed, white hat. The minister got so mad he ad-libbed an irresponsible speech threatening to "fight fire with fire, blood for blood". Meanwhile Pardi leaned on a metal police barrier, watching with amusement as the plan of his political opponent backfired before him. But the incident had a profound effect on my father, who stated bluntly that he would never forget this insult to his father. The minister was Edward Seaga.

There were other repercussions to Mardi's creation of *Bogle*. The new studio, built with a higher roof to accommodate the statue, was made of zinc sheets which Mardi always intended to replace with wood one day, for if the sun shone it was unbearably hot, and if it rained she said she could not hear herself think. She put in an air-conditioner, which was also noisy, and though it helped with the heat in the short term, it was almost the death of her. Soon after casting the fibreglass mould for *Bogle*, she started getting severe attacks of bronchial asthma which were said to be related to allergies. They filled her with terror, for she had a traumatic fear of weak lungs because of the death of her father due to pneumonia. It took many hospital visits and medical tests before it was discovered that the allergy was to the fibreglass, and many more years before her baffled doctors figured out that she was still breathing the residue, which continued to be circulated by the contaminated air-conditioner.

I spent two years in London, from September 1964 to the summer of 1966. I had been sent there to "see the world", get to know my mother and "just settle", Mardi would say with sibilant exasperation, so as to do well enough in my exams to get into university. I was seventeen when I went, and I needed to get away from the self I had become. I was very difficult, and knew I had a nasty streak. I craved attention and surrounded myself with people and gossip. The stronger the bonds of good example, the readier the strands of advice offered me by my family, the harder I fought against them. I wished to be the complete antithesis of what I knew them to be. In short, I pursued a shallow, vapid, frivolous life.

"As a child you had a sort of flame," Mardi said to me before I left, in exasperation. I cringed with shame. "You could pick your way between what is true and what is false. It's now covered over with all your own confusion..."

We were at the table, and Pardi was next to us, winding the clock on the sideboard. I hated Pardi hearing her criticisms, for I hoped he still thought well of me.

"...and by people who haven't any real values. There, I've said it!" And with that little gem, she got up and left. Pardi just went on winding the clock.

I swung precariously over successive emotional crises of my own making. Like Chicken Little I had always expected the sky to fall on me, and I vaguely believed that it would happen when I met my mother—or that my mother might be the sky that fell. Our eventual meeting would therefore have less impact on me than I anticipated.

My father took me over to settle me in. When we arrived at the address in Clanricarde Gardens which had been given to us by the rental agency, my father looked astonished. He checked the piece of paper again before letting us through the black door with the number 23 in gold numerals. This was where we had lived fifteen years ago, when I was a baby. We stood there wondering what the coincidence augured.

Michael, who remained for six weeks, was unbearably irritable. He had recently given up smoking, after two heroes, Nat King Cole and Edward R. Murrow, both died of lung cancer. His mental image of these two men, one at a piano and one at a typewriter, had always included a cigarette languishing from their lips. They died within months of each other.

He must have been the only man in history to give up smoking, from between sixty and eighty a day to zero, cold turkey, irrevocably, twice in a weekend. Shortly before leaving for London, he arrived at Nomdmi to spend a weekend with his parents on the same day he quit smoking. He was accompanied by a crate of green-skinned apples to appease his craving.

"Oh, Michael," his mother implored, "this is going to ruin the weekend!"

And Michael, always anxious to please Mother and Dad, decided to smoke again for just those two days and stop cold turkey again on Sunday night. He did it. And he became like an electrical appliance with a short, one that shocks you every time you touch it.

While in London he was often out, either working or meeting Barbara, who came over separately on a clandestine trip to be near him. She did not stay with us. One night when my father was out, I found letters from her in his room, and in a fit of jealousy I have since regretted, I burned them.

My mother, Jacqueline, lived in a quaint mews flat off the Portobello Road where her legendary fastidiousness was constantly challenged by a German shepherd called Beau Beau on whom she doted. I was in awe of the witty, unsentimental humour of both her and my sister Anita, the latter struggling to keep depression at bay after a recent personal tragedy. I used to visit them alternately on weekends, and distinguished myself at one dinner by announcing to the all-white table of guests, "I'm coloured you know." To which my mother drily replied "I don't care if you're green, eat your supper!"

I thought my mother's face very beautiful and, though there was only a mild resemblance, something in the way her expressions seemed to ignite reminded me of my grand-mother. The resemblance ended there. I was amazed by the domestic efficiency of my mother, who also had a demand-ing job in the city. She cooked beautifully, and instead of terracottas, her oven produced her superb "puddings from Yorkshire". She was smaller than I had imagined, and I felt I had discovered the source of aspects of me that were uncharacteristic of my paternal family, ranging from a too-ready gregariousness to a love of bread with butter and jam. I shared her compulsion to create an aura of busy unreality around myself to ward off the intrusion of any personal tenderness. In those days we failed to get nearer to each other than the interplay of our own, invented subsidiary characters. I am sure of one thing. If I had not been told, I would still have known she was my mother.

I found England both familiar and surprising, uplifting and depressing. So much of the landscape fitted the litera-ture and art that had been imposed on us as a colony. But there were times when some small event jumped up and smacked me in the face. White waiters! My first visit to a Wimpy Bar amazed me. I suppose I had never really thought about it before, but why didn't white people hold trays in Jamaica?

I spent a useless first year out of my depth at a private school in Holland Park, where I learned, more than I ever had at home, what it was like to feel British disdain. For the first time in my life I became self-conscious about my Jamaican accent, uncomfortable about my colourful taste in clothes and even sheepish over the postal code of my ad-dress. My confidence was somewhat boosted by a gift from Barbara, a smart black coat with a fur collar which, although it must have been much too big for me, I was very proud to wear. And I was comforted by the fact that most English teenagers could not dance!

In my second year I moved to a quiet country school that catered to foreign students. There I was haunted by the English countryside, which made Blake's *Songs of Innocence and Experience*, and Wordsworth's lonely summer cloud, come alive for me. The dense moisture of the place, the mists and worldly weepings, the unused envelopes whose flaps stuck themselves closed like brown rotting leaves, my shoulders always too cold at night, the search for a fireplace as compelling as yesterday's search for mountain sun, were like a thousand Februaries at Nomdmi. In a state of chronic homesickness that thrived in the gloomy landscape of such poignant beauty, I resorted to corresponding with my old friend Pardi, writing gullible, romantic poetry and tackling the necessary work.

"How goes the world?" wrote Pardi. "Be sober, but not all that sober. Knowledge can always take sparkle—sparkling ignorance is another thing!"

Two students at the school started me thinking about Africa. Douglas was still there. We had only discovered about Roy's traumatic operation when Douglas brought his younger son back to Carmen in Jamaica. The operation had been a success. Douglas had then collected his elder son, Norman, who accompanied him to Rhodesia. There my cousin had to enter the country through a separate line set aside for blacks. Douglas was of fairer complexion and was shown to the line for whites "for they said he was a bore," Norman wrote me, perplexed. This inauspicious gateway led to a time of confusion, pain and anger for Norman, until UNESCO moved them on to Zambia, then Ethiopia, where Norman looked so like an Ethiopian he was quite at home. Pardi wrote that in Jamaica the PNP threatened to boycott the Queen's visit if England did nothing about racial segregation in Rhodesia.

"This multiracial Commonwealth is now pure hypocrisy," Pardi noted, "so why have a queen?"

Pardi had visited Ghana in the glorious days of Nkrumah for its independence celebrations in 1960. A federalist at heart, he was fascinated by the Pan-African dream. But the high point of his trip had been meeting a man he sat beside on the long journey from London to Ghana. He said talking to him had been an inspiration. The man's name was Martin Luther King, Jr.

They met Jomo Kenyatta, whom Mardi described as the most conservative man in all of Africa. She said he wore false teeth, and when he wanted to impress his chiefs he clacked them and rolled his eyes.

Douglas had added a fresh insight on a trip through London when he told me, "Julius Nyerere is the only one with the right idea: the extended family in Africa. One has to recognize the concept of the tribe as inevitable."

And then one night a shattering thing happened at school. We were together after supper watching the BBC news, and there before our eyes was the *coup-d'état* in Nigeria: "He was found shot dead at the side of the road in a ditch." The minister of Finance had apparently lain where the crowds now gawked. Eboh's daughter was one of the two African students in my school. She got up like an ancient queen and walked slowly, regally from the crowded room.

The other student was a daughter of Krobo Edusie, memorably called Lucy, whose mother had reputedly received from her father, a Ghanean minister, a bed of solid gold.

"How tragic about Nigeria," Pardi wrote. "Who are the rest of the world looking back in its own history to judge these new nations whose very traditions sometimes pass over into modernity with all the appearances of misfitting. Golden beds sound crude, but ostentation was in the tradition of African chiefs, and Indian princes make golden beds sound trivial, and even the Queen wears a tiara etcetera."

I returned to Jamaica with an inkling of Africa, a knowledge of op-art, a cockney accent and a place in Sussex University which I never took up, opting for the Jamaican university campus. I convinced my nationalistic family that this would display faith in our own system and, at a time of cash-flow crisis, would also cost less. My real reason was simply a wish to return home to my friends, and to avoid the English climate, which I detested.

I had never seen my father so happy before. Mardi said that she had, and so recognized his condition.

"Michael's batting those imaginary cricket balls in the air again," she explained. This is what she said he always did when he was in love.

Mardi would look at her younger son quizzically, the way one might approach a mirror with the suspicion of finding something embarrassing. She recognized so much of herself in him. Oh dear, she thought, here we go again! She hadn't seen him act like this in a long, long time.

Michael's whole being reflected the mood of his heart. He exuded a joy, a kind of shining, a radiance that was catching. Before this, as far as I knew, he had never been happy in his relationships. It seemed to me that initially, in his need to satisfy the object of his fascination, he would develop an irritable compulsion to please her. This would later be replaced by a restlessness, perhaps a reflection on the neediness of those with whom he became involved.

Mardi would despair, "But no one can ever live up to Michael's evaluations...no person could ever be *quite* as intelligent or *quite* as talented as Michael's heart designates her to be!"

But this time he was indeed happy. Barbara became his world.

She got her divorce, and they decided to marry. I arrived in time for the wedding. A large party of friends witnessed the ceremony at Barbara's father's smart town home. Her dress was aqua, her hat and veil were aqua, her shoes were dyed to match, even the flowers in her bouquet and around the house were sprayed aqua—a fact that mortified Aunt Muriel and entranced me, for I had a fond memory of such coloration on Easter chicks. Strangest of all for Pardi was the sight of the aqua cake. He referred to the occasion as the "blue ceremony"; Barbara said, "Well, let's face it, it can't be white—and blue is better than scarlet, Pardi!"

I was requested to match. I ended up wearing an aqua A-line dress with sleeves of embroidered cutwork, and raised eyebrows when I shortened the hemline to the bold and fashionable mini length I favoured.

"At least she's just showing her knees this time...at her father's last wedding she produced a tooth!" Aunt Muriel observed.

I vaguely remember the honeymoon, at a gracious north coast hotel, for my brother Joseph and I were there. In my mind I have an incongruous picture of Barbara in a diaphanous, full-length beach coat over a white two-piece bathing-suit with a white fishnet midriff, and a huge white straw hat over her large dark glasses, walking elegantly over the sand in high white sandals.

"Come and swim," Michael called from the water, where Joseph was practising diving between our father's sprawled legs under the water. I could see how much weight Michael had gained. He was almost two hundred and twenty pounds, a statistic he blamed on giving up smoking.

Barbara stopped and double-shaded her eyes. "Oh, I'm not going into the water." She shivered and clutched her crossed arms as if she was cold, and shied away from the swiftly disappearing frill of a wave, then gingerly, uselessly, lifted the coat as some sort of explanation.

"Why won't you swim?" I asked her, finding her apparent coyness tedious.

"I can't swim. You know," she confided, "I have an uncle who always says he has never seen a fish walking down King Street, so he doesn't see why he should be swimming in the sea." She laughed. "Maybe I didn't learn because I fear being engulfed...oh, that's just a grand excuse for being a total coward!"

I suspected that, like me, she didn't want to get her hair wet.

I was initially ambivalent about her. Part of me welcomed the style she brought into our lives, for I was very impressed by her good looks and tasteful clothes. My father moved back with his new wife to Ebony Hill. Now everything in the house matched. The living-room appeared overdressed in floor-length curtains and a complete living-room set with aqua sofa and matching aqua chairs, a shiny oblong dining-table to replace the unsteady, gnarled one, and new dishes and glasses and cutlery and linen.

"I think I make a house look too much like a wood carving," Mardi remarked regretfully when she first saw the refurbished room.

I envied Barbara's poise and composure, and sometimes tried in my own circle to imitate her, but my nervy, neurotic nature would get in the way of the façade. On a more personal level, I was deeply jealous of her, and resented her closeness to my father.

I am not sure whether she breathed new energy into the family or whether her arrival simply coincided with a resurgence of our own, but by 1966 there we were: Pardi and Mardi at Nomdmi inventing a new way of life, she sculpting in Mini, he up and down the hill as he faced yet another general election; my father, to a large extent encouraged by Barbara and his certainty of his strength with her at his side, looming ever larger in public life, and I settling into my first year at university, living on campus.

Michael and Barbara transformed the study below their bedroom into a studio flat for Pardi and Mardi whenever they came into town. Having no kitchen, they were given a standing invitation to eat upstairs, but they usually had their meals next door with Aunt Muriel. Mae the cook was now fairly stable after receiving electric shock treatment at the mental hospital, except for one occasion when she turned up at the table to serve dinner in one of Aunt Muriel's finest cocktail dresses; Aunt Muriel signalled her brother and Mardi to pay no attention.

Pardi installed a two-burner gas stove to boil water for his coffee, having discovered the wonder of Nescafé Instant. He saw this phenomenon as invaluable to modernity as sliced bread. Mardi invested a great deal of time trying to master the boiling of a perfect three-minute egg. She finally insisted the process could not be done in three minutes but only in five, which Miss Boyd explained was due to her not boiling the water first.

"But I can't, dear," Mardi explained, "for the eggs simply burst!"

"If you put salt in the water they shouldn't ooze," Miss Boyd suggested, but Mardi liked to crack open her eggs herself, so she persisted in placing the eggs in cold water. Now she claimed to be able to cook, a boast which the family saw as further proof of the power of her imagination over reality.

It was on one of Pardi and Mardi's short trips to Ebony Hill that they found Barbara overjoyed with the news that she was expecting a baby, a discovery that astonished the mother-to-be; she had been told by three different doctors, with as many reasons, that she was infertile. The last one had suggested she keep a pet.

In 1967, only five days before nomination day, Michael decided to run in the next general election to be held that February. He took the plunge in Central Kingston, a newly created constituency that had been so gerrymandered by the JLP that it was now considered to be far from a safe seat for the PNP.

The decision came after a talk with Barbara that lasted most of the night. It was really the denouement of a conversation Michael had been having with himself all his adult life. Mardi described it as "the agonizing search through his own self-doubts". He saw it as his struggle with the long shadow cast by his father.

The doubts about himself were never about what he could or could not do. He knew only too well his own capabilities.

They were about what he wanted to do and, ultimately, what terms he was prepared to live on.

"I suppose when other boys were purchasing their heroes for a shilling in a comic book, I had my hero alive beside me right there in my home," he explained to Barbara that evening. "Comics you outgrow; the characters fade as they become diminished by one's own growth in proportion to them. Now you try doing that with a living hero!"

Barbara's perspective always seemed to come from the other end of the shadow. As though she were looking back from fifty years later.

"I think it's your destiny. I think, when it's fulfilled, you will find your father's shadow is beside you."

Sometimes he could feel his mother's spirit in him fighting to be free—free of the expectations of others, of his expectations of himself, of that great yoke of his conscience; most of all, free of the example, heavy with its share of triumph and disappointment, of that shadow.

"And at the end of it all, one is likely to get kicked in the teeth...like Dad."

"Then we'll just have to get a nice new set of teeth," Barbara concluded, unperturbed.

He made the decision not really because he was convinced, though her conviction was comforting. More because he felt drawn by a tide. Maybe that was what happened with destiny. Maybe it didn't have to be right or wrong, it was just ordained to *be*.

"Central Kingston" was to become as familiar as the house names. It was a campaign of violence, guns having made their way into the hands of political thugs in the ghetto areas.

During the last weeks of the campaign, Pardi and Mardi stayed in town. Mardi was in a state of quiet desperation. It troubled her to witness the parade of pomp and glory as the JLP ministers displayed their trappings of power—official cars and titles and functions and circumstance—dispensing their favours, or not, throughout a somewhat perplexed little island. Although she liked her husband's left-wing agenda, which seemed like the shake of a fist at the powers that be, she was not optimistic about the result. She knew they were fighting the inevitable two-term tide, and the JLP were due to win.

Barbara's enthusiasm was clearly a source of inspiration to Michael, but the flesh seemed weaker than the spirit; Mardi noticed that Barbara was often alone upstairs resting in bed.

One afternoon Mardi found Barbara in her bedroom dressed in a simple red sleeveless shift that hung over her melon-shaped stomach. Mardi suddenly saw the outline of every bone in her daughter-in-law's body, as though the wind had sucked her skin tight over her skeleton. For a moment she saw Barbara's figure as though it were leaning to one side—not bending or inclining, more as though it were broken, the snapped stem of a plant. And her eyes looked sunken, too—but when Barbara smiled at her they seemed to resurface, and became so alive that Mardi wondered if she had imagined it all, and looked away.

By the time Michael came into the room to collect her, Barbara was intact, tall and slim in her red smock, smiling with concerted valiance. But Mardi could not get the outline of bone out of her head. It reminded her of moments in her work when the truth of a piece replaced whatever she had envisioned before. It reminded her of anatomy classes, and the hard, white indifference of bone.

"It's all so very strange," she said to Pardi that night as they lay head to head on a pair of single beds along two adjoining walls of their son's studio flat. The crickets were shrieking outside, and the noise seemed to echo in the room.

"How so?" he asked. He could see sharp stars between the louvers above his head, where a wind passed like someone friendly and freshly bathed, leaving the generously sweet smell of the tuberoses his wife planted beneath the window—her only intrusion on her son's garden, for she said cows didn't like their smell and would leave them alone.

"I think Barbara is ill."

Pardi too had noticed a new fragility in his daughter-in-law. Whenever he came to Ebony Hill alone, he would go up to see her. He loved his visits to Barbara. He could always hear every word she said. She was often in her room, just lying there, dressed as though she had originally intended to face the day. She would brighten as he came round the door. He would sit at her dressing-table, on the little frilly stool, swivelling this way and that. He had the warmest twinkle she had ever seen from a man, the deepest reservoir of thought and concern and, except for her own father, the fewest complications of ego.

Michael, though it was his room too, would come formally to "visit", and favoured an upholstered chair that he always had to clear of her clothes before he sat down.

Douglas, dropping in on his holiday returns from Africa, would sprawl flat on his back on the bed beside her, his eyes fixed forward, his hands clasped on top of his paunch, and proceed to gossip. Barbara liked being alone with him; he reminded her of a pot that was slow to boil. You had to let him warm up. His mother, she felt, was always finishing his sentences for him.

"She sees the doctor," Pardi now said to the bundle of grey waves that was all he could see of his wife. He found the nearness of her head reassuring, their proximity like a dormitory coziness. He never had dreams when she was with him in this room.

"She makes Michael so happy," she said softly.

"Yes, I know."

"This afternoon she struggled out of bed to go with Michael to Central Kingston... apparently the constituency named her president of its women's group. Under that baby she's shockingly thin, you know... she came in from that meeting and just collapsed into bed. Michael had to get her clothes off for her. He's so worried..."

"Yes. But once she has the baby..."

"The doctor's a bit worried about her too. So they may decide to pop the baby out with a Caesar, and have a look-see, Michael says." She said this in her "let's jolly things along and they'll work out okay" voice. She shortened the term "Caesarean", as if she thought this would make the news seem less threatening to him. His concern seemed to make his breath come slow and heavy, and he sighed.

"I didn't know that. When is the baby due?"

"In April."

Pardi thought for a minute. He had planned to lay out a grape arbour up the hill, but had postponed it because of the election. He wanted to try the fruit up there despite the warnings of his agriculturist friend, Lecky, who said it was too high and too moist for grapes. They couldn't fare worse than they had in town. But that would have to wait.

"I think we'd better stay put, then," he suggested gently. "Michael may need support."

Sometimes at night in that room, Pardi could imagine from the sounds beyond the gully that he was still at Drumblair. The dogs barking, some preacher railing at God or a Four Roads congregation, or was it a politician? The boom of surly, defiant sounds from the rum shops, the drone of night trucks stealing sand from the gully bed. His own heart loyally pounding in his ear.

Mardi gave a little cry that was neither despair nor woe. It sounded to Pardi more like one of those times a memory surprised her, like when a mule suddenly stopped in the path, and Ivan said it had seen a duppy.

He put his arm over and held her upside down shoulder. "I wonder why the tuberoses smell stronger at night?" He didn't expect an answer, and was surprised when she said very precisely:

"Because that's the only time the world listens."

And Pardi, who could find no logic to her answer, stood at the familiar edge of that other life, the way he lingered after each chapter of a D.H. Lawrence novel, enriched but damned to his own sure world.

※

After five years in opposition the PNP lost again in the general election in February 1967. It was a campaign that took place against the backdrop of the Western Kingston Wars, which began in 1965 and resulted in a state of emergency being called in 1966; it was characterized by political tribalism. Each side blamed the other.

Michael narrowly won his seat; out of ten thousand votes, the margin was in his favour by only forty-three, after several recounts. Pardi, in a safe seat, also won his, so now they were both members of parliament.

Seven weeks after the election we were gathered at a hospital, where we awaited the birth of Barbara's baby by Caesarean delivery.

The maternity wing of the Nuttall was a new structure at the back of the hospital. The rooms were arranged around a courtyard, which made the atmosphere breezier, brighter and somehow more frivolous than that of the solid original building, whose solemnity cowed visitors into whispers.

"This is where I will die, isn't it, Norman? With a dry martini in my hand, listening to the love stories of silly young nurses!" Mardi always said this when we went to the Nuttall.

"It's hardly likely you'll be in this wing, dear."

Barbara had been wheeled out of the new wing on a gurney, all covered in a green sheet, with a lopsided green cap on her head. She was giggly by the time she left, for they had given her a dose of something "to dry out her secretions," said the matron, whom we all knew only too well. The corners of Barbara's mouth had tell-tale traces of white where the drug was already doing its job. My father held her hand as he walked beside the gurney, and the little group of orderlies and family followed the wheels with their *gathub, gathub* each time they crossed a seam in the concrete, down the darkening corridors of the older building, which housed the operating theatres.

Barbara's family went back to her room to wait. Pardi and I left Mardi sitting in the car in the parking lot and went in search of something to eat. By the time we returned from the visitor's canteen with a pack of potato chips and some weary patties, my father was pacing up and down the parking lot, looking up on each turn towards the surgical area.

"What will you call the baby, Michael?" Mardi asked as I divided the snacks. My father wasn't hungry.

"David...if it's a boy." He was kicking up dust.

"Suppose it's a girl..."

Michael looked irritated, but Mardi was determined to distract him.

"...have you got *her* a name..."

"Well...I suppose...Ruth, or Sarah. We like both. Barbara said if it was a girl, she'd wait to see which one she looked like." He paced off and took a cantankerous turn at a dusty bed of pink ram-goat roses that circled the roots of an old tree.

Pardi and I began a game of Twenty Questions...animal, vegetable or mineral—to pass the time, and every now and then Michael would join in to ask a brief question and come hurtling down with an answer, sometimes right, sometimes wrong, before setting off, tight-jawed, on his marking of time.

An orderly, recognizing Michael, came rushing across to him, taking one of his hands in both of his.

"Joshua, we proud of you, man. Congratulations on winning your seat!"

Then he saw my father look self-consciously towards the car and, seeing Pardi there, he released one hand to wave, and called, "Sorry about the election, sir." Turning back to Michael, he said, "In my heart he will always be the Father of the Nation."

Sitting in the car, Pardi reflected on the recent election with mixed feelings. He felt that Michael had become more relevant to Jamaica than he was. The country had a new profile of protest. Black power had brought with it a new breed of "angry young men" with whom Michael seemed better able to communicate. Pardi had never been a patient man, and his intolerance of what he considered foolishness was legendary. He thought reducing the country's problems to the issue of race was taking too simplistic a view of the complicated consequences of colonialism. It was Jamaica's tragedy that the equation of white with wealth and black with poverty provided such a facile but essentially useless interpretation of history.

But it wouldn't be his responsibility much longer. That had been his last election. He had made one final, energetic effort, and he had no further force left to spend. It was time for the next generation. He had made up his mind to retire, but he had told no one yet, for fear the party might feel he was setting a hand for his son.

He saw a steadiness and strength developing in Michael now, as though Barbara were the metronome he needed to pace his life, the magnet that pulled his restlessness to base, the comfort zone needed to calm the splashing of his soul and allow deeper philosophical tides to guide him. For the first time since adolescence, Michael seemed comfortable with just being alive. He hoped to God Barbara was all right.

Michael suddenly broke away from his prowl and walked towards a figure crossing from the theatre to the maternity wing. We all looked over to see a nurse holding a small bundle of green hospital sheet. My father intercepted the nurse at the steps. In the few seconds it took us to join him, his face had become embattled.

"But to do *what?*" he was demanding of the gentle nurse, who held what could only be a baby, though we couldn't see its face.

"Do what?" Mardi echoed, looking first at my father and then at the nurse.

"They've found something," Michael said in angry confusion.

"Mrs. Manley," the nurse said, looking imploringly at her, "I can't really say, you will have to talk to Doctor. It seems they have called another surgeon...Doctor will be out."

Pardi missed this interchange. He walked straight to the nurse and gently pulled the folds of green cloth to reveal the face of the new child, who seemed peaceful enough beneath. "My, my," he said softly.

"She's a baby girl," said the nurse.

Michael looked down at his baby daughter, and his face softened.

"You are a Sarah," he said.

Mardi, though distracted by worry, slipped a sleuthing hand behind the small neck, looking for the familiar sink just beneath the back of the head which she considered authentication of the Shearer line. She gently fondled the infant's "cubbage hole". "A Swithenbank," she acknowledged, as if it were a roulette number she had always expected to turn up.

"What is the baby?" asked Barbara's mother, who emerged eagerly from the maternity wing with Barbara's two sisters in tow and settled proprietorially over the bundle.

"A baby girl," repeated the nurse, who was relieved that the attention now centred on her small charge.

It seemed that we waited a long time for more news, two families drawn together through circumstance; Barbara's hovered near the nursery wing, ours prowled uncertainly where Barbara had disappeared.

But in fact it wasn't very long till the orderlies wheeled her out, and the doctor explained that they had found a growth, and that a fine surgeon from the university had come in to see and he would operate in a week. In the meantime they hadn't attempted to take anything out. There would be tests, and they would know more.

Barbara's mother and sisters came in and out of the room. Mardi was amazed at how few questions the mother asked; she appeared to cope on autopilot, her stalwart faith having kicked in. Barbara's father looked devastated.

Michael sat outside the room, on a low wall edging the walkway of an open quadrangle, waiting for Barbara to wake.

Barbara may have had an inkling before Sarah's birth that there was trouble ahead, but Michael felt it was when she was breaking the surface of sleep, lapsing in and out after the anaesthetic, that she realized something was seriously wrong. She must have sensed the worry in the faces coming and going around her. When she realized she was holding Michael's hand, she turned for reassurance to his eyes, which he tried to keep steady and truthful.

They had always maintained that truth was to be the basis of their relationship, whatever happened. It was to define the terms of their life together. "This is the only way," she had said, and he had tried earnestly to meet that challenge. They both felt that in their other relationships it was unreality that had finally undone them. There was a side to Caribbean life that set men and women in a ritualistic dance, changing steps, changing costumes, changing masks. They did not want this.

The baby was fine, he assured her, and I think she is a Sarah. Yes; the doctors had seen something, there was a growth, they would remove it and do tests. A second operation was due a week later. Keep steady, he told her, we'll get through.

Over the next week Barbara braced herself for the up-coming ordeal, trying to engross herself in the immediate joy of their daughter. When she first saw her, Barbara said she had the sensation that the whole room contracted, and all she could see was her face. She was relieved, she said, to discover that the baby was an extrovert, for it would have been difficult if she had been a loner like Barbara herself.

"Oh Lord, how can you know that already?" asked her mother, who felt labelling the baby somehow diminished her innocence.

Barbara told Michael to expect a long operation, and reminded him that, whatever the eventuality, he must never break faith with her. Whether the outcome of the surgery was good or bad, they would face it together.

Her small, bright room was inundated with flowers. The thin curtains competed with flouncing mauve and aqua blooms. Michael brought a large table fan that paused with its head tilted at an odd angle at each end of the rotation.

"It gives me a crick neck watching it; I want to move its neck the other way," observed Barbara.

We all visited in relays. Pardi and Mardi stayed in town and brought gin and tonics each afternoon at six. We arrived with cards and played rummy on the side of the bed, and when Sarah came to be bottle-fed by her mother, Pardi would pick up one of the "penny dreadfuls" that Aunt Muriel had lent the patient, and Mardi would set up her grand demon patience with two packs of cards. One day we even brought an orange-meringue pudding that Zethilda had made for her and handed us surreptitiously over the fence, though without Zethilda's accompanying admonishment: "Lawd Gad, missus, no mek dem open her up...if you let in fresh air, growt' wi' eat you up!"

When the day came, we replayed the waiting game during the operation. It started at two in the afternoon. We loitered at the back, between the old building and the new wing, and twice we went over to the nursery to visit Sarah.

"Kenny is there," my father said to no one in particular.

Kenny was a friend of my father. He was also a fine doctor who had turned to politics when he got bored with medicine. He was one of the newcomers who had worked fervently to shape a more radical party, to save Jamaica from what he called "me too" politics, in which both parties mimicked each other and offered the same things.

"Oh, he's such a dear. Now I feel better, knowing that," said Mardi uselessly. We were all nervous of Michael when he was worried. He was not a person one comforted. He was too proud and impatient, and his pragmatic nature made sympathetic gestures profoundly irritating to him. Mardi, who had made an art of providing the sympathetic gesture and was now trying to curb the instinct, was attempting to appear practical.

"I thought Kenny was ear, nose and throat," noted Pardi.

"Well, dear, he's turned to plastic surgery now," Mardi explained. "He does wonderful noses, I'm told."

Pardi looked bewildered.

"He changed his specialty," she said with finality.

"He's there as an observer," said Michael, who shared his father's need for straightforward answers in life. "He's my great friend . . . I asked him, Dad."

It was six hours before Kenny came out. I remember the afternoon in stages of light moving towards evening, when the parking area seemed to pull yellow strands from the building to alleviate its grey. I felt the time in heavy intimacy: I noticed the lengthening of the shadows of branches, or a roof, as a shape reached and passed a stone or a piece of paper on the ground. But by six o'clock there were only the beams of electric lights. Friends came and went, but the families stayed on.

When he finally emerged, Kenny was still wearing his operating gown and cap, which were splattered with blood. He was a small but commanding figure with a limp which, if anything, made him seem more decisive. He gave his accustomed smile, heartening and vivid, but his eyes looked steadily into Michael's fierce, questioning stare. He motioned to him, and Michael followed him a few feet away.

"It's bad, Michael," I heard him say, and then I could barely hear his soft talking—"spread like wildfire..."

And then my father shouted so hard we all jumped, "No!"

"It must be cancer," I whispered to Mardi and Pardi.

"Dear God," muttered Pardi, looking down as though to find some unused area of earth to start his own prowl.

After long years of practising medicine, Kenny must have been accustomed to this. He spoke calmly through it all, as though he were the surgeon working on the minutiae of tissue, sure that the surgical clamps were in place and would do their job to stem the flow.

It was cancer and it had spread, no question about it. The surgeon had done a fine job. They had had to remove part of her colon. They hoped they had caught it all, but they would have to wait for the tests. They would do all they could. There were specialists he knew abroad. They would try to buy time; Barbara could try various treatments. But his opinion was clear from what he did *not* say, the way he refused to reassure us. These measures were appeals that might stave off the final judgement, but ultimately they would not carry the day.

Soon afterwards Barbara herself came out, still and grey on the clattering gurney, with tubes and a drip, and was transferred to her bed in the maternity wing. A pump was attached to something, and every now and then it made a horrible mechanical sound that I could not believe related to anything human.

I sat on the low wall outside Barbara's window. I found myself thinking of the strange way things fell off a shelf during an earthquake, how the walls shook and you could hear the earth rumble, and you could see trees lifting and falling if you stayed calm and watched, and yet something quite heavy would just seem to bow itself over the edge and fall, as though the fall were the only gentle, silent thing left in the world. And sometimes it would do it when the shelf didn't seem to move anymore, but as though it had thought about it, and decided just to tip over as an afterthought; or maybe it imagined that was what was expected of it.

This time, Michael sat dead still in the deep visitor's chair. His elbows rested on the wooden arms, and his index fingers pressed his pursed lips as he stared at the frosted window slats, probably composing a way to deliver the truth to his wife.

There seemed to be movement in her mind long before Michael considered her back from sleep. When she did wake, she seemed uncertain whether she had, and kept asking if this was a dream.

"Someone was talking to me...about humility...must have been God..."

She fell asleep again for a bit, and then struggled back again and this time seemed quite clear-headed.

"It is cancer," Michael said, feeling brutal. "It has spread, and they have had to remove some of your colon, but the surgeon hopes he's caught it all."

She looked as if she'd been hit in the jaw by a heavyweight boxer. Her face shuddered, and then her eyes searched the ceiling as though for comprehension or escape. She still had a grey pallor, and her face looked bare and frank without the splashes of eyebrows and the usual deep black pencil outlines.

He told her that he had decided to take her to New York, to the Pack Institute...one of the best in the world for cancer, Kenny had assured him. In fact, Kenny had already gone to make the arrangements.

"We'll lick this thing together," he told her.

"We will?" She said it vaguely, and then closed her eyes again. He wondered if she meant it as a question, or if what sounded like disbelief was just her voice succumbing to drowsiness.

"Now I'm a semi-colon," she said and went back to sleep.

He was ashamed of his own cowardice. This was the only time he had ever felt reluctant to be alone with her.

15

Two
Ducks in
a Pond

The funeral was in June, which Mardi found entirely inappropriate. Not the service, but the reality of a death in June at all, much less the death of anyone so young. June was, after all, the middle of the year, the early edge of summer, when the June roses stuffed their pink and white cheeks, and children stole guavas from the remaining backlands, their pockets trailing an elastic strap from the slingshot within, and you just had to hope that, boys being boys, they wouldn't actually raid a nest for helpless young birds, but would wait to get their parents and make them orphans instead.

Mardi fanned herself with the small white pamphlet whose only ornamentation was the stencilled outline of a single lily beneath the alarming words:

Order of Funeral Service
Barbara Manley

The church was packed. The small mutterings of ushers trying to get people squeezed in to fit, and the hum of the fans overhead, were more immediate than the traffic sounds of Half-Way-Tree, which reminded one that, just outside, commerce, traffic, ill-tempered motorists, whistling peanut-vending bicycles, filthy-lunged country buses coming to town, men at the side of the road spitting and hoisting their crotches as though to confirm that they were still really men even if they were unemployed or simply vagrant by disposition—all this was still going on. Life, the inescapable road, would still be out there when this gathering of heart-broken and curious and polite mourners returned to the afternoon.

It was three o'clock on the ninth of June, 1968. The service should be starting.

Mardi sat in the row behind Michael. His hair had been recently cut with what must have been a barber's razor, for the line, when it appeared over his collar, which was whenever he looked down or across at his two older children on either side of him, was so straight it looked artificial. It made Mardi think of him as a little boy, when he got his hair cut the day before each new school term.

It is said that, to a mother, a son is always a little boy. In the past Mardi had been able to mend and fix, to make each little cut and fall-down "get better". This afternoon Michael's vulnerability was an unplugged drain down which she felt herself falling. Her sheltering spirit spread uselessly, for his pain was more defined and self-contained than mourning. Mourning one could mop up and absorb like a big spill. But this—and she smiled as Michael looked back at his father, then at her, to check if they were all right—this was a tense incubation, the way sprinters crouch to collect their thoughts and prepare their muscles for the moment of launch.

Over the altar was a stained-glass window shaped like a huge domed door with inset panels. As a child Mardi had imagined that a similar window in her father's church in Penzance was God's door leading up to the sky. Churches always made her feel as if she was being herded and couldn't get away. She remembered having to get tidy on Sundays, scratchy dress and tight, buckled shoes. She loved to hear her father's voice as he gave the sermon, but it took what seemed like a whole day, and she didn't give a damn about anything else in the service. She wished she could get out to the fields to jump hayricks.

She looked up. Overhead were the usual scenes of madonna and child, shepherds and kings. The madonna held her attention. This was an Anglican church. Having returned to the medium of wood, Mardi had just finished a carving of Mary for the Catholic church. The legend of Jesus' birth held no particular interest for her; her fear and fascination were inspired by the single godhead of the Old Testament.

Hers was a very different Mary. It was Mary looking down into a son's tomb. At first her working drawings had shown Mary with her hands up to her face in horror or surprise, or to keep the knowledge out of her head. But when she approached the wood, she couldn't get it to co-operate. She felt its grain fighting her, sulky and stubborn. And then one day, suspending her will, she followed the wood and let it guide her hands. A different Mary emerged. The face held little expression, offering an emptiness that sorrow or memory could engrave over the years. The contorted figure was rooted in despair. The arms hung straight and stiff from the lifted shoulders, in reluctance or dread. By contrast, the body's unconscious leaning, the dislocated bend of the head, suggested a spirit snapped like a stem. Only the hands held on to any hope, as though cradling their loss.

Mardi recognized her. She was the leaning, broken figure that had struck her that afternoon when her daughter-in-law was pregnant. She was sure she had seen in that moment the shadow of Barbara's death.

She looked across at Barbara's mother. The families sat in opposite pews, as if this were a wedding, their friends gathering themselves obediently in the rows behind. Then there was a block of pews headed by the government ministers. Hugh Shearer, the prime minister, was there; he had come to lead the JLP government when Donald Sangster, who had taken over from the ailing Bustamante, had died. Shearer had shown both public and personal kindness to Michael during Barbara's illness.

Aunt Vera, the family's genealogist, had always thought Shearer was our cousin. Mardi agreed. Looking at his tall frame and wide shoulders, she wished she could get him to turn around one day so she could feel the back of his neck and determine for sure if he was a relative. Michael had been very fond of him since their union days, when Shearer had been his counterpart in the rival union.

In the fourth block of pews, that peripheral one where no one anyone knew ever sat, there were now dignitaries of one sort or another, and Barbara's associates from the tourism and advertising world.

The organ music was so soft that I didn't notice it until it stopped. As the church rose to its feet in a wave, altar boys came down the aisle, and a priest with incense swaying, and the closed, rather ornate coffin that oddly reminded me of too-shiny shoes was wheeled in and left just in front of my father.

The organ suddenly crashed into sound.

Jesus lives! thy terrors now
Can, oh death, no more appal us;
Jesus lives! by this we know
Thou, oh grave, cans't not enthral us.
Hallelujah!

Mardi could sense Pardi's exhaustion beside her. He was not a figure of devastation any more. He had become like a ruined city, the remains of an old splendour dreaming on, forgotten, through eons of dusty centuries. Nothing much more was likely to happen. A brick or two might fall off a wall in the next century; there might be evidence of a tourist's visit in a wrapper of gum or, better yet, a scratched initial. But the agony was gone as his voice followed a phrase or two of the verse, as she felt the comfortable lean of his arm in its soft grey suit with the gentle, familiar smell of his cupboard, or was it the Mennen prickly-heat powder?

Of all the family members, it was Barbara's mother who most rose to the sense of the hymn's occasion. My brother, Joseph, now eleven, ignored the pamphlet and the singing, standing with an impervious, soldierly gaze as though to defend the sorrow of our father. Michael took refuge in the concerted wail that now surrounded us, dabbing at the edges of his eyes and nose and refolding his handkerchief before attempting to put it back in his pocket. I took it from him, deciding he might need it again. It was part of my clucking over him, a duty I had been allowed to perform in the days since Barbara's death.

I had been at the other end of the island, in Montego Bay. I was playing Anne Page in that year's Shakespeare production, *The Merry Wives of Windsor*. The news of my step-mother's death, which I received as I left the stage, saved me having to explain why, in an attack of stage fright that greatly outweighed the significance of my minor part, the audience had failed to hear my comparatively few lines.

The first time I really grasped that Barbara was gone was later that night at a small airfield where I waited for an army plane to fly me to Kingston. I was seated in an empty, very dusty hangar on a tin pail that a soldier had turned upside down for me and offered as a seat. From a radio somewhere, I heard Louis Armstrong's voice rasping about what a wonderful world it was. The presence of his voice in that hollow room was profound. I tried to match my information with the words, and that's when, incongruously, it hit me. *Barbara is dead.*

I had seen Barbara for the last time the night before I left Kingston. I had come from the university to say goodbye. I walked in with a friend who happened to be wearing a paisley tie, which Barbara admired. She said that it reminded her of ducks, whereupon she recited a verse she apparently remembered from her childhood.

Two ducks in a pond,
What a funny thing.
To remember for years
To remember with tears
Two ducks in a pond.

At first she seemed quite amused by this, and then she looked at me thoughtfully and said, "The funny thing about ducks is that they appear to glide so smoothly on the water, but underneath their big feet are paddling like hell to keep up."

Although centred around tragic circumstance, I would miss these afternoon visits to Washington Drive. Pardi and Mardi had lost their tenant and moved back down to Regardless. I used to come to Ebony Hill to bring my laundry and to play with the ebullient Sarah, who bounced rather than bobbed, and stomped rather than inched her way round the rails of her crib in Joseph's old bedroom.

Sarah disliked being physically overwhelmed. She displayed a good-natured impatience with affection, and seemed to derive pleasure from fending off sentimental approaches. With Pardi it became a game. She would lie in wait for him, ready to thwart his efforts, chortling at her handiwork when she'd knocked his glasses askew or twisted his nose. One night when she wouldn't go to sleep he sneaked a minute drop of gin into her milk bottle, and everyone remarked on his uncanny knack with his granddaughters. We all stopped to say hi to Sarah during our nightly visits to Barbara, when the house was busy with the parade of doctors, nurses, well-wishers, friends and Barbara's family. And Hoad. The Reverend John Hoad.

Barbara's illness followed its own schedule, and could be absorbing and, to be honest, even as exciting as an election campaign. There were the good-news days after some test or a drop in her fever, when we would see the dismantling of her drip, and the scary bad-news days when her blood count was down or her yellowness (so much an indicator of her state that Barbara had started painting it in her pictures) had returned, and there would be a new doctor or an extra nursing shift, and the contraption suspending her drip would be reinstated beside her bed. And there would be Reverend Hoad, tall, and somehow indecisive in features and colouring and speech; he was a Barbadian Methodist minister who had married Barbara and Michael, and christened Sarah.

He now stood at the altar beside the bishop, preparing to read the memorial address, holding his prayer book but looking around at the gathering with compassion, almost fondly and with a hint of apology, as they dutifully repeated the twenty-third psalm:

The Lord is my shepherd...

His eyes could have been grey or blue—even a pale yellow, I sometimes thought, but this was probably due to his spectacles, which looked like yellowing plastic. They were transparent eyes that remained thoughtful and sceptical, and lacked any trace of fanaticism. He had that wide, diphthonged, almost Somerset accent which, for reasons I never grasped in philology, white Barbadians share, but the edges of his speech were less fierce and blunt, less phlegmatic, than the usual Barbadian accent. He spoke slowly, holding his jaws open, as though helping his words out of his mouth as one would an elderly person out of a car. But though he showed evidence of great simplicity, it was not a simple mind he had, but rather a simplicity of spirit that reflected his Methodist tradition, which avoided icons and statues and pageantry, the "graven images" of religion, keeping itself free of most elaborations.

...He restoreth my soul...

Lulled by the familiar meander through "the valley of the shadow of death", Michael watched the tall pastor with what might have been a combination of affection and a certain envy. Over the last few months he had listened on the sidelines of his wife's relationship with the minister. They became close, and if he was there, Michael felt oddly adrift and uncomfortable during their long conversations.

"You are both contemplatives," he said to Barbara once.

"Why, what are you?" she asked in surprise.

"I suppose an activist," he said.

There was no sense of Barbara in the church now. This funeral, a pageant with the words of worthy saints and the promise of heaven, was to Michael no more reminiscent of her life than the necessary paperwork of her death certificate, handed to him apologetically by the doctor, had been reminiscent of her departure.

My father told me years later that he felt he really lost his wife on their second visit to the Pack Institute in New York, seven months before she died, in November.

Not that the first visit had been easy. Within weeks of Barbara's second operation, the infant Sarah developed meningitis. A continent away, Barbara was starting experimental cobalt therapy at the Pack Institute. Michael could barely bring himself to think about her terror each time she had to approach the small therapy room. The first time she went, she had with her only a small prayer book that Hoad's wife had sent for her, and the doctor's assurance that this would not hurt, and that the consequences would be bearable.

The news of the baby's illness devastated her. She was far more upset by this than by any of the gruelling side effects she had to endure from her own treatment. Michael felt at times overwhelmed by circumstance, and would find himself at Saks Fifth Avenue buying dresses for his wife as though purchasing good news or time.

But it was the second visit—after it was clear that Sarah was over the worst and would recover without lingering damage—that he felt had devastating significance.

He was called in for a meeting with the doctor, who told him flatly that they were only buying time. The cancer had spread to the vital organs, and was of a most virulent nature. He couldn't say exactly how long she would survive, but he expected no more than six months.

"Never, in all my years in this profession, have I found it advisable to tell a patient a prognosis of imminent death.

Always give them hope. The human spirit must be allowed that."

And with that, the human spirit in Michael—which through all this, fuelled only by hope, had managed to thrive and remain creative—was dealt a fatal blow. He had enough pragmatism and little enough mystical faith to accept the best scientific opinion. His spirit floundered as he faced a problem without a solution.

"My advice to you is never to tell her."

But he had promised her truth.

During a tormented walk down Fifth Avenue, Michael again took refuge in Saks and purchased a stunning gown designed by Tiffaud, white with a geometric blue design. Its asymmetry attracted him; it hung on the mannequin from a single bow on the right shoulder, and fell dead straight with no waistline. It was just like her, he thought—starker for its embellishment, and with a fundamental style and angle all its own.

He brought it to her in the hotel room later that day, as though he were bearing tribute. Her eyes lit up as she opened the box and separated the dress from the packing tissue. Looking down at the gown across her lap, she caught him off guard as she asked him directly, "How was the meeting?"

"Fine," he said too readily, lifting his voice higher than necessary. "He's very pleased," he lied. "The horrid stuff seems to have done the trick."

She looked at him. He couldn't look at her, so he looked at the gown.

He knew in the back of his head, like a traveller who senses he has taken the wrong turn, that he had made a mistake and that each step after that was a waste of time.

That night as he lay beside her in bed, where she appeared to be reading, he had a battle with his tears. He thought he had won until she said to him, "You've got something in your eye." It was an act of complicity. "If you look on the shelf in the bathroom, you'll see my Murine. It will help. Try it."

From that day on, he felt he had lost her. He said he often wondered if he had robbed her of any option but blind faith.

... thou art with me,
thy rod and staff they comfort me. ...

Reverend Hoad used to visit Barbara. He had first come to see her at her mother's invitation. He arrived in early December, when she was surrounded by the Manley family and a pile of new books she had brought back from New York.

"Look, I have all these new books. I must be planning to stay a long time in my bed if I'm going to read them all," she said.

"Then maybe you won't need this, but I'll leave it anyway." Hoad placed a small paperback on Zen Buddhism beside her.

He had not expected to visit her again, and was surprised when three days later she called him.

"I *love* your Zen masters." She sounded as thrilled as a child. "When can you come and speak to me about them?"

His visits became a regular afternoon item, one which he probably depended on as much as she did. She gave so much of herself, and he seemed to be irresistibly drawn, whether to her mind, her beauty, her sorrow or her tragedy. He seemed somehow to be ministered to, in ministering to her.

One afternoon many months later, just before Sarah's first birthday, Hoad arrived with a large book, and found the home in a state of commotion. Barbara was sobbing on her husband's shoulder in the bedroom, and Sarah, in a nanny's arms, appeared to be hysterical. When Hoad came in, everyone looked at him as though he were somehow to blame for whatever had occurred. I drew him aside and explained.

We had been playing cricket on the lawn when we heard Barbara scream from the bedroom. She was on the huge, low bed, playing with the baby, when Sarah lunged out of her arms and fell to the floor, hitting her head on the side of the bed. Barbara didn't have the strength to hold her or catch her, or even pick her up.

"Oh, God, I can't even hold my own child," she had sobbed.

Later, when I walked him to the door, I said to Hoad, "I'm sorry, you haven't had much of a welcome. I think the whole family is feeling a little bit angry with God at the moment!"

"I understand," he said with more certainty to his tone than usual.

"I'm sorry we pressed you so hard. You are like God's ambassador, and we are outside the embassy staging a protest demonstration."

"But that isn't quite right." He looked squarely at me. "I'm not in the embassy, defending. I'm out here in the street too—protesting. I too feel the burden and pain."

He turned round self-consciously, as though his tall frame might be taking up too much room. He looked first out of the window and then down at his sandalled feet, and sighed.

"What's more," he added, "I don't think God is in the embassy either. He's out here with us in the street, afflicted in all our afflictions. He's with us in our search for meaning, instigating it, prodding us on."

I had only meant to be mischievous, but now I felt slightly embarrassed. We were a family that felt uncomfortable talking too seriously of religion.

Hoad had placed the large, grey book beside Barbara's bed. She found it after he left. It was the Book of Job with startling modern illustrations. A piece of paper was placed inside on which Hoad had written the words:

"God is subtle, He is not malicious."
—ALBERT EINSTEIN

The art book became a permanent fixture on Barbara's bed. If she wasn't leafing through it, sometimes sitting up alertly, following one of its stark outlines with an attentive finger, then it was within arm's reach.

A week later, when Hoad had visited many times and Barbara had either not mentioned the Book of Job or remarked only tangentially on some point of artistry in his gift to her, she abruptly returned to the theme.

"Job got better. Everything was restored to him."

She had been doing some painting herself, and her most recent was a small picture of Sarah, her vivid eyes glued to a fishtank in which one glorious goldfish expanded its tail. The canvas seemed dominated by the child's intent stare. Did Barbara feel that in Sarah's eyes she was like this imprisoned, beautiful, useless fish? Hoad stood looking at the picture, his back to Barbara, apparently collecting himself.

"I am not getting better, John."

"Who then is Job?" he asked.

... world without end. Amen.

Reverend Hoad climbed quietly up to the pulpit, pulling with him the eyes of the church. He seemed to stand there for a long time, and I couldn't help asking myself what would happen if he just cleared his throat and left his podium. I knew this was a thought that crossed my father's mind whenever he had to make a speech; he had a terror of words not coming, or of words coming out in a stammer. He had learned to cope with this, maybe his deepest fear, but he said that each time he had to make a speech it caused him equal dread.

"On behalf of Bishop Clark and myself..."

An inviolate space spread itself around Michael, growing in size with each word of Hoad's speech. Each word was one more word gone. Barbara's world was slipping away. Somewhere in the last six months he had lost track of his own life too. He thought of their bedroom and knew he could never go back there; the memories were too profound. One day Barbara asked Hoad to arrange for her to take communion. She was too weak to come to church, so he brought it to her bedside, where he found her fully dressed. She had obviously thought much about it beforehand, and had a candle burning on the night-table. They followed the Alternative Order in the Methodist Book of Offices. She cried as he read Psalm 51, "that the bones which thou hast broken may rejoice", but then she rallied and they carried on to the end.

Michael felt unrelated to what he saw as Barbara's religious revival, a quest she described as "being brought back to my faith like a bucking bronco." I suspect that he left the question of faith, like the mountains, in the background of his life. "They abide," he would say, the issue of their certainty out of his hands.

"I often wondered what her secret was..." Hoad's sermon moved with flat but powerful feet along its loving journey; the eloquence of his thought was striking, the more so because the predictability of his voice reassured one that what he said was not contrived.

Michael was packed. Sarah was already gone; she would be brought up by Barbara's parents. He felt a deep pluck at his stomach, and consciously resisted it. After his experience with me, he had made a promise—which he had kept with Joseph—that he would never take a child away from its mother again. This promise was now adapted to the new situation: custody would at least be on the mother's side. Even if he was tempted to resist, he knew his political life would deprive Sarah.

In any case, Barbara had asked her mother to keep Sarah in the event of her death. It was shortly after that day she dropped the baby. In fact it was Mother's Day. Barbara had had a nightmare in which Sarah died. When Hoad arrived, she had obviously been crying.

"I'm broody," she said with a guileless charm.

She showed Hoad a small pencil drawing she had placed in a book beside her bed. It was of two figures, one smaller than the other. They were bell-like, maybe angels. The larger one hovered behind the smaller.

"Mardi calls it 'the ancestor'," she said, looking at the creation as though it were not hers.

"I see Sarah, and I see you."

"What am I saying, then?" she asked.

"I am with you always...," he suggested.

She looked troubled, but seemed to be attempting to settle herself.

"What will happen to her?" she asked, with more curiosity than distress. "She will have gifts of art and intelligence. It's in her genes."

"What would you want to happen, Barbara?" Hoad asked. "You need to think about what would be best for her."

"Best for her, best for Michael. Sometimes I wish I could just die quickly and set Michael free."

If Hoad felt alarmed by her words he didn't show it.

"Do you think Michael isn't free now?"

"Sometimes I watch him prowling up and down. He seems too big for this house, certainly for this room. He's like an imprisoned panther! Maybe Jamaica itself isn't big enough for him," she chuckled with wry resignation. And then her face went very dark and quiet.

"Are you worried about Michael?" he asked.

"I know it's hard for him. I'm always so tired. Sometimes I feel us both in here in our cocoons of gloom; we are together, but each of us is alone beside the other...two"— she took a deep breath—"two alonenesses."

That evening Barbara sent for her mother.

"If anything happens to me..."

"Nothing will happen..."

"I want you to bring Sarah up the way I would. I want you to let her be whatever she wants to be. I want you to let her marry at nineteen and have five babies, if she wants to!"

Her mother clutched at invisible rails of denial, for support.

"Do you hear me, Mummy?"

"I hear you, but..."

"Promise me!"

She promised.

The evening of Sarah's first birthday party, after the guests had gone home, Barbara was propped up on pillows in bed, still in a white linen dress and stockings, among Sarah's birthday presents. Heavy makeup made her angular features so pronounced that they appeared graven in bone. She looked intense and dramatic.

"Shall I put these away?" asked her mother. "We can open them tomorrow."

"Tomorrow!" gasped Barbara. "No! I have no guarantee of tomorrow. We'll open them right now!"

With that she set Sarah to work, the child tearing open everything in sight and Barbara delighting in every inch of debris. It had gone better than expected. She and Hoad had discussed beforehand the likelihood that the occasion might be an emotional trigger for her; she might be devastated by the thought that she wouldn't be around for the second.

"Enjoy the party," he advised. "Go away and cry if you must. Then come back and enjoy it again."

"But *everyone* will be thinking that this is the last time this, and the last time that," she worried.

"Then think Zenwise," Hoad told her. "How much time does it take to eat an apple? With the answer..."

"...it doesn't take time, it takes teeth," she finished, and they both laughed.

From the pulpit Hoad's voice became so personal, I looked up to see if he was still reading. He was.

"...she once said that an hour with him was like a day with anyone else, and a day with him was like a million years without. He brought out the latent possibilities in her, and she enhanced his own courage and freedom to be himself."

I wondered how my father would carry on. How he felt watching all these people, with their expectations of him.

What mattered wasn't whether Barbara would have made a good political wife or a bad political wife. It was just that she would have been there. A kernel of happiness for him.

He was leaving for London the next day, for a two-week break that he couldn't afford but would have to find a way to afford. He had already composed a letter for Hoad which he left with Mardi.

My dear John,

Where does one begin?

You were so wonderful throughout. You saw the shining truth of Barbara from the very start. So did I. What you probably never could know was that she was the light of my life and my world. Not the world of union negotiation which I could win any time without her. But the world of simply being alive and knowing that was worthwhile.

When Pack told me it was all over last November the light went out and it will never turn on again. I do not have the courage to die with her because the selfish, sensual man will cling to life at any cost. I am, I fear, more survivor than idealist. And I am a coward.

But you who loved her can know that I tried to give her the best of me. In the end, it was only the flowers each morning but I gave them with my heart as a tribute to a great lady. She would have made such a contribution to Jamaica.

I am glad you helped her back to her faith and I hope you are both right—only for her sake.

I do not know and so I must weep inwardly—and even sometimes on the surface—because I have no alternatives to the sense of loss.

You have all long since claimed her as your own—
in faith—in God—in the wonder of what she was.
But for me she was simply the light and it has been
turned out. The world will never be the same again.

But you—I will always treasure your kindness and
your steadfastness which I know helped her so much.
And for sending her on her way—with style and with
truth.

And these, style and truth, were her greatest
qualities. May I humbly bless you for that—and
thank you in the name of a "great human being".

Michael

"Those of us who shared the last steps of the long agonizing journey that ended last Friday…" Hoad looked at
both families as though for support.

Barbara racked with fever, Barbara in between fevers. "I
am all mashed about," after another round of tests. The drips
in and the drips changed. Vitamins or pethidine?

"If it is His will, I want to die well, John."

"Pray for those who are around you, Barbara. Will you
do that?"

"I'll try."

"She's retaining fluid," Pardi observes, his hand gently
surrounding her ankle.

"My shoes will be too small for the funeral," comes the
weak voice from the bed. And a small, wry smile. So she can
hear us.

"You really love her, don't you?" asks Mardi before sleep.

"Indeed," says Pardi, smiling at the thought in the dark.
"Enormously."

"Do you know there is a little mad old lady quarrelling, quarrelling every day when Auntie Mu goes out?" She is babbling like a small child now. Maybe she's delirious.

"Not altogether, Reverend Hoad, for Mae next door is quite mad." Mardi explains.

"I only wish to let in the truth, John. But then I ask myself, how much can I let in? How much light can I bear?"

"Do you mean in the sense that 'No man shall see God and live'?"

"Yes. I am afraid. Very afraid."

She worries that her illness is making her intolerant. I told her, writes Hoad who has started to keep a diary, her intolerance is a need for things that matter, for time may be short.

"Don't talk if it's difficult. Just do little puffs," Hoad tells her one day.

She smiles and forms a small blowing motion with her mouth. The nurse offers her ice.

"Little puffs of blessing," she says weakly but distinctly, after the cold comforts her lips, and then she settles down to sleep.

But she doesn't sleep, Michael says. She's afraid, she's terrified.

"John, am I dying yet?"

"Not yet."

And then one day, fiercely and wide awake:

"Michael is Job. I suppose God wants Michael to learn humility."

"Checking the infections will simply lead to more grotesque sufferings," concludes Aunt Muriel.

Less medicine. More sleep. More and more yellow.

"It's her liver."

"She's sinking."

"Michael had to go for a meeting. Call Michael."

"Can you hear me, Barbara? Can you speak?"

"Yes, but it's difficult to say 'Rev...er...end'."

Her smile is left to fade.

The congregation stood for the final hymn, combining the smug stance that life's survivors bring to any funeral with the voice of jubilation, the resounding relief of all church-goers on reaching the end of a service.

Jerusalem the golden,
With milk and honey blessed...

Michael had despaired when he received a call telling him that gunmen had attempted a union takeover at one of the bauxite plants. The unions were fighting for control in this prosperous industry. He dreaded leaving her, and begged her to wait for him. He had no choice but to go.

"She is sinking fast," came the message to him later that day.

He drove back from the centre of the island in half the time one would have thought possible, moving the road out of his way, its miles slipping into oblivion beneath him.

When he arrived, her family were in the room along with the doctor and a nurse. Hoad was not there. Her being seemed dismantled and vulnerable without the attending drip. She had passed through the final yellowing, and her face seemed beyond that, as though it were recovering from a bruised black and blue and the colours were dissipating. She was very far from fear now, and it looked to Michael as though all her decisions had been made for her.

Like a child who won't go to sleep till it says goodnight, she had waited for him.

"You're tired. Try to rest."

He leaned over her and took her hand in his, holding it and watching her from another world, from a long-ago, many-bends-before, riverbank. She opened her eyes and looked thoughtfully at him. He looked for terror there, then he looked for peace. He found neither; just a quiet if disapproving resignation, a well...that's it then.

"Goodbye, bright flower," he whispered.

The white shape of the nurse closed in. He shifted slightly and saw that Barbara's eyes now stared past him at the wall behind. No longer bright. No longer there. Just so, he thought. She had gone.

Exult, O dust and ashes;
The Lord shall be thy part;
His only, His for ever
Thou shalt be, and thou art.

16

THE VERGE

"FAILURE IS FINAL, but we must proceed." Pardi recited this on the veranda at Nomdmi, with his hands folded patiently on his lap; Pardi could not remember where he had heard it. Facing Mardi and himself was a young Trinidadian graduate student who had wandered over from Bellevue.

"Who said that?" Pardi asked the young man.

Pardi had announced his retirement on July 4, 1968, his seventy-fifth birthday. He had surprised the party with the news during his speech at a formal banquet they laid on to celebrate his three-quarter century, thank him for his years of service and with luck raise funds for the organization.

Pardi fumed, for he considered the occasion an unnecessary fuss. Mardi reminded him that, after thirty years leading the party, he deserved it.

For more than a year after the election in 1967, and all through the final months of Barbara's illness, Pardi had been preparing to retire. He was frail, his blood pressure was high and for Mardi, watching him, ageing was taking on a familiar face. Its proximity, its traceable fallibility, made her recognize her own frailty for the first time in her life.

At the end of the birthday banquet, the PNP gave Pardi a powder-blue Mercedes-Benz. All through the evening he felt the strain of having to appear to enjoy what he ought to enjoy, and what everyone else was enjoying. In a very profound sense he felt it was time to go home. But he had to make his speech.

Speaker after speaker rose and made eloquent noises about him. They spoke about him sitting there as though he were already dead. The speeches were full of wit and humour, of remembrances and elegiac tributes. They fixed him firmly where he belonged: in the past. And that was just how Pardi felt it should be.

Beside him at the high table his wife seemed to be translating the evening and the speeches for him. She would laugh and press his arm, or pressure his thigh under the table; she whispered when she thought he hadn't heard something; then she passed what she felt should be his feelings and reactions on to the crowd with nods, smiles, little confiding moments with some large lady who had been a key delegate in the party, or had helped start a clinic in a constituency, or was an indoor agent on polling day. Some she knew, some not. What she did know was that everyone in that room was caught up in the refrain of tribute to her husband.

"And looking back, Mr. Chairman, over the years, may I declare that they have been great years. I have known all things in politics the hard way. I am glad. I would not have chosen my road in life in any other way. I affirm of Jamaica that we are a great people. Out of the past of fire, and suffering, and neglect, the human spirit has survived—patient and strong, quick to anger, quick to forgive, lusty and vigorous, but with deep reserves of loyalty and love, and a deep capacity for steadiness under stress, and for joy in all the things that make life good and blessed.

"Bless this dear land and bless our people, now and for ever more."

Later that year he mustered his strength for his last farewell to public life at the Party's annual conference which he addressed in the arena at the National Stadium. It was a deeply moving occasion in which he recounted the grand history of the party in a voice now slightly rumpled from its attic of storage. He spoke of the years creating the infant nation, the challenge provided by Independence to rebuild the national spirit, and the failure of the present government in meeting this, as they moved unimaginatively into what he saw as merely a new guise of colonialism.

Thirty years. 1938 to 1968. Full circle. A political revolution.

"I will...close a very long chapter in the book of my life, but I cannot imagine a life that was lived without that chapter...when the wheel turns it rests on different soil...the difference between birth and subsequent growth...life does not start from scratch...the present derives from the past...."

There he stood before them...a moral old statesman who loved his country. It was as fundamental as that. Beneath the brave words which affirmed the achievements of his own political career, lurked the crumpled memory of each defeat. And although history was on his side as he recounted the irrevocable strides which had brought them to nationhood, his shrunken frame was testament to his disappointments; it was difficult not to think of them as he spoke, since for every milestone there had been an attendant shadow cast as though for him.

He outlined the responsibilities of the next generation of the party whom he charged with social and economic reform. And then he summed up what had been his own.

"I say that the mission of my generation was to win self-government for Jamaica. To win political power which is the final power for the black masses of my country from which I spring. I am proud to stand here today and say to you who fought that fight with me, say it with gladness and pride, mission accomplished for my generation."

There in the arena at *his* stadium, the vast crowd exploded. Michael who would soon be persuaded to run in the race for party leadership, was there to receive what he was destined to make his mandate. He crossed the platform to embrace his father who seemed in that moment lost behind the large frame of his younger son. To Mardi it was symbolic of the passing on of a legacy of love, politics and, inevitably, pain within our family. To me it was a sloughing of skins, an inner shuffling of selves or fates, a natural metamorphosis in the life of the family.

To Michael it was simply his father's moment of triumph for which he hugged him in an intimate applause, and he predicted that the phrase "mission accomplished" would "resonate in the corridors of national memory". In this speech Michael had found a crescendo he thought a befitting climax to his father's work.

And with his public farewell over, one might have safely expected that Pardi could now settle peacefully back on his laurels with satisfaction, visited by devoted family members, appreciative friends, colleagues and countrymen, his legacy assured, warmed gently by the sunset of his life.

Pardi had built his own study at Nomdmi during the year they lived there. Mardi suggested this was where he must one day write a book.

"A book?" Pardi was perplexed.

Although she agreed with his decision to leave politics, she felt it necessary to find a different name for retirement. She hated the word as much as he did. She recoiled from the concept of voluntary withdrawal—into what? An exile? Worse yet, a void? A dissipation? She wondered how the human mind could embark on any journey without a destination, even if it was simply moving from one room to another. How could it just give up? So she had conjured up an alternative.

"Norman has decided to write a book," she started telling friends. "Norman *is* writing a book."

"Your story, you know," she nudged. "A sort of chronicle."

But he had no plan to write any book. He was not a writer. He had lived his life. If a biographer wished to make something of that, so be it. That was another thing.

The study was a long cement-block room with untiled concrete floors. Its entrance faced the first of Mardi's named peaks, Dilmoon, with large glass doors through which Pardi, when he was seated, could see only the tops of the mahoes and pines staggered down the side of the valley below. My father could never understand why they wouldn't just cut down the trees to provide a view.

Pardi thought it was a very private room, for it was disconnected from the house and sat on the verge overlooking

Morgan's valley, brooding among the trees. Inside, it felt lonely to Pardi, its emptiness echoing till the sound escaped valleyward, as though the single entrance were a large drain through which everything washed. Mardi got a round watsonia lily mat from Bellevue which she felt would soften the room and absorb its echoes. It proved to be more successful as a dragnet for dust.

Pardi covered the walls with bookshelves, on top of which he centred the second maquette of Bogle; its purpose bestrode the room. He chose a small wooden desk that had been in his bedroom at Drumblair, and matched it with his swivelling wooden desk chair. The desk was the least pretentious one he had, and seemed not to require too much ambition of anyone who sat there. He brought an old reclining chair over from the house, and a cupboard he had made himself.

One day Mardi was surprised to discover one of her old carvings on the wall. It was a bas-relief three and a half feet tall, on a thick plank of mahogany, which she had started to carve soon after the 1938 national unrest from which her husband's political life had proceeded. Pardi designed a way to hang it with a brace, and Ivan, with help and a great deal of difficulty, managed to hoist the heavy carving onto the wall.

Three heads stared from the wood, surrounded by gouged-out flames; each head faced a different direction. They were Shadrach, Meshach and Abednego, who in the Book of Daniel are cast into flames by King Nebuchadnezzar for refusing to worship a golden calf, and emerge unsinged. Mardi had called the carving *The Fiery Furnace*, but when it was complete she sensed in people an indifference to the piece. When a photographer asked her if she didn't intend to finish the work, she quietly but firmly stored it out of sight and forgot it.

She had no idea how he had unearthed it. She saw that time had not diminished its sense of defiance. Its place on her husband's wall now seemed its triumph. She wondered why he had chosen to put it there, but felt she shouldn't ask him, for fear it would break an important spell. Sometimes when she entered the room its presence inspired her to recite her favourite quote from Lawrence—"See, we have come through."

In the odd way one remembers the place where one receives bad news, the room reminded me of Aunt Vera. News of her death came by a telegram which Pardi opened one afternoon when he was sitting quietly working on his upcoming retirement speech. She had died of whiplash, reported her daughter Pamela to Aunt Muriel, who thought it was at least mercifully quick.

I had handed him the telegram. "Your Aunt Vera has died," he said and he kept looking at the telegram for a long time. I remember I was looking at geraniums; I may have picked them and brought them to the room, or maybe they were already there in a vase. Red geraniums with a sticky smell. My great-aunt's sometimes stern face now came to me gentle, as she had looked when I had last seen her in London where she roomed at the YWCA. She had given me a sensible pair of walking shoes, finding the ones I wore unsuitable for "these devilish pavements". And for me this study became the place from which the family proceeded without a vital digit. Pardi suddenly rose to take the news to his wife, as though it were properly intended for her instead. I went with him to the main house and ran up the stairs, with an alacrity I always accorded the communication of bad news.

"Aunt Vera is dead!"

"Oh, not *now*, I'm washing up!" Mardi shouted incongruously from behind the closed upstairs door.

Aunt Vera's homecoming was unceremonious, for her remains arrived in an envelope carried, inexplicably, by my mother's first husband, Bob, who happened to be travelling to Jamaica. My family had gone to meet a coffin, and were visibly deflated when Aunt Vera emerged from Bob's jacket pocket.

"She wished to be sprinkled over the mountains at Nomdmi," Bob explained sombrely, in his lay preacher's rumble.

"Absolutely not!" Mardi was emphatic. "I've had Vera in my hair most of my life, I won't have her there in death as well!"

Aunt Vera was placed in an urn and, contrary to her express wish, buried in the cemetery in a spot near Barbara. Cremation was a new phenomenon to Jamaica, so some curious acquaintances who went to pay their respects asked if she was really that small, or wondered why she had been buried upright.

Just after the study was built, Parboo, a maverick Jamaican artist of Indian descent who was a close friend of Douglas, paid an unannounced visit to Pardi at Nomdmi. Not to Mardi—he was explicit about that.

Parboo drank too much and lived too much. He was physically small, with a restless, eager, often quarrelsome resonance that exuded from the light in his eyes and the gleaming of his teeth in a round face. Mardi always said that his person was a mere abbreviation of his being.

He arrived on the hilltop with his comparatively serene American wife, who was also an artist. It was strange that what would have been an intrusion to Pardi and Mardi at Regardless was seen as an event at Nomdmi.

Mardi dreaded unpopularity. She was so eager to win Parboo's truant heart, and to expose herself to a new generation of artists, that she provided ponchos and pot luck on a cold, windy mountain Sunday, while Pardi gave a tour of the study. The boisterous artist surveyed its incongruous modernity, called for a rum and some paint and proceeded to transform the bleak outside wall facing the cottage with a bright mural in orange and green and black, colours left over from a recent repaint of Nomdmi.

Pardi loved his wall. He often wished he could see it from inside the study. Mardi found the vivid colours and bold outlines exciting—if not confrontational, certainly challenging. Just what Norman needed intellectually, she decided.

So there it remained, a cheerful and surprisingly uncontroversial design, in harmony with the mountain top.

Between Nomdmi and the gate, the rebuilt Mini was the halfway mark: the place where Pardi would wait for Mardi to invite him to see her work, or simply to emerge, shaking her short grey hair free of whatever she was doing, for her midday drink.

In a small clearing near Mini there was a large old mahoe which had come down during the hurricane. It was the tree under which, as a child, I used to bathe in the Norman Washingtub mobile bath. In later years we often sat on the natural bench provided by the fallen trunk. Hardening and drying over the years, its bark always made me think of the hide of a pachyderm who had somehow got stranded on his back, feet in the air, on this mountain, and bore the frustration of his handicap in silent immobility. Above the trunk a greenness sprang from a fissure, as though staking its claim, and flourished in joyous contradiction. In the mornings, on her way into the hut, Mardi had taken to beating her breast with a closed fist as she passed the fallen-down tree, and asserting: "A refusal to die!"

Mardi noticed that Nomdmi had returned to that seamless feeling of total inactivity. For a while, when they were actually living there, Mardi feared it had lost this quality. Now even their breathing coming down the path seemed an intrusion, or the sound of solitaire's musical note, or rats unparcelling the crisp underbrush.

Although Mardi visited Mini, she was not in a working mood. Nowadays she wondered if her carving had taken up too much of her life. She had a strong if desultory maternal instinct that she summoned at times of need, but she kept it as an emergency self, for she knew that in everyday life it might overwhelm her family.

At times she felt in love. Not with anyone, but just the "in love" she had felt in her younger life, when all around her poets were writing poetry and there were artists in love with wood or paint or clay and Jamaicans had fallen in love with Jamaica. And now she saw it all come full circle: a genuine Jamaican art movement.

She had started writing letters to the scattered members of the *Focus* group. Some of them answered her, occasionally including poems. Mike sent her a few verses he must have written clandestinely during his self-declared years of poetic abstention, and George, who had written virtually nothing, sent a sudden deluge of pained love letters.

She needed to mother some creativity other than her own.

Pardi was getting so frail. His breathing was more laboured, his walk slower, his deafness appalling. Even when he coughed it sounded weaker; only his temper remained indisputably charged. She found more and more that she had to tend him. As she listened to the silence around her, she would try to will the flow of her husband's spirit onto the page.

But every time Pardi started to write, he felt awkwardly pompous. There was something in his soul that disliked talking about himself. Maybe because of this, he found an erudite voice leaning over his shoulder and telling the story for him, as though it were a third person referring to itself as "I".

"My father was the illegitimate son of a woman of the people."

He had always dreaded the fate of both Lot's wife and Eurydice. Now he looked back in a contemplative search, he found there no new worlds to conquer, only the irritating discovery of endless buried fragments he had not wished to disturb. "Only a dog goes back to his vomit," he'd sometimes say.

He tried to muster enthusiasm for the project for his wife's sake. Two young history graduates from the university were hired to do research. They retrieved their findings from the dispassionate graveyard of history, bringing his memories back piece by piece, bone by bone, sorted, bottled and labelled.

Now and then he sat with the students in the afternoons over a drink. He longed for their opinions of the history that had fathered them. They were solid and righteous, and brimmed with the arrogant omniscience of youth. They waited for him with disapproval as he reached out over the years, shaking their neatly trimmed Afros and clucking pronouncements from the safe rim of hindsight.

"It was a great mistake," they said of this or that, and their hairdos agreed.

"You should have" or "you should not have", but they only offered this if they were asked, otherwise staying politely within the mandate for which they were paid. They did their work competently.

Many young Jamaicans were sympathizers of the new Black Power movement. Whatever their complexions, they wore high Afros, colourful dashikis and Jesus sandals. Black Power, with its mission of restoring black self-esteem, was a powerful antidote for our past. Some of its sympathizers thought deeply about our history, our need for change and what was positive and constructive for the future. Others simply looked defiant and talked about heads rolling, or appeared to be insolently biding their time. They expressed discontent with everything. They saw compromise in what had been called change, sell-out in what had been considered negotiation, and traitors in some of those who had been our heroes.

At first I was in awe of the movement, excited by its audacity. I wished to be part of it. It was a way to establish one's credentials on campus. I did all I could to endear myself, even washing my hair in baking soda to make it frizz, always aware that my rather fair skin and the name of Manley singled me out for suspicion.

At the start of the first term of my final year the student body called a protest march. A Guyanese history lecturer had been unjustly declared *persona non grata*, barred from re-entering Jamaica because of his "subversive" teachings. I hoped that the outrage students felt against the JLP government would impact favourably on their opinion of the PNP. But I was trapped in what the movement called "the old mind-set". Their disillusionment was with both political parties, who were felt to have evolved from white cultural roots through white education, no matter what they fought for.

Caring not a jot about either the issue or the slighted lecturer, I saw my opportunity to pledge my allegiance to those aloof beings who treated me to their indifference; I set off on the protest march. I saw a police baton split open the head of a friend beside me, and experienced the unforgettable inner scorching of tear gas. Hours into what turned out to be an historic and bloody affair in which three people died, I ran towards a water hose held by a kindly gas station attendant who was spraying the jet at the burning faces passing by.

I thought I had won my spurs.

In a newspaper the following morning was a picture of students running towards the hose, with a report stating that even the opposition leader's granddaughter had fled the march on discovering the real issues.

Pardi was outraged. "Do the students not give us hope that they will serve a real purpose in our community when they show a live interest in matters that are of profound concern to democracy and the principles of human rights? What did Ghandi spend his life doing but practising civil disobedience? And what did Martin Luther King live and die for?"

My written explanation to the students was generally ignored, and I remained an outsider to all but two of my peers: a haughty Trinidadian who felt that the soul was lit more by poetry than by politics, and a Jewish friend whose father had escaped the Communists in Czechoslovakia.

Criticism against both political parties raged on campus. This led to the inevitable protest newspaper. *Abeng* was a slim tabloid produced by some of those whom Pardi called the "angry young men" of the university. *Abeng* was an old African word for the horn used by the Maroons to summon members of the tribe.

My dilemma grew with the first issue of *Abeng*.

I wanted to be part of a generation that repudiated our history, but to attack our two-party democracy I would have to tear down Pardi. Moreover, I was not convinced that I should emulate these people. As far as I was concerned, most of them had not earned the right to destroy Pardi's name. Yet I still wanted to be accepted by them. I resented them for writing what they wrote, but I hadn't the guts to say so.

I hated myself for being such a coward. I hated my family for being the kind of people that I couldn't rebel against without complications. So I resorted to nebulous belly-aching: "Why shouldn't they disagree if they want to, and who do you think you all are that everyone has to worship you?"

I knew they were wearing Pardi down. And I believed I was disappointing him.

"It's bewildering," said Mardi, clearly affronted.

"Well, they are disillusioned. It's not personal. They don't really have an argument with me. They have an argument with history; so have I," he tried to explain. "We just see different ways of proceeding. It's an old argument, and not a very clever one. It's based on the premise that even the best things we inherited through the colonial system are to be repudiated. They come from a source of our history that was contaminated, so every aspect must be damned."

"These young hot-heads were in their cradles when we were struggling for universal suffrage and workers' rights and self-government! Who the hell do they think got the British *out*?" Hearing her, I suddenly thought with embarrassment how incongruous Mardi would seem to my fellow students —standing there looking Caucasian, delivering her theatrics against British imperialism in her flawless English.

"Their argument is that we are replacing the old system with a variation of the same system. I do not agree, but it is a healthy sign for Jamaica that there are young Turks fighting about these things."

Despite what he said, Mardi felt that the sunset was proving to be less golden than expected. "They will break his heart!" she decided.

In February the PNP voted for a new president. The contest was between Vivian Blake and my father. Blake, a Queen's Counsel like Pardi and a lover of racehorses, had always been close to Mardi and Pardi. It was rumoured that on more than one occasion he and my father had loved the same woman. He was considered a moderate in comparison to my father, who was seen as radical because of his union background. Blake had fought the battles of federation and the recent election side by side with my father, in support of Pardi.

I arrived home on the eve of the party conference with a copy of the second edition of *Abeng*. There on the front page was a picture of Pardi with the two vice-presidents contending for party leadership, Michael and Vivian Blake. The caption was crude: "P.N.P. Choice: Black Dog or Monkey".

Mardi gave a little gasp. "Not that wretched rag again!" As Pardi's fingers, contaminated by the cheap ink, followed the text, his hands faltered.

"Oh *God*, that's all we need this afternoon. *Why* bring this awful rag home, Rachel?" Mardi used my full Christian name when she was angry with me. "I wish you'd just not bring it into this house!" Her face disarranged by rage, she walked over to Pardi and took the paper away, as though to rescue him.

"Chut" was all he said, as firmly as his old voice could, but it was strained. I went to stroke his head, but he brushed away my hand with a lifted arm that felt like steel.

I kept alternating between affection and pain, acutely irritated with them for not seeing things in a way that would make the students forgive them, for not being heroes the students could revere like Marcus Garvey or Malcolm X, for not being something *other* than the middle class people I had now realized we were. All the shelves with their classical music, the books of Jung and Freud, Bertrand Russell and Browning, Hopkins and Lawrence, seemed an irritating anachronism to me.

"It's time we start speaking *Jamaican*, and teaching dialect in schools," I pontificated, espousing what I heard at university.

Pardi was watching me. He said nothing.

"You don't understand," I shouted, facing Mardi. "You were brought up English." Then came the cruellest thing I could have said to her. I knew this, but I couldn't stop myself. "You are only a quarter black!"

"So are you, for that matter, my dear," she replied. I had brought that on myself.

"The point is, you can't use the oppressor's system to free yourself. You have to go back to your own roots..."

"You won't find many of those, I'm afraid...and certainly not in someone else's field," Pardi said flatly. "But no doubt we will go on digging, in futile search of a time we lost. It was a betrayal, but that's that. It's the past."

"You can't go home again," Mardi quoted grandly.

I felt tears of frustration in the back of my throat. I wanted just to be part of the life I belonged to, with a point of view that rhymed with everyone else's, in a world where I looked like everyone else. I wanted not to be torn to pieces by conflicting views and ideals, not to have to decide between low ground and high ground, just to flow with something greater than myself that would not even notice it had swallowed me.

My father was elected party president—whether as black dog or monkey, we never knew. Like two old matriarchs, Mardi and I heard the news over the radio at Regardless. "Here we go again," she said on a sigh, but she was very proud. Though I was joyful for him, I knew that my life would continue in five-year cycles, with good years and lean years, and that the family's recurring pain was unlikely to end.

Pardi liked the students who visited from Bellevue, the university retreat next door to Nomdmi. Their trespass was part of a code of mountain informality and exploration. They came to pick ortaniques, not to argue history, and when he was there they always left with a bag or a box of fruit. They were usually post graduates, though now and then he met final-year undergraduates swotting for exams. Pardi invited them onto the veranda for a drink and took the opportunity to quiz them.

The older ones were often glib, the younger ones brash.

"I don't know who said that," admitted the uppity English major in his lyrical Trinidadian accent, and then, with callous insensitivity, he went on to surmise, "People with big egos can live by the sea, but people with small egos should live on mountains."

However he interpreted this, Pardi took no offence. "Who said that?" he frowned sceptically.

"I did," the student said with satisfaction, a smirk pulling down the corners of his mouth.

Pardi appeared not to believe him. He had recently been given a wristwatch by his constituency, but its place on his wrist was only a sign of affection; whenever he needed to know the time, he fished into his shirt pocket for his old fob watch. He did so now. It was after six o'clock, and getting dark.

Mardi had turned on a light in the dining-room. It sent a ghostly beam through the window and down the path, sinking the veranda where they sat into deeper darkness. She saw the wooden chairs hunched like lonely shoulders in the dark, and for a moment she imagined Pardi not being there. Not there at all. As if her life was continuing but she was there without him. She imagined her footsteps coming back from the gate without him, attempting to pick up courage, like a child moving faster and faster from its fear. She became so frightened she swallowed, as though she had stalled and needed to start herself up again.

The student, whose father was a retired high court judge, took the time check as an Edwardian signal of dismissal, and bade them farewell before Pardi could check it again. He descended the crumbling stone steps and disappeared around the side of the house through the guava trees, retracing his steps over the trampled bracken and sticky burs. He carried a box of deceptively ripe looking ortaniques, and no doubt the hope that he had dug a mark deep enough to leave his signature in the bark of the old man.

Mardi, still shaken by her imaginings, was thinking what a lot of her life had simply been her husband. He was almost her faith, and her conscience. In a way he had taken the place of God for her.

"What does he know," she observed haughtily once the student was gone. "Trinidad doesn't have *real* mountains!"

17

SEPTEMBER
SECOND

"WELL, THAT'S THAT, then," said Mardi, and it was more by the fold of her arms in front of her, a gesture unusual for her, than by her actual words that I knew, possibly we all knew, that an era had ended, a way of the world had ceased, poems wouldn't be poems any more, or painters really artists, or music journeying contrapuntal as hips towards the wordless, transforming flight of Philomel, or pines sighing, or solitaires crying from an inviolate solitude. All that was now debased. It was July 1969, and man had arrived on the moon. Mardi's moon. Which didn't have a man in it, and wasn't made of blue cheese, but was actually a woman, an echo of the sun's flame, who established her own nocturnal domain; a woman I had always assumed was mad, rather like the woman in the attic at Mr. Rochester's house in *Jane Eyre*.

"Dem lie, dem lie like Lucifer!" Zethilda spat this out without once closing her distracted mouth, so that it seemed her eyes, darting back and forth from the television set to each of us, were actually pronouncing the words.

We were at Regardless, watching an annoyingly snowy, ethereal picture on a small black and white television, since the grander original one had been relinquished in Pardi's gesture.

"One giant step for man..."

"Dem lie, Barrista...nu listen, Miss Ray, dem wi' mad you!"

Mardi stood watching through unsympathetic eyes. Pardi sat back, hands propped on the armrests, fingers pressed to the narrow groove above his lip as though they were made to fit there. His eyes looked only mildly interested as they watched something he deemed irrevocable.

A dreamy figure that could have been the Michelin man or St. Nicholas in a snowstorm drifted through the crackling, indistinct screen.

"Jus' lik 'ow dem seh dem 'ave Santa!" Zethilda mocked.

Mardi looked bristly and defensive, as though guests had arrived unannounced. "I'd rather not have seen this," she said.

Pardi looked across at me.

"Well, Pie?" he seemed to say, but he actually didn't say anything. He didn't speak a lot nowadays, just seemed to attach his eyes to some comfortable point on the horizon and focus as though trying to keep his balance. I had become impatient of his poor hearing, embarrassed by his stumbling and bumping into things. The day before, he had knocked his knee on the glass-topped coffee table and I had turned on him. "Why can't you look where you're going? You don't make any effort."

"You know, if I thought it was that...if I thought my mind just wasn't in control...I'd shoot myself!"

I knew that he meant this. I knew his mind was still like iron, while the rest of him melted around it, the flesh softly falling away from the bone. But I couldn't bear to watch the physical manifestations of his age. The teeth in the glass, the slow dust-on-tile shuffle of his tired old shoes, the edges of yellow wax on his hearing aid, the small wet spot on the toilet seat or the front of his pants. I didn't want to see any of this. I didn't want my friends to see it. I didn't want to know how it all turned out. And I knew I would never forgive myself for what I had just said, or for feeling what I felt.

"What a waste of money," I declared, looking at the screen. Actually I couldn't connect with what I saw there. It did seem unreal, maybe because the picture was so bad or maybe because it suggested those science-fiction movies we knew not to believe. But I was young enough to know it *was* real. It was the moon of my geography lessons with Miss Batt that was there on the screen.

But it wasn't the same moon that had followed me through my youth, like one of my ancestors. That moon had looked down on me from the window at Drumblair, though as a child I believed Nomdmi was its home, for it was brightest there; it had chased me in cars till I got carsick making sure it still followed me; it had been the subject of many of Mardi's carvings and drawings, and of course all her childhood stories to me, in which there was never a man in the moon, always a woman.

"We have gone too far," Mardi said sadly.

Pardi placed his hands in his lap. The fingernails were long, and as he gazed at them I was reminded of something I had heard: that a person's nails and hair go on growing after death.

"Dem lie!" Zethilda repeated. "No man cyan go to de moon, Barrista, not even a 'mericaman!"

"Why is that?"

"A God light lef' on at night, sah...man doan 'ave no business in dat!"

She swatted the back of the chair disagreeably with a yellow duster and went on cleaning and complaining all the way back to the kitchen.

Her departure stirred the air, and I caught a whiff of a putrid odour. I looked up to see Batiste gesticulating at the door.

"What is it, Batiste?" Mardi asked, sniffing exaggeratedly.

Batiste smiled amiably from the door. "A dead cat in de kiln."

"Same t'ing, a sure sign, dat...a de end o' de world coming. Man nu fi tell lie 'bout no moon...." Zethilda stood in the doorway with a gleeful look, her eyes for once shining with vindication. Her every prophecy was fulfilled, and the dead cat was the signifying omen.

"That damned cat! I forgot it," said Mardi.

A few days before, someone had inadvertently driven the car over a cat belonging to my Czech friend, who was still in university. I had arrived at Regardless very upset, with the squashed animal in a plastic bag, and Mardi had tactfully stuck the problem in the kiln so everyone could forget about it. But she'd forgot to tell Batiste, whose job it was to bury animals in the garden. Now she explained the anomaly, and asked him to dispose of it.

"Have you heard man has landed on the moon, Batiste?" asked Pardi, as Batiste stepped out on the veranda. The gardener came back to the door.

"What, sah?"

"Man has just walked on the moo-oon." Mardi lengthened the word as though making it eternal. She was reassured by the fact that Batiste evidently didn't care.

Batiste stepped forward to think about this for a moment, scratched his head and cocked it to one side. "De moon t'ing? Miss Tildy seh a dat weh cause de cat to dead in Modor' stove." He started to laugh so hard that he had to excuse himself, chuckling on his way out to retrieve the body for burial.

The smell trailed after him.

Batiste decided to bury the cat at the site of the plastic Aztec god, between the roses and the plumbagos. He propped the bag against a stone in the circle of a garden bed, covered by the speckled shade of the woman's-tongue tree, and began digging. Pardi, who had moved out to the patio for peace, watched him for a while and then moved slowly over the lawn towards him.

"Nice place to bury," Batiste acknowledged. "Look over 'pon Drumblair." He looked up at Pardi for recognition of a common bond.

"Indeed," Pardi agreed.

"You no gwan bury 'ere, sah, you 'ave to bury down a Race Course!"

Batiste was referring to National Heroes Park, with its memorials to Garvey, Bogle and Gordon. Pardi didn't like memorial parks; the red and yellow cannas made him think of rows of war dead marked by stark white crosses. They reminded him of his brother Roy.

"God forbid...under cannas. I hate cannas."

"Better roses," Batiste agreed.

Pardi looked over to the right and shaded his eyes from the relentless shine of Aunt Muriel's flat white roof. "You know, doctor believes in reincarnation...that we become something else in the next life."

"Nex' life," Batiste scoffed.

Pardi ignored him and shuddered. "I'd hate to come back as a canna."

Years later, my father could not remember why he came over that evening, but he vividly recalled sitting with his father on the patio. Pardi looked as though he had thrown himself into the chair as one would toss taken-off clothes. He sat in a sealed zone of silence. He looked at his son with a frown, not so much of dissatisfaction—more the way one shies from sudden light. Michael couldn't think of anything to say and, feeling awkward, he sat there trying to decipher the name on the cover of a book spread-eagled over the wide wooden arm of a chair.

"Michael, I am *bored.*"

That was what Pardi said. The final word was expelled from the collapse of his diaphragm, arriving with such violence that Michael instinctively flinched. And it made perfect sense to him; his father who filled every waking minute of every single day. The endless hours of work, of research, of practice, of knowing the whole heart of a case, of a problem, of the law or the rule, the sum or the context, caring in every way that caring counted; who entered every event of a sport, and ventured all those he could, specializing in all things, who braved the extremes and still couldn't sleep those few hours left at night; the activist who filled even holidays with a boat, or planting one tree and cutting down another, sometimes the wrong tree, the carpenter, the punter, the farmer, the institute maker, the mouth organ player, and he still found time every night to read...the philosopher...

Here, after all those years and wearing and tearing, his body, exhausted, betrayed him. That's how Michael understood it.

Michael held onto this memory as though it were a bead he would require later, when he came to string together the story of his father.

July had started with our birthdays; Pardi turned seventy-six and I turned twenty-two. When I suggested to Mardi that we pool our resources to buy him either a pair of pajamas or his annual red shirt, I found her response puzzling: she looked startled. Although she quickly regained her composure, something in her spontaneous reaction made me think that, in a rare and indiscreet moment of practicality, she had judged the gift futile. As though dropping a marker in the sand against the wash of time, I gave him instead a photograph taken of myself the year before.

Our friend Jessie, sister of the late novelist Roger Mais, threw a big party spanning the generations to celebrate our birthdays. Jessie's hillside house was full of flowers, which made Mardi cough a lot. Just after Pardi and I cut the cake, I slipped a disc in my neck. I had attached many hairpieces, lavishly curled, to the top of my head. Then, clad in a sea-green gown whose shoulder straps kept slipping off, I thrust my chin up in the air to receive an embrace. From that position, I tried to retrieve a dress strap, and felt a pain in my neck—the sheer weight of my hairpieces had caused the accident. We had to return home, where a doctor manipulated my head and someone held my feet firm till I felt a snap in my neck.

That was the first time I heard it: a piece of music that seemed to be arguing with itself. It sounded desperate. It reminded me of a bird locked in a room, looking for an open window, looking for a way out to its freedom. Its effect on me was haunting. Pardi was listening to it in the living-room.

"It's Mahler's tenth," Mardi said in exasperation, as if I would understand some cryptic implication in this, and she stroked my ankle as though that would soothe my neck.

"Don't you like it?" I asked.

"He wrote it while fighting his final cardiac illness," she explained. "Pam calls it Mahler's heartbroken farewell to life. He keeps playing it...." She made a decision, which brought her instantly to her feet and to the doorway.

"I do beg you, dear, please turn it off...it makes me so terribly sad...why do you listen to it? It's like listening to hear if your heart will stop."

He turned it off then, but the sound of that music often filled the house after that, and like a wistful coda, it followed me all through July.

The day after the moon landing, before I left, I received a slip of typed paper as slight as its information; a lower second degree. I handed it to Pardi like a truce.

"Thank you for everything," I said.

It seemed to please him.

"Pie got her BA," he said very quietly, as though I were no longer there in the room with him, maybe no longer even part of his life, but with a tenderness that expressed both the joy of our years of comradeship, and something other. Maybe regret, maybe nostalgia.

"What will you do now?" he asked.

"I'm going to have a ball in the Bahamas, and then I'm going to become an air stewardess," I declared defiantly.

"Then you can use your Spanish," he said, with unintrusive satisfaction.

"Well, I'm just going to have fun and travel the world."

His eyes disturbed me. He reminded me of an old grandfather star that had been in the sky longer than the others, for his light was dimmer and yet somehow more unyielding in its steadiness—or maybe he was just farther away in the universe.

"You know"—and he stopped to clear his throat and blow his nose, rubbing it impatiently as though it got in his way—"one eventually discovers that the least interesting premise upon which to base a life is oneself."

※

Mardi always said that Zethilda cooked Pardi his last supper. The items of food changed year by year, story by story, depending on what Mardi felt would have been good for him, or suitable at that time. It was always a soft supper, for by that time his partial upper plate, which included his front teeth, was permanently in the bottom of a glass, in some liquid that smelled like Listerine.

His last supper was a few days before he died. He came out and sat at the table for it, I'm told, for I wasn't back yet. He probably had steamed fish. Manley men never seem to be partial to fish, disliking the tedious business of small bones. And I don't remember him being partial to steaming or boiling unless it was to do with a diet fad. But Mardi had always felt fish was recuperative, light food. Since this is the menu she most often remembered, I imagine he did get steamed fish.

After that he announced matter-of-factly that he had a train to catch, and went back to bed.

He never got up again.

During the remaining days he frequently asked her for a time table.

"But why, Norman?" Mardi enquired. "What train? We don't want you to go anywhere, Norman, we need you here," she pleaded.

She tried to get him to write in his diary. She felt she must keep him awake, keep him conscious—as though he had taken an overdose of something.

He co-operated once or twice, and each time simply wrote lists of ortaniques for grocery shops, or copious lines detailing gallons of gas for the Benz, or kerosene for up the hill. One day he made a note about something to do with the party which he must speak to Michael about. Another day he wrote that he wished "Rachel would do something sensible with her life" and "When is Doug coming home?" On another, "Uhuru needs worming."

The doctors kept coming and going. His blood pressure rose higher and higher, his delicate ankles were bloated from water retention. They believed his kidneys were failing. He hated hospitals, and the specialist felt that admitting him would serve no purpose, and that he would be more comfortable at home. I don't think anyone actually said he was dying. Neither did Pardi. He knew how to keep his own counsel.

The last day of August was a Sunday. September the second was the day of the by-election to fill the seat in St. Andrew South left vacant by Pardi's resignation, and Kenny McNeil, who was often called on to give Pardi medical advice now, was contesting the seat for the PNP. Michael had been extremely busy with the by-election, checking each day on his father over the phone, and on one occasion having to organize money for Mardi because Pardi kept signing his cheques with mathematical equations or dates and times. He came to visit him that morning and was surprised to find his father in a hospital-style bed, but apart from a very insistent vein throbbing in his temple, Pardi's face seemed quite relaxed. He almost looked well.

"How is the voting going?" he asked, and Michael noticed that his voice trembled.

"That's not till Tuesday, Dad."

"But I thought..."

"No, today's only Sunday... remember.... elections aren't on Sundays...."

"But surely..."

When Michael returned that evening, two doctors were there and Pardi once again asked for a train schedule. He looked much weaker.

"Why go by train, Dad? Wait till tomorrow—it's late now and it's raining—tomorrow we'll take you in your own car. Don't you want to go in the Benz?"

"No, Michael, I have a train to catch."

Mardi followed my father out the room. They would handle it all gently, they decided. The doctors and Michael left.

Mardi went back into the room.

"Norman, where do you want to go in that train, where is the train going?"

"I don't think I know—I'm not quite sure—but I have to catch it. My suitcase is there and I know just the clothes I want to wear—they are there in the cupboard. I must catch the train."

"Why don't you stay with us—we all want you—don't bother with the train—stay with us."

He was silent for a long time and then he looked at her very tenderly, penetrating her every nerve and fear.

"No—life here costs too much."

He had made his decision.

I arrived at the house late on the Monday night with an infected foot. I didn't see Pardi that evening. Mardi, who seemed overwhelmed and confused, said he was sleeping. As we sat on the old couch, she latched onto incidentals: the plane? How deep in my leg were the sea-eggs? Did I see that long island, Eleuthera? Not with any real interest, but as though they provided a diversion from something frantic within herself. I sensed she wished that the world would go home and I would just settle, settle down and sleep, "I'll make you a cup of warm Milo"; that the night would settle under the watch of the announcing crickets, the wakeful dogs, the peenie-wallies' flashing beacons. I felt my presence was depriving her of something. She wanted the house back for herself.

She wanted the night back. She must be in the middle of a carving, I thought, for the gestation of creativity always made her veer wildly between resentment towards the world and guilt.

Early the following morning, I crossed the narrow passage to their room. The room had changed; the hospital bed and a handsome nurse in white had transformed it into a set. My grandmother sat on the other bed, a silent audience, peripheral and detached from responsibility. Uhuru lay on the floor.

The early English upbringing which Mardi had long since subdued or discarded would surface at the oddest times, almost instinctively, to meet a moment, reducing it to a sub-terfuge of bland but respectable superficiality.

"This is Nurse Morgan, dear."

The nurse smiled brightly and soon after that left the room.

Pardi was in his blue pajamas. They seemed so familiar and unforeboding. For a while I just kept looking at the pajamas, comforted by the safety of the cotton and the soft colour. Farther up on the bed lay his face, whose sleep had no peace. I remember it well. Although his eyes were closed, there seemed such struggle, such determination behind them. Yet I knew instinctively that for us there would be no re-sponse. I sensed no hope in the room.

Mardi sat noncommittally beside the storm battling be-hind his face, his chest giving an occasional arabesque of breath, his once beautiful hands filling up till the skin shone beneath the polite cuffs of his sleeves. Looking at her, I felt suddenly angry. But looking back at me was a greater rage than my own. Her lips were fixed into that state of disap-pearance common to the family. They were fixed the way she fixed them when, sometimes failing to get her own way in manipulating us, she would announce her intention to pack it all in and die. And I realized that he was defying her; in his dream he was a runner struggling over a last hurdle, waning muscles struggling to fulfil the will's final intention. She knew his struggle was not for life but for death.

I saw his brush, the blue-backed, nylon-bristled Addis that he loved to scrape against his skull. It was lying with its familiar grey strands on the bookcase beside his bed. I picked it up and brushed the hairs clinging damply to each other. I wondered why he had fever.

"What's wrong with him?" I asked.

"He's simply given up." Mardi shrugged matter-of-factly, almost arching one unarchable grey eyebrow. I didn't know anyone could die of simply giving up, but she had the sharp edge of anger that made her on occasion brittle and nervous, which I disliked. I did not understand what I saw as Pardi's surrender; maybe I did not want to.

I stopped brushing after a while and squeezed the swollen fingers of his hand, and without looking at his face—let there be no last time, I thought—I left the room.

She wasn't in the middle of a carving. She had done no more than sketches in a small notebook she now kept beside her bed, along with her big diary, which she had moved across from the studio. Sometimes she drew, sometimes she wrote. When she drew what she meant to be future carvings, she either outlined large stones across a river or swept her charcoal around large wings that flew over water or hills. One of these wings she discovered belonged to a man who at first she thought was Pardi, but when she drew him turned towards her on the page he had no face, and carried a small figure safely tucked into one protective wing.

And now, on Tuesday morning, she had seen the face, implacable and beyond appeal. She knew it was the face of an angel, and she knew why he was there. She felt the tears so near her heart that, when she remembered her husband's presence and checked to see if he was aware of what was happening, she was surprised to find heavy wells in the corners of her eyes. She squeezed them away with her thumb and index finger and, quite without meaning to, she trailed them damply onto the drawing book before her. The tears mingled with the traces of charcoal. The smudge, shaped like a wishbone, seemed to her like the desire of her husband's endless sleep. She recognized it as the frown on the forehead of the angel.

Tossing her head, she reached for her diary. She did not want him to know she had cried. If the future was so upsetting, she would turn to the past instead.

She wrote:

The clouds are hanging low over the house in the mountains and the air is still and very silent...no sounds at all. A man has walked slowly...summoning the end of his strength...from the house to the glass-doored study that stands a little distance away.

Gravely, he moves to the desk and takes a seat in the swivel chair; his long sensitive hands move to the drawer and quietly he opens it...bending to look inside. He closes it...and gently he touches the objects on the desk...slightly rearranging them with care.

With great effort he pulls himself to his feet... and moves to the bookshelves, drawing his fingers across the backs of the books on his way to the great plate-glass doors.

For a long pause he leans against them, his eyes going far across the crumpled mountains that are his country. He stands quite still...his face and particularly his eyes brooding and withdrawn.

The woman beside him can bear it no longer and draws him away down the path through the pine trees to the waiting car. He alone knows it was goodbye.

She turned round and walked over to the window. She moved close to the grey louvers and wound the handle at the base till the opening before her tilted up to the sky and she could squeeze the metal edges out of her vision.

"There, now…" she said, with a note of optimism that barely made its way through the drowning in her throat.

It was a bright, tense morning with an everyday, harmless enough looking sky which she gratefully breathed in—a sky that, having produced no hurricane by September, was reluctant to call attention to itself. There were only a few small, white, tightly packed clouds.

It was hard to imagine that anything could bring about the end of the world. There were so many worlds going on simultaneously. If you missed one show, you could join another, even if you had to sit through some of what you had seen already.

It was too late to panic.

Whatever journey he was hell-bent to make, he'd caught his damn train.

On September second.

She must inform the family. They would have to keep it quiet till the polls closed, for it might affect the vote.

She picked up her drawing-book.

Before she reached the door, she stopped for a moment beside the bed and lightly, for she thought it wasn't hers any more, touched Pardi's hand.

"Kid…I *did* see that horse!"

And without looking back she left the room.

No one seemed to agree why Pardi died. The doctors thought it was renal failure. My father thought it was boredom. I feared it was a consequence of my not loving him enough.

Douglas thought it was probably his final nervous breakdown. His father's death had come strangely to him; rather than taking him away, it had given him back his father. He was in Africa, asleep in his bed, when something woke him. There at the foot of the bed was his father, his father who through the course of his life Douglas never once remembered anywhere near his bed or even in his room. "Dad," he said, surprised, and started to get up, but his father told him to stay where he was. "It's going to be all right now, son," he said, and very slowly, as though not wanting to leave his son, or to frighten him, he faded into the darkness.

To this day Douglas, the family sceptic, swears that the vision came to him at the exact hour that his father died back in Jamaica.

Although publicly Mardi always blamed Jamaica for Pardi's death—"He died of a broken heart," she'd say—I think it was really her husband she blamed. She felt it was the most stubborn and bloody-minded he had ever been. It may have been the worst battle of wills they ever had.

I walked into the small blue room that had been their bedroom. The door opened slowly, unwinding ribbons of breeze. A new light entered with me, slightly altering the shadows. An inner life of its own repose had been disturbed, as though eyes half awoke for a moment and then rested again. The fat white telephone lay curled like a dog asleep without a master to call.

The beds faced each other from opposite walls, their linen bedspreads, bright blue with yellow pineapples, neatly wrapped around them. They were the comfort and conclusion of so much, and muffled the energy and agony already spent, like circumspect housekeepers.

The familiar cupboard, with its wooden sliding doors, sprawled across the far wall. I wondered what was left of Pardi's belongings, and tried to move one of the doors. I had forgotten how heavy and uncooperative they were. I shoved harder, leaning my shoulder against it with a heave, and it ground along its dusty rail reluctantly. Some of his shirts and suits hung over wooden frames. In the gloom of the inner floor the size-eleven leather shoes, narrow and laced, hosts to years of such strength and elegance, now cracked around damp envelopes of air. The old man's feet were gone.

This room had contained the last of a great sorrow, but also the memories of an extraordinary journey. I had been only a very small part of this, and yet this was everything I knew, everything I was. A door had been closed; though the breeze would return to flirt with the curtains, or the light slant in to reveal a new shadow of dust, some sustaining, glorious occupation was now complete. I was old enough to vote and I had lost my grandfather.

I could hear again the sound of a mallet composing its phrases against wood.

The road disappearing, the wings of a journey, the implacable face that takes with it only one soul, says Mardi.

The Lord giveth and He taketh away, says wise old Batiste as he tends Pardi's roses.

Better 'im over dere, Zethilda consoles.

Oh, I miss the old house, says Miss Boyd, while she straightens her hair and readjusts the pins.

Aunt Muriel says she should have been next. She doesn't care about life any more.

The pea-doves have a new call: "A...ny...one...there?..."

Only the ghosts of Drumblair.